Breathing Space

A novel of 70s London

Judy Hindley

ISBN 978 1 914076 23 7 (paperback)
ISBN 978 1 914076 24 4 (ebook)

Cover design by Wheelhouse Design
Typesetting by preparetopublish.com
Author photo by Stuart Owen

For John and Anna

With special thanks to Sarah Singleton and Brian Utton

PART ONE

1

Autumn, 1976

It wasn't until the night of the move to their new home, where she and the children were to live alone, now, that Jessie was struck with the full force of what she'd done.

It was November, the worst month for such a move, just as the darkness closed around you. She could imagine only too well how lonely it will seem, now that the clocks have been turned back, and it will have been long dark as she struggles home through the weather from the train, the neighbours all withdrawn indoors or hurrying past almost fearfully, huddled into their winter coats…

But in fact, on the day itself the movers had left by early afternoon, and so the first thing she hated was the autumn sunlight.

Hatred was an emotion she kept encountering now, in the most unexpected and painfully unwelcome places. It was one of the many surprises of her situation.

The sunlight made it all so drearily normal: the chaos of packing cases jammed into the tiny hallway; the dingy, humiliated-looking furniture heaped willy-nilly in each small shabby room; stained mattresses denuded of their coverings; sofa-cushions squashed out of shape under heavy shelving units; scarred legs of chairs poked ignominiously upwards. And then, the garish clown print they'd bought long ago as students, picked in a hurry from a bin at some cut-price outlet, which of course the removal men had plucked from its perch on the pile of rubbish and given pride of place against a wall, atop a stack of cardboard boxes.

Now the clown's lopsided face mourned at her with lugubrious familiarity, the sunlight brightening its blues and reds with mocking cheeriness as she squeezed between the crates and cases and pushed aside the heaped-up bales of bedding and winter clothing, abandoned coat-hangers sliding and slithering underfoot. She fumbled and hopped her way from the front to the back of the little house, after the movers had left, unconsciously seeking some kind of vantage point, a height, a clearing – until she suddenly realised that this was what she was doing, and that there wasn't one.

The movers had arrived at dawn. She'd had only one day's leave, midweek, to get it done. To begin with, it all went very fast. She was propelled by adrenaline, faced with the arrival of the removal van after so little sleep: the final packing case labelled at 3am, she'd collapsed into bed without even washing her face. The last night in that big, sunless bedroom which they'd only inhabited, after all, for eleven months. But after the physical exertion of the day, she slept for those few hours like a stone.

There were still so many final things to do. Reading the

meters, turning off the water, stripping her bed – remembering to run next door and finally (with shame, after all this time) leave the note for the barely befriended neighbour to hand to the teacher who'd been so kind to Ella, back in the summer term, when he'd discovered her huddled in a corner of the playground, weeping for her daddy… Then, the alarm clock had to get stuffed into her already swollen handbag, because she'd need to be able to lay her hand on it, for school and work tomorrow, and then she remembered there'd have to be a towel and soap and washcloth added to the carrier bag with her toilet things, and then, the kettle. Which she'd just have to carry.

And all this time, it wasn't bad that the day was dawning clear and pink; as the upper rooms of the emptying house were bathed in brightness it seemed appropriate. It had the glamour of emergency.

She rode in the cab of the removals van, perched high, with a regal view of the coloured tops of cars, the secret interiors behind first-floor windows, the abrupt, foreshortened lettering of shop fronts. A little numbed and silent now, she was relieved when Dave and Ian spoke across her, and she had only to smile at a witticism now and then and give herself up to the movement of the van, to the novelty of this aerial view, the low, dingy, brown-brick streets of south east London curiously gilded in the early sunlight.

Early on, they stopped at a café for breakfast. This was a huge, greasy, succulent fry-up, doused with squirts of a thin, bright scarlet sauce that mimicked ketchup, and accompanied by cups of that mahogany-coloured tea that she had loved from the moment she encountered it when she first came with Danny to England, some eight years ago (so excited and hopeful then, with baby Ella, and Ben a bright-faced five-year-old). Old-fashioned, British railway tea, so strong that you could almost chew it. They all lit cigarettes, and the smoke curled blue in the shafts of sunlight, and Jessie sat there mute between the comfortable, burly men, and wished they never had to leave. This was a good bit.

She was aware of how she kept clinging to the good bits.

After this, it was the Blackwall Tunnel under the Thames, with its dull, synthetic glare. She became conscious of a certain excitability, an edge of hysteria, her own sensations unnaturally highly coloured, sharpened against that long duochrome and then the abstract architecture of the exit ramp.

But then, as they ground their way through the endless urban drabness of east London, veering up yet another treeless stretch of council buildings, dipping down yet another road sunk between concrete flanges, the excitement wore off; she lost her bearings; her companions gradually fell silent. They joined the great river of traffic on the North Circular, rounding onto the home stretch. Here were the alien territories of north London, where she was to live now. Here the encompassing cityscape was built in a different shade of brick, the red and white frontages taller and narrower, more decorated, the lintels and stone copings cut to patterns of a different series, the differences, which she had got to know just a little, over the past months, having acquired a distinctness in her mind like that of some new spice she'd learned to recognise but couldn't name.

Finally, here was the turn-off from the main road, and then the turn into the street that would be her address, and then the house itself.

In the summer, when she had found the house, so long ago now, the street was dense with green, the houses hidden by it. Now the crowns of the trees were quite transparent, lit with the coloured shards of a few last leaves, individual and clear. She hadn't seen the street, in daylight, since before the heavy winds of late October. Greenlea Avenue. It was a different street now.

'Keep going,' she said. Then, 'Here,' she said. 'Here it is.'

Had she not seen it before in such strong sunlight? Or had it become more obviously shabby, over the long months of negotiations, while men she knew mainly as telephone messages cleared out the furnishings, ripped up the floorboards, gouged the plaster to run the new wiring along, injected chemicals into the walls.

She pushed through the gate. The privet hedge was rank and overgrown. Weeds sprang from between the flags of the crazy paving, and the paint peeled off in curling shreds on the little porch. She opened the door to a heap of junk mail. Behind her, the one called Dave blew through his lips in a noise of astonishment. She turned to find him peering past her down the hall.

'This is it?' he said. He caught her eyes, with a rueful smile. 'Putting a quart into a pint pot, isn't it?'

'I guess,' said Jessie, with a nervous laugh.

Deserted, the house looked smaller than ever. A frayed runner of carpet led along the narrow hall to a curious maze of doors that opened, directly ahead, into a cramped, narrow scullery. Just beside the entrance, an equally narrow stair led straight up to the open door of the toilet.

'Never mind,' said Dave. 'We'll manage. You have a good look round and then come back and tell us where to put it.' And he made off.

The place was filthy. The dust of dereliction and various kinds of builder's rubble mingled with a more personal detritus: a length of yellowing net curtain, a soiled old bed-jacket, broken plant pots dribbling earth, together with empty drink tins and cigarette ends and even the crumpled, greasy paper wrappings from somebody's fish and chips, presumably one of the men who did the clearance.

It appeared that all they'd actually cleared away was the furniture, things that could be carried off in bulk. Much had been simply left to lie where it dropped or rolled – the small, poignant, dirty, spoiled and broken debris of the two old lives that had wound down towards their endings here. Plastic lamp shades, so brittle that they cracked. Tins with faded labels. The perished tubing of a shower attachment. The grimy, flattened packaging of some ancient personal appliance, unidentifiably obscene.

Silently, she moved from room to room, climbing the stairs to wander through the bedrooms, surveying the dirty windows, the dirty, littered floors, the sad, old, nasty wallpaper.

Downstairs again, she opened a cupboard in the kitchen, and ancient medicine bottles tumbled out, their shoulders dim with dust.

'Ready, now?' Dave asked hopefully from the doorway.

Strange how the paltry-looking heaps of their possessions, so diminished by the van's cavernous interior, became unwieldy even as they approached along the path, and nearly impossible as they were squeezed in through the door.

Of course, she had hopefully labelled crates and cases – kitchen, back room, front bedroom. But once the appliances were manoeuvred into the kitchen, nothing else could be crammed in, and the other things couldn't go upstairs until the beds did, and inevitably the double bed was problematic, given the dimensions of the stairs. Soon the whole process seemed to become almost entirely provisional. It was like some nightmarish brainteaser, because nothing could happen until some other, equally unattainable thing had happened first, and at times, it seemed as though she simply milled almost aimlessly from room to room, reduced to an attempt to sweep out the corners before anything immovable went into them.

Other moments, she panicked. So much muscle and energy engaged in putting the wrong things on top of each other or in places she knew she'd never be able to move them from, and she should be making use of all this energy, this valuable strength. But now, however much she ran from room to room, trying to undo the damage here or guide the dispositions there, she could not keep up. The decisions came too fast; the movers themselves were on a roll, she felt, hardly in charge of their own momentum.

'Sorry miss.'

'Excuse me, miss.'

'Could we just…'

They smiled apologetically at her, shouted with relieved, loud energy to each other as they hustled past her, heaving the gross fragments of her exploded life into the hallway, round the corners, up the stairs, until somehow they'd managed to cram the lot of it, that whole van load, willy-nilly into these small, dirty rooms; and then they left.

So now she stood there among the packing cases, realising there was nowhere to go, because this was it, this was the arrival. This was what she'd been aiming herself towards, with such forced, wilful energy, for all these months.

She reached down and gathered up the metal coat-hangers that had almost tripped her up a moment before. Once they were in her hands, however, there seemed no obvious place to put them down. She thought she remembered that there was a hanging rail in a little cupboard in one of the upstairs bedrooms, but she was daunted by the thought of working herself all the way up there, over the obstacle course of heaped-up furniture, on such a speculative and minor errand. Instead, she shoved them between the back of an armchair and a cardboard box stuffed with condiments and kitchen staples, then made her way towards the kitchen sink. Perhaps the thing to do was scour the sink: just to get one thing clean and ready for use.

Then she realised she had no idea where the box with the washing-up things and the scouring powder was. She looked in a box sitting on the kitchen table, the table having been jammed sideways between the small, deep sink and the vast fridge-freezer brought from the other house, but it was filled with toys and children's board games.

In any case, her energy was gone.

She found the clock, at least, and checked the time. In less than twenty minutes, Ella would be delivered for the first time to this house from her new school. Then, shortly after, Ben would be getting home as well.

She was terrified at the thought that they would find her like this, paralysed with uncertainty. She wasn't ready for them. The impetus of the past months had deserted her.

It seemed now that that had been the easy part – the way it's easy to smash a glass, to slap a face, to throw a bomb, presumably – the quick, large gestures of destruction. All those separate moves in the dismantling of the family, though each had loomed, at the time, so terrible an obstacle, seemed in retrospect to have been fuelled by drama, by an emotional charge that was now exhausted.

She wasn't ready for them. They had a right to some degree of order, or at least of purpose, energy, determination, but it had all abandoned her. All her energy, whatever self-belief had kept her going, all these months since that queer, almost weightless moment of decision back in March.

She had done this. She had brought them here, to this rickety dwelling with its crazy paving and the queer, crabbed scullery, the plumbing wrapped in ancient rags, the dated, ugly wallpaper, the rooms where nothing fit – and an alien neighbourhood to learn their way around, all over again, for the second time in scarcely more than a year.

Because it was hardly more than year since they had moved to start their last new life. Danny had finally made the decision he'd hung fire on for so long, as though for years he'd been reserving some last commitment to their marriage. He'd finally moved them into that big, solid house, in its enclave of affluence, and in only a year she had wrenched the whole thing apart, and brought the children into this.

Late that night, she woke up needing a pee. Having managed, at the end of that long day, to install Ben and Ella up in the bedrooms, she had gone to sleep in a single bed, downstairs; now she would have to make her way up to the toilet, navigating the unfamiliar darkness. The grimy, meagrely covered floors felt inimical to her bare feet, and the cold house was suffused with the clinging smell of the chemicals used in the damp treatment.

A part of her had looked forward to the darkness, to the night, as though it was a safe place you could hide. But then you woke up and realised there was nowhere safe any more. Climbing the stair, shivering and scared, felt like a penance.

'How strange,' said her mind. 'How strange.'

As she went up and then down the cold, dark, queer-smelling stair, the cool little phrase repeated itself, as though from some detached observer in her mind. *How strange.* A distancing, to ward off terror. She made her way back to that small, lonely bed.

For seventeen years, his body had been her home. For nearly half her lifetime.

2

Surely there had been, at some point, a gleam of purpose. She remembered the sensation, but she could no longer believe in it; it had been so corrupted by irrelevant fantasies, angry justifications. Yet until the morning of the move, she had thought she was up to it. Could you really be so radically diminished by your surroundings?

But she felt, now, that this was the real her: the self of the other house had been a lie – an illusion promoted by the flattery of its dimensions and solidity. That big, generous entrance, for example, which seemed itself a declaration of unhurriedness and ease, and the wide, shallow stair to the first floor, up which you could glide, boasting a landing before it squared itself to the next few easy steps. Then, to the back and front of the living rooms, those walls of glass, looking down into the crowns of trees in one direction and, in the other, out at the distant, tiny, glittering towers of central London.

Standing at that window, you had the city almost literally at your feet, its lights a thousand little stars crushed against the darkness. Even by day, the angles of the nearby buildings, the careful landscaping, screened from your view the blighted streets stretching down into the tattered hopelessness of the shopping district. Even visually, you were protected.

Magpies and jays and woodpeckers – large, astonishingly coloured birds – flew up to the rustic porch outside the dining room. The Grove, their own little private wood, was accessible only to the people in the development. There was no sunlight, this side of the house, but you looked out on trees. You could hang nuts for the birds to squabble over. You could scatter crumbs and watch the jays alight and walk among them on their proud, stiff legs, so close to you.

It was easy to get used to the comfort of it. The house was spotless, and everything fitted, everything worked, everything answered so readily to your convenience. There were deep, roomy cupboards in nearly every room, capacious cupboards, heavy, quiet doors that opened at a touch, shut tight with a soft click. There was a separate laundry room, a facility she'd never expected after leaving North America. She'd never even, in fact, much wanted it, but how luxurious it seemed now, when suddenly they had duvets and stacks of bed linen, and you could just skip down through the big, warm house to do the laundry instead of struggling up the road to the launderette.

Neatly ordered in these big cupboards, their rather scant possessions seemed more substantial. Even their minimal furniture seemed almost elegant, grouped on the dull, soft, creamy carpet that ran through all the house, lapped to the edge of the skirting board in every room. She liked how clean and empty the big rooms looked, even cumbered with packing cases and emerging stacks of books. She would have liked the rooms to stay like that. In the early days of their marriage, when they were allowed to dream (when they were only students, and anything was possible), she had been entirely captivated by a slick *New Yorker* ad – it was spread over two whole pages – for a certain hideously expensive sofa, posed in splendid isolation on a sweep of beautiful bare floorboards. What she liked was in fact those wide floorboards, the proportions of the room, the stave of sunlight angled from tall, deep windows at the back… *That's what a house should be: a space to dance in.*

She'd told him they'd have a house in Chelsea, one day. Arrived in London all those years before, houseless and nervously excited, crammed with suitcases and children into one of those comical tall black cabs, they had been driven to the station along a sunlit stretch of river looped with handsomely ornamented bridges, flanked by wrought-iron dolphins and antique lamps, bordered by great solid, gracious buildings. Down a side-street, there was a glimpse of little houses, people-sized houses, with small-paned windows and brightly painted doors, all similarly smothered in a luxuriance of foliage, and she'd cried out.

'Danny! That's where we're going to live some day.'

That gleam of purpose. All she could remember of it now was how the thought had begun to haunt her: this is wrong. It shouldn't be like this.

Once, during the summer, with the woman who had become her confidante during that period of limbo after the split, she had broken down.

Arlis and her husband Marty, one of Danny's colleagues, had been with him at a party the night before; he was looking well, they told her.

At first, the word had been that he was hyperactive. He talked about himself too much; people were bored with the trivialities of his little personal concerns; they made ho-hum faces, rolled their eyes, were surprised at the callowness he was revealing. Arlis reported this gleefully to Jessie, who heard it with a mixture of relief and painful tenderness. Apparently, they were glad to see him taken down – quick, flippant, handsome Danny. She was sorry they were glad.

Arlis said that he had lost a great deal of weight. 'He's anxious,' Arlis had suggested, then. 'He isn't even drinking; he's too anxious. He needs to be in control.' That had been in the spring, just after the break-up.

After this, he'd had a few strokes of luck.

Now Arlis told her, in a tone of surprised goodwill, that Danny seemed very well; he seemed relaxed. She offered this information as though he were just a mutual acquaintance. She said, 'He's really getting his life together.'

Jessie said, 'Well of course, he'll never really doubt himself.'

'He's not the type,' Arlis said offhandedly, opening a kitchen cupboard, continuing with the meal she was preparing.

Watching her from the doorway of the little galley kitchen, Jessie waited. She waited for the attention to herself that must surely follow this exchange. In a moment, surely – when she had finished spooning out the olives from that jar, perhaps – Arlis would put down the spoon, the jar. She would turn round, she would fold her arms, lean back against the kitchen counter, offer a face reflecting the emotion unacknowledged by the tones they used.

Waiting, Jessie felt the pressure rising in her lungs and towards her throat.

Arlis put down the spoon and screwed the lid back on the jar. She turned around. 'Hummus?' she asked, brightly. 'Some of my famous hummus? It's coming out of our ears, I made so much of it.'

Jessie stared at her. 'Of course, I know that's how he is,' she burst out finally, her voice cracking. 'I always figured, if we ever did split up, I'd be the only one who went on wondering, the only one—'

'You had to do it,' Arlis interrupted.

'Only I guess I somehow had this hope,' said Jessie, the tears beginning to slither down her face as it came through to her how deeply this disregarded hope had sunk its roots into her heart. 'All the time, I must have had this hope.' She turned her face against the door frame, gripping its edge between thumb and knuckle as the sobs took hold.

'The hope is unreal,' said Arlis. 'It won't happen. You need to face that.'

'I don't know how to stop,' said Jessie, her voice choked almost to a whisper.

For a time, then, it really seemed as though she didn't, that perhaps she couldn't, any more than she could stop this flood of tears, now it had started. Although it was so childish and out of place, and in half an hour people would be arriving for the evening.

By the time they had this conversation it had been five months since Jessie first made her way to the flat in Bloomsbury on her own, desperate for adult company, the night she came to the decision.

Danny was away. There'd been a letter from him – it had been waiting when she got back from work, with its foreign stamp and the familiar black, looping script which over the years had carried, in her eyes, such emotional freight: so longed for, so desirable; and which gave her now a stab of sick unease. In the week since he'd left, she'd managed to avoid the knot of questions raised by the thought of him. In a burst of rebellious spirit, she'd managed to enjoy herself. She had gone out; she had giggled with Ben and Ella. She'd had some unexpectedly happy moments. Now there would be a reckoning…

She read the letter twice, and then she sat for a while. It was not like thinking. It was more like letting an impression take. Then she rang them. She was having a crisis, she told them; she was thinking of leaving Danny. She needed to talk.

That was the first time.

With a few isolated exceptions, she did not share confidences outside her marriage. She wouldn't have shared them with her oldest friends, or with her family, but in any case, the family and the very few old friends were all back in America, thousands of miles out of reach. So this was a peculiar move for her to make. It was also one of the few times she had left the house in Albion Grove to go out somewhere on her own at night.

She rang a mini cab to take her to the Tube. This was an extravagance. Normally she would have walked and caught a train that would connect her to the underground. But in the months since they had come to live here, their former disciplines had slipped, and she was not sure why. Were they really better off now? Or had they never been quite as hard up as she'd thought? Or were improvident gestures maybe another feature of the recklessness that had begun to colour the way they lived?

For a moment she contemplated this unwieldy journey: the trailing through the dark streets, the unsheltered waiting on the platform, the lurching, jolting carriages travelling patiently across the miles to central London and the underground connection. But a sense of crisis gave her licence. Soon she was shut into the warm interior of the mini cab, and then she was dropped directly beneath the red-and-blue badge of the Tube entrance, sucked into its bright machinery, connected directly to the city's heart, where they both worked, but visited only rarely out of hours.

As she sped into central London in this fast, well-lighted capsule, as she walked the streets from the stop at Warren Street station to the Goldmans' flat, she wasn't rehearsing what she would say to them, wondering what they would make of it, anticipating their reactions. She felt, for the moment, absolved: the novelty of the journey, the rush of sheer volition, briefly freed her from that grey tangle of doubts and fears, supporting the flicker of a new idea that it could be different. Just as she had begun to feel: *It shouldn't be like this.*

She mounted the step to the heavy door of the ground-floor flat, and pressed the button of the rather elderly bell. In a few moments, the door swung open and there was Marty, giving her just one quick, searching look before the kiss on the cheek, and the hand on the shoulder; and with the slightly stagey gestures of his usual welcome, he ushered her inside.

3

She'd thought they would talk about money.

She thought of these friends as particularly knowledgeable people, shrewd, astute. After all, Marty was an economist, like Danny; his stock-in-trade was the importance of information, rational decision making. Arlis had been in social work for years. They had each, in different ways, known what it was to struggle. Now a childless couple in their mid-thirties, they lived an easy, sociable, time-rich life in central London, but they both had stories of coming up the hard way. They had experience, a wide acquaintance. They would know things.

What little she herself knew about British divorce law came from an article in a short-lived glossy feminist publication she'd come across eight years before, just as they were packing up to leave for this apparently savagely misogynistic country. It would be hard; that was all she knew.

Sitting across from them in the comfortably shabby, book-lined sitting room, after the various routines of welcome, she looked at her fingers. Then she looked up at them. She took a deep breath. 'Well,' she said. 'So I'm going to leave him. I think I have to. I think it's time.' They looked back at her, waiting.

'But I don't know what the situation is. I don't have any idea how it's going to work. I don't – do you know much about divorce law?'

'No,' said Marty, immediately, with a brief shake of his head.

Arlis said, 'It varies. It depends on circumstances. It depends on all sorts of issues.'

'So – how do I find out?'

'There are ways to find out, that's not a problem,' Marty said. 'But – just a minute; look…' He ran his fingers through his thick, curly hair. He was Danny's oldest friend. The three of them had known each other since university days, long ago in Chicago. 'What's going on? Do you want to talk about it?'

Jessie looked from him to Arlis. She hadn't imagined it would go this way.

Arlis leaned forward and tapped the ash from her cigarette. She tilted her head, looking earnestly at Jessie, her face creased with attentiveness. 'Tell us,' she said.

What had propelled her was an impulse to find out where she stood. Her going to them (the phone call, the unprecedented evening journey across London) was a declaration of intent; she meant to confront the facts. She wanted to bite down on the pain, to swallow her disabling, bitter fury at the injustice of what (from the little she knew) a wife embarking on this course of action would face. To know what she would have to deal with.

And then, it didn't go that way at all.

Later that evening, she tried again to broach the question of her circumstances, but Marty said, in answer to her appeal, 'What can I say? I just don't know what the situation is. And you know, Jessie, people don't arrange these things just by the rule book. The law is a last resort. It's for people who aren't talking to each other.'

'It's only… If I have to find somewhere to move to, I'd have to rent it. I don't have any money. And with rent control… Wouldn't I have to get a furnished flat?'

She'd been steeling herself to face it. Surely Marty knew what she meant. She remembered the dingy, claustrophobic premises she and Danny had confronted when they arrived in London, on their first real house-hunting forays. Given the provisions of rent control, anything they could afford had to justify the phrase 'furnished lettings' to protect the landlord from being stuck with this tenancy in perpetuity at the current rent: hence the scenes of ungainly, overstuffed furniture crowded round the bulk of a gas fire…

Marty grimaced. 'That's possible.'

She met his dark gaze steadily. 'Then do you—'

'But that's nonsense,' said Arlis. 'A wife with children stays in the marital home.'

Marty threw his hands wide. 'I told you, I don't know about divorce law. Jessie asked me about rent control. And I don't know a lot about rent control.'

'Jessie, you have rights,' Arlis persisted. 'What are you thinking? You've completely lost your confidence.'

How their positions had reversed, over the years. Jessie could barely remember the small, silent, dungareed Arlis of the early days, when she was first with Marty, hidden in curtains of fair hair from which emerged little urgent puffs of cigarette smoke, like a stubborn sign of life. Now she was heavy, fashionable, outspoken: the shoulders back, the hair upswept and curled. She wore scarves and brooches and was in training to be a psychotherapist.

'Jessie, there's hope,' she said, with a hand on Jessie's arm, as she ushered her out at the end of that long evening. 'You're quite young still. You're attractive, you've started a career. Look,' she insisted, 'don't be so concerned with the practical issues. You're too anxious! It's not going to be that bad!'

The solicitor had reinforced this view.

The one she saw was the one who'd only recently handled the house move, and it later occurred to her that perhaps this embarrassed him. But she didn't know any other solicitors, so she'd just rung up Dunwoody and Barnet on the number she'd scribbled in her address book the previous summer when Danny had called on her to nag them. The secretary gave her an appointment in just three days. She was relieved. She wanted Danny to get a letter before he started back home, and there was not much time.

The first evening after seeing Arlis and Marty, she had talked to the children. She had some questions about the changes it might mean for them. She had to ask them how they felt about it. But it was easier than she'd expected. They'd had those happy hours together on the weekend; she'd felt almost defiantly happy with them, sitting on the new chairs round the big, new table, in the new house, watching the big, surprising birds fly over from the tiny wood. They talked about the birds. They enjoyed the birds, together.

That gave her some reassurance as she sat in the quiet, well-lit offices of Dunwoody and Barnet. But she watched with some suspense as Mr Dunwoody read the account she'd written. It had been odd to see it written down like that. Everything it said was true, but after all, there are so many ways to tell a truth. When she herself read it over, she didn't see anyone she recognised. It was not her voice, describing Danny. It wasn't him these words described. Now she would see the reflections of this story in a stranger's eyes.

When he'd finished glancing through it, he put it down, resting his fingertips on it, and turned to her a bright, neutral gaze. 'Yes,' he said. 'It does seem to be an irretrievable breakdown.'

Jessie nodded. So that was what she'd said, then.

'Well then, I suggest that the next move is for his solicitor – does he have a solicitor?'

'No, he… actually, I wanted to discuss the situation with you.'

'I'm sorry. I understood you'd decided to ask for a separation.'

'Well, but I have to. Don't you think so? Only – what are the implications?'

He continued to look at her, enquiringly.

'I mean, the financial situation,' she continued.

He blinked. It seemed, somehow, a hideously embarrassing question to be raising.

'I mean…' She tried again. 'What am I entitled to? I'm going to need to make arrangements,' she said, apologetically.

'You understand these things take time. There'll be time to work all that out,' he said.

'But the basic—'

'You want to know about the legal situation,' he suggested.

'Yes,' she said, relieved.

'Let me just explain it to you in broad terms. Broadly speaking, the law is simply interested in minimising the disruption to all parties. Our aim is for both parties to retain, as near as possible, their position prior to the divorce – or separation.

'Both parties,' she said.

'Both parties,' he confirmed.

The letter to Danny was more difficult than she'd imagined.

She wanted it to be simple, matter of fact. No emotion, no explanations that could then be brought into question – most of all, by herself. She wanted there to be nothing she couldn't be sure that she could keep on meaning.

It was very hard to get there.

She found herself writing about his future dealings with Ben and Ella, how they could organise holidays – painting cheerful, reassuring pictures, for her own benefit, really, but even more, just to fill out this terse communication.

She brought this draft to Arlis, who'd become her confidante after the night of her decision.

Arlis looked doubtful. 'Jessie, you're too responsible,' she said.

They talked for a while about Jessie's over-responsibility.

Was that the word, really? Jessie wasn't sure, but she could see, now, that what she'd said was wrong. His life henceforward, his holidays with Ben and Ella, were not going to be her business.

At home the next night, after supper, she tried again.

She didn't even know how to begin.

'*I finally realise…*' This wasn't true. It wasn't as though she'd come to the end of a line of reasoning, a process of considering. *I can't… I feel…* Every softening phrase that she came up with seemed, on reflection, saturated with self-pity.

As for *we must* or *surely we need to* – that was like the draft she showed to Arlis. She couldn't speak for him now. There was no *we*.

At last, she thought of telling him of what she'd done: that she'd been to see the solicitor, Mr Dunwoody, about a separation. She said, '*It's time to cut the knot.*' She added, though it seemed both posturing, and untrue (but she needed to underline the fact that she was taking responsibility for this decision), '*I want to be free.*'

4

Winter, 1976

Horst Buchardt paused on the doorstep of the little house, looking sideways at the front-room window. Then he stepped back down and walked over to it. He put out a finger and flicked away a sliver of dried, curling paint. He shook his head. He said, 'You see, it's very bad.'

'Yes, that's another problem,' Jessie said. She waited for him to turn back to the porch, but he bent to examine the window frame more closely.

'Very bad,' he said again. 'You must do something about this very soon.'

After a moment, Jessie said reluctantly, 'You mean it needs redecorating?'

'Oh,' he groaned, as though wounded by the term. 'Oh, dear. You see, the paint is not just decoration, on a house. A house is not a woman.' He turned to offer a large, fixed, genial smile; Jessie laughed obediently and immediately the smile dropped from his face. 'No, no; you need it for protection from the weather.' He sighed, and looked up gloomily at the dank, drizzling sky. 'You must get it done before the winter.'

But it was already winter, and she had no more money.

'I don't have enough money to get it decorated. They said in the survey that it wasn't absolutely necessary. I think they said—'

'Think for yourself.' He raised his hands expressively. 'The water gets into the fibres of the timber. The frost comes. It freezes. Water expands, you know, when it freezes. More splinters. More cracking of the surface paint. Look,' he instructed, turning to scratch away the flaking paint and dig his fingernail into the naked wood beneath. 'See? Already the timber underneath is soft. Soon it will be rotten. These window frames are very expensive to replace. I don't know if such window frames are available.'

Jessie was silent.

'Well!' said Horst. 'We were going to look at your boiler.' And they went inside.

During the summer, there had been a time she'd thought of buying a much larger house. It was just round the corner from Greenlea Avenue, in Mountfield Road: a house from an earlier period with more generous proportions. She'd first come up to view it, with Horst's wife Maggie, and later with Marty and Arlis as well as Horst, and there was a pleasurable buzz among them all. It was an interesting, ambitious project: a property with serious problems but considerable attractions. It had large, high-ceilinged rooms, a cracked chimney, a bathroom with a hole in the floor, a hallway in which people could pause and chat and look about, with a sense of leisure. Jessie had enjoyed carrying around the rather important-looking set of keys. She even began to make arrangements with a firm of builders to discuss the costs of renovation.

She'd first come up to the neighbourhood at the suggestion of Maggie, whom she'd rung for help about the question of schools. Ben would have to leave the prestigious public school in which he'd been installed for the past three years, and how this would work was one of the imponderables to be juggled. Did Maggie know anything about the big south London state school, down the road from where they lived in Albion Grove? Maggie did. She rather thought such a switch shouldn't be attempted. Not in the same area – their own area.

Maggie was assistant head at her school, and exuded competence.

'Oh God,' said Jessie, after a while.

'Look, you don't really want to stay around there, do you? Can Danny afford to keep you in that house?'

Well of course Danny wouldn't want to, but Jessie had thought, perhaps, a lodger…

'You know, Jessie, the schools up here are excellent. I never understood why Danny preferred south London. Well, property is cheaper, granted, but you pay for it in other ways. And anyway, there are some nice little properties around here.'

'And the schools?'

'Why not come on up and have a look? What about Saturday lunchtime? Have a bite to eat and a little look-round.' Maggie had said invitingly, in her voice that was a deep, rich purr, with such alluring undertones of dry amusement. 'Bring Ella,' she said. 'The boys will take her under their wing. And I'm sure Ben will have his own engagements.'

Jessie was comforted to be so deftly managed, though she

was wrenched by the vision Maggie had invoked of Ben's life, full of sociable activity. Ben did not, in fact, have his own engagements. But, on the other hand, he wouldn't have wanted to travel up with her and Ella to north London.

So this was how she first found herself discussing schools and houses with Horst and Maggie, in the big airy kitchen of their house in Greenlea Avenue, one sunny Saturday.

Horst's contribution was rather academic. What a difference it made to the character of the environment, he pointed out, when and where the big demographic changes had occurred; had Jessie noticed this, eh?

Maggie said, 'I'll just have to let Horst waffle on to you for a moment while I speak to Josh about his piano practice. Sorry Jessie.'

Horst said, 'I'm being very useful! I'm watching the coffee drip.'

Maggie disappeared into the garden, where her two boys had persuaded Ella to join them in kicking a soccer ball around the large, well-kept lawn.

Jessie said, 'I do know what you mean. We went to France, once, and it was so different.'

'Ah, in France,' said Horst.

'Danny said, what a happy coincidence it was that just when the new housing was so ugly, the French population shrank. I would never have thought of that. And here, that was just when the population rose.'

'It exploded. And then there was a building boom,' said Horst.

'And it was all so lumpy. Miles and miles of it,' said Jessie, wonderingly.

'Yes, that was the period when this house was built,' said Horst. 'The ugly time. Mid-thirties.'

'Ah,' said Jessie.

'Very ugly,' he repeated, with a laugh.

'What's this?' said Maggie, emerging from the garden.

'We are speaking of our ugly house,' said Horst.

The Buchardts were older than Danny and Jessie. Their house, though indeed the exterior was not beautiful, was utterly comfortable, easily accommodating a piano, an acre of clever shelving, big, neutral, welcoming, over-stuffed furniture in the child-free sitting room in front. Behind it was Horst's study, and across from that, in the kitchen, looking out through French doors to the garden, the capacious blonde-wood table to which the children had been summoned for juice and biscuits.

Here they all gathered later for bread and cheese, and bowls of Swiss packet-soup, while Maggie continued her run-through of all the conveniences of the neighbourhood, to which, it seemed, a number of her divorced friends were migrating.

There was the Tube, of course, and the bus service really wasn't bad (though Horst, who used it, gave a snort at this). There was a cinema within reach, which sounded jolly – there were no cinemas within miles of Albion Grove – and in the other direction a place with the peculiar name of Chix-Chox, where you could have a cheap meal with your mates when you were fed up with feeding your family.

Some of the points she emphasised seemed odd, at first. For example, down the main road there was a branch of an exclusive chain called Waitrose, apparently a much-prized class of supermarket, though Jessie would have to take a bus to get there; but there was no Marks & Spencer within miles, unless you made your way out to the big new shopping centre – but never mind, you could stock up on a season's socks and underwear all at once in any case, hmm?

After a while, Jessie began to feel subtly flattered by this implication that she belonged to some freemasonry of intelligent consumers, capable women, so independent that they went off to cheap restaurants just to dine with their own particular friends, all on their own.

And there was a house or two for sale in this very neighbourhood. Maggie walked round with her to the house in Mountfield Road.

'Very promising, wouldn't you say?' said Maggie. 'It's a local agent, too,' she pointed out. 'You could just pop up and get the details. Ella will be all right here for another hour or so, won't she?'

En route to the agent, Jessie turned off to see the schools. It only needed a very slight diversion, because the primary school really was just round the corner, as Maggie had promised – round the corner, past a side street, and across the road, there it sat, a small, low, modest-looking building with some pretty shrubbery, ringed about by its playground. Just beyond it rose the main building of Christ College, the boys' grammar school. Maggie had said there was a very good grammar school for girls, too, in the same catchment area, and of course, they were sending their own boys to St Elfrid's Primary, and later on to Christ College.

The College was an older and more serious-looking structure, but still only moderately sized. And the schools were both so close. You could walk there in ten minutes. You could walk home with friends.

Jessie went across and stood for a moment beside the low gate to St Elfrid's. Then she walked round to get a closer look at the boys' school. Not that you could tell much, from the outside. But Maggie was such a knowledgeable woman.

She went on to the estate agent, and then back to Maggie.

She didn't really know the Buchardts very well, though for years they had been elements of the same social scene. Perhaps they had met first at a party, in the old days, when people danced. She thought she could remember a younger, more slender version of Maggie on one of these occasions, standing a little apart, raising a single well-marked eyebrow (she could do this) at Horst's rather extravagant flirtations. Then of course they met at faculty functions in the warren of hastily augmented buildings of the university where Horst and Danny held positions, and as the years went by, they would meet now and then at dinner parties, and sometimes at larger parties at each other's homes. Under these circumstances, people often become like landmarks in a neighbourhood, elements by which you navigate or whose presence offers the simple reassurance of the familiar, though you haven't really looked at them for years.

When they began to spend much more time together than they'd ever done before, Jessie was sometimes startled to realise that Maggie entertained a view of her that was quite skewed. Once, for example, Maggie was floating the idea that they might go one day with a friend of hers to the Welsh Borders. She and the friend were planning to attend a teachers' summer function, but they could leave Jessie for the day at Hay-on-Wye, to look at books.

'To look at books,' repeated Jessie, temporising.

'That's the big place for antique books, you know – collectors' items. That's what you like, isn't it?'

Maggie was distracted, at this point, by the demands of a child, and Jessie didn't feel obliged to disabuse her. But she felt guilty of social cowardice at not doing so. If only she knew even a little bit about old books. There had been some childhood favourites, inherited from a much older cousin, that had that particular, nice smell, between the pages…

It was like that time, meeting Danny in the Three Tuns, once, after an exploratory outing to a poetry reading. The couple he'd been drinking with had been interested. Their faces brightened; they wanted to know about the event she'd been to, and she was sorry to disappoint them by not having liked it. They tried for a while to find some common ground: what about Betjeman; surely she loved Betjeman? But at the time, she didn't know this Betjeman, and the two of them were reduced to reciting bits to each other.

During the period when Jessie was negotiating for the house in Mountfield Road, she had become a focus of interest. There was that day when Marty and Arlis came up, to add their ideas and impressions, and all five of them went round the house. The men spoke to each other about load-bearing beams and joists; they examined the dust and became technical together. Maggie and Arlis pointed out the picture rails, and the particularly pretty ceiling rose in the front room, from which the frayed wires of the decayed electrics dangled. For Maggie, however, the main discovery was the amazing toilet bowl in the upstairs bathroom, which she declared a late Victorian original.

'Look, look!' she said, in her inimitable husky voice. 'They painted the inside with violets; isn't it wonderful. It must be worth something, don't you think?'

Up and down and round about they trooped, through the echoing, dusty rooms, brushing aside cobwebs, stepping across broken floorboards. Jessie peered into the back garden, in which a great cast-iron bathtub sat submerged by thistles, and her heart felt leaden.

Later they all sat round the Buchardts' kitchen table and discussed the project.

The other four argued it out among themselves, while Jessie listened, trying to grasp the situation. On the whole, Horst put up objections, to which Marty occasionally added. Meanwhile Maggie, who was particularly enamoured of the house, insisted on the case for it. 'The place has real potential,' she said. 'I'm sure Jessie could make something of that house.'

Jessie found herself on Maggie's side of the argument.

Over the next few weeks, she came back several times to explore it further. She sat at the Buchardts' kitchen table, making notes of problems to investigate, drawing up efficient little lists of building firms, jotting down the phone number of a workman Maggie thought she could vouch for.

When she saw the house a second time, it was as though her imagination had grown into it. Moving through the empty rooms again, on her own, she began to see herself there with Ben and Ella, even if it was a somewhat romanticised version of the three of them. In particular, she visualised a stately Christmas tree in the corner, by the fireplace, in the high-ceilinged living room. 'Can you think what it will cost to heat these rooms?' Horst had exclaimed, but the women had brushed him aside. Perhaps they, too, already saw the Christmas tree.

On her next visit, she was struck for the first time by how attractive the house front was (unlike the Buchardts'). How proud you'd be, if it was your house. Even the front door, though its paint was faded, looked impressive, with its old brass knocker, and the deep porch was sheltering and hospitable. *Jessie's house*, she said to herself. She imagined people arriving, for a party.

In particular, she imagined some of her own colleagues, as well as Danny's: her friends, coming to her house. She imagined Oscar, the man she worked for, arriving with his beautiful Swedish wife. Britta would say, in her delicately accented English, 'So this is Jessie's house?' with respect in her voice, as well as some surprise.

It was the sort of house where you could imagine people gathering.

5

Spring, 1976

Later she wondered how that solicitor had managed to allow himself to deliver those bland assurances – and how she could have allowed herself to believe that they meant anything at all.

How could 'both parties' manage to set up households each the equal of the one they'd shared?

How could each of the two halves of a pie (a pie which was not very large to begin with) equal the whole of the pie itself?

What was he talking about?

However, it wasn't until some time after her first interview with Mr Dunwoody that she learned of the one-third–two-thirds rule. Legally, what was due to a wife was just one-third of the couple's joint income and one-third of their joint property.

The maintenance for each child was a small, fixed amount, regardless of the father's income.

'One-third of their joint income,' she repeated. 'Their

joint income? You mean, if the wife earns more than half of what her husband earns, she owes maintenance to him?'

'This is all highly theoretical,' said Mr Dunwoody.

'Very highly theoretical,' said Jessie. 'Since the wife has probably been home with the children anyway, running the household, not building a career.'

'Exactly.'

'But that's outrageous,' she said.

Mr Dunwoody looked faintly uncomfortable. 'Well,' he said. 'I'm afraid it's just the law.'

'All right. All right. I can see that in a way it was my choice,' said Jessie, groping for some rationale for what was happening to her. 'Why should anybody be supported by their partner, if they split up? But surely the fair thing is how you support the children. Surely their maintenance should be based on Danny's earnings. Five pounds a week, you said. I can't believe that's right.'

'Five pounds a week for the first child. It's rather less for the second child, and then there's a bit of a sliding scale.' Mr Dunwoody looked again at the papers in front of them, and for the next few minutes submerged them both in an accumulation of meaningless calculations of amounts so small that Jessie couldn't take them in. It was like being beset by gnats.

He looked back up at her. 'Let's not panic,' he said. 'We haven't received your husband's proposals yet. Most men turn out to be rather more generous than the law requires.'

The odd thing was that no one seemed to share her sense of outrage.

Arlis listened assiduously to her account. But at the end, she only sighed and shook her head, dropping her eyes to scrutinise her cigarette. 'Mmm,' she said. 'I don't know what to say. It's difficult.'

But – hadn't Arlis realised?

'Jessie, it's not my area,' said Arlis. 'I don't deal with the legal side of things. As far as I know, the wife and children usually stay in the family home. Unless they're in a refuge, of course.'

On her sofa, across the room, she had now put out the cigarette, and shifted into a self-protective curl. One hand supporting her plump elbow, she chewed her fingernails, looking across at Jessie warily.

'It's just – I can't believe it,' Jessie said. 'He must be wrong. He's got it wrong, he must have. Maybe he's only good at house conveyancing.'

Arlis uncurled. 'You need to look around,' she said. 'Ask someone else.'

'Who?' cried Jessie, fighting a bubble of hysteria. 'Who do I know? I can't keep taking time away from work. I can't keep being late home for the kids.'

'Calm down,' soothed Arlis. 'Don't be so defensive. You worry far too much about the kids; they're fine. Look, Marty'll be back here any minute. Have a cigarette. You can wait five minutes, surely.'

But Marty, too, was at a loss. 'Arlis, how should I know somebody?'

'The law department?' Arlis ventured.

He gave her a look.

Jessie had gone through it all again. Although she knew it would be out of character in Marty, she found herself trying to rouse his indignation – to invoke some satisfying blaze of fellow feeling. It wasn't right. Surely it was so wrong that it could not be true.

For a moment, indeed, he seemed quite shocked. 'Ouch,' he said, feelingly, passing his hand across his eyes.

'Marty, she needs a new solicitor,' said Arlis.

'Wait a minute. Wait,' said Marty. He continued to knead his forehead. Then he looked up at Jessie. 'Is that what you want?'

'I need to know,' she said, uncertainly.

'You don't think you can believe this guy?'

'How can I?'

This was where Arlis interjected. Surely he knew somebody – Marty must know of someone who could help.

And Marty didn't.

'Oh, there'll be somebody,' Jessie said, recovering herself. 'I'll find somebody.'

'Sure you will,' said Marty.

She'd have asked her boss – Oscar knew everybody – but he was away on a lengthy selling trip. The guys in the design department, on the other hand, were not the kind of people who knew people. They were friendly and streetwise, and they said (as she had feared they would), but why don't you ask Marjorie? She'd know. Or Henry, Henry'd definitely know; ask him.

So she went back to her own department, now ruled by Marjorie with the unofficial support of Henry.

She didn't believe that Henry and Marjorie were sympathetic to her situation. Well, Henry and Marjorie were not sympathetic to her. None of them were, in her department. There was a history. Even Peta and Annabelle, the two younger women, kept their distance. If she mentioned her life at all to them, these days, even something funny one of the kids had done, say, she could almost see the interest shutter in their eyes.

But Henry and Marjorie were, if anything, more egregiously wary, though there'd been a moment, when she first broke the news, when she had thought that they might soften.

'I'm very sorry to hear that. Very sorry,' Henry had said, with likeable readiness. He fixed on her his very round blue eyes with a solemnity that might have seemed to commiserate. 'It's so difficult for the children.'

And Marjorie said, 'This is very sad news. I'm truly sorry, Jessie.'

They continued to gaze at her from their desks, facing her, in silence.

Jessie said, 'Well, it's been coming for a long time.'

This seemed to break the spell.

'I don't imagine that would make it any easier,' said Marjorie, in a curiously reproving sing-song; and with an air of relief, she picked up her paper and shook it out, turning to the Positions Vacant page (as she did, each morning), eyes screwed against her cigarette smoke.

The next morning, Jessie found on her desk a freshly updated schedule, with her own deadlines brought forward by a week.

'Jess, I know what you're going to say,' said Marjorie, before she could raise a protest. 'But I think we really have to do this. We can't afford another slip-up. We need to pace you.'

Except for Henry, they'd all worked together for three years now, but Jessie had been there from the start. She herself had dreamed up all the projects they were working on. She shouldn't have found herself so entirely unsupported. But there were ongoing disputes between her and Marjorie about her schedules.

As for solicitors, Marjorie referred her to Henry.

Henry was deeply disapproving.

'But you already have a solicitor?' he confirmed. 'Then I really don't see how I can help you.'

'But you do know somebody?'

'I do know people, yes. But I don't think you can do that – can you, Marjorie?'

'Mmm,' said Marjorie thoughtfully. 'Perhaps you're right.'

'What you'd be doing – isn't it…?' Henry folded his arms, and used a Latin phrase.

'Is it?' asked Marjorie.

'I think so,' he said.

'It might be in the *OED*. Well, the big one,' said Marjorie, reaching for it. The dictionary was always kept close at hand, for the crossword puzzles.

'I don't understand. Doing what?' said Jessie.

'Well, as I understand it, what you're asking someone to do is to give you advice that may run counter to the advice of a fellow solicitor. When you're actually in his care.'

'But if he's wrong—'

'If you don't trust the man, you shouldn't be with him,' Henry said robustly, and the round blue eyes looked almost hostile.

So she had to plead.

'Well, I'll see what I can do,' he said at last, unpromisingly.

Eventually, it was conceded that there might be a way around this difficulty. She might possibly, just possibly, have a chat with someone, who would be seeing her as a personal favour to Henry. She would be seeing him (Henry briefed her sternly, when he had arranged this interview) on an entirely informal basis, just as a chat.

'You do appreciate,' he said again, 'you can't just shop around for a solicitor.'

The actual exchange between her and Freddie Benedict was quite brief. She sat on an enormous leather chair, in the expensive city office, and gave him her prepared statement. Given that she was considering the possibility of a separation… believed she knew the outlines, but if he could clarify… and surely, surely, what she'd heard about child maintenance… here she departed from the script… this business of a fixed amount, no matter what the circumstances—

'You're American, aren't you,' he broke in.

'Yes, but—'

'I'm afraid you're going to be terribly disappointed with us,' he interposed. 'No great alimony settlements, I fear.'

'Alimony,' Jessie said. 'Oh, no. Of course not.'

Had he heard what she'd been saying? He sat four-square to her, his large, flushed face presented to her, and yet he seemed, somehow, to be under duress; to be paused in flight.

'I do understand the position of the wife,' she repeated, hurriedly. 'I understand that. I mean, it's odd, but –' hastily back-tracking – 'I do understand the principle. Why should I go on being personally supported? I mean, just for having been a wife?'

He stared at her wordlessly.

'But the point is, children are a different issue.'

'Yes.' Unexpectedly, he nodded.

'I mean—'

'I think you mentioned that you're acquainted with the rule there.'

'Well, I heard something.'

'Yes?'

'Only it can't be right.'

He waited.

'Five pounds a week.' She laughed. 'It can't be right. I mean – for a professional man? I mean – it's ludicrous!'

At this point, his phone rang. He answered it. It was a very, very long conversation. He smiled into the telephone. He hunched over it, twiddling a pen, smiling companionably in its direction. After a while, he sat back in his chair. He put down his pen, and she hoped that at last the conversation might be over, but it wasn't. He ran his fingers through his hair, luxuriously. He laughed. Again, he bent above the phone, his fingers curled around the desk edge. The call continued.

At no point did he look in her direction.

She began to wonder if she should really be there. Was she meant to leave? She tightened her clasped fingers, waiting.

At last, he was saying his goodbyes. The strengthening

May sunlight was golden in the seamless window behind his desk, suffused through the linen staves of vertical blinds; by the big clock to the right, above the door, twenty minutes had gone by.

'There you are,' he said. He brought down his two hands smartly on his desk, in a gesture of conclusion. 'That man earns fifty thousand a year. And he only pays five pounds a week for his child.'

'You see?' said Henry, when she had told them of the outcome. 'Aren't you glad you didn't ditch your solicitor?'

6

It would become the summer of the heatwave, when even the perennially green lawns of the London parks eventually crisped and browned, and the great ornamental lakes shrank; and all through the months of this amazing weather, the remaining pieces of Jessie's broken life, not yet fixed into their new positions, seemed continually to rearrange themselves into patterns suggesting new alarms or hopes, unstable as a heat mirage.

But in April, it just seemed an unusually lovely spring. For a few weeks, while Danny was still away, Jessie managed to put aside her speculations about what would happen to them all; she didn't know (as Marty emphasised); why not save the worries till she knew?

She had turned to the Goldmans, Marty and Arlis, several times after that first phone call. One Sunday, they invited her with the children. Once she went back in the evening after going home to cook a meal and settle Ella down with Ben; another time, one Friday, she even stayed the night, waking early to get home for the Saturday routines. She had dropped by after work as well, once, when she was struggling to write to Danny. She didn't mean to stay long – didn't really stay that long, perhaps an hour? – in any case, she'd not infrequently been kept that late at work and had to ring home asking Ben to put the casserole in the oven, say, or scrub potatoes. But it was odd to walk back through the fine old Bloomsbury squares toward the first link of her commute: under trees just starting into leaf, past the big central bookshops with their lavish sequence of displays, and then the few really splendid shops of furniture, where the windows showcased just the one fine thing or two, in a well-positioned spot of light.

At this point, of course, she had not yet managed to complete the letter, but she meant to be very clear, direct, straightforward. There'd been enough emotion. It was time to move; she was fortified by this intention, and the signs of spring – the lengthening days, the small, bright leaves and fretted twigs – felt promising, and new, and raw.

She sent the letter to reach him in the last few days before he left. Then there was another week of waiting.

She was expecting him to arrive back on a Sunday. On Saturday morning, as she went down for the post, she felt a thrill of apprehension: what she'd done seemed increasingly real and frightening as the time approached for a response to it; but there was only a letter from her parents, far away in California.

It seemed a vulnerable object, this neat little envelope from Planet Yesterday, where they did not yet know her news.

She went up and began the Saturday chores.

In the weeks that Danny had been away, she and the children had begun to weld into a unit. From time to time, she fell into long chats with one of them, or even (though less often), both together. They had flights of silliness. They made noise, sometimes, with a freedom not circumscribed by Danny's thinking, for which he so often needed to commandeer the living spaces. At times, it almost seemed to Jessie as though she was finding access to new reserves of energy. One Saturday, she even sang, trying out an ancient repertoire of folk songs and old jazz classics as she mopped and vacuumed. Was she whistling in the dark?

One or two stray little girls ran up and down the stairs with Ella, up to the living rooms on the first floor, and down the trendy exterior back stairs to the patch of garden shadowed by the little wood. Oddly, they didn't explore the wood. Once they made a guinea-pig assault course on the meagre lawn, with some bricks and a plank they found, and a pillow from which Jessie had to shake out guinea-pig droppings, later on. Another day, Ella went off with her new friend Sasha and Sasha's mother to a jumble sale, and came back radiant with pleasure, in a skirt and jumper she had bought herself, with her own pocket money. It being England, they had their uniforms for school, and Jessie, who lacked the dedication of a good consumer, tended to forget about buying clothes until a situation forced the need upon them.

Ella wore her new outfit the day they all went to the Goldmans, and Arlis was much amused. 'Ella has more sense of style than you have!' she exclaimed. 'Jessie, Ella could give you lessons!'

In fact, Ben and Ella were both looking very nice, that day, pleased with the special attention.

Arlis pursued her gambit. 'Ella,' she said. 'Couldn't you take your mum to St Mary's jumble sale?'

'It won't be there any more,' said Ella, her face slightly shadowed. 'A jumble sale is just one day.'

Arlis laughed. 'You'll have to find your mum another jumble sale.'

She had mounted a campaign on the subject of Jessie's wardrobe. It was one of the signs of Jessie's subjugation as wife, she thought, though that was wrong. Danny loved to dress her up.

After lunch, that Saturday of waiting, Jessie and Ella went by bus to the vast new supermarket in the shopping centre, one of those retail centres that were beginning to spring up everywhere like plastic fungi. Jessie was still not used to getting the groceries at this place. Of course, it was only a version of what was happening even faster back home in the States, yet it seemed to her alien and unfriendly, like an object so flimsy it was bound to break before you even got used to it.

In the neighbourhood where they'd settled when first in London, there were shops just up the road, five minutes away, a long, miscellaneous parade; there'd been little hardship in bringing home your shopping in a trolley or even hanging from a baby's pushchair. The children had the freedom of the neighbourhood. It was a rackety, characterless neighbourhood, a little new development tucked in among a heterogeneous array of older homes and shops, but it had seemed to small-town Jessie poignantly urban.

Albion Grove, by contrast, was quite isolated from commercial life – from any public life, really. The streets that led to the station were residential, lined with great, silent trees, and walls, and the blank façades of purpose-built flats. In the other direction, falling away downhill from the wooded enclave of the smart, new town houses where they lived, was an area that would once presumably have boasted a variety of shops and cafés, even a street market, but was now an acreage of urban desolation, the shops almost entirely boarded up, enlivened only by the occasional pub or betting shop. It would have been impossible to shop on foot, and Jessie was obliged every Saturday to make the shopping trek by bus.

In the evening, she did some ironing.

It was very strange to find herself doing this. Was she already becoming a calmer, more effective person? Ironing was so often an emergency exercise, with someone panicking or scowling while she did it, yet here she was, working her way through one after another of the pieces laundered just that morning. She could even glimpse the bottom of the bag – even imagine emptying the bag.

Ella had said, when Jessie tucked her in, 'It's good we cleaned the house today, when Daddy will be coming home tomorrow.'

'We're not sure,' said Jessie.

'But we think so,' Ella said.

Jessie said, 'Tomorrow afternoon, it's Sasha's birthday party.'

Ella said, 'He'll probably be here when I get home.'

Jessie ducked this comment. She had talked about the situation with Ella and Ben. She'd already said how much she didn't know.

She picked up a lock of Ella's hair, just washed for the

birthday party. She said, 'Your hair looks nice.' It had lost its baby silkiness and the blondeness was winter darkened now. But Ella's colouring was still extraordinary: the skin so white, the brows and lashes black, the mouth almost unnaturally red, like a scarlet rosebud.

She kissed the little scarlet mouth and Ella's arms whipped suddenly round her neck. For a moment, they held each other, tightly.

'Sweet dreams,' she said finally, kissing the plump little cheek once more, and then at last, as Ella squeezed her eyes shut and made a show of burrowing down into her pillow, she saw the rosebud mouth relax, the corner curving up, almost contentedly. And it occurred to her that she could iron the dress Ella would be wearing to the party.

She went down to the laundry room and set up the iron in the entrance way. When she'd finished the dress, she thought she might just do another bit. Then she kept going.

After a while, Ben arrived back from a walk. She didn't know where he found to go, on these walks of his. He didn't offer information and it felt wrong to probe, perhaps to reveal the loneliness in which he found himself in this neighbourhood.

So she said only, with false brightness, 'Did you have a good walk?'

And he said only, with a look clearly intended to be cheerful, 'Oh, yes, thanks.'

Then he kissed her goodnight and went on up to bed, and Jessie continued with her task. It occurred to her that she hadn't smoked a cigarette since early evening.

The entrance hall opened into the big main bedroom as

well as Danny's study and the stairs and laundry room. She had got a stack of wire hangers from the bedroom wardrobe, and as she worked, she hooked the finished items to the top of the door frame: first Ella's dress, and then the big and medium-sized and little shirts, some cotton trousers folded over, two of her own skirts, pinned up with clothes pegs. The collection grew. She began to be aware of the comforting smell of the hot iron on freshly laundered fabric, the soft thump of the iron, as in her mother's kitchen, back at home.

It wasn't a cosy place to work, this empty space under the glare of an overhead light. But there was a section of the wall where she'd thought you might put a bookcase one day, and you might put a lamp there, too. Perhaps a plant. You might hang a picture over it.

Though she had felt no special fondness for the house before they moved there, she had found that it began to open out to her, though only a corner of it at a time. The galley kitchen, she'd realised, was actually wide enough to comfortably allow a tall stool (if you had a stool), which you could perch on while you chopped and stirred, as in her favourite kitchen, the first of their married life. She'd thought she might hang bunches of herbs from ceiling hooks there, and how from this envisioned perch you could look past the herbs into the wood, or onto the balcony where the birds came hopping. You could have herbs in pots, too, or a planter, and a proper bird feeder.

It had occurred to her that you could have a great pot of geraniums by the front door, a huge, round pot, she imagined it, sky-blue.

These scraps of vision for the house had fed her confidence.

The house itself had fed her confidence. She felt important as she ascended that wide, softly carpeted stair. It was as though once you had something – security, for instance, and support – you were equipped inside, and then you could do without it. As though it had really made her a different person, and after this, she could face what she might have to face.

7

With Ella away at her party, Jessie spent most of Sunday afternoon in Crystal Palace Park, alone.

Though the park was quite close, it had never seemed part of their neighbourhood. They'd never explored it as a family, and she'd never been there before by herself. In fact, though you were aware of its presence (the tops of its trees, for instance, and the rise from which the giant structure of the TV transmitter towered), in all the months they'd lived in Albion Grove it had eluded them, like a sorcerer's enclosure.

Once, on one of their rare family walks, they'd spent some fifteen minutes on the park's perimeter, having come across its iron railings. Jessie urged them on. Surely, surely, this would lead them to a gate. But it was midwinter, already very late – they never managed to get out until it was nearly sunset; the chilly dusk soon gathered. Thwarted, they'd turned back again.

Today, taking a new direction, she came across an entrance, and found herself on a great tract of lawn, near playing fields and low, unenticing shrubbery. She was disappointed at how unremarkable it was. Where was the crystal palace? But the day was sunny and very mild, unusually warm for the end of April. She sat on the grass and smoked, conscious of these good auguries, and tried to enjoy the unaccustomed liberty. Here I am in the sunshine in a park, with nothing at all to do but just relax.

Gradually, she realised she was frightened.

It had been very late by the time she went to sleep the night before. After finishing the ironing, she had dawdled, almost exhilarated. For a while she lingered in the darkened living room, drinking whisky, looking out at the distant lights of central London, smoking and daydreaming. Perversely, her mind still ran on thoughts about the house, and in particular the kitchen. She could get strings of onions, like the ones brought by the onion seller man, massive ropes of braided onion stems slung across his old iron bicycle. Would there be an onion seller man, here? Maybe somebody could get them for her. She could hang smoked sausages as well. There she would be, perched on her tall stool, in the midst of this aromatic plenty, stirring something in a great iron pot… Of course, it was just a daydream, but it was so pleasant. And after all, who knew? Almost against her will, she'd been affected by Arlis's mantra: the marital home…

In the morning she was awake again at seven.

She put on the kettle and got the Sunday paper from the doorstep. There were several interesting items in the review section. She found herself dreaming up possibilities for new projects that she might get taken up at work, one day – so many that she began to scribble down some notes, but then she stopped herself. It was like that, sometimes: ideas branching out from one another, like the jerking growth of plants in clever nature films. At those times, she felt tremendously hopeful and excited, as though this self of hers (of which at other times she was so doubtful) would now be permanently carried by the current of ideas, and never trouble her again.

But she was determined to stay calm, and in control. There were things to be done, and you still had to do them. And she was proud to be up so early on a Sunday, even before Ella.

For a treat, she made American pancakes, and they had a proper big Sunday breakfast. They were quite chatty together, for a while, and then busy. She helped Ella wrap the birthday present, and let her have a go at curling the ribbon round the scissor's blade, and Ella was elated at finally managing – once! – to create that magical cascade of ribbon ringlets. She tried to talk to Ben about his vexed biology homework.

She didn't recognise the level of anxiety she was experiencing. She thought it was energy.

By two o'clock, Ella had been collected for the party and Ben had gone off by bus on a lengthy expedition to their former neighbourhood, in hopes of meeting up with one or two of the old friends he'd kept in touch with there. Jessie thought she should go out, as well.

She didn't know when Danny might be expected. They hadn't had that sort of parting. She didn't want to be there when he arrived, as though waiting for him. She felt a little defiant on this score.

Now, in the sunshine, in the park, she began to be afraid that he would find her there.

This was unreal, she knew. They'd never even been to this place together. How could he find her? Why would he think of looking for her, here?

Why would he want to?

Where she sat, the grass had been invaded by areas of close-growing groundcover, almost flat to the earth: cushions of thickly growing small, round leaves with the occasional miniature blue flower. She fingered the little leaves, and traced the stem of a tiny flower, plucking one and then another of them. Would they last, if she took them home to Ella? She plunged a hand into one of these cushiony areas and then, on an impulse, she leaned over and put her face into the grass, inhaling its scent, feeling its prickly warmth.

Suddenly, with a thrill of alarm, she jerked upright and turned to face him.

But he wasn't there.

Now, she was frightened. She had felt compelled to turn, as though he had called her name. She had been so sure that she would see him striding towards her, hands fisted, those wide shoulders swinging, the dark eyes forbidding. Her heart was thumping.

She would have thought it conventional to be afraid that he would hit her. She liked to think that she was strong (though of course, he was a big man, and very tall), and after all, she had hit him, too. But now she was physically, unreasonably frightened. She felt, unreasonably, that she no longer knew what he might do.

Above stretched a bland, pale sky, interrupted only by

the great thrust of the transmitter; round about stretched the institutional greens of grass and shrubs. She felt foolish, sitting there alone on that strange lawn.

She thought she had better get used to this. She would get used to it. Scared, self-conscious, she tried to concentrate on the feel of the warm sun on her skin. She took a deep breath. Soon, she lit another cigarette.

It was a very long afternoon.

At the end of it, she felt nauseous and headachy after so many cigarettes, so little sleep, but she'd stuck it out. She'd made the experiment; she had not just stayed at home and waited for him. As she finally drew near her door, she was intercepted by a neighbour, full of apologies, with a letter. It had arrived on Friday, *sorry*; all the post had gone awry that day. A temporary postman.

So there was a letter from him, and after all, he wouldn't be coming home.

The letter was brief and business-like. Her decision had been a relief to him, he said; he didn't think there was anything he needed immediately to come back for. He'd see a solicitor himself, and be in touch. He didn't mention Ben and Ella.

8

On Monday, Jessie rang Danny at his office. The term would have started, so she knew there was a good chance she might find him there, and her own office was empty for the moment.

He picked up the phone immediately. 'Jessie!' he exclaimed, when he heard her voice, in a tone of such innocent surprise that it seemed like welcome. She was struck through with a pang of intense relief. His voice was as dear to her as ever, its freshness and energy. In comparison, her own seemed peculiarly nervous and uncertain.

It appeared that, for the time being, he was staying at the Goldmans'. He referred to this with dry amusement, as though it was some Noël Coward comedy they were all involved in. He didn't mind about the sheets, he said, with just the hint of a lascivious reference to the night she'd spent there.

No, he really didn't need anything from Albion Grove; he'd been meaning to buy some new socks and underwear, in any case. Perhaps a few new shirts, as well.

But what about Ben and Ella?

Well yes, he said; they'd have to come to some arrangement.

'Well, this week,' she began, but he interrupted her. He was completely tied up this week, with the new term beginning, and he didn't know how long it would take to find a flat for himself. He had some ideas. In fact, he might already have a lead, but it would take some time, as she could well imagine.

'But Ben and Ella – you'll see them before that, won't you?'

'Jessie, I need to get a place first.'

'But I don't mean having them to stay. I mean, see them.' She felt, by now, totally off balance. 'Danny,' she implored him, 'they'll want to see you.'

'No, no, no,' he said, as though reassuringly. 'It's much better for them to see me when I've got organised. Much better.'

He'd be in touch, he said, into the silence. Then, she was all right, wasn't she? The Goldmans had assured him that she was fine. He was very glad she'd had the Goldmans to support her, and he hoped he'd return them to her before too long. Well, he hoped so for his own sake, too; he didn't know how long he could put up with Arlis. In any case, she was all right for the time being, yes? Well, she was to take care, then. And he'd be in touch, he said again.

Ella asked, 'Doesn't he want to see us?'

Confronted with this unanswerable question, Jessie was filled again with the mix of rage and grief and helplessness that had been threatening since she put down the phone that afternoon.

She'd avoided telling them until they'd had their supper. Then she'd said, as though casually, well, she'd spoken to their dad and, after all, he'd got back yesterday, and he was fine, and he was staying at the Goldmans', but she didn't know yet when they might be seeing him. Really, he thought it would be best if he got his own place, first.

Ben just nodded. He looked at her with a wry half-smile – really, just a grimace of acknowledgement – and nodded, and then he got up and started to clear away the dishes and wash up, which was his job that night.

Ella, however, insisted on clarification.

'You mean, he's not coming back here?'

'No.'

'He's not coming home at all?'

'No – not back to this house – no.'

For a moment, Ella said nothing more. Perhaps she was letting this fact sink in. Then she began again. 'Couldn't we go and see him?'

'Well, that's the problem; he doesn't have his own place, yet.'

Ella waited, with a look of puzzlement.

'It won't be long,' said Jessie.

Ella said, 'We could go up to his office. Why don't we do that? We went up there before, once.'

'Well, I guess he doesn't think that's a good idea. You know, the term's just started, and it's all very rushed, with all the—'

'Doesn't he want to see us?'

'It isn't that,' said Jessie.

How could she keep on saying this?

Ella stared at her.

'But I want to see him.'

'Yes,' said Jessie, finally. 'I know.'

'And doesn't he…' Ella's voice cracked. 'He doesn't want to see us?'

9

As it happened, Danny didn't spend many nights on the Goldmans' sofa. His first stroke of luck came within days of his return: Janice, the friend of a friend, had just married and moved in with her new husband, and handed on to him her old flat in central London. It solved a problem for Janice, and provided a happy outcome for everyone involved. It was a rent-controlled flat which she had, herself, inherited from another family member, and though she could no longer make much use of the place, it was too valuable a possession to relinquish, so she sub-let to Danny. This would be good for Jessie, too, it was pointed out to her, since financially there would be that much more to go around.

Since the sub-let was illegal (though undoubtedly customary), and since Janice as the leaseholder wanted the option of an occasional night or weekend there, close to the theatres as it was, and because she knew Danny, and possibly, too, because he was Danny, she asked of him only the same peppercorn rent she had herself been paying. Thus, Danny's rent was almost exactly (as Jessie worked out, later) the price of Jessie's weekly commute. But Danny was exempt from transport costs, now, since he could walk to his office or to his classes in less than fifteen minutes, as he told her with delight when they were again in regular communication.

The flat had no amenities, no central heating, not even a fridge (but when you had no heat, you didn't need a fridge, he joked); it badly needed doing up; he would be starting from scratch. It had a small extra bedroom where the kids could stay, occasionally (at least, when Janice and/or her husband weren't making one of their rare visits). Two small floors, it was, above a small, dark tobacconist, on a short, lively street just off a main thoroughfare, and just round the corner from – well, nearly everything. Funny little shops and restaurants, a traditional fish and chip shop (the best in London, Danny would later boast), old churches, theatres, small old parks, the National Gallery, the British Museum, the Thames itself…

Danny was particularly entertained by the fact that he was profiting from a black market in rent control, a system which theoretically he so deplored. But this was exactly how to bring down a system that was intrinsically unfair and vulnerable to abuse: you just went ahead and abused it till it sank. It was almost Marxist, wasn't it: a delicious thought; you were just advancing the inevitable downfall.

Well, Jessie knew that this was how he would regard it, what a joke he'd think it; and of course, Marty, who shared his excitement at the critical possibilities of the new economics they embraced, took the same position.

But was it just a satire of a false solution – or of any attempt at all at a solution? That bracing realism she'd once delighted in seemed increasingly underpinned by a glee at human cupidity that unsettled her.

During the time before Danny established some routine contact with the children, Jessie managed to keep track of his general whereabouts and welfare through the Goldmans. Arlis had rung her late on Monday evening to mention that he was staying with them for a while – to fill her in, and to warn her off. Jessie had been grateful to hear her voice; she'd assumed that for a while she would lose this link.

'Jessie, I'm sorry about this,' said Arlis. 'I know you've relied on us. But I don't think it will be for very long. He's already had a lead about a flat.'

But though she began in this spirit of compunction and apology, the social interest of the situation won her over. Soon she, too, was making jokes about the pre-used sheets, the ex-marital sofa (a witticism of Marty's which she repeated with heavy jocularity); how they were all playing turn and turn-about. Even Jessie was drawn in, seduced by the sheer, companionable gossipiness of this treatment. She felt wistful thinking of the three of them in that big, friendly flat, drinking whisky together, eating a lingering late supper; and Danny being amusing about his interesting situation, charming even to Arlis, probably. Perhaps, even – who could know? – he would warm to Arlis. Taken out of herself, she could be childishly delighted and engaging, and after all, Marty liked her…

She thought of the new intimacies that might emerge, as they had done so rapidly when she herself had flown to Marty and Arlis. Perhaps Danny, too, would have moments of openness with Marty; would perhaps confide…

'Danny?' scoffed Arlis, when Jessie began to suggest as much, in a later phone call. 'Those two, talking about emotions? You must be joking.'

But Danny's bachelor flat became available almost immediately. By the end of the week, he had bought a duvet and a camp-bed (useful later, for when the children stayed) and begun to establish himself there. For these details Jessie was indebted to Arlis, who had them from a friend connected to Janice. Listening to the various names woven through this narrative, one or two them teasingly familiar, as though they had all once met at parties, Jessie envisioned a whole social world from which she appeared to be excluded.

Arlis and her friend were particularly delighted by a version of the transaction in which Janice had first negotiated key-money and visiting rights, and then swanned off on her honeymoon, leaving Danny to clear the debris of a raucous wedding party, though Jessie later doubted if it could possibly have happened this way. If it had happened.

'She just swanned off to the Canaries!' Arlis repeated, with considerable relish. 'She left it a mess!' She assured Jessie that at present the little flat was still so bare and dirty that Danny couldn't possibly have the children stay.

Then, in a different key, she added, 'Give him time, Jessie – he's very anxious.'

'Anxious?' Jessie repeated, wanting to hear more.

'He's lost his family,' said Arlis.

'Yes. Of course,' said Jessie.

'It's bound to take him a while to settle.'

'Oh,' said Jessie. 'Sure.'

She had begun to be visited by spells of furious defiance. Well, she would manage, then; she'd manage by herself; she'd provide the parenting on his behalf as well as on her own; she would win out.

At work, the same spirit energised her; she'd recently taken a number of initiatives that were daring to the point of rashness. After all, she could not resist. The ideas were too good. She couldn't bear to subject them to the flattening scrutiny that Marjorie would impose.

Marjorie had been her manager for two years, since just after the little company's first twenty months. Those first months had been a crazy time, a period in which Jessie had shot from the position of general gofer to Oscar and his then partner (just the three of them, mocking up covers and titles – sometimes hilariously – for a non-existent list of mass-market children's books) through a chaotic period in which the partners disappeared into smoke-filled rooms while Jessie roughed out the first books on her own and temporarily became, herself, manager of an ever-larger staff that included Marjorie. Then, out of the messy birth-pangs of this effort, it was Marjorie who emerged as manager. Jessie, however, still allowed herself (at least, sometimes) to consider this development to have been a rather meaningless, if sometimes painful and irritating, glitch – an organisational technicality, which was bound in time to be corrected. When the new little company had got its feet. When more reviews of her own books came through…

So what if she could not yet see how everything would

work? Surely her ideas had proved themselves: the reviews, the sales, had been a triumph, though so belated... She deserved another chance to innovate...

It was strange that, just as it seemed the tide was turning on her once again, new problems emerging and piling up in her life, her mind reacted by going almost into overdrive. At times, now, she could hardly type fast enough to get down the details of these new proposals, and her typing was extremely rapid. Surely now they ought to recognise – Oscar, at least, would recognise...

And if they didn't, she'd have to take the initiative herself. It was a time for risks.

Dear Dad (wrote Ella),

Can I please come and visit you? I miss you very much. Please tell me when you get a new adress. I hope you are well.

Love,

Ella

By the time Ella came to Jessie with this letter, Danny did have an address. Jessie found an envelope and stamp and let Ella write it out herself, in her own best nearly-nine-years'-old handwriting.

To herself she thought, ah, this will get to him.

She was still half-consciously waiting for a moment when they would all meet, and it would be like a family, though it was the end. They would share the pain of it.

She was still half-consciously haunted by scenarios in which she met him herself, and he saw at last that she was serious. He would ask her why. Not challenging or dismissing her, not as a prelude to debate. Just, why?

Not long after Ella's letter reached him, Danny rang.

He sounded almost breezy. He wasn't, of course, properly set up yet, he told Jessie. He was full of detail about the arrangements that were needed, to make a home of this neglected pied-à-terre. It would take a while! But naturally he was looking forward to seeing Ella, and Ben as well, and perhaps they would like to meet him for a pizza.

Ella was very happy. Ben said it would be nice to meet Dad for a pizza.

This was more or less all you expected Ben to say, these days.

10

Jessie broke down only once, that summer. That one time, with Arlis, showed how dangerous it was: it might be impossible to stop, if you let go. And there was only once when she realised how scared she was; and after all, the fear had been peculiar to the day, and hardly rational.

But from time to time, she was conscious of a sense of grief that was like an enormous bruise, so that the most commonplace events and random memories could make her wince.

She hadn't wanted to lose him, not for ever. Really, it sometimes seemed, she had only needed everything to just stop, for a while, to let her breathe and find out how to think straight. After all, she loved him. She was bound to him by a thousand threads of hope and memory. Once, they had been going to do so much, together. They were going to think great, liberating thoughts, create some fine new moral synthesis – find some entirely new way of being happy. He was her great, true love.

This grief could exist right alongside flashes of hope,

ambition – even exhilaration; let alone those much more frequent times of being enraged and newly hurt, bewildered, and humiliated by him. And right alongside the most ignoble, burning fits of envy.

Anger made it easier, at least temporarily. Sometimes, over the particularly tumultuous months preceding the break-up, she'd experienced the clarity of outrage; and what a relief that was.

Once, in January, under the influence of such a moment, she'd gone to her friend Lucy, ringing her late one evening with a cry for help. It was the one other time she'd done such a thing: perhaps even a rehearsal for that terminal phone call to the Goldmans, the unconscious prelude to it.

There were many first times, during those odd months. Everything was breaking apart, yet seemed also, perhaps, about to come together in some new way. You didn't know. You couldn't tell, from one day to the next. At times, there seemed no way of knowing whether any action either of them took was an impulse of healthy spontaneity that might save them, or came from a darker, more destructive source.

But Lucy's voice on the telephone had seemed like sanity.

With some reluctance, she called out to Danny, just before she left, that she was going out. Lucy was coming to collect her.

'Go right ahead,' he called back.

She made her way down to the garage area, where the cars came in, and waited there under the cold, blurred darkness of the city sky for Lucy to drive up.

It was odd how they always lived in houses that were particularly set up for people who had cars, and they never had one. Of course, in London you shouldn't need one, but then again, in this part of south London, you really did, and the vagaries of public transport, particularly across the width of it (it seemed most routes led into central London, like spokes of a wheel), made the few miles that separated her from Lucy seem impassable as desert. Particularly now, of course, since Lucy had acquired a baby and a toddler, while Jessie had at last got herself a job, even a career, though she still felt herself so much less experienced than Lucy – as though she was much younger, though she wasn't, really.

Lucy pulled up and reached across to open the car door, peering up at Jessie with a diffident, wry smile. 'Are you all right?' she asked.

'Oh, I don't know.'

'Is he being an utter bastard?'

Of course, she knew that Lucy actually liked him. She also suspected that Lucy's husband had his own (perhaps uneasy) depths. It seemed an almost comradely remark.

'Yes. Yes,' she said. There came a sob, though it began as a cracked laugh, and she pressed a knuckle to her forehead.

Lucy sighed. 'Oh dear,' she said.

'I'm sorry,' Jessie said. 'It's so good of you to come round like this. I'm sorry.'

'Never mind,' said Lucy, gently.

They made their way in silence for a while, along the deserted late-night streets, and gradually, Jessie found herself growing calmer. Lucy asked about Ben and Ella. Was Ben okay? Was Ella still so happy at her new school? Lucy remembered about things like this.

The sleeping house was very cold; it was so late that

the radiators had all shut down. The two women sat in the kitchen with their coats on, while the kettle boiled, and after a while, Lucy lit a burner on the cooker top, for heat. Jessie had never known anyone do this before. She was amazed to think that this little circlet of blue flame might be expected to make any difference; but it did.

So they stayed on in this friendly kitchen, lit only by a small, shaded table-lamp, and the long, cool glow from the cooker top and the single gas ring, from which Jessie lit cigarette after cigarette as she went through the details of her demeaning story. What he said and what I said, and what he said then, and how I'd thought. And how I don't. But what he did that other time, and what he said, then. And so forth, and so on.

Lucy watched her with a look of challenging directness. Once, she reached out for a cigarette, though she put it out after just a few inhalations; when they first knew each other they both smoked; nearly everybody did, then. Once, she crossed her arms and gave her head a shake. Her rather bony, lovely, deeply freckled face was still to the point of sternness.

At last she said, with fierce protectiveness, 'Jessie, you must just remember, you are right! He is wrong!'

Taken aback, Jessie said, 'I'm right?' What was she right about? How could him being wrong mean she was right? This was a recurring problem for her.

Lucy couldn't say. Jessie had a sense that there was something here that was important, maybe crucial; but she couldn't put her finger on it. Nor could Lucy, who seemed to know it without needing to articulate it.

Lucy said, 'He's only trying to get the better of you. He's

just winding you up; you mustn't let him. He's just being cruel. I had a cousin who used to do that to me all the time. She's older than I am, and I was so fond of her.'

'But why do people do that?' Jessie asked.

'Oh, why?' asked Lucy, with that wry, knowledgeable look she had, which made Jessie suddenly feel that perhaps they lived in different universes, after all, since she still asked such questions, whereas Lucy seemed to have already settled them. Lucy got up to put the kettle on again. 'Or would you like a drink?' she asked. 'I can't, because I'm going to drive you, but go on. It's better for you than a cigarette.'

'But do you mind if I smoke another cigarette, as well?' asked Jessie, with a sense that this was probably as childish as her metaphysical questioning. Lucy only laughed, and poured out the whisky, and put a little pitcher of water on the table next to it.

After this, Lucy drove her home again, and Jessie found that she was feeling better. She felt more ordinary. Nothing had been decided, nothing solved, but she still felt better, and perhaps she should have tried again to talk to Lucy. Perhaps she should have called on her again, the way she had that night; perhaps she might have learned what Lucy knew, or seemed to know. But at the time, she hadn't known how to ask.

To her surprise, Danny hadn't condemned this midnight flight. She had expected a certain look of outraged contempt, but no – almost the opposite. He seemed, if anything, amused. He seemed to think that this was quite endearing: two females huddling like this for comfort.

He said, 'You were complaining about me, weren't you? Isn't that what women do, together? You're supposed to complain about men, aren't you? I like Lucy,' he said, apparently irrelevantly, but maybe not.

Jessie had never wanted to be part of it: that thing of complaining together with other women about men. She had always disliked the notion of those old-fashioned conversations in which women (and probably men, as well) got together to moan about the shortcomings of the opposite sex. The idea of the cosy huddle, of referring to 'men' in that special, scornful tone of voice, offended a deep instinct of sexual loyalty. She would not surrender the interpretation of her man to other women. She refused to view his unique and impossible behaviour in terms of some ordinary sexual stereotype.

And then it seemed that perhaps Danny wished she had.

11

Early in the 1970s

Once she had said to him, 'If I just knew what it would take to make things work between us. It occurred to me, if I had to stand on my head three times a day, I'd do it. You would too, wouldn't you?'

At that moment, she'd believed he would. She'd thought he was equally dismayed by what kept happening to them. Why did these griefs descend upon them? It was one of those times when yet another scheme for harmony had somehow crashed into unreasonable and obscene chaos, like a train wreck: cues not taken, quips misfiring, gestures misinterpreted; till all at once they faced each other over a black pit of mistrust.

What she meant was, that she refused to believe it had to be this way. It was not to be accepted that they couldn't devise some negotiation of their differences. There was so much at stake, between the two of them. The lovemaking. The talk.

What talk they used to have, sometimes, jumping from abstraction to anecdote, spiralling into giddy reaches of delighted speculation. Intellectually, their imaginations touched; and how very wonderful it seemed, that her peculiar bent towards intellectualising, which had led to such anguished, adolescent isolation, had brought her this desired and rare-plumaged person.

True, he based his arguments more on history, or theories of history, on theories of society, on politics and political life. Hers more often referred to people, experiences, novels. But he was that rare male who read novels too, and soon they could talk about the characters that peopled them as though they were an extensive body of mutual acquaintance. 'But don't you remember, Ivan loves Alyosha, even though their worlds are so entirely antagonistic; that's the point. All three of them really love each other; yes, they do, Danny!' She would be pulling out the book to read him bits to prove it; the individuals themselves as familiar as neighbours – or in most cases, more so.

For a long time she entertained the thought that perhaps you might put a case for what you believed – what you thought might be so – through fiction. It might be the only way. If you couldn't call on evidence, you could – perhaps – create plausibility. You could show how it might possibly be.

He liked her having ideas like this. He believed she could do it, too.

They talked about things like what a self was, and how communication happened; whether it did happen; and if so, how did you know? They talked about absurdity and truth and solipsism and what was required as a basis for action; about what the Greeks called *virtù*; about goodness, and whether it was possible. About the natural, and whether it existed.

Is plastic bad? Is wood good? In fiction it's arguable (she thought). She thought perhaps she could make that case.

Early on, when they'd first met – she an idealistic, small-town seventeen-year-old on an astonishing scholarship, he an older, foreign, late-entry student at their university – he had said to her, 'We don't have anything in common, really. You're not really interested in any of the things that interest me, like history and politics. You're interested in love and God and poetry, but I don't believe in God, and poetry leaves me cold. What interests me is how people organise their lives.'

How people organise their lives. It seemed to her that she had been waiting for just that, just such an object, vague as it was; and he said it with such a grand, free air, as though accustomed to surveying a large prospect.

People's lives. Poetry seemed peripheral compared to this. She imagined some radical inclusiveness, a mass of material embracing mysticism, sex, devoted love, ambition, passion – she was thrilled by so generous a vision. She imagined them working side by side on this absorbing project. You would understand why people did the things they did; you could share everybody's life…

Then he fell in love with her, and she was touched and astonished by it. He wanted her with him constantly; they even studied together; there were times, at first, when they even studied hand-in-hand.

Together they submerged themselves in the most challenging material their studies offered. Together they read of Dostoevsky's Grand Inquisitor, Shaw's impersonal Evolutionary Will; they read of Nietzsche's Superman, who so devastatingly fingered the element of cowardice in conventional morality; together they staggered under the great, sodden load of the century's two most powerful reductionists, Marx and Freud.

But as they considered these problems of human purpose, Danny focused increasingly on the questionable influence of the unacknowledged ego. What horrible things people do in the name of right and goodness – the rescuers, the ideologues! He observed that, surely, this is what came from not being truly self-sufficient. You shouldn't need to do good to bolster your own unsteady ego. You shouldn't need some great cause that might involve people dying in crusades or labour camps. How arrogant to try to do good for other people – as though you could live their lives on their behalf!

He drove home to her with considerable force the insidious and pervasive influence of these agendas: the way they flattered individuals with a sense of purpose, even as they freed them from responsibility for their own lives.

There were certain scalding episodes in which he pressed home these themes with particular reference to Jessie herself: to certain family dynamics she'd been uneasy about (for instance), not to mention the historic scandals of the Catholic church, an institution to which, as an adolescent, she'd been deeply attached. Why had Jessie never faced these things? Was she content to go on living in a dream-world? Wasn't it time she began to notice other people – notice what they were up to: that basic striving for position, for advantage? To refuse to acknowledge those motives in yourself was bad enough, but to refuse to see them in others was to make yourself a victim, complicit by default. Like Jessie's depressive mother, for example.

Well, like Jessie herself, it seemed, for she, too, fell briefly into a spell of depression that would recur for years: she lost weight; she lost touch with friends; she lost her really excellent four-point grade average. It was almost as though she had lost herself, though she'd never have admitted such a phrase. It was like the extinguishing of a light she'd unconsciously been living by – some light of trust, or hope, or self-belief – not to mention that belief in God which she had continued childishly to cherish and which it seemed (given these revelations) was no longer tenable. Which it was even cowardly to mourn.

Meanwhile, Danny was captured by economics.

As luck would have it, their university was known, at this time, for the most charismatic economist of his generation, one who proposed a system that gained its power in part through the rigour with which it excluded everything which could not be analysed within it. It was a masterpiece of framing, and within its strict boundaries, allowed for marvels of clarification, a quality that Danny was particularly drawn to. His delight in this machine for problem solving was all-absorbing. It now eclipsed any other concern about social purpose, absorbing those other questions into this new confidence in ways to optimise individual purposes, which it seemed you could all but ensure mathematically. And thus the original project seemed to empty; but by this time, their attachment was intense.

After all, what a glamour he'd had, when she'd first been with him – how everything about him seemed to possess a *mana*.

Once, before he had quite allowed her into his life, he'd

taken her to a film, and in the interval, when he went off to the men's room, had given her his RAF scarf to hold. It was a heavy, striped silk square, unlike any garment a young American male would have worn. She held it in both hands and sank her face in it. It smelled of him – an amber, animal scent that sent a tingling warmth all through her body. Of course she had loved him first, but all her friends were half in love with him as well. To begin with, at twenty-three, he was so much older. And then, he was an Englishman, and he had done things. He had been in business, flown an aeroplane. He'd been the lover of an older woman.

Jessie had never met anyone like him before

She was fascinated by his teasing, his intrusive and challenging remarks. He had a restless, lively social intelligence, picking up clues people off-handedly let drop in odd remarks and gestures, weaving these threads into theories of their origins and prospects – from the class-conscious England of the mid-century, he brought also the heightened alertness of the stranger: the things he saw implied a range of experience she had never guessed at. She loved the bravado with which he would toss onto the table some large mocking generalisation (*Oh, Americans are all so earnest…*).

Then, from time to time he would let fall grains of information about himself which seemed to her pungent as incense: bird-nesting as a child; the wood he played in; certain glamorous tales of London, where he once knew a painter who kept whole strings of salami draped from the ceiling in his kitchen so you could just slice off a chunk whenever you wanted, and a man with a butler and a very complicated name, who had invited him to play a game of chess in bed…

Like her, he had been a rather solitary, bookish child, a voracious reader all through adolescence; they began to read each other's books. *Oh, but don't you remember, Ivan loves Alyosha…*

Later, as married students with a proper home, they became a draw to Danny's single colleagues in the graduate department, particularly Marty, and when the three of them met again in London, in Marty's bachelor days, they renewed the habit. In the few short years before he was joined by Arlis, Marty often came for supper with them, travelling all across London from his flat in Highgate, and he'd stay the night, half of which they spent in talk, over whisky and cigarettes. It was always an extension of the same kind of talk, ranging between philosophy, history, economics, personal stories: how you know what you know; why you do what you do – as though together they found themselves in a country in which there was always more to explore. In the morning, Marty thrilled the children by blowing smoke-rings and walking on his hands for them, and later they would all go walking together in the park, still talking.

Years afterwards, Jessie and Danny were still having this sort of conversation, especially when they'd both read something that excited them.

There was, for instance, a particular quasi-novel that gained considerable prominence, involving a psychotic breakdown, an American road trip, endless ruminations about truth, science, the infinity of hypotheses by which any event could be explained. The protagonist figured it was just a matter of how you sliced it, how you organised the data, and this affronted him. There was no 'truth', only the slicing knife.

'No wonder technology seems such a solace,' Jessie said. 'It provides a rationale for the slicing knife.'

'So why this hatred of technology?' asked Danny, who had once accused her of being at war with the whole of industrial civilisation.

Well, she'd said, perhaps it's precisely because it has that edge; it fulfils that secret desire for demonstrable certainties. It gets some kind of special position in the hierarchy of arguable truths – some unfair advantage that nobody acknowledges.

Though he disagreed with her altogether about technology, he liked the point, that there are hidden emotional subsidies to certain arguments. It was one of the things that most engaged them both: this secret emotional content of a debate.

Then she would say, but aren't there felt truths, that might somehow be debated and conveyed; could there be rules for this debate? And aren't there truths of intention, too, as well as just description? Like, when somebody asks you how you are, there are numbers of emotional questions being asked, not the least being, just: are you my friend, today?

They had this particular conversation, that started with motorbikes and Zen, while they were still in bed one Saturday morning. It carried on through innumerable cigarettes, through one after another cup of tea, while Ben wandered in with his bowl of cereal, and Ella climbed into bed, between the two of them.

'When are we going to get up? Get up, get up!' Ella demanded imperiously, but they said to her, it's nice in bed; it's cosy; why don't you get your own book?

Ben sat on the floor leaning up against the wall, watching

and listening with considerable interest. He was particularly interested in truth. He said, at one point, 'Stories aren't true, but they're not lies, either.' Then he and Danny and Jessie all looked at each other for a long moment, considering this.

Then Danny said to him, 'But don't you think, sometimes, *that couldn't happen*, and what you really mean is, *that's not true; Biggles wouldn't do that.*'

'Oh, Dad – I don't read Biggles any more.'

Ella, who by this time had wriggled out to go and look for a book, came back and said, 'Daddy. Listen to this: an insect has six legs.'

'A demonstrable certainty, I guess,' said Jessie.

'Not at all,' said Danny. 'Somebody might have pulled off a couple of them.'

'Oh, Daddy, no!'

'Oh, Danny!'

'Well anyway, a tautology. It's not a prediction; it's the definition of an insect.'

'Oh,' said Ben, with that dazzled look of his when he got hold of a new idea, as though he'd received an unexpected gift.

So this conversation which had so absorbed them turned into one of those rare festivals of family affection, as though what bonded the two of them was in itself so strong it could provide the architecture of a family. It was what she relied on. In the absence of so much else (community, a shared commitment, the friends and family all left behind in another country), it was what there was.

And indeed, again and again, over the years of their marriage, they had gone on rediscovering this hope: that they could create some quite original plan for being happy.

12

April, 1976

To her parents, when she finally wrote about the separation, Jessie adopted a tone of confident equanimity, almost as though announcing a move forward – another step towards being a grown-up, like getting the job. She used all the disarming, neutral terms. She said how fully she and Danny would share Ben and Ella's upbringing, how amicable the parting was. I'm sure you realise how hard we've tried, she wrote. And, we feel it's time.

It was so much easier to write than the letter to Danny. Although it would be two weeks, at least, before she had a reply from them, it was with a sense of relief that she sealed up the pages in the blue-and-red-bordered envelope. The task of telling them had weighed on her.

Of course, they were so much less exacting than Danny was.

We have every faith in you, they wrote back heartily; or in fact, nervously, as she could not but know. They were very sad about it, naturally, but they were glad, particularly for the children's sake, that Jessie and Danny meant to keep up a good relationship. Her dad himself wrote, with unexpected (and even questionable) warmth, you know, we always liked the guy – although, as she knew, this was hardly true – or at least, not always.

Her biggest worry had been about Ben's school, but she had tackled this at once, soon after having that first chat with Ben and Ella about the separation.

She and Ben didn't talk the way they once did. The boy who had once been such a chatty character, such a famously persistent talker, seemed no longer to have very much to say. He had become remote. Sometimes, in company, as he sat in silence, he twisted his hands together.

She'd called to him while he was finishing his evening chores, and he sat down with her, and she said how she had to tell him that it would probably be impossible to afford his school fees, if she and his father separated – as it seemed to her they ought to do, as she and he and Ella had all discussed – and now, she was terribly sorry, but she had to explain what this would mean, financially; and how would he feel about this?

He said, 'You mean, it might be good if I left the College?'

She felt a fresh stab of compunction. 'I'm sorry. I'm really sorry. You'll probably have to. Would you mind a lot?'

'Oh, no.' To her astonishment, he laughed – a snort of surprise, or perhaps relief.

'You wouldn't mind?'

'No,' he repeated. 'Not at all.' He sighed, now, and then laughed again. 'Oh no.'

'But don't you like it there?'

'I hate it,' he said.

'My God,' she said, after a moment. 'I didn't know.' She stared at him. 'Why didn't you tell us, Ben? Why didn't you ever say so?'

'It just seemed so ungrateful. I felt so rotten,' he said, suddenly almost loquacious. 'It cost you and Dad so much for me to go there. And it was all my fault. I thought it would be so wonderful. Remember all those books I used to read, those stories about kids who went to public school – remember the stories about Billy Bunter?'

'Billy Bunter?'

'They were just fairy tales for little kids; of course it wasn't like that, but why would it be? How could I have believed that?'

Now she remembered. They were schoolboy stories from the early 1950s, like the stories Danny had grown up with. She remembered the two of them bantering about these stories; it was one of the few things they had shared, like Biggles.

'You were only nine,' she said.

'I was just so gullible,' he said. 'I was so stupid. And then we moved down here, because of that.'

'Well,' she said. 'Not really.'

He looked puzzled; she herself wasn't sure what she was saying. After all, that's what they said to everyone: they'd moved here to be closer to Ben's school.

'Well, but the point is, you wouldn't mind changing schools? You might even like it?'

'I think it might be good,' he said

'Oh Ben,' she said. 'Oh, I'm so glad!'

The shock of his revelation was outweighed, undoubtedly, by sheer relief. She was struck by the flash of a recurrent, stubborn hope that, after all, who knew? Perhaps some things might actually get better.

This whole, horrible problem of The Schools! The question of schools had darkened their lives for years. Its curious exactions were a source of continual shock, to Jessie, as of some hard, unfamiliar object you kept on bumping your shins on, in the dark, resembling in this the equally mysterious obstructions of the British class system, to which it seemed so painfully related.

Child of a looser and more open culture, she found it hard to adjust to the fact that after about the age of eight, school and learning, here, were no longer a delight, a field of exploration, but instead a curious sort of battery in which her children were required to stuff themselves with quantities of unrelated fact, to regurgitate banalities, and to perform feats of handwriting and arithmetic which seemed to her ludicrously onerous. The worst of it was the assumption, impressed on her especially by Danny, that you could not escape this painful drudgery except by way of mastering those other games of prestige and class: it was only money, connections, privilege that could bounce you back into that happy realm of excellence and freedom, where learning was a joy, again.

Why should this be? Why did you have to prove yourself, so stupidly? Secretly, rebelliously, she harboured a belief that it could be different – since it so clearly ought to be. There must be places. There must be others. If you allowed yourself to believe, they might appear.

She said as much to Arlis. She had dropped round on the Goldmans after work the next day; she couldn't refrain from sharing her relief. Even before investigating what next to do on this front (after all, at this stage, everything was still to do – she hadn't spoken yet to the solicitor; she hadn't even begun the fateful letter), she had to share the astonishing outcome of this first step. The problem of the school fees now looked solvable. Ben might actually be happier.

'I wondered,' she said. 'I had wondered if he was really happy there.'

'It isn't doing him any good,' said Arlis authoritatively, though actually, she could not have known.

'Jessie, relax. Sit down,' said Marty.

But Jessie said, 'No, I must go; I can't stay long,' still standing just halfway into the room, clutching her handbag, her briefcase, the bag of vegetables she'd picked up at lunchtime.

'Well, put down your bags, at least!'

'Oh, yes!' she said, with a laugh at her own distractedness. Then she reached for a cigarette in the pack he was holding out, and bent towards him for a light; but still she stood there, musing. She felt almost unnaturally disburdened, almost dizzied by it. 'Of course, I don't know anything about the situation, really; I don't know what the alternatives might be – well, I don't know where we might be living, after all; but still…'

'State schools can be excellent,' said Arlis.

'I can find out. I can ask around.'

'There's a lot to find out, and you can do it,' Marty said, emphatically.

'Oh yes,' she said, with a wondering sort of emphasis. 'I can, I can. It's just such a relief,' she said again.

For at that moment, she was overcome by exhilaration, and had to share it. It was like getting the job, she told them. Still on her feet, she found herself launched into that story – that amazing tale of unexpected openings, when it turned out there were all kinds of options, after all, all sorts of ways to manage things. 'And I'm good at that,' she insisted, remembering those heady days, putting aside for the time being (or even re-categorising) the many ensuing setbacks and complications. 'I'm good at finding ways to make things work. Everything worked! Well, anyway, for a while; until—'

'Jessie, you don't have to convince me! You're very bright!' said Marty.

But Arlis broke in, reprovingly. 'Marty, she's just discovering herself! Jessie,' she told her, in a voice that was soft with professional solemnity, 'you're reclaiming your own perceptions.'

'I have to go,' said Jessie, suddenly conscious of how far she had strayed from duty. She looked around for her bags, and picked them up again. 'Well, anyway,' she said. 'I'm seeing a solicitor tomorrow. That'll give me a better idea where I stand.'

At which Arlis called out indulgently, 'Oh, don't worry, Jessie!' and Marty said, kindly, with a comforting hand on her shoulder, as he saw her out, 'Keep us in touch. You know we always like to hear from you. You're always welcome.'

Of course, that first interview with Mr Dunwoody brought no further information whatsoever – that first time, he didn't so much as mention the infamous one-third–two-thirds rule that made such a mockery of his bland reassurances about her finances – nor was it particularly helpful to write out her case for his benefit.

She couldn't resist making it a case, an argument based on the wrongs done to her and her own rightness, but this was ultimately quite unsatisfying. It didn't account for him at all – for Danny – let alone herself: she didn't like her self-depiction as an injured wife; and at the same time, she was indignant that such injuries as she could document seemed to have no relevance and spark no interest. It felt very odd to sit across from this relative stranger and watch him reading the statement with which she effectively terminated her marriage. She discovered that she was trembling. She realised that she had unconsciously assumed that it would feel very much like arranging to have Danny murdered. And then, his only response had been that bland, impersonal remark about how it seemed that the relationship had broken down.

And was that all? Wasn't he even going to take her side? Or, on the other hand, try to argue her out of it? Wasn't he even going to say to her, as Danny had when, on occasion, the subject had come up between them, 'Don't you realise what this will mean for you?' – implying stringencies that she refused to believe, and hadn't dared investigate.

What did it mean for her?

He parried her every attempt to get a firmer grip, leaving her only the abstract consideration that if so experienced a professional was as willing as Arlis to reassure her that her situation was tenable, then it must be so.

Meanwhile, she had done what needed to be done. An official letter would ensue, as a result of this conversation. The step was taken. And so she allowed herself to put aside that set of fears and worries, for the moment. Everything was still to do, but she felt incrementally stronger, lighter; and she meant to sustain that easier, lighter mood with Ben and Ella.

It was not that hard. Those first few sunny days together, the weekend that Danny left, had set a tone, and now it was as though the children, too, were ready to lighten up and be ordinary. To talk about jokes and school and telly, friends and playground gossip, and whether (for example) the barbecue set that had just arrived from Jessie's parents could really cook a chicken on just six balls of wadded newspaper. They all tacitly avoided the subject of the separation, or referred to Danny only with the most natural matter-of-factness. Of course, it was possible that they didn't quite believe in what was happening. They certainly never thought he wouldn't be coming home to them again, not ever. Even Jessie never thought that. In the absence of any harder evidence, it seemed possible that things might continue mostly as they were. Or they might even (as Arlis kept proposing), might even, actually, be better.

13

'Look, I don't say there's nothing to worry about,' said Marty. 'Perhaps there's plenty to worry about,' he conceded. 'However, a person's stock of emotional energy is always limited – even yours, Jessie. You will be using your undoubted imagination to invent many wonderful answers for problems that may not, in fact, exist.'

'Oh, you're right,' said Jessie.

It was the day she'd gone round with her letter to Danny to discuss with Arlis, but Arlis was not yet home.

'More coffee?' he offered, picking up their cups.

'Oh, Marty, thanks.' She sat up a little straighter, looking round again at the room in which they sat: the great, heavy table, the heavy, comfortable, unmoving chairs, and on the wall that faced her, that familiar etching – a tiny, beautifully precise rendition of an arch, a column (some fragment of European architecture of quite another century), in its wide mount and frame of dark, aged wood – which had followed Marty through the London years, from the first scruffy two-room flat in Highgate.

The things in Marty's flat all seemed like friends. In fact, most of the furniture came with the flat, the warden's flat of a university hall of residence. But she liked that very quality of gentle wear, of having borne many years of comfortable use, like the things of a family, or a considerate and friendly public.

'But you know,' he continued, beginning to chat as he returned with the coffee pot, 'I sometimes think, perhaps some people need to exercise this mental faculty. Some people love to worry.'

'Oh, yes,' she laughed.

'Perhaps there is some imaginative faculty that must be exercised, you know? It must be, in a way, let off its leash; it must be given a little chance to have a run. Jessie, this does not apply to you! This is – well, this is people at the opposite end of the imagination spectrum, you might say. Well, on the whole.'

'Like the spinster who thinks there's a man hiding under the bed—'

'Well now, this may involve a different under-utilised faculty,' said Marty, with a comical shrug; and they both laughed. 'But that's for Arlis to say. This is her territory.'

He had a way of referring to Arlis, now and then, that served both to distinguish himself from her and to link the two of them, as though he enjoyed the reassertion and redefinition of their partnership – in fact, as though he found this whole situation of partnership continually interesting. It was one of the things she began to notice, seeing the two of them in this new light – seeing them in her new character (as though it was this which changed the light): not yet quite single, perhaps, but a singular being, with uncertain edges, broken away from the unit they'd known so long, and from the shelter or confines of which she'd known them. From time to time, there was this little jolt: who were they, actually? And who would she be herself, now?

She began to have glimpses of a marriage she'd never seen before, and glimpses of new aspects to the two of them, and she enjoyed this. It was something you seemed to get so little of, as an adult: this kind of third-party or familial intimacy with other people. As a child, her domestic world had been so much more populous, with neighbours and relatives continually dropping round, and you never knew when you might get new glimpses of the wonderful secrets of their lives (peering into the fridge, for instance, apparently unlistening, while the mothers conferred over coffee at the table – or even, sometimes, edging into the doorway from the other room, when you overheard them talking). She didn't consciously compare these situations, but there was something in this enlarged domesticity that had almost the quality of coming home, as though she was only returning, now, to a place that really belonged to her. Surely she was meant to live this friendlier, more spacious life. It was like those first days in the job. There was meant to be more fun. There were meant to be more people in her life, in all their lives – hers and Ben's and Ella's.

She would find herself almost assuming, sometimes, that this new life included Danny. That it didn't, would occasionally be a shock.

She was to see quite a lot of the Goldmans over the next months.

Later, as the spring progressed and developed into summer, it began to be expected – at any rate, by Arlis – that Jessie would be establishing a new life, a new social world; and Arlis set herself to encouraging this venture. Hadn't Jessie ever been interested in other men, for instance? Inviting confidences, Arlis related tales of her own years as a single woman, stories of considerable fascination to Jessie, who had gone so directly from girlhood to motherhood. They exchanged memories of these different girlhoods; they discussed their families, their crazy mothers. During those halcyon hours of unusual leisure, when the children first began to spend the odd night with Danny – during those days of waiting, when all the arrangements for the future still hung in suspension – Jessie frequently found herself in these long, confidential chats with Arlis, comparing their different experiences, in a way she hadn't done since university, since the very first days, before she had become so entirely at one with Danny.

It was fun to have a girlfriend. They would dress up, sometimes, examining Arlis's latest bargains, exploring the remoter reaches of her wardrobe, Arlis drawing forth the occasional offering for Jessie to try out, suggesting a new persona.

Sooner or later, on such occasions, Marty would wander in from his study, or arrive back home from a drink at the student bar, after his last classes, with a greeting that invariably suggested that to see her, Jessie, was a glad surprise. He always had news to tell, a story to share, something he'd read, even news of his internal weather: 'I find I am stuck at exactly the spot I was stuck yesterday, so it was time to quit!' Or even news of how there was no news: 'The gossip is all the same. Bernie is grousing about his overload of classes, Allen is trying to cuddle up to Mac, Mac is getting fatter. Georgia might be going to the States next year.'

'She was going to the States last year.' This from Arlis.

'As I say, the gossip is all the same!' Marty repeated, as though this in itself was quite deliciously amusing.

Then he would pour out a generous whisky, and Arlis would go off to the kitchen. She had only recently taken up cooking and was enchanted by it, particularly in discovering how sympathetically it met her glee at bargains. 'Soup costs nothing! Garlic croutons – nothing!' She loved the shopping and the haggling – she and Marty often spent the Saturday mornings at the street markets – and had revealed a talent like his for peasant delicacies, the delights of tongues and tails, hearts and livers, treated with great tenderness, as well as wine and herbs and butter, splashes of vermouth.

These were little islands of bonhomie for Jessie, on which she sometimes relaxed into the dangerous fantasy that she had discovered the new life already, as though it was a whole safe continent. It was so pleasant to share the leisure of a childless, cultivated couple, to imagine that she shared the same resources. It was delightful to get the chance to engage with Marty in flights of speculative chat.

To begin with, the talk had been mostly about her marriage, and about Danny, and at first, of course, they had mostly listened.

There was a lot of background to go into. Why they had taken this course and not that; what had been the understandings; who had most regretted or most benefited from certain crucial moves: interpretations of what Danny would have called the power base. She was surprised at Marty's baffled look when she used this phrase.

'The power base?'

'Well, you know,' said Jessie. 'Money – options.'

Arlis made a sound, a sort of 'Psshh!' of simple indignation; rolled her eyes, and sat back on the sofa, as though detaching herself altogether from such foolishness.

Jessie looked back at Marty. She said, 'You have to recognise these things. It's only realistic, isn't it? Women with children are dependent, aren't they; all societies have to deal with this. According to the circumstances, one person or the other can be more dependent – well, particularly a woman with a child; it's like fighting with one hand behind your back.'

'Oh yes, yes,' said Marty. 'Of course, it's true: one person may have a stronger economic base. But Jessie, a marriage is not a war.'

She looked at him.

'Well, perhaps sometimes it is. But this is not, shall we say, the conventional formulation. I mean, not while the relationship is happy.'

There would come such moments, every now and then, when she would find that certain things she took for granted, certain attitudes in which she'd worked to train herself, seemed to come to them as a complete surprise. Sometimes she thought they hadn't really thought about it. Sometimes she wondered if she had, herself.

And then at other times, on tentatively offering some hard-won idea about Danny which she expected to have to justify or explain, she would be met instead with a surprised, 'Of course.'

'Of course he did.'

'Of course he was.'

'You never realised?'

'You didn't know?'

They sometimes seemed to her both more clear-headed about Danny, and more sympathetic towards him. He seemed, in their eyes, more genuinely vulnerable, though in different areas than she had seen herself. They had a different view. Arlis had lived in this country all her life; Marty knew the academic scene from a different angle; for years they had both been part of that world of work which she herself had only joined so recently. Through this, she began to see him in a different light, sometimes, and at moments, felt closer to him than she ever had before. It was not until later that she realised the extent to which this had shielded her.

They discussed him like a man in process, a life in process. They talked as though they all still mattered to each other, were irrevocably connected, like a family – it resembled the lull that can occur in the period just following a bereavement, when sheer intensity of focus seems almost to recreate the presence of the person lost. She would forget she'd lost him. At the same time, there was an interest in Jessie herself, which could be quite heady. It was very pleasant, this interest in her own self, her situation, her possibilities.

So it was that, oddly enough, in those first weeks there were times when she was almost gay.

One day, on an impulse, she unearthed her copies of the lead titles of the Otford launch – the books finally published the year before – and took them along the following Sunday to show the Goldmans. It had been three years since she'd come up with this approach, with what became the Otford approach – way back at the beginning, when she was almost entirely on her own; and at the time, she'd been so excited about it.

She was both alarmed and gratified by their response, especially Marty's. Arlis, as ever, was more measured. While Marty exclaimed, and enthused, and drew her out on how she'd laboured, working out the prototypes – the struggles with Oscar that ensued, the impossible schedules, the terrible crises (sketched only briefly, as though they were past, and won) – Arlis remained absorbed, murmuring little noises of assent ('Mmm, mmm,') and nibbling her fingernails as she turned the pages.

At last she said, with a note of surprise, 'But this is good. This is very good. Children's books. I thought—' She shrugged, leaving Jessie to imagine what she thought.

Jessie said, 'It's a departure, isn't it. There's nothing like it, is there. It's got class.'

'And Jessie, this was you? You did this?'

'But you've got nothing to worry about!' exploded Marty, flinging out his arms. 'How can you worry, when you do things like this? Soon, we'll all be saying, we knew you when!'

'Oh, well,' said Jessie, with a rush of deprecation. Suddenly she felt frightened and even fraudulent, and she was not sure why; later this would be one of those themes that kept recurring in her long sessions with Arlis: the false self,

Arlis would comment, sombrely, with a nod of recognition, using a term she'd apparently come across in the current phase of her psychotherapy training.

The point was, they didn't know. They only had her word for it. And yet, there was nothing forced about their reactions. Clearly, it wasn't just politeness. She was good. And the new ideas…

There were moments of crazy optimism. Visions would flash across her mind as she walked down to her commuter train (for instance) in the morning, when the late-spring light was fresh.

The first of her new ideas had developed into the possibility of a series, the series into a programme: she could imagine already how powerfully it could be marketed. She would be a success, yes, just as Marty said: the children's future would be assured; they would have sunny, happy holidays on their own together. She would take them on cycling trips in France (she'd never cycled as an adult, but why not?). In her images of happiness, they were always in the countryside together, in the sun, walking a cliff path under sweet-smelling pines, or cycling down one of those white, empty, poplar-bordered roads that she recalled from their one memorable holiday in France.

Surely the company needed new ideas.

She'd been disheartened when it seemed that Oscar expected them to churn out identikit reproductions of her first project, after it proved so exceptionally successful. She'd had a lot of opposition to overcome when she broke the mould with the second project, though she was sure it would prove – in time – equally successful; and then the one that followed (it was so long before the sales and the reviews came through!). She had to assume she'd face a similar struggle. But surely it was important to keep innovating. They had a mission, didn't they? In the end, Oscar would be glad.

14

Of course, she knew it was risky to play with new ideas. Her schedule for the current project was extremely tight; Marjorie would be snapping at her heels. But this part of the job, dreaming up new projects, new approaches – this was the part she loved, the part that gave her the energy to keep on going.

In any case, she hoped to use outside writers, now, which would lighten the workload. It would be a step-change in what was called the Otford method, though in fact, it was Jessie who'd come up with it, and only because there were no examples, at the time, of what she wanted. Oscar had meant to use freelancers – this was how these mass-market visual books were done, he had complained.

But now the books she'd imagined had been published; she could point to them, and she herself had experience on her side. Now it should be easier to work with outsiders, and she thought this was something she could handle. She was good with people on the outside.

With this in mind, she couldn't resist some tentative

contacts with potential writers, possible researchers, on evenings when Ben and Ella were with Danny.

A couple of the people she got in touch with were young, bright, educated but unconfident mums – much like herself, only a few years back; two more were oddball academics she'd met at parties. Alone, her hand went irresistibly to the phone; on the other end, she could almost hear the enthusiasm catch, like a fire beginning to kindle up and crackle. There were times when she got so excited she then spent hours typing notes on the ideas raised – though also, at times, uneasily aware that she had perhaps left her contacts with too much hope.

The trouble was, there was so much else to keep on top of, and sometimes, it would blow up all at once – solicitors, the separation settlement, the initial upsets of phone calls or letters from people who didn't know, the emotional surprises. And still to come, perhaps, another move, house-hunting, getting a mortgage, and then the schools, Ella's, as well as Ben's.

By what had seemed at the time a stroke of luck, Ella had fallen in love with her current primary school. It was small, and sought after, and only three-quarters of a mile downhill from Albion Grove.

Though she'd have only a short time in this cosy refuge before the problem of the secondary school would again cast its long, cold shadow, it was a wrench to think of taking her away. The staff were young and numerous and enthusiastic. At this school, Ella had told her, they had thinking lessons. Ella was enchanted. She went off to school as though it was a party. She got herself up and dressed without a murmur. Thinking lessons!

Nearly every night, now, when Jessie collected her from the teenage babysitter, Ella had stories of this wonderful school. From the time she was little, she'd had a taste for mathematics: for numbers and puzzles and conundrums; it had inspired her first teacher to spend many an evening inventing special problems to engage her. Now she explained to Jessie about maps: about different kinds of maps, what you were doing with a map, what it was for. Had Jessie ever wondered how you did a map? Had she ever wondered what a map was? Jessie heard her out with an unsettling mix of feelings.

The decision to leave Albion Grove was not at all straightforward. For a while, Jessie entertained the notion that she might have rights to it. As Arlis kept insisting: the marital home… It was nice to have this space, these lordly views, the little balcony at the back. She'd begun to like how it made her feel: the sense of substance and stability.

But the first conversation with Maggie had unnerved her.

In her relief at discovering how Ben felt about the College, she had hoped their lives might open out. Perhaps the bad reputation of the local secondary schools had been exaggerated. They would be less pretentious; perhaps it was only that.

She had bursts of confidence, imagining how different it might be.

Perhaps these schools were simply less traditional. Maybe there'd be more modern history, for example, instead of classics, and normal timetables instead of Saturday school, and less weird terminology like *exeat*, which had so baffled her. Perhaps they'd have girls, there, too, which was more normal, anyway, and surely nicer for an adolescent boy.

Perhaps (it had then occurred to her) someone like Maggie Buchardt would have some information about all this.

That was when she'd phoned Maggie.

Maggie was wonderfully uncurious and matter of fact about the split itself, which Jessie appreciated. She went straight into practical information about schools and houses, about London and transport and differences of educational provision. Maggie assured her that the area they lived in was in fact, educationally, a sink. This was even partly because of those little peaks of privilege – the College and two or three other fee-paying schools – which sucked away any children whose parents could afford them.

'I'm not saying there might not be some advantages,' said Maggie, finally. 'It would be a much more relaxed environment, academically, and who knows – for some boys, this can work. Not everyone flourishes in an arena of rampant competition, despite what your dear husband thinks – and mine, to some extent.'

'I wonder,' Jessie said. 'I'd like to see him under a bit less pressure. When he was little – before we came to England – he was so bright. I never thought we'd have to worry. Teachers loved him.'

'Ben seems a sensitive sort of boy,' said Maggie, which was observant of her, since she hadn't met him since the days their husbands brought them to institutional Christmas parties; and Jessie said as much.

'Well, that's my job, dear,' said Maggie. 'But, that being so, what is much more worrying is the social side. He'll be known already as a College boy; and I promise you, boys of that age – in those sorts of circumstances – they can be vicious. And they'll pursue him, never fear,' she continued, dryly. 'Can he defend himself?'

'I never thought,' said Jessie.

'Well, he'd have to learn,' said Maggie. 'They'll have seen him in that uniform, and then, the accent…'

Oh yes, the accent.

'I'm afraid he'd find himself a marked man,' Maggie said.

'Oh, God,' said Jessie.

After which Maggie had asked her, why on earth did she want to live there, anyway?

Jessie discovered her bank account was overdrawn before two weeks had passed after Danny's arrival back in England. There'd been unusual expenses, like Ella suddenly needing a new Brownie outfit; and there'd been things like the taxis and the extra babysitting. And the whisky, too. And so forth. Then there arrived the chance of getting a whole month's shop at Sainsbury's at one go, courtesy of a neighbour with a huge estate car. Wouldn't that make life easier? insisted the neighbour. Surely Jessie didn't want to schlep along there every Saturday by bus. Only you see, it had to be this Friday night, because, because… So Jessie had rung Arlis and arranged a short-term loan, without giving herself time to think too much about it.

This particular period of financial insecurity didn't last long. Soon afterwards there was a note from Danny, very polite, saying that naturally, for the time being, he would go on paying the mortgage and the phone bill, and the standing orders for utilities, and he even added a small increment in acknowledgement of the unusual circumstances; the rest would continue to be covered by Jessie's salary from Otford. Jessie was able to pay back most of the loan from Arlis, and the immediate situation was stabilised.

But it was odd, how raw and new she felt, going through the everyday routines. Things she had always done seemed to take place, now, in a larger, emptier space, like a kind of bubble, untethered to a past or future. The things seemed easier sometimes, and sometimes more difficult, but different. It wasn't the first time she'd run the household on her own. Since they were first in England there had been periods when Danny had worked abroad for several weeks, even a month or so. Only a few years back, just after she started full-time work, he'd been away for the best part of a year, and she'd taken pride (at least, to begin with) in her ability to manage. Why should this be so different? Live in the moment! people kept advising.

In May, she asked Phil and Lucy round for a barbecue, without reflecting that she'd never done such a thing in the whole twelve months that Danny was away on that sabbatical.

15

With the spring so far advanced, it was still light outside; that was partly what had given her the idea. But she hadn't finished any of the preparations; she'd stayed too late at work. She hadn't even changed her clothes or brushed her hair. She was hurriedly putting a stack of plates out on the table, to create a sense of welcome, when the doorbell rang.

They'd been round before, of course, in the winter. Danny and Jessie had given several dinner parties when they first moved in. The Seymours had seen the house when there were candles on the table, the buzz of other people, Danny to look after them and give them drinks, the children looking in to say hello. Jessie remembered her surprise at quite how well Ben and Ella had conducted themselves, the way they looked – so graceful and unselfconsciously friendly – as though expanding like plants in sunshine under the unaccustomed stimulus of sociability and cheer. But, even as the real sun enlarged its compass, they both seemed to be getting lank and pallid; now they were like forced plants that have been grown too fast, indoors. Ella's hair was badly in need of cutting, the fringe so heavy she seemed to peer out from beneath it like some small, hunted creature; and Ben, she realised, was becoming spotty.

None of them looked their best.

She'd thought it would be funny to try out the American barbecue that was supposed to work on rolled-up balls of newspaper. This was the excuse for her impulsive invitation. It gave a reason for Ben and Ella to be involved; it was a novelty – a joke, she'd thought. She found herself laughing far too much, as she grew more flustered and more harried in an effort to pretend the joke had worked.

She'd taken the Seymours first into the living room, because it had the view, and it had the drink and glasses in the cabinet in the new, clever shelving. Then she'd had to leave them there while she went back to the kitchen for the ice and water. Ben was down the back stairs in the small, dull yard, fetching the barbecue, which they planned to try out on the balcony. Ella should have been putting out the knives and forks; it was supposed to be her job to set the table. But that would have left Phil and Lucy completely on their own.

When Jessie got back with the pitcher and the ice, she suddenly realised with some dismay that they'd dressed up. They had that look – perhaps a freshly ironed shirt on Phil, and Lucy with her dressy boots and earrings – as though it was a proper dinner party. There they stood, gleaming and expectant, in the middle of that bland, still under-furnished room, entirely alone except for Ella.

Lucy asked, inevitably, 'Can't I do anything? Don't you need some help?'

Of course she did, but now she could not think what, so she said, ridiculously, 'Oh, Ella's going to set the table,' and then they all trooped into the kitchen/dining room, to be companionable, and eventually Lucy took over the chopping of the vegetables that were supposed to be a platter of crudités. Jessie tried to keep her mind on the potato salad, otherwise nothing would be ready, while Phil went out on the balcony to confer with Ben, and Ella extracted Peter the guinea pig from his big box to introduce to Lucy.

Lucy said, 'I think he's more interested in these carrots.'

Peter the pig squirmed energetically in Ella's arms, his twitching nose stretching urgently towards the vegetables, and Ella and Lucy debated his preferences.

'I think he wants the celery,' said Ella.

'I think he wants it all,' said Lucy.

'He thinks it's a party.'

'Well, it is a party,' Lucy said. 'But not for you,' she told the guinea pig.

Presently they relented and decided to give him his own special party dish, in which Ella laid alternate strips of carrots and celery with mathematical exactness while Peter Pig, temporarily liberated, made panicked dashes from here to there across the floor.

His box had been commandeered for the stockpiling of newspaper-firing, and on the balcony Phil and Ben now peered at the instructions for the barbecue. They discussed the question: exactly how do you form these balls of newspaper? Do you just loosely scrunch it? Do you try to wad it?

Lucy said, going out to them, 'You know I don't believe in this at all,' and Jessie (back in the kitchen, still involved in the potato salad that she should never have attempted) was tremendously relieved. This was the kind of thing that Lucy was supposed to say.

'We've rehearsed it,' Jessie called to them.

'Just with hamburgers, though,' said Ben.

'Well, hamburgers,' Lucy said, dismissively.

Jessie had cut up the chicken as small as seemed in any way feasible, not entirely trusting this outlandish venture. All the same, there ensued an anxious forty minutes, with all of them grouped together on the little balcony, peering down occasionally through the smoke to watch the pink, translucent flesh become opaque and pale, with the occasional startling red thread of blood.

Phil said, holding out the instruction leaflet, 'Just six balls of newspaper – that's all we gave it. I believe what I'm told.'

Lucy said, 'But did they say which paper? Did they?'

Ben said, hopefully, 'It smells nice.'

'That'll be the marinade,' said Jessie.

'Or the printers' ink,' said Lucy. 'Vaporising.'

'I did wonder,' Jessie admitted, after a moment.

Stricken, she glanced from Lucy's narrow look of kindly mockery to Phil, who shrugged. 'It's inescapable,' he said, in that nice voice, with its faint, warm trace of a northern lilt. 'Chemicals,' he explained. 'Why fight it?'

After which the conversation moved with lugubrious ease to a number of shocking statistics about industrial pollution, but then suddenly, Ben said, 'I think it's ready, Mum.'

He and Phil forked all the pieces over, to make sure, but he was right. It was cooked through, and the skin was crisp and golden. So it was really a very nice dinner in the end, though

Jessie couldn't think where everyone should sit, and there was almost a problem here, too. She said to Phil, 'Pretend you're carving,' and put him at the head – struck suddenly by the sense of an ominous symbolism were it to be herself, now, at that end of the table, or (even worse, somehow) were she to have put Ben there. At the same time, she thought what she'd said was unnecessarily contrived and silly. Luckily, Phil, with his easy chattiness, simply took up the subject of carving and dishing out and how people did it; what they had done at home, when he was young; what it would be like in really big families, where you had to look sharp to see you got your share. Ben looked a little less remote than usual, and Ella sat close to Lucy, smiling up at her occasional asides. Really, it was fine. But how had she managed to believe it would be easy?

They'd left by nine-thirty, just after Ben and Ella had gone up. They mentioned the babysitter. She hadn't considered they'd have to get a babysitter. They'd got a babysitter, and they'd come all this way, in their good clothes. She was embarrassed at how she'd over-reached herself. There was so much to learn. Even about things she'd thought she knew already.

And of course, she missed him. For a moment, leaning afterwards against the railings of the balcony to smoke a cigarette, she felt it like a sudden, angry ache. She missed his presence, his partnership, the crucial social element he'd have added. She had a flash of anger at how impossible he had made it for her to have him at her side, there. She missed the person she'd have been with him.

16

What would it mean to be a single woman? To be genuinely single, lacking even an absent husband?

Jessie was surprised at how much she minded these social losses, like there being no one to entertain another couple while she cooked for them. She felt exposed. It was as though a door had been left open, somewhere; the uneasy awareness of a draught from somewhere, and then you realised this was going to be permanent. It was going to be like that, now. She hadn't expected she would mind so much. There were lapses of something more than confidence, as though she could sometimes forget quite who she was, what she was about, or could expect of herself. There were times when she seemed to forget such fundamental things as what to wear – mornings when she stood and looked at the things in her wardrobe and seemed to have no idea what to do about them.

Once, early on, under pressure from Arlis, she had gone with Ella to another of those local jumble sales and bought a skirt. Arlis told her it had been an excellent buy; she even recognised the label. Fingering it, she exclaimed in happy triumph, 'You see? In an area like yours? It would be mad if you didn't look at jumble sales!' In her enthusiasm, Arlis found one of her own jumpers to go with it, another sale trophy, with a sort of tie affair in the low-cut V of the neck.

Jessie had gone to her with the skirt one April Saturday (one of the first free Saturday afternoons), and was standing barefoot in this skirt (which did fit perfectly), wearing the new jumper, while Arlis ransacked her wardrobe for accessories, pulling out scarves and rummaging in drawers heaped up with beads and brooches.

'Marty!' she cried imperiously, catching sight of him as he came into the flat. 'Come and see Jessie. See the new Jessie; doesn't she look wonderful?'

'Very nice,' said Marty approvingly from the doorway.

'See how little it takes,' said Arlis, briefly abandoning her search to indulge in another survey of the project. 'Clothes are magic. She looks *wonderful*.'

Marty shrugged. 'Well, you know, I always think so. You both look wonderful! But I like to see you playing.'

'Playing!' said Arlis.

She gave up the scarf idea finally, but accompanied her gift of the jumper with repeated, firm instructions on how this outfit should be carried off.

'Do you have any shoes with a little heel?' she asked. 'You need a heel for a skirt like this – some kind of heel, just a little bit of heel, and you have to wear stockings. I mean tights, of course, but fairly sheer…'

'It's going to feel strange,' said Jessie, though she was not sure why. It wasn't as though she never wore a skirt.

'You'll be fine. You'll be all right!' Arlis encouraged her.

On Monday it rained, but Jessie did not delay the trial. For one thing, the washing machine was acting up, so it seemed she really had nothing else to wear. She silenced her doubts by telling herself that there was no alternative. Anyway, how much of her energy could she be expected to spend on clothes – at a time like this, especially? It had been, for the most part, a busy, fractious weekend, frayed by a number of minor breakdowns and unexpectedly tedious chores.

But later she wondered how she could have been so stupid.

At home, they didn't have a full-length mirror, so she never saw exactly what she looked like; but she felt it. There was something wrong about the skirt, something about its length or maybe the shape of it, and the jumper was limp; it was one of those rainy days when the air is heavy with humidity and the fabric stuck to her. It was a nondescript colour, a sort of greyish-brown, and the floppy stuff of it stuck to her inner arms, and it seemed as though when she took off her raincoat in the office and went upstairs to the design room, where she had recently installed herself, she got a couple of startled looks before the guys looked back at what they were working on, after the most minimal hellos.

She tried to focus on her own work, and not be self-conscious. What did it matter? It was only clothes. But she hadn't expected, going down for coffee, to collide with Oscar and encounter Tony, Oscar's friend and hers, once. That unforgettable look.

'Oh. Jessie.' (You? she could almost see him thinking. This is you?)

'Oh,' said Jessie. 'Hi.'

He'd have been told about the separation, she imagined. He'd make his own assumptions.

She nearly stumbled, and felt herself go scarlet. He forgot to say hello.

They dispersed in a muddle of confused intentions, Jessie going off without her coffee, pretending she'd been heading for the loo. There were these moments of unexpected misery, no less intolerable because she was so ashamed of this degree of misery from such a cause. Her clothes.

But in her social dealings, too, she found herself stumbling not infrequently, as though she'd entered a terrain with an unexpectedly demanding surface, wearing the wrong shoes. She didn't know what was expected of her, and was angry when it seemed more than she could supply. She didn't know what she herself should expect of herself.

How awkwardly, at one point, did she turn down an invitation for a Sunday gathering in north London, with some of Danny's colleagues and their partners. It would be just a nice, relaxing afternoon, it was explained to her; the couple were having some friends round to watch sport on television; surely an afternoon off would do her good?

She knew they had probably seen a lot of Danny, recently, and this was their equalising gesture, it being the weekend he'd taken the children to his mother, in the Midlands. They wouldn't like to be refused, she felt, having so readily taken up this opportunity; and she did not know how to do so. She didn't want to say she wasn't up to it, which in any case was not the truth. Danny would have had no problem with the truth. 'Travel two hours to watch your television!' he'd have said (if he was disinclined to do so). 'You must be joking!' And then he'd have sparred enjoyably with the guy, and no harm done.

Jessie did not know how to do that.

She was embarrassed at how little she wanted to spend her Sunday trekking up to Kentish Town to look at television with this group of people, maybe even if it wasn't sport, but especially at the cost of leaving untouched that great slagheap of problems in which she might yet make some inroads, if she kept at it. She would regret it if she went (she thought). She would almost certainly arrive there late, resentful, sullen (she felt it already!), and quite unable to enthuse about this game they all got so excited by. However, she'd also regret staying home. There she'd be, nagged by the consciousness of having been, perhaps, ungracious; thinking perhaps they'd never repeat this invitation – after all, this was the first time they'd extended it – and that she'd mind. In fact, they never did ask her again. And in fact she didn't mind, because by that time there was too much else to mind about. But this was the beginning, when it seemed that life might yet retain its familiar contours, and in which such slights and differences would be sorely prominent.

Thus harassed, focused entirely on dissembling her state of mind, she never thought when she rang them back to offer a note of simple, warm regret. It didn't occur to her – perhaps she was too angry. She attempted a smooth and airy tone, such as she fancied Danny might approve of, saying, oh, sorry, but she thought she'd better give it a miss, this time. As though there'd been, or would ever be, a sequence.

'Well, if you're sure,' said the voice on the other end, a little coldly.

'Oh, thanks very much, but – yes, I think,' she said.

Then this guy, Marcus, said, well then, excuse him, but he had to rush; they still had to get to the market – they tried to make it to the street market on a Saturday – and Katie was calling him. 'Don't be too much of a hermit, Jessie!' he finished, heartily.

Which suggested that after all, she hadn't even really carried off the pose.

Arlis, too, berated her for an unhealthy lack of social gusto.

'What do you mean, you're going through your bills? On a Saturday afternoon – with the kids away? Jessie – it's summer – the sun is shining – you've just lost a marriage of fifteen years! Come on – you can't just hide away at home with your head stuck in paperwork!'

But that time, too, Jessie was obstinate. She was less anxious about losing contact with the Goldmans, and it was no longer always fun to spend a weekend afternoon together.

There had been, at first, a couple of wonderful days exploring central London with them. Once they took her to lunch in Soho with another single, younger woman, to a Chinese restaurant, where they sat at a large round table in an airy, spacious upper room, and were served a variety of dishes she'd never before encountered. Another time they introduced her to various auction rooms in Fitzrovia where they were buying furniture for a flat they were fitting up, and it was revealed to her where you found the old, solid kinds of furniture she liked, and how cheaply you could sometimes get these pieces (if you looked out for them, as Marty emphasised). A couple of times they met for a drink at a pub with tables on the pavement, where they told her they often brought their Sunday papers. As the weeks passed, however, and then the months, these excursions lost their power to refresh. She no longer wanted to tag along while they considered furnishings. She stopped being entertained by the auctioneering – though it could be so funny when Marty told the story, later, if she had dinner with them, that she wondered at her inability to see the fun of it when it was happening.

The occasional evening meal with the two of them was a comfort. Sometimes, when the children were with Danny, she stayed over, and in the morning it was all too easy to linger on, drinking good, strong coffee, listening with Marty to Puccini while Arlis flipped the pages of her newspaper with little exasperated noises at what the government was doing, or some politician. Then it would be, why not stay for lunch? Why not stick around a little longer and perhaps take a wander into Chinatown?

'Oh Jessie, you weren't going to your office?'

But she'd begun to find that if she allowed her visit to the Goldmans to extend itself into that ramble into Soho, she did not feel rested and restored by it; she felt anxious. Saying goodbye to them afterwards, watching them wander back to the comfort of their safe routines, she felt a pang of separateness and dissatisfaction. She was ashamed of this dissatisfaction. It seemed she did not know how to be simply idle. Yet there were periods when – sometimes quite abruptly – nothing urgent was required of her.

There was a lot of waiting. She would find herself

waiting for some response from Danny or his solicitor, or for the arrival of forms inexplicably delayed, or (later on, during the brief insanity of negotiations for the house on Mountfield Road) for the reports from builders, surveyors, plumbers. There was even a period when Danny unexpectedly left the country for ten days on a consultancy, and the first outlines of an agreement dissolved again into uncertainty, and suddenly every initiative was blocked.

At those times, she knew that what she should do was concentrate on work: she should keep her head down and focus on her deadlines. However, she'd reached a point when she was going stale on the current project. It was a familiar stage. She needed to renew the first enthusiasms, talk to someone who would really listen, find new approaches – even, perhaps, just go and walk around the block, to shake her thoughts up; but this was not allowed. And there were no colleagues to whom she could open up. They didn't see what she saw as problems; she could see they found her distress affected; Marjorie would merely ask her to take shortcuts: why was she such a perfectionist? Really! Jessie, you're not Leonardo. This was the real battle. How she dreaded Marjorie's response: the weary sigh, the unnatural cheeriness. She didn't believe that Marjorie was right. She didn't believe that Marjorie was on her side.

But who was on her side, now? Oscar didn't seem to care any more, and Alison, his business partner, who had once been such a delightful co-enthusiast, who had shared so many of her pet hates as well – Alison had been lost to her for some time, now; was completely absorbed in whatever Oscar was absorbed in.

And after all, Marjorie was only saying what so many of them were saying: don't try so hard, don't make such heavy weather of it; Jessie; relax; you can't work properly if you don't relax… The implication was, she wasn't cool. She wasn't (as had been so frequently observed of her) well organised. Why didn't she take a lover, have some fun? Why couldn't she just relax and enjoy the summer?

17

As the summer progressed, Arlis made it clear that she thought that Jessie used her responsibilities, especially towards the children, as an escape from finding a new social role.

Sometimes this was expressed by means of a hint, a raised eyebrow, a way of repeating Jessie's own words with a sceptical emphasis, but sometimes it was more overt, especially in relation to Ben and Ella. Children were so often used to satisfy their parents' emotional needs.

And indeed, the children themselves seemed to have accepted their new regime almost unquestioningly. They didn't seem particularly distressed. They didn't seem worried about what was happening, or might happen. Returning from visits to their father, they seemed untroubled. On the whole, they seemed to enjoy this part of things – the novelty of eating out, for instance: the delights of fancy crêpes and upmarket hamburgers in central London; and then also, perhaps, just the chance to be with Danny on their own. They didn't say that much, but what was there to say? Dad had bought a bed.

Dad was thinking of buying a stereo. They went with Dad to look at a sofa that he might get. They spent a night at his new flat. It was okay, they said.

Ella said, importantly, 'He's not going to get a television. When we visit him, we'll play chess.'

Jessie was struck by a vision of the three of them, serenely companionable, in a way that had been achieved so seldom in their life together, as a family. A quiet, lamplit room in that enviably bohemian little flat of his, so near the Strand…

'That won't work,' she objected, childishly. 'You can't all play chess; it's a game for just two people.'

'Scrabble, maybe?' Ben suggested.

Ella said, 'Not Scrabble. I'm going to play chess with Dad. We can take turns,' she pointed out, quite sensibly. She now referred to him as Dad.

What a self-sufficient unit they had seemed, when Danny took them to Wales, once, with his widowed mother. It was the summer of 1973, the first summer of her job with Oscar, and Jessie had asked to stay home on her own, the first week. By the time she joined them, they had created a mini-culture in which she seemed to be only a tourist, or perhaps – at most – an honoured visitor.

The children had become wonderfully well behaved.

'Shoes off!' commanded Danny, as they approached the cottage, after bringing her from the train.

Ben and Ella sat down with alacrity on the steps.

'Mummy, you, too,' said Ella.

Everyone was taking off their shoes.

Ella said, 'It's because our shoes might be full of sand,

and we would track it inside, you see. Of course, you don't always have sand in your shoes, not if you don't go to the beach; but then if you do, you don't forget and get the house all full of sand.'

'Oh, that's a good idea,' Jessie said.

To which Ben added, encouragingly, 'That's the good thing about rules. You don't have to clutter your mind up; you just do it. I think that's a good thing.'

This was the talky, bright-faced Ben of three years earlier, a young, happy Ben, who conquered the apple tree outside his bedroom every morning, sliding down to it from the pitched roof over the entrance and coming in for breakfast through the kitchen door.

Gran was making jam from blackberries they'd gathered from the hedges; after supper, they walked the dark lanes to where the starry night was broken by the abrupt, quick, half-seen, haunting stir of bats, flitting from the dark crown of an enormous oak. When Jessie woke in the morning, Ben and Ella were on milk duty: gone to fetch the morning milk and butter from the farm to which the cottage was attached. After breakfast, Danny sent the children flying again to get their beach things. They were being good troops. The two of them seemed delighted to be good troops for Danny, as though it was a game they had been waiting all this time to play, and Jessie was delighted to see how happy they were, at having this special time with him. But where did she fit in?

As they wended their way in the rented car along the farm track to meet the road down to the shore, they came to a barred gate, and Danny braked. Jessie began to open the door, but Danny put out his hand to stop her. 'No, no, no,' he said. 'Sergeant major in charge of gate?' he said, not turning round. But already, Ben was out of the car and running to the gate. Holding it open, he stood to attention, his hand raised in salute, and as the car rolled past, Danny returned the salute unsmiling, touching his forefinger briefly to his forehead.

It seemed to Jessie that she could almost feel the pleasure and importance radiating from Ben's energised young body, as he came tumbling back into the car.

She had arrived in a state of unusual exhilaration, elated by the adventure of solitude. Having at last begun to earn something, she had seized the chance to negotiate this week to finish a piece of fiction she'd been working on. Perhaps this, too, might have a future. She felt so much more confident, she told Danny. She thought she could finally begin to finish things. She'd begun to engage with the world. She was learning to sell herself. Just making the case to him was an example of it.

She had waved off the family one August Saturday, and then plunged happily into the rewrite of a bleak, slender novel about existential despair and emotional emptiness.

She felt entirely at peace. She saw no one at all (except for strangers, the crowds in the summer park); she spoke to no one except when Danny phoned her in the evenings, from a callbox down the road from the Welsh cottage. He missed her; he was excited by the strange country darkness, and the bats; and she was embarrassed when he rang, because she'd actually forgotten him – the actual, physical person – and hadn't missed him at all.

She wasn't really convinced that this novel was a

commercial proposition. Allowing Danny to get that idea was almost a lie, or at least, a moral risk. But this would be her responsibility. She thought if she could just keep going, she would discover something.

Quite frequently, as she strode about the streets and across the common after a day's work, purposely emptying her mind, these ideas sprang up into the space. She would note them down, sometimes: the story of a witty suicide; the story of a mugger's victim who invokes a different, murderous accident to prove a point about implication and significance… She carried a notebook in her pocket and would jot down these surreal and violent fantasies and then, looking up, catch sight of the shifting flight of a flock of birds, perhaps, and be filled with joy. She found herself laughing out loud at the eager, toppling run of a two-year-old chasing a striped ball across the common. It was as though her exertions on this questionable project rinsed away self-consciousness so thoroughly that she was restored to innocence.

She thought that Danny would enjoy this paradox.

At one point, it even occurred to her that these scenarios (like the novel) were a matter of posing a question – perhaps an important question – and this was worth doing, wasn't it. Danny would understand. He might be the only person she knew that she could count on to understand.

She went out every day, at the end of the afternoon, walking all through the neighbourhood village onto the common and across into the great park by the river, given up to the pleasure of sun, streets, trees, people, birds – with a pure light-heartedness she didn't seem to have experienced since adolescence. Then, at home again, just exercises, bath and supper; and in bed, an hour or two reading P.G. Wodehouse, which Ben had recommended, and which was like another dose of sunshine. Lying in the middle of the bed, with all the pillows to herself, she sometimes put down the book and wriggled her toes with pleasure.

This was probably also because it was all just so unusual.

At the end of the week she hadn't completely finished, after all, but she allowed herself not to mind. It seemed to her that the experiment was a success, and she packed up her files again with a sense of completion. In any case, she'd already put out feelers for another free stint; there might well be further chances; and she was ready for the family holiday by the sea.

To go off alone on the train to Wales was another adventure. She bought a newspaper at the station and enjoyed sinking into it, having the time to follow through her responses to bits of it. There was an editorial that projected a future technology that horrified her ('*George helped himself from the refreshment dispenser to a dry martini and some microwave-heated snails…*') – she was soon writing passionately, once again, in the little notebook she'd slipped into her handbag. But after a few heated sentences, she shut up the notebook, as she'd learned to do in order to preserve that delightful sense of energy, and went down the rocking carriage to the corridor beyond, where you could lean out of the opened window with your face in the rushing wind of passage. There, startlingly, she saw a cow frisking in a meadow, great swollen body on delicate little legs, twitching a small, stiff tail with a tassel on the end. The train stopped, suddenly, beside a field. Daisies and green blackberries, sunshine on a million wildflowers, and a small, isolated, grey electricity-supply house, chalked over with messages, reading:

He was here.
Who?
You know. All mouth and welding kit.

She was filled with a sense of the boundless strangeness of the world, a sensation that somehow seemed like hope.

Of course, it was probably also because of the job with Oscar.

It wasn't that the job was all that promising or exciting yet. Much of it was just routine typing and filing, and even the research bit was not that interesting. At that stage, the title of her job was 'secretary–researcher', and what this really meant was that she did everything that Oscar and his partner Alison didn't have time to do. She went to bookshops to see if any new books were showing up, in the area that Oscar had his eye on for this new company, and she went to the education library to see if there were theories to back up what he and Alison were thinking of doing, and she spent quite a lot of time in the central library looking at books that attempted something similar. On the whole, she found this activity depressing. Most of the library books, the educational books, had a stale, preachy air that made her feel forlorn, and the mass-market books in the shops (their other target area) were cheap and horrible. Oscar's own favourite series (the hugely popular little books that had made his name, in his previous company, and got him the vast financial backing he now enjoyed) seemed to her astonishingly empty. However, she was willing to understand what made them work (Oscar's books, at any rate) – to find out how this new game could be played. She was willing to entertain these claims of his.

From time to time Oscar would call her and Alison to sit round with him and think up a new series of books, or what ought to go inside them. 'Come on, chaps!' he'd say, and Jessie loved it, that they were chaps together, and anyone might make the coffee, not just her. Sometimes they had pub lunches, and drank pints of beer, together. On rare occasions, Oscar would stomp around, or sigh, going through figures at his desk and groaning. Other times, however, he would almost dance round the office, unashamedly whipping up his own confidence – and theirs, if possible.

'We're the best! We're the best gang! Well, okay,' he might say, 'so there's only you two and me, okay. So, you're in at the beginning! You're in on the ground floor!'

Another time, he might call to her and Alison, 'Right; come on, chaps, we've got to think up three lists of titles to show the bank.'

Then they would gather round a table, with notebooks and biros and cigarettes and coffee, and dream up titles and blurbs for non-existent books.

'Okay, okay,' he said one day, pushing his glasses up to the bridge of his large, commanding nose, 'we need a series title. What about…' He suggested a couple of possibilities to which neither Jessie nor Alison could find any response but a thoughtful, 'Hmm,' and a studied gaze into the middle distance.

'Or what about…' said Alison; but this again fell flat.

They sat and smoked for a while in silence, Oscar staring down at the tiny, abbreviated outlines on his notepad, Alison doodling the usual bunches of grapes and ribbons and clustered flowers down the page of hers, Jessie poking her biro into one of the punch-holes in her own.

Suddenly she sat up and made her own contribution.

The others sat up, as well.

Oscar repeated it. He looked at Alison. All of them looked at each other.

'Fantastic!' Oscar cried. 'That is fantastic!' He rose from his chair into a brief, almost violently enthusiastic victory dance. 'Marvellous,' he said subsiding. 'Okay, let's see then; that will be…' He went on for a bit trying out this term on the list of titles they'd been working on, trying out how it sounded as a whole. But when that was finished, they all just sat around for a while, marvelling at how well it worked, how well it meant what you wanted; all the things you could potentially do with it; until suddenly it occurred to Oscar that it was so very good, this series title, somebody else might be using it already, and he got on the telephone to consult about it, and then, when it turned out it was okay, nobody else had got it, to confer with another solicitor friend to make sure nobody could.

After which, Jessie went back to typing up Oscar's letters as usual, but with a new sense of hope – a buzzing, fizzing hope that perhaps she really could make something fresh here, something worthwhile.

During this period, she also got to look at samples of artwork that came in, and she was asked for her opinion – for why not? She was a member of the public, a mother of children, articulate – yet it was very flattering, all the same.

It wasn't always easy. Once, Oscar became completely infatuated with a truly nasty series of sketches, which he hung up over his desk in the centre of the room (they were still, at this point, all in one large room, in which Oscar kept rearranging the furniture), and these crudely coloured drawings assaulted your eye the moment you walked in the door. The worst part was how he kept leaning back in his chair to gaze at them, calling over his shoulder occasionally for support in his adoration. 'Jessie, don't you think these are marvellous? They're marvellous!' he gushed insistently; and for the ten days before these sketches quietly disappeared, her confidence in him was badly shaken.

At another point, however, a small, fair, smiley man was introduced to Oscar by a mutual friend, and left a portfolio the two had mocked up on Oscar's vague description of the new series – the one Jessie privately considered hers – and from the first moment, she would have put her money on it.

'What is it?' asked Oscar, when the young men had left, and the three of them were staring again at these mock-ups, now positioned in three different places on a desk. 'Does this work?' he asked, picking up one of the drawings and holding it closer to his face, and then at arm's length again. 'Why do I think I like it?'

'Mmm,' said Alison, tentatively. 'The colours are very clear.'

Jessie said, with sudden conviction, 'It has authority.'

Oscar gave her a sharp glance, and then he put down the mock-up and stepped back to view it from a distance. 'Yes,' he said. 'Yes, it does. You're right. Yes. Yes.'

She felt as though she'd won a medal.

By the autumn, just two months after the holiday in Wales – a matter of weeks since Danny had left for Germany – she had a new job title, and she'd been given her head, at last. She was to put together the first few illustrated double-page spreads, and she was almost on her own. Oscar and Alison had moved into their new room; they were already hiring staff for another series (a fatally cumbersome, resource-hungry project, as it turned out); and for a while, she got to do just as she liked.

She'd had few hopes of the job, when she first took it. It was just that when she'd rung about the ad and Oscar said he was thinking of practical books for children – books on how to do things – she had felt an unusual sense of solid ground. She'd tried so often to do the projects in the books she'd got for Ben and Ella, and they'd been impossible; the books had seemed almost cynically bad, as though the publishers couldn't care less about the people who bought them. It must surely be possible to improve on that, because she would care.

So when the chance came to try, she was ready for it.

She chose one of the illustrations Jim Collins had brought in that day, and hung it on the pinboard above her desk, for inspiration. There was something inexpressibly jaunty and direct about this drawing: she felt as though it lit up a path for her. All she needed was to find a scrap of text, a tone of voice, that would match the vitality of this bit of drawing. It was like a pitch-pipe, a tuning fork.

Already she could imagine it out there in the world, a spark of aliveness and energy among the drearily worthy, the wearily commercial, and she was so excited to think she could make it happen.

18

Winter–Spring, 1973

She'd turned thirty-two before she got the job with Oscar – her first real job, her first experience of being out there on her own in the working world, where people earned their livings and had salaries to depend on (or be dependent on, if you looked at it that way).

Sometimes it seemed almost a miracle. Even as it had been borne in on her that she would have to find some paid employment – some way to contribute to the household – she'd begun to fear that perhaps she'd become quite unemployable.

Of course, she'd had numbers of jobs as a teenager. In a big family with a smallish income you were expected to earn your clothes money, not to mention pocket money. Then, too, her father had insisted that she learn shorthand, as well as typing. She hadn't wanted to do that. She had meant her life to be about thinking: about learning, and imagining, and writing. She'd had grand, hazy notions about finding something wonderful to share with people, something she'd surely find out there, once freed from the suffocating anxieties of home. How fatuous she'd been, at that age.

But the typing and the shorthand had proved useful. She'd worked all through the university holidays, and then, during the years after Ben was born, when she was finishing her own degree and Danny getting on with his PhD, she'd even, for a time, held the title of editorial assistant on one of their university's house magazines. But however skilfully she presented it, however beautifully she typed up her account of it, no conjugation of this stop-gap employment added up to something resembling a career.

This was baldly pointed out at her first interview.

She'd gone to a big employment agency in central London, where she'd assumed the decent jobs were to be found. She'd dressed up in the trouser suit that still looked good, and at first, she thought she might carry it off.

To begin with, the interviewer treated her as an equal. Her manner was almost warm. As they exchanged the initial pleasantries, Jessie began to think that perhaps it would be much easier than she'd expected. The years spent home with children – well, of course, the woman said, and smiled encouragingly.

Then Jessie handed across the carefully typed-up CV, and the nice woman began examining its contents. After a while, she brought up a hand to the back of her neck. She glanced at Jessie with a look of apology.

'It's not so much the child-rearing gap itself,' she said. 'The fact that you haven't had a job for the last ten years… You can imagine, we come across this problem quite a lot. It's just, with you…' She knitted her eyebrows, and said, with an appealing shrug, as though she could only hope that Jessie would understand her difficulty, 'Well, you'd never really had a job before that.'

Jessie tried to betray no response to this damning insight. She kept on her face a bland, enquiring mask. She was hungry for a cigarette.

'Let me have a think,' the woman said, quite as though there'd been something mentioned that she might think about. 'We've got your phone number? I'll let you know if anything comes to mind.'

For a while, all the same, she persevered with the agencies. She could remember the time when she had been a bright girl. Danny remembered. She'd been showered with honours, once. She ought to be doing something. She ought to have already done something.

She had meant her life to be about thinking – about thinking and writing and imagining…

At one time, she'd had a lot of support for this. She'd got that surprising scholarship as a result of this ambition; she'd got to study with people who believed it was worthwhile, just to think, and question and imagine. Even with a baby on her arm, she'd managed to go on doing it, and get a good degree; but there the money stopped: there was no career path for what she wanted to do. It was left to her to do this thinking on her own, stranded helplessly (as she then found herself) in the unacknowledged isolation of motherhood.

All the same, she did a lot of it. She read certain literary periodicals voraciously, a range of contemporary thinkers; she attempted essays; she tried writing stories, too, in hopes of embodying ideas she couldn't otherwise express, though she mostly resisted the impulse to write poetry, because nobody read it, did they. She wanted desperately to be part of things, part of the conversation – part of the world from which she seemed increasingly remote, as time went on.

So she struggled to get her head around how things worked, those forces of power and control that Danny had so indelibly impressed upon her, but the question that haunted her was their relation to emotional truths – strivings and yearnings that she sometimes felt could change the basis of that whole system; could illuminate that very need for control and power; because (in the end) what was that control and power for? What satisfaction was to be got from it?

And yet, was that really her question – how to be happy. Was it anything but self-indulgent, to be focused on this question? And where was she, after all this questioning and thinking, but unemployable?

She was ashamed of the time it had taken her to explore this problem of employability. All those years of trying to identify what it was in Danny's thinking that seemed so powerful and yet so deadly – those crisp, neat, inarguable categories of cost and benefit – all those years of pondering grand abstractions about society, human nature, social purpose; and when it came right down to it, what did she know? What did she know about the world? What could she do, to make herself useful to it?

Danny could be quite caustic on this score.

Another agency was more impressed with Jessie's early, long-ago achievements. She wondered if the girl had read quite through her CV, but didn't ask. This time, she got an interview with a personnel officer.

Again, the interviewer had that attractive combination of competence and friendliness. When she spoke of critical paths and programme analysis, Jessie picked up the jargon and returned it with a sort of social competence – the way you do at parties – surprised at her own cool glibness: perhaps she could actually do this, after all. The woman went hopefully away, and seemed to genuinely regret, when she returned, that there was no job for Jessie at the moment. But yes, she would certainly keep Jessie's details, and the company was growing so rapidly that it would not be long. She spoke encouragingly of getting started again, as though she had done it, too; others had done it; it was all quite possible.

By this time, Jessie was so grateful and relieved, and so pleased to have passed, at least, this initial hurdle (by hunch and guess and the stretching of every faculty), that she told the woman she knew she could pick the job up quickly; why, as a matter of fact (she confessed) she hadn't really known the meaning of several of the terms they'd used, and yet she—

'Which?' said the woman, with a look of fractional withdrawal.

Jessie realised it had been a mistake to say that.

'Why – report editor?' she said wildly, picking out, in sudden panic, a term she had, of course, perfectly understood; that anybody would have understood.

'Really?' the other woman said.

'Yes, well – could you explain again exactly what this entails?' asked Jessie.

Then she listened as though intently to the unnecessary reply – trying to meet those baffled eyes with a look of confident enquiry – while all the while, the hope ran down inside her.

In any case, Danny would not much want her to have a job like that. He had married a girl with promise. Since she had clearly failed with all that thinking and writing, down in the makeshift study, since she didn't seem about to earn any money, or even some kind of name for herself – what exactly did she mean to do with her life, he wondered?

Jessie began to doubt that she was fit for anything.

She read the situations vacant ads, and tried to make sense of them.

She tried to imagine doing the things that people did out there, in a world that seemed to her largely pointless. She tried to imagine thinking up advertising slogans, remembering the names of different kinds of typeface…

She was abashed by the sheer stamina of people who earned their livings out there in this world; somehow, she'd reached a point where she didn't see how she'd ever be able to do these things.

She'd never been clear about exactly what their financial situation was. It was Danny who got the salary and paid the bills, and though they discussed these questions, it had always been a matter of Danny noting down, in his quick, large, definite hand, various estimates and rounded figures to obtain a bottom line, or sometimes (more rarely) a small future surplus that they might play with.

He liked that term: play with. Coming from him, the word 'play' seemed to emphasise movement, freedom, like the play of a fishing line (though he didn't fish): not playfulness, but flex, and scope. He didn't like to mess about with details: why should he bother? He'd pointed out to her, in the kinds of ads that spread out over several columns in *The Times*, the salaries that would be available to him in industry. In this frame of reference, her own possible contributions or small economies seemed too paltry even to consider – seemed, even, unrealistic. A job hardly mattered in view of the sacrifices that would be entailed. Why was she thinking of it?

Yet sometimes, on the occasional trip to central London to meet him for a night out, she would see a woman commuter with a purposeful step, a look of bright alertness – a professional woman, carrying a briefcase – and feel a pang of longing. She wished this were Ella's image of a mother, someone sallying forth into the world with a look of confidence and self-reliance: her own person.

Then there arrived this offer for Danny to spend a year away at the institute in West Berlin, just as the decision about Ben's school confronted them. Now, these financial unknowns that had never quite seemed worth clarifying were closing in around her like a trap. The question of a job – she'd almost begun to give it up, but in West Berlin, she'd no longer have the choice. She realised she'd have to try again. She'd have to find work here, and stay on in London, as she'd done before when Danny was away. But Danny was fed up with these discussions of what Jessie should do. What she should do was come with him to West Berlin. Ben would go to the expensive school, without the scholarship; Danny was ready to pay the boarding fees for Ben; but there was no way he was going to try, as well, to support two households. Jessie and Ella would come with Danny, and he'd rent out the London house for a decent sum to visiting Americans. Soon after this discussion he went away for a weekend residential seminar.

A few days before, a friend who'd come round for coffee had told Jessie she was thinking of getting the odd night's work at a local care home. She said the money was so good it was worth the disruption, and you didn't need any special experience or skills. What made her think of this? Oh, she'd just looked through the situations vacant ads in the local paper. She waved at Jessie a copy of this meagre tabloid, and then showed her the actual ad, the actual figure of how much you could earn.

After she'd gone, Jessie got out the bills from the cubby-hole in the desk where they were kept. She found the stack of bank statements, to double-check. She made a note of the mortgage payment (but Danny would have to cover this, in any event). Then she added up the figures for the various utilities, over the year, and averaged them out, including the standard phone bill, and in less than half an hour, she had a figure for what she'd need to earn, each month, over and above her usual housekeeping budget, to run the house.

She'd never done this before, and it only took half an hour. She was astonished at how it felt to have taken this tiny initiative.

She went out and got her own copy of the local paper, and began to examine it. There were several jobs she thought she could handle, some with short hours, and close enough so that she wouldn't need to make elaborate arrangements for looking after Ella.

Then she looked at advertisements for rooms, in this paper

and *The Times*. It had occurred to her that it would take very little to fit out that makeshift study, in the back of the unused garage, to serve as a room for Ben on breaks and holidays, while she herself moved into the small third bedroom and Ella into Ben's old room. This would mean that she could rent out the big main bedroom – to a student, possibly. It could be fun, she thought. It could be company.

She checked through the figures again and it all worked. On this basis it was perfectly clear that she could do it; she could easily maintain herself and Ella.

Oddly enough, the fantasy of the briefcase had evaporated. A little job down the road – they needed an assistant at the local chemist, she had noticed – and she could be sauntering back to Ella at an early hour. Perhaps sometimes they'd have a meal, just the two of them, at the small Chinese restaurant she often passed on her way to the supermarket: this idea had a peculiar charm. And then, in the evenings she'd be free – to read what she liked, think what she liked, work at whatever project took her interest...

Danny was won over by this show of decision and clear-headedness. At last she was acting with independence, and this was interesting. She was being a real partner, finally – she could see this, and she could see why it mattered to him. She had enlivened the future with a new set of possibilities. It wouldn't be all just up to him to make things happen.

In fact, what began as a discussion of facts and figures, she having lassoed a reluctant Danny into sitting down with her at the kitchen table for just five minutes while she explained her plan, turned into an hour, two hours, of increasingly absorbing chat, over numberless cups of tea. If she was really going to be a proper wage earner, things could be different; they could look differently at all sorts of things. But to begin with, think what fun it would be to meet like lovers, over the year he was away. Of course, he would be coming home for family visits – and he hoped she would bring Ben and Ella for a month in summer – but in between, they could have the odd weekend, just the two of them. They could rendezvous in Amsterdam, perhaps Boulogne… It would be like exciting little honeymoons.

As for the job itself, surely she might lift her sights a little, he suggested. What about taking another look at *The Times*? Not the big, impersonal agencies; after all, she wasn't really a secretarial type; but what about the small ads?

He even found a few, right away.

But it was so wonderful, as always, when that barrier of disagreement between them melted away, and suddenly there was everything to tell each other. During the weeks of coolness, it had begun to seem that they shared nothing; that whatever there had been had all dried up (and when it was like that, you almost couldn't remember what there had been); yet now, whole worlds had opened. She could see how he must have missed her, from the eagerness with which he wanted to tell her, now, about everything that had been going on with him in the meanwhile – thoughts and feelings, but even silly stories, too; something bizarre that had happened at the university, and then this article that had struck him, in the papers – and she had read the same article; she also had been moved; how astonishing that was…

As for her, he now seemed to want to know about her.

She could tell him things, all sorts of things. He touched her cheek; he held her hand and watched her face with love.

It was reading week for Danny, and they'd been sitting since lunchtime at the kitchen table. In a burst of energy, they decided to go down to the deli in the village, and look for German delicacies to get an idea of what there might be to brighten Danny's bachelor meals in West Berlin. This was the long-delayed fulfilment of a fantasy dating from their poor student days, when they used to window-shop at the deli in their neighbourhood and make lists of all the good things they would sample one day, when they were rich and could afford them. It was very peculiar, this idea of 'affording' things, because of course there had been many times, since, when they could have, but they never did, and suddenly, they both realised that they ought to.

So when the children came drifting in from school, they found the two of them exploring a great festive heap of sausages, jars of herring, a peculiar loaf that smelled of aniseed, pickles, half-wrapped cheeses, a bottle of Schnapps, too. And music playing.

19

August, 1976

Three years later, seated across from her in an expensive little restaurant in central London – the first time they'd met each other on their own since the separation five months earlier – he was asking her, 'Why did you do it, Jessie?'

But it wasn't the straight question that she'd wanted.

It seemed it had all been for nothing. All the times she thought she'd finally won through, solved the problem, found the answer. It was as though she'd never tried, or cared, or meant it; or, worse, couldn't even control her own intentions.

She'd had very little sleep, the night before, but had been buoyed up by a giddy sense of exhilaration, going off to meet him – escaping from Marjorie, from the telephone, from the uncorrected briefs in their ominously thickening folders on her desk. She was glad of the new shirt she'd bought. She thought it looked confident, and carelessly expensive, and it gave new currency to the skirt, which, though a great deal older, had also, once, been an act of considerable daring, but it had paid off; it had worn very well. She had bought shoes, too, with just the shallowest platform to give height to the shapely little heel, so that your legs looked long and slender, and she knew she had pretty legs. It was one of the things she liked about the summer, that you could show off your legs.

The hot sunlight of that extravagant summer poured into the streets, as she left to meet him, and she felt almost gay: unreal, defiant. Why shouldn't she have good things, occasionally? He had chosen a small, expensive-looking restaurant on the Strand, quite near to where she worked, but in a direction she didn't usually take. It had thick, old, small-paned glass in the windows, and an immense oak door. Opening that door, you stepped onto beautiful wide floorboards, black with age, and into an ambiance of gentle voices, gentle noises – the chink of cutlery softened by thick linen – and a smell like the distillation of good cheer: garlic, butter, woodsmoke, wine… a smell of such powerful assurance, it might have been a strong arm round your shoulders.

It was like the essence of that holiday they'd never had again, a promise that had kept on dancing just ahead, over the last few years, like an *ignis fatuus* over the marshlands of fairyland. That happy time when they would relax and be reconciled.

For over an hour, they seemed to be playing at having this whole separation business be a game, almost a lover's game. And then a pause developed, and he was saying, 'So why did you do it, Jessie?' with that quizzical, almost kindly look. 'Why are you so determined to be a loser?'

She had had too much wine. She shouldn't have been drinking wine at lunchtime. She probably shouldn't have been here at all, at lunchtime, but as the months had passed, as one after another plan had crumpled, she'd found herself struggling to maintain momentum, and it was at this point that he had asked her out to lunch.

So she said yes, though it was midweek, and she had too much on, and she knew she shouldn't.

But as July drew to a close, she found herself doing this. She invented outings with Ben and Ella, even taking them for Sunday lunch, once, to new acquaintances who lived in the far hinterlands of southwest London, from which they didn't return till midnight, having missed the bus on the last leg of their journey. She accepted an unsettling invitation for a drink with Oscar. She got in touch with a man who'd been in love with her, the year before.

She also went out and bought a number of things she thought they needed, including some new clothes that Arlis had become convinced she should invest in, since she couldn't seem to deal with jumble sales; she then had to persuade the bank manager to extend her overdraft. She was expecting a decent settlement, she told him grandly.

For a brief time, this was true, about the 'settlement'. Her views enlarged and shrank under the impulse of sometimes wildly varying pieces of information and misinformation: gossip about Danny's plans relayed through Marty – changes of heart, of mind, and fluctuations in Danny's circumstances, too.

For he, too, had been tantalised by new prospects. In June

he had been approached about a particularly highly paid consultancy, six weeks in somewhere alien and surprising, like Dubai; when this fell through, he was sufficiently shaken to ring her up one night, confused and rather drunk. He talked for hours, that night; they made a plan to meet; but the next day she panicked and called it off.

After this, when they spoke, his voice had hardened again. This lunch date, a month later, had a different character. Perhaps it was just a demonstration of how lightly he could now extend an invitation; that was what the tone suggested. In fact, she had no idea what it was.

'Well, it's a free lunch,' she said brazenly to Arlis.

'Jessie, you're learning,' Arlis said.

It was still assumed by them all that she had a lot to learn.

The truth was, of course, she was at sea. She might have known that it would end the way it did. Another glass of wine, and yet another, while the lunch hour illicitly extended itself. The waiter had taken away her desecrated plate – cigarette ash fallen on the last florets of broccoli, the remnants of sole in a puddle of its lovely sauce – and now he was pouring another glass, from another bottle, bringing yet another pristine ashtray. And Danny was saying, 'You had me in the palm of your hand. How could you do it?' Saying, 'Are you actually scared of power? Is that what happened with Oscar, too?'

Even now, she could always be drawn into engagement with him. Particularly this endlessly self-referential talk about each other and themselves together, about the relationship – about their own, and about what a relationship could be; about herself, and how she had come to be this way.

'Is it your background?' he would say. 'Is it your family? What is it, Jessie? Why do you need to do this to yourself?'

The week before, she'd finally given up the Mountfield Road house.

It was a wrench, because she'd not only enjoyed the fantasies about it, but also, by now, invested time and energy in it. There'd been phone calls to lenders, agent, workmen and surveyor; roughing out notes for a variety of different building plans; attempting to work out a schedule and a timescale; trying to get an estimate of the costs involved, and how it could all be financed.

Maggie had been sure there was great potential for letting rooms. Early on, one Saturday afternoon, there had been a delightful hour or so drinking coffee with her and Horst while Maggie, between spells at the cooker – efficiently slipping a dinner-party casserole into the oven – leafed through the local paper exclaiming at the rents you could get, for lodgers, and calling out figures for Jessie to scribble in her notebook. Now and then, giggles and shouts and thumps were audible from the neighbouring rooms in which Ella was engaged in some boisterous game with Joel and Aaron.

'So where are we?' Maggie would say, returning to check those figures. She brought round a heap of potatoes for Horst to peel, while she resumed her seat at the kitchen table for a moment. She lit a cigarette, and picked up Jessie's notebook. 'You wouldn't be offering breakfast – laundry – any other little service, would you?'

'God, no,' said Jessie, with alarm.

'Oh, you're quite right; it would be ridiculous, in your

position. Now, Elaine does bed and breakfast – you've met Elaine: two doors down? She usually does a student, during term time. Of course, she only has that little part-time job at the library. Poor Elaine! By the end of term, she's invariably involved in some extremely bitter feud.'

'But she is so mean!' cried Horst. 'She insists on the breakfast, just for the extra charge, and then she gives them these horrible packs of biscuits—'

'Peak Freen,' said Maggie, with a certain relish, 'because they're the cheapest you can get, in their own little packs.'

'Horrible, tasteless biscuits,' Horst continued, 'and a very small packet of jelly, and she leaves the tea outside the bedroom, getting cold, because they aren't allowed in the family rooms, you see—'

'Pathologically mean,' said Maggie, comfortably. 'It must be said. But no, no, no; I was only checking. Quite right – keep it simple.'

'But it is not simple,' Horst demurred, with a doleful deepening of his voice. 'It is never simple. There must be advertisements, references, interviews – remember, this is a stranger coming in your house.'

'But Jessie knows that, Horst; she's an old hand; she's done the lodger bit. The question is,' she resumed briskly, 'how the figures look. What's the bottom line?'

'Well of course, there are actually several unknowns. But, given what Horst was saying, about the mortgage payments—'

'Ah now, don't be frightened by that figure. You know Horst, surely! And of course, you'll have to get them to knock a few thousand off the price, hmm?'

At this, she turned her dark gaze on Jessie a little sternly, and Jessie frowned with the effort to look as though she'd been contemplating this very operation.

'But obviously, you'll wait till you've got yourself some ammunition. I'm sure there'll be plenty to pick up from the survey. And you'll need estimates from a reliable builder. But I'll introduce you to McEnroe; he's a lamb,' she finished, in tones of deep approval.

For nearly two months, Jessie tried to believe in it all. She was scared of the work involved, all the different tasks and imponderable contingencies to which the others referred so lightly, but she was caught up in the excitement. To be the owner of such a handsome property – to be in a position to rent out rooms and get an income from it – this idea gave her a gratifying sense of substance, and to the others there seemed no doubt that she could handle it.

There'd been the question of how much capital she'd be left with, for the deposit. Maggie thought she could surely do a deal with Danny, flog it to him as an investment with agreed shares he could cash in at a later date.

Arlis thought even this was probably unnecessary. 'Jessie, come on. You're in a powerful position. What can he do? The children must have a home. Think what you'll be saving him, in school fees. After all, you could just sit where you are: no court would oblige you to move from the marital home.'

Jessie wondered what it would be like, to get to say this to him. She pictured saying to him, coolly, 'You realise, I'm in a very powerful position,' like one of those movies in which the man and woman are equal partners, sparring.

There were some shocks relating to this question. The first was the discovery that, after all, she wouldn't have to try to bargain with Danny, or cut deals, because he was offering her all the equity of their present home – anything she could make from the sale of it, after paying off what they owed.

This was an unexpected development. She hardly knew how to take it.

'I've had some good news,' she told the Goldmans, dropping round to them after work that day, with the solicitor's letter.

Marty gave her a quizzical look as he took the letter, but on reading it, exclaimed, 'But this is very good news!'

'It is a surprise. It's not what I expected.' In fact, she felt peculiarly upset. 'He's being very generous,' she said, uncertainly.

'Rubbish,' said Arlis indignantly. 'He has no choice!'

Marty gave her one of those looks of his, but let it pass. 'The point is, the coast is clear,' he said. 'Now you have some basis for making plans. Now you can get things moving. How much capital do you think this house will bring?'

When Jessie told him, he looked very pleased. 'But this is good. This is excellent,' he said, rubbing his hands with satisfaction. 'This is not riches, but it is adequate.'

So now, she began to feel happy, too. Within days, she'd begun a flurry of arrangements, and for some time, she felt excited and important.

But the next shock was when it was pointed out to her that she'd forgotten the second mortgage on Albion Grove, though it was by means of this that Danny had paid off some rather hefty debts, including the remainder owed to their university for his doctorate, and had furnished the house with many things that were new, and matched, the way he wanted. This brought down the figure by a substantial chunk. When Marty discovered this, talking to Danny late one night in the student bar, he was so upset that he got drunk, as Arlis related to Jessie, later. Danny had made some passing reference to his wife's mad plans: that was how the subject had come up. That was how the information had come out.

Jessie was devastated. Suddenly, everything was hard again, just when she'd started to relax a little, and entertain these fatuous hopes. She felt tripped up and tricked and furious, all the more so because there was no one to blame – certainly not Danny. Whatever the amount might be, by law (as her solicitor had explained) she had no right to more than a third of it.

For several nights, after this, she lay sleepless, itching all over with this objectless fury.

At last she calmed down, and then, with Marty's help, did the figures again. It was all just possible, though with the maximum mortgage. And after all, the renovation didn't all have to be done immediately, did it. You do these things in stages. She could prepare the rooms for lodgers with a lick of paint; get hold of some second-hand furniture – so cheap to come by, if you kept your eye out, looked in at the auctions now and then (why hadn't she and Danny ever done that, Arlis wondered) – and surely, Jessie's own salary was bound to rise. Look at how well those books of hers had done! And with all the new ideas she was so excited about…

Oh yes, those ideas. Yes.
For a while, she shut her eyes and ran.
Sometimes, that was what it felt like.

20

Shortly before, she'd finally rung Tony Wentworth.

It was nearly a year since she'd first met him, at the party in 1975, held to celebrate the publication of the first two series of Otford books. Those titles that Jessie had cut her teeth on – struggled with, fought over, come to grief about – would at last be appearing on the market, some fourteen months after the final proofs had been corrected. In the meantime, and while they all waited for the completion of Oscar's own pet trilogy, she'd revived and gone on to bruise herself on another, even more ambitious project; now she was down, again.

The dark times kept on happening, even after she'd found the job at Otford's; they struck her even as she was finishing a project; now, she was so miserable she could hardly speak, though she should have been happy – she should have (surely!) felt like part of the celebration. There were her books, at last – big, shiny stacks of them – but she wasn't excited about it, now. She couldn't imagine why any of it had seemed to matter.

The preparations for the party – held in the main office at the end of the afternoon – made a break in routine for which she was marginally grateful. It helped to do physical tasks. Desks had to be cleared, extra chairs rounded up from adjoining rooms, bottles and glasses unpacked from the crates brought in from the off licence by the guys in the design department, Max and Johnny. Other colleagues busied themselves looping swags of coloured crêpe paper from the window sashes and arranging flowers here and there, in beer mugs. Oscar had asked a number of friends and acquaintances whom he had at various times consulted or who had supported the operation, over the last two and a half years, and his wife brought in tray after tray of tiny sandwiches, encased in great sarcophagi of silver foil.

At four-thirty, Oscar finally made a noise with a steel rule against a wine-bottle, to get everyone's attention, and began a speech, using that special, smarmy voice he saved for such occasions (which, oddly, no one ever seemed embarrassed by). He began, as always, with the story of Oscar and its upward trajectory, but soon moved on to congratulatory reminiscence and even congratulations, including a few jokes about Alison's preferred new mode of production – she being now heavily pregnant (and indeed, soon to gently lapse from this paper role of partnership). Then they all drank to the publication of the first two series, and to the future success of Otford Publications, and then the gathering broke up into smaller knots of conversation, and people began to move about, and mingle.

That was when Jessie found this man beside her, asking her about herself. She couldn't think why he was bothering to do this. There was no particular need to be polite to her. He didn't seem to be stuck there, and no one had brought them together. He just began talking to her, asking her what work she did there, how long she'd been there. He seemed surprised by and apparently interested in the answer.

'In at the beginning. That must have been quite hair raising – knowing Oscar. What was it like?'

'It was all right. It was fine,' she said, beginning to remember. 'It was strange, at first. I thought Oscar was very strange. When I came for my interview, they hadn't even got any desks, yet, just a sofa. There was a big vase of paper flowers in that fireplace there. And a kite on the wall. One of those Japanese kites, like an insect.'

'A kite,' he said. 'How very apt!' This made him laugh. His pleasure seemed so good-natured that Jessie began to smile as well; but as he returned her glance, she found herself turning away, with a stifled sigh.

Then they were both quite silent. She had dried up. She didn't ask him anything about himself. She didn't feel up to pretending that she cared.

'Look, you need a drink,' he said suddenly. He laid his hand on her shoulder very lightly, so that she looked up. 'May I?' he asked, putting out the other hand for her glass.

He made off across the room towards the drinks table.

Newcomers had continued to arrive, and it had now got crowded. He stopped several times to speak to people. Then Oscar's wife, Britta, waved and smiled at him, came across to him, drew him away with her to meet someone.

Jessie looked quickly round for social occupation, but no openings presented. Few of the outsiders she'd worked with had been invited, people like the trembling little elderly ex-scoutmaster, the messianic young biology teacher. Instead, too close for comfort, the firm's first educational advisor was holding forth, author of several series of those dull, empty, lavishly produced small books whose ubiquity in the libraries had so seriously discouraged her, back in the beginning – books with titles such as *Wood*, or perhaps *Containers*. He had captured the nice woman who ran book groups.

Ah, what to do? What to do? Oscar and Alison, of course, were each at the centre of congratulatory groups: noisy, amused, repellingly complete. Max and Johnny had formed a companionable huddle with a tall, fat, friendly-looking boy who had recently come for an interview, but she could tell, even from across the room, that they were talking motorbikes; indeed, even as her gaze discovered them, Max fixed his hands on a pair of juddering phantom handlebars. As for her colleagues, the people she worked beside – the people who had, actually, once worked under her management – she'd become uncomfortable with them now.

She hadn't thought she minded being demoted, losing her job to Marjorie. She'd got to see through those first books; that was the main thing. She'd never wanted to manage people. In a way, she'd almost welcomed her independence (what she'd assumed would be independence). She hadn't seen why it should make much difference. But gradually, the atmosphere had changed. The others developed jokes she couldn't share, a certain lazy, easy-going culture. The way you told your personal stories, where your desk was, what you ate for lunch, became important, as though you were all in primary school. Her own intensity about the projects became redundant.

She could hear snatches of banter from them, now. Beautiful Annabelle was in fits of giggles, flirting with the print buyer; even Peta, beside a more than usually expansive Henry, was becoming pink. Standing alone without even a glass to hold, Jessie felt almost paralysed with self-consciousness.

The nice man was still engaged with Britta, having got only a little closer to the drinks.

Jessie began to panic. He mustn't suddenly remember her, look round for her, see her so obviously alone and waiting for him. He mustn't find himself forced to leave his friends and rescue her.

She was saved unexpectedly by the production director, who wandered up with a look of dismayed preoccupation. He began at once to grumble unhappily: it seemed that no one had remembered that a vital sample of artwork needed to go off for repro, and now Oscar was badgering him to meet somebody. When Jessie offered to organise a courier he was hearteningly grateful. Soon she was safely alone in the production room, making the phone call, taping up the package. Then it was easy to just slip away downstairs through a different entrance, without even re-entering the rooms full of party noise, and this was why, when Oscar called on her to give lunch to Tony Wentworth, two months later, she had no idea who he was.

She was working on a new project when Oscar buzzed her that day, calling her down into his office to ask if she would meet this friend of his, on the off chance that there might be some work for him.

'He's a good chap,' said Oscar, with an oddly defensive

intonation, running his hand down over his lanky fringe before dropping it heavily on his desk again. 'His problem is he's rich. He's never had any need to earn his money, and he doesn't really know what to do with himself. Too much intellect and too much time – one of those chaps who can argue himself out of anything. Should I cut the grass? Is this the best thing to do for the world? Of course, he doesn't actually cut the grass.'

'But what's his specialty? What does he do?'

'He doesn't do anything, poor chap. He can't decide on anything, that's what I'm saying. Well, he got a first in philosophy once, that's probably what did for him. And then he did a history degree – he did write a novel, years ago, but his heart wasn't in it. I don't think he's done anything at all, since then. Basically, he needs a job. And his wife's just left him; who could blame her, really? Stuck out in that huge old pile in Wiltshire.'

'And so – does he live there on his own, now? In the country?'

'Not at the moment, no; he lives in town. Well, I told you, he's very rich. Anyway, just have a chat and see if you think he might be useful, anywhere. Take him out to lunch; you'll cheer him up. He needs to know he can still chat up a pretty girl. I mean, you know, just lunch,' he qualified, dryly. 'I'm not a dating agency. And you're still married, aren't you?'

'Of course I am. Oscar, you know I'm married.'

'That's okay; that's fine; I'm in favour of people being married. But he isn't really around much, is he? Wasn't he away for a year or so?'

'Just on sabbatical. He's been back a year, now.'

Oscar continued to gaze at her, rather quizzically, over his spectacles.

'Now and then he goes off on consultancies,' she added.

'Well, that's fine, then. Well okay, about noon tomorrow, right? I'll give you a bell.' And he turned back to his desk.

This request was not unusual, though perhaps a little more so than it would once have been. Oscar was ever and again bringing in yet another of his friends, particularly in the early days – some with private incomes, several with the kind of job you could do two or three of, at the same time; just occasionally someone between jobs, or (as this one seemed to be) in some sort of difficulty. He introduced them with a variety of motivations and excuses: to write a proposal, to consult or comment; just to chat. The company itself was still quite small – though of course, geometrically enlarged since she had joined him and Alison – and Oscar was still new at it.

She had sometimes wondered, in the first days, if Oscar really knew quite what to do next; yet he managed to create a sense of perpetual forward motion, through whatever means. He was continually inventing new initiatives, pretexts for action, a sense of urgency, and he knew the magic of sheer social energy – people knowing about you, being excited with you; people coming and going; new projects being vaunted and paraded, which he could then extinguish ruthlessly when a more promising avenue seemed to open up.

So this was what brought her together again with Tony. It was a shock, when she went down into Oscar's office the next day, to realise that this was the man she'd escaped from at the party. She could see it was even more of a shock for him. His reaction, though instantly covered up, was visible.

When she recounted all this to Arlis, a year later – the fragmentary first meeting, the unusual impression she seemed to have made, and then what followed, Arlis listened impassively, with a wise nod from time to time. 'Hmm, hmm,' she said.

'He was feeling vulnerable. Marriage splitting up – you were a fantasy. Jessie, you have that sort of persona; you're very pliable. Men can impose their fantasies on your image.'

Jessie didn't like this interpretation.

'Jessie, there can be real bits in an affair like this! There can be real affection! You just need to be aware of the fantasy element. But Tony has warmth. He sounds very interesting – a complicated man, but interesting.'

Jessie thought that in fact he was very simple, despite what Arlis said, what Oscar said about him. She thought he was almost dangerously simple. He seemed a man longing simply to be loyal: devotedly, single-heartedly loyal, but in need of a single, integral object for this devotion. She thought this was what was dangerous about him. Though she remembered every touch of his hand on her own hand, on her arm, her shoulder, it was some time before she gave in to Arlis's urging that she should contact him again.

But afterwards, what she remembered most poignantly from that period wasn't Tony. What she remembered, because it was one of those moments that seemed to stand in a clear space, in a higher altitude above a too-familiar turbulence, was how happy she had been that morning, quietly working on her own. Just that moment, that very moment before the internal buzzer on the phone rang, with the call from Oscar.

It was late summer, but a dark, rain lashed day, which

perhaps made the bright room seem peculiarly secure and safe. Henry had just burst into the room, drenched and energised by the weather; there was a lively exchange; some kind of joke. She couldn't remember what the joke was, just that when she looked up, she discovered on Henry's face a look of such undefended good spirits that suddenly it was easy to be joining in the laugh. The opening door brought the smell of coffee from the new machine Oscar had recently – so wisely! – installed in the cubby-hole kitchen beneath the stair. She found herself stretching and yawning, in a wave of wellbeing, and then thinking, with surprise, 'But I'm okay, now. I'm alive, again.'

A part of her had been flattered and interested when Oscar called on her, but another part didn't want excitement, but to have been left just a little longer on her own, working quietly at her own pace, with her head down, because it was precious to be alive again, at the end of that deadly summer.

21

August, 1974

The person she had slept with, in fact, was Oscar, which she realised would be considered by most people a politically stupid act, if not actually perverse. In the context of the work scene at the time, you might well have thought this, given that he had just demoted her. But there had been also her own, separate, personal scene, which so outweighed those developments as to render them incidental to her emotional economy. She had used him. That was what it boiled down to. And if this, too, was politically dangerous, it was perhaps less so because (at the time) she was so entirely unaware of it: either that there might be any imbalance in the transaction, or that it might possibly have been anything more than that.

She had been shocked and frightened when he made a pass at her, during the painful winter of 1973, the winter of her first year at Otford Publishing.

It hadn't even occurred to her that he was attractive. He was odd. Even his looks were odd, almost a caricature – the shaggy hair that fell below his collar, fell into his face, fell even between his eyes, sometimes, giving him a curiously cross-eyed gaze, as he so imperiously ignored it; and then, those very round dark eyes which he would widen as he brought his face right into yours, saying things like, 'You understand, I'm really astonishingly successful!' Which was how he had introduced himself to her, when she came to be interviewed about the job, and she sat beside him on the tiny sofa in the otherwise almost empty room, and he launched straight into an exposition of his own unusual brilliance and achievements, and she was simply astounded by his unselfconscious egotism.

But before long, she began to realise how much she looked forward to him. More and more, she enjoyed his energy, the comedy of his almost self-parodying rages and enthusiasms, and above all, the rapport that developed between them: the way he got her jokes, the way he clearly relished how she got his jokes. She began to realise, guiltily, that it was more pleasant to think of him than of Danny, whose letters from West Berlin had become increasingly dissatisfied, and bleak.

There came a time at which, falling asleep at night, it was images of Oscar that occasionally sweetened her last, drowsy thoughts. She imagined his hand on her shoulder, or even on her own hand; even, perhaps, a particularly warm, sweet hug…

Instead of which, he had suddenly mauled her, in the dark garden at Alison's engagement party.

There were French doors that opened onto a small terrace, but no one was out there, because it was winter and too cold. One moment, she was flirting and laughing with him, standing beside the open door; the next, he had taken her arm and was drawing her outside, an attention which flattered her. But then, hurriedly, he was pulling her right away from the angled light that fell from the room inside; and then, outrageously, he picked her up in his arms and ran. In a moment he had carried her bodily behind some shrubbery, and setting her down, began to kiss her, fondling her with such greediness that she immediately pushed his arms away, hissing at him to stop it, stop it – stop!

He stopped. He apologised, in that horrible, smarmy voice. They drew apart; she took a deep breath; she brushed down the pretty dress she had been so pleased to find occasion for. Slowly they sauntered back towards the terrace, at a calm, impersonal distance. As though with one accord, they paused together on the terrace, and as they did so, someone called from inside: quick, they're opening champagne – and the incident was erased, like a ripple in a stream.

She was so relieved. It wasn't until later, safely at home and in bed again, that she was hit by a wave of shame and humiliation. She felt punished for her fantasies. She was horrified at what Danny would have thought of her.

What happened between them later in the summer might have been happening to different people.

It was by then a different era. She had come back alone from the family holiday in Germany to a sunny, empty London (the children staying on with Danny and his mother, two weeks longer), and found that her role had changed. In her absence, she had been relieved of her post by Marjorie.

Even her desk had been moved while she was gone; but the truth was, this desk had stopped being any kind of home;

the days of camaraderie and jokes had long since passed. The single, empty room had multiplied, spilling out into further rooms as other enterprises that had occupied the building failed and vanished; and even so, the desks were crammed together and heaped high with papers to accommodate the ever-expanding staff.

Now, once again, Jessie was spending most of her time away from the office, looking for new projects. Once again, she was browsing the dead matter in the libraries, the cheap, tacky volumes in the bookshops, and trying to dream up something on her own.

But the good thing was being on her own. She didn't have to timetable the short-lived Bubsie, or listen to Annabelle; above all, she didn't have to edit Marjorie, which had been extremely painful to them both – Marjorie being so much her senior, after fifteen years on women's weekly magazines, and, though she tried to hide it, so violently conscious of her loss of status that sometimes, as the two of them bent together over Marjorie's inept first layouts, Jessie could not help noticing the trembling of her hands. Loneliness was a small price to pay for being liberated from such a false position.

On her first day back, Oscar had called her to join him and Marjorie in the room that he now shared with Alison. When he broke the news, Jessie was unsurprised. She'd somehow known it wouldn't be good news. She sighed, but then she shrugged; she said that actually, she was quite relieved.

'Why?' asked Marjorie, in a markedly tight, cool voice.

Jessie was taken aback. She said, 'Well, you do have more experience than I have. You know about all those technical things,' she added, with a generalising hand movement, barely aware of how dismissive the gesture was. 'You know about typesetting, you know about typefaces, you can work out schedules…' Why was this woman being so ungracious? Under the circumstances, it seemed unnecessary.

Oscar looked from one to the other. 'Well, that's all right, then,' he said, briskly. 'Don't worry Jess, your salary stays the same,' he added expansively, referring to the tiny increment on the tiny sum that had preceded it; 'this won't affect your salary – for the moment, anyway.' He turned back, blandly, to his figures and calculator, altogether missing Jessie's reaction. Of course it shouldn't affect her salary. She was good; she was a prototype-maker. Why should she want to be a manager, as well?

She had come back from holiday with a sense of stony resolve. Physically, she felt restored by the time away among lakes and forests, by having the burdens lifted. She thought she felt stronger.

The winter that had followed that first mellow, hopeful autumn at Otford Publishing had very soon become a tunnel of misery. One setback followed another: domestic disasters accompanied by a pummelling of impersonal, but no less disruptive public upheavals: the problems for Ben, the problems for Danny; and then the coal strike, the energy crisis, the three-day week, the train strike – well, a train strike, which unfortunately affected only Jessie, so that she seemed forever tripping over an obstacle invisible to her colleagues – on and on it went, together with the endless juggling of lodger and housework and groceries and meals and laundry, not to mention sitters for Ella – time with Ella – time with Ben, who was spending his weekends home again – and all the while, her own driving passion to get those first books right, not just done, but right… Until, by the end of it all, there was just a last frenzy of panic and patch-up, to meet the deadlines which then became so swiftly meaningless; and getting through the last days of holiday packing in a state of mindless exhaustion and unease.

For, soon after Christmas the marriage had gone wrong, too, in a new and terrible way. After all, there had been no lovely little honeymoon weekends to break up the separation, just a single rendezvous in Amsterdam, when things were already bad and couldn't be discussed. And they couldn't be discussed on the brief, rare phone calls, which instead might even end in crippling coldness. And not in letters. The worst mistakes of all had been in letters, and thus irrevocable.

She'd arrived back in London determined to find a lover.

How do people do this?

There was just one person who occurred to her as a potential partner. He was a bachelor colleague of Danny's, a kind, attractive loner who often had a pretty girl on hand, but at present, she knew, was on his own. She used to flirt with Frank at parties, in a friendly way, and once, when an opportunity presented itself, he had kissed her, with memorable gentleness and sweetness.

But when she rang him, she was disturbed to notice that he did not sound smooth and casual, as she had imagined, but rather breathless.

It was about this movie everyone was talking about,

she told him. Danny had mentioned it when she saw him, recently. Had he seen it yet – if not, would he come with her?

It might have been different if it had been another movie. It might have actually been worse. If it had been an easier, more enjoyable film, they might have relaxed, and spent some time together afterwards, and gone to bed – unless she'd actually panicked and turned him down – and either way there would have been awkward consequences and emotion.

However, this was not a movie to relax you, even if you understood it. She did not understand it, and was too embarrassed to say so. It was a dark, claustrophobic film, emotionally obscure, about a middle-aged man involved in an elaborate surveillance operation focused on a supposedly vulnerable, adulterous couple who turn out to be murderers: protagonists veiled in layers of deceit, distrust and treachery, and among them all, who could you care about?

She supposed it was also about Watergate, which she also didn't care about. At any rate, she couldn't pretend that she was shocked. It seemed to her that very few things shocked her, now. It seemed she had no particular expectations. She seemed to have no sense of what you could allow yourself to expect, or even hope for.

As for that world out there, the world of politics – well, the grey sludge of history was made of cheating and lying, wasn't it?

Sitting there in that cinema, next to Frank, she was stiff with self- consciousness, afraid of revealing the depth of this passivity; she wasn't surprised that when it was over, they walked off in silence. In the dull, end-of-summer darkness, he delivered her to her door, driving all the way over to her side of London – the wrong side for him – and neither could find anything to say. She thanked him; there remained several feet of space between them, in the car; and he didn't reach across it to kiss her goodnight, and it didn't occur to her to invite him in for coffee. She felt chilled by the sense of having exhausted a source of goodwill which she realised, now, she had foolishly counted on; and what had given her the idea she could do that?

Before the film, they'd met in a pub next to her office, and coincidentally, Oscar had offered to buy her a drink after work that day and had seen that she was meeting someone – the two men had met each other, before she went off with Frank – and several times, the next day, she caught Oscar's glance.

Shortly afterwards he found an opportunity to ask her if she wouldn't like to meet for a meal on the Friday, after work.

So now, another option opened up, but Oscar was a completely different case. He made all the running. This time, he was entirely gallant; he all but courted her. He bought her a wonderful meal; he paid her compliments. He used his phoney, smarmy voice a lot; he wasn't funny and outrageous, the way she had so enjoyed, once, but it didn't matter; that was no longer relevant. Together they wandered down to Trafalgar Square; they watched the fountains and the people enjoying the season's lingering warmth; he put his arm around her shoulder, and then he said, as though suddenly inspired, why not find a hotel room, Jess – why not have an adventure, together?

'Why not?' she said, and he reacted with delight.

Hand in hand, they made their way back towards Bloomsbury, where very soon he found a nice hotel, small but reassuringly well appointed.

In the lift going up to their room, he put his arm around her shoulders, gave her shoulders a squeeze, smiled down at her as though she were a child; and this was the attitude he sustained throughout, coaxing and reassuring.

She was surprised at how calm it was. It all surprised her.

He excused himself for a moment, while they waited for drinks to be brought up to the room. When he emerged from the little bathroom, damp from a quick, gallant shower, she discovered an immediately trusting feeling towards his body – not a beautiful animal like Danny, none of that muscular, lithe grace, but just a friendly body, square and stocky, under its pattern of springy fur.

When they embraced at last, between the crisp, alien sheets, she was surprised by the friendliness of this unknown nakedness, the warm kindness of its presence, closely holding her. She smiled with relief; for several moments, they lay smiling at each other.

'You're so – tender,' he said, and a puzzled look crossed his face: almost a scowl.

At just the right moment, he turned off the light.

Then she found that her skin relaxed at the contact with that skin – her body warmed at the contact with its warmth. To her relief, she found that she responded.

Of Oscar she'd had no expectations, and she had assumed it was the same for him. She had a husband; he – after all – had a wife, of whom he spoke with careful admiration, not to mention two adored small children, all still abroad on holiday, like her own family. She was surprised to find that he was shocked when she insisted on leaving him, later that night, to return alone to her own empty house; she was surprised at how painfully changed he looked, when she next saw him in the office. There was a clumsiness about him. His face was puffy and his eyes were reddened.

But as for her, she felt she'd done what was necessary. She had relaxed the talons of this need that Danny felt so burdened by. She could perhaps be lighter, freer with him, now.

She had – she thought – released him.

By the time he returned from West Berlin in mid-September, she was prepared with a whole bright, new façade of independence – new clothes, bright prospects. She thought she had regained her confidence.

Though it didn't work, of course, any more than any of the other solutions that she thought she'd found.

22

Summer, 1976

The summer she left him, there were times she thought she knew what she was doing.

There were times when she arrived home at a reasonable hour, one of those sunny evenings, and as she greeted Ella and Ben, and began to sort out the household and cook the evening meal, she thought: we're all right together. We have fun together; we can do this. She felt strong enough to enjoy getting through the tasks. She thought she would know how to make a good life for the three of them. *I couldn't handle him*, was how she put it to herself, then. She would have liked to maintain this modest formula: not blaming herself, not blaming him. It was a relief to be liberated from anger and regret and hurt, though it was shameful to realise, later, how much these sunny periods were sustained by fantasies.

A certain week towards mid-July had been like this. At last, a framework seemed to have been established, and for the moment she'd done what she could about the Mountfield house. She'd got over some of the first, distracting frenzy of ideas on her new, private Otford project, and begun to make more headway on her current work, despite the inevitable run-ins with Marjorie. Recently, meanwhile, there'd been no disturbing news of Danny. He was even planning to take Ben and Ella on a visit to their grandmother, and she was comforted by the idea of this plan. It would give her a break without arousing the little devils attendant on so many of the novelties of their new relationship.

Getting home on time from a decent day at work, she could actually keep her mind on one of Ella's long, detailed accounts of the classroom pet corner, and discuss whether Peter the guinea pig might get to visit it, one day. She felt relaxed enough to find ways of bringing Ben into some kind of conversation with them, which was extremely cheering.

Occasionally, they sat together on the balcony after supper, in the warm, light evenings. All the evenings were warm, that summer, and although on this side of the house, the north side, they were cut off from any direct sunlight, they had privacy, and the little wood to look at.

A couple of times, Jessie found herself telling stories about her own family, now scattered all up and down the west coast of America.

By now, all but the youngest of her siblings had left home, and soon the last remnants would be further scattered. It didn't seem right to tell the kids, yet, but she had just heard that her parents, too, had once again split up – it seemed to have become a pattern. Her mother had gone on the rampage, as she did, now, between spells of the old depression, and her father had taken the youngest on a desperate pilgrimage to various other siblings, while he figured out what to do next. It was all a mess. It went on and on being a mess, in increasingly painful ways.

But Ben and Ella had happy memories of California. What they remembered from their only visit, some years before, was things like spending the night outside in sleeping bags in the backyard; waking to the quick flit of a hummingbird just two inches from your face, and your grandpa squatting down beside you – he could be so entirely charming to small children, so full of things to share; such a performer.

They remembered the tortoise that bumbled out from under the squash leaves in the vegetable garden, the old dog that begged at your knee for cookies, while your grandma scolded; they remembered the magic of picking your own breakfast fruit from the backyard trees, dead sweet and falling-off ripe.

Danny had stayed behind in Ontario, working on the project that had brought them there for a six-month stint, but Jessie, coming back to her family with the children, for the first time in seven years, was fêted and celebrated. There were barbecues and picnics at the beach and streams of friends and relations dropping by for chat and coffee and homemade cookies, pies, fruit cobblers. The youngest of the little sisters, just fifteen, adopted Ella, who was immediately absorbed in projects of jewellery making, dolly tea parties, and numbers of feminine pastimes that Jessie had never quite got the hang of, emerging radiant with delight, to display toenails and fingernails gleaming with pink nail varnish, hair elaborately braided up with ribbons.

Other siblings lived wonderfully colourful hippy lives with their spouses in a nearby university city, one lot in an old house right in the midst of an avocado grove. Spending a weekend with them, Jessie was torn between fascination, shock, distaste and admiration for this new culture they inhabited. They were so funny, and beautiful, and feckless. The girls wore clothes plucked from the rubbish bins left out by the wealthy students. They lived on beans and many free avocados and fish caught by the guys, one of whom wrote a passionate free newsletter about The System, and how it was ripping them off. They thought they were owed.

The couples who didn't live in the avocado grove lived in subsidised housing, and their lives seemed so happy and comfortable that Jessie couldn't see how this ripping-off was happening, only being there for a weekend, and struggling with the jargon, the new information, the unfamiliar references. A thing that particularly bothered her (this being sunny California) was that there was even a heat lamp in the bathroom of the subsidised apartment, to turn on in case the toilet seat felt too cold.

There was also the way every discussion seemed to revolve around Vietnam, not the hows or whys, which seemed too well understood among them to need rehashing, but just the fact of it, as though that fact was the bedrock of this new stance – as though, it being so uniquely evil, protesting against it was in itself a way of life, needing no further justification; while back in England, apolitical Jessie had had no sense of the dimensions of this protest.

But the idyll suffered a frightening interruption. Ella was bitten by a dog – a lovely, shaggy young dog, owned by a lovely, shaggy guy who had dropped by to share some dope –

and it transpired that this animal, its thick pelt redolent of the sage-covered nearby hills, had not been vaccinated against the rabies which infested those same fragrant hills.

Before leaving (after a flurry of soft-eyed, fulsome apologies and demurrals), its owner reluctantly gave Jessie the phone number of his vet, just to reassure her – she was so panicked! he observed, with what he obviously considered a comforting laugh – but the vet, when contacted, asked angrily for payment of a three years' overdue account, mainly for two other dogs; and no, he had no record of treating Wolfie.

There followed a long, agonised wait in the corridor of the city hospital's emergency department.

As she waited, Jessie's heart increasingly hardened against her siblings. Even as she talked with Ella about the enchantments of the house in the avocado grove (there was actually a beehive in an outside wall, whose intricate society you could observe through a glass set into it) – even as she diverted her with chat of new delights to come, memories of other family let-downs came rushing back to deepen her anxiety and fear.

The dog had bitten Ella on her face. Its tooth had punctured the skin just next to her lip. It had drawn blood.

How it happened, Jessie'd had only a flickering glimpse. They'd been bedded down in quilts and sleeping bags on the floor, and woke – with a happy sense of holiday – to the feel of soft air and old, soft quilts, the fragrance of sun-warmed wood, last night's barbecue, a trace of incense, and some immensely friendly, aromatic herb that was probably cannabis. She heard low, male voices on the porch outside, and through the opened door, this large, hairy animal came wandering in towards them.

It was just in that drowsy moment of waking up that she felt four-year-old Ella stirring and sitting up, with a cry of delight – which instantly became a scream.

Then there was pandemonium: the dog barking, the guys bursting in with shouts and curses, the scuffle and clatter as the creature was dragged outside, its toenails skidding on the wooden floor.

The doctor didn't make light of her panic; she almost wished he had. He spoke to Ella with smiling sweetness, and made her smile, in turn. But the very tenderness with which his hand cupped the little face, as he examined it, pierced Jessie's heart.

Then he outlined the dilemma they faced.

Because it was, it seemed, a dilemma. The site of the laceration, the fact that it was the face, was obviously a bad thing, he observed. But soap and water was astonishingly effective; she'd washed it immediately with soap, she said? Yes, that was very good. Because he was extremely reluctant – extremely reluctant, he repeated – to subject this little person to a course of rabies inoculations. Did Jessie realise what this treatment would entail? He described it briefly and unemphatically, but as he glanced at Ella, Jessie saw his eyes blink shut for an instant, in what seemed like a flinch. Her stomach twisted.

He thought it was probably unnecessary, he said at last. He really thought it would probably be all right. But of course, it was Jessie's choice, whether or not to chance it.

'You think it will be all right,' Jessie repeated, desperately wishing for more certainty than this.

'Any symptoms would show up in twenty-one days,' he said.

Happily, Ella almost immediately forgot this episode. However, the twenty-one days closed over Jessie like a term in jail, and as long as that threat remained, she couldn't allow herself any softening towards the cause of it. That would have been collusion. The idea terrified her, as though it would lay them open to the worst.

In particular, she hardened her heart against her brother Joey, because Wolfie's owner, Sam, was a friend of his, and she had already heard too many jocular references to how the two of them had bent and side-stepped too many rules and laws, and the others shrugged, because they, too, did many of those things themselves, and anyway, after all, the government…

It seemed you couldn't know when you could count on them, what rules they would think worthwhile to follow. What promises they would think worthwhile to keep. Even her father – maybe first of all, her father.

Joey had come up to them, when Jessie joined the family barbecue afterwards, saying of Ella – with his usual smiling swagger, 'Hey, I thought she'd have half her face torn off!'

But when Jessie's hand flew up in outrage, he caught it easily before it hit him, and immediately, their father interceded: 'Hey, now, Jessie!'

'But Daddy, don't you realise—'

'Come on, honey,' he objected, 'let's not spoil our family get-together!' And putting a commanding arm around her shoulders – with a squeeze that made it impossible to pull away – he drew her off towards the picnic table. There was no acknowledgement of what she was living through, of what Ella might be facing, of the casual, lazy carelessness that had caused the threat that still hung over them.

They were sloppy. That was what Danny said, about her family. So playful, imaginative, sweet, but not to be counted on – Danny'd had his own experience of that. And then, they evaded, manipulated, didn't own up… He put it down to their politics, a certain lack of personal responsibility: it was always something else that was to blame (ill health, bad luck, the government).

So much for communes. So much for peace marches.

'Why don't we go there?' Ella asked. 'Can't we go back again?'

'We will,' said Jessie. 'We'll go back, some time.'

She didn't mention the impossible cost of airfares, or the fact that the beloved young aunts and uncles lived somewhere else, now, let alone that the cosy grandma had taken to drinking in local bars, while Grandpa, high on cortisone and frantically averted guilt, was at present planning his escape.

She talked instead, shamelessly, of what good times there'd been, growing up there. She told stories of the various houses that they'd lived in, best of all the rickety house by the railroad tracks, with rabbits and chickens and a treehouse, and a bramble patch so big they hollowed it out inside to make a hide-out. And about the camps they made, the clubs they organised, the shows and circuses they invented to amaze the neighbourhood. About creating secrets and surprises for each other, and especially for their parents, and how they didn't even mind the washing up, because while they were doing it, they sang.

What a long time ago, what a different world that was, like something you might read about in a magazine.

She'd forgotten about the singing. Walking home one evening, after reminiscing with the kids about those times, it occurred to her that there might be a solution here for Ben. He had a good voice, she'd been told (one of the very few good things the College ever said to her about him), and he seemed to have an unusually good ear. He'd once had lessons in classical guitar, and though he didn't take to it, he still had the guitar.

What about playing folk music? she suggested to him. What about playing rock music?

He got out the guitar and she got Ella to sit with them and try some songs – old family songs, and folk songs from university – while he attempted to pick out a chord or two. It was an agonising process, the first few times, and Ella complained about it forcefully. But he started practising, with the determination he could show about something that interested him, and soon she was greeted by the sound of his guitar on arrival home from work. In a very short time, he could strum a real accompaniment, with just a few halts and pauses and having to start again. Even Ella was mollified, though largely because she thought she and Jessie could now stop singing and talk about something interesting, like getting a kitten.

One day, in a surge of inspiration, Jessie went out at lunchtime and hunted down a Beatles songbook. This turned out to be a triumph.

She'd finally rung Tony. After all, why not? One of the books in the series she was dreaming up would be perfect for him, and he had such a wonderful magpie mind, full of the kinds of fact that children love. It could be just the occupation he'd been looking for. Of course, he might be busy, by now; perhaps he'd found some compelling interest of his own. But if not, they could meet and talk.

So much had happened since they'd last met that she'd forgotten what had bothered her about him – an attractive single man, who liked her, and whom she liked – and of course, it was great that he was wealthy.

It would be such a coup, wouldn't it.

And no, he hadn't been too busy. He wanted to hear more about her project. They arranged to meet.

She was surprised at how happy she felt, to hear his voice.

It wasn't as though she was entertaining specific fantasies. As she told Arlis, all it took (it seemed) to renew her zest for life was just that contact, that particular voice, that sense of interest. Wasn't it amazing?

'But of course,' said Arlis, who had been urging the move for a considerable time, and never missed an opportunity for instruction: 'When your own needs are met, you can be generous!'

23

As luck would have it, the call to Tony had caught him just on the point of leaving for three weeks on holiday – in fact almost walking out of the door, he said. He seemed uncharacteristically abashed and flurried.

'Oh, but it's – Jessie,' he interrupted himself, pronouncing her name in a register that moved her disproportionately. 'Jessie, how are you? You're all right? I've heard about—'

'I'm fine. I'm wonderful,' she said.

'I didn't know,' he said. 'I wondered. Oscar mentioned it, of course, but you know Oscar; I could hardly ask for details. I just didn't – but you sound well.'

'I'm fine,' she said. 'In fact—'

'God, I'm so sorry,' he said. 'I've actually got a plane to catch; would you believe it? I feel so—'

'Oh, don't worry, Tony, please! I'll let you go! Only, I've finally got a project that I think you'd like – in fact, it's something we used to talk about. So I was hoping—'

'You've got a new project?'

'I shouldn't say that; I haven't done the proposal yet; it's just ideas. But I'm really pleased; I think it could be brilliant. Oh, but I'm sorry; I know you're in a hurry.'

'But Jessie, that's wonderful. Could you just… Look. I've got two minutes. Quickly, tell me.'

So she did.

'Well, we should meet,' he said, when she'd finished her summary. 'I've got my diary open. Let's meet for lunch when I get back.'

'There,' he said, when they'd got the date. 'One o'clock, at the Spaghetti House, right?' There was a pause. 'Jessie,' he began again, with a sudden change of tone. She heard an intake of breath. Then he finished rapidly, 'I'll see you soon. I've got to go… Take care,' he added, gently.

'Goodbye, Tony.'

He was still there. 'Goodbye,' he said.

Then he was gone.

You could not help wanting to be happy. You could not help wanting to be cared for.

It was nearly a year since she'd first met him, but she didn't count that time. The fact that she'd made an impression on him then made her uneasy. She had felt so flat and empty, at that party – so cut off, like a cold ghost at the feast. It bothered her, that men could like you when you were like that. What was it that they liked? Where was she, when that was going on?

And why had Oscar wanted her to meet him? What was he up to?

'Have you met my American girl?' he'd asked, introducing her to Tony.

She didn't like being stirred by this kind of speculation. She hated the way her vanity was teased, let alone her ambitions. Now that she'd finally regained a taste for life, after a spell of such aridity, she wanted only to keep her head down and do her work. It was more than enough. You really didn't need any more than that.

And of course, she was right to have been wary.

Yet to begin with, what surprised her most about Tony's company was how easy and unthreatening it was. Having lunch with him that first time was just so innocently companionable.

First of all, he'd made Oscar cancel the reservation at Mario's, suggesting instead the Spaghetti House round the corner, which it seemed he knew. ('Mario's. What was he thinking of?' he remarked confidingly, as they emerged into the street. 'I'm looking for work; I'm not going to invest in Otford Publishing.')

He asked immediately, where had she got to, anyway, at that party. She explained about the emergency in production.

'I kept expecting to catch sight of you again,' he said. 'I carried your drink around for half an hour, at least. A drink in each hand; not easy.'

'No,' she said. She immediately warmed to him.

'I drank them both, in the end. I saw no alternative.'

He stopped, then, to point out a curious feature in the façade of one of the buildings they were passing. As they strolled off again, he looked around with interest at the little courts and alleyways, remarking how long it had gone on, the association of market and theatre, in this area.

It occurred to her that he'd been living mostly in

the country. Had he never spent much time in London?

But before she could ask, he began to tell her numbers of interesting things about the streets and buildings that they walked among. He turned out to be that sort of person. He kept looking back at her, his look enquiring: Was she interested – really? He wasn't boring her?

'But you should write about that,' she said, when they were finally seated across from each other on the plastic banquettes of the empty little restaurant. 'That sounds like a wonderful project.'

'Oh, no,' he said immediately. 'I'm not a writer. I don't have a creative bone in my body; not at all.'

'But you've written things. Oscar said you wrote a novel.'

'That was a mistake. No, sorry,' he added quickly. 'What I mean is, writing it was a mistake. Or maybe publishing it.' He looked at her, worriedly. 'Maybe I had to write it. I was quite young. But I didn't have to publish it,' he finished, with a vehemence that invited her to laugh.

He rested his face, for a moment, on his hand, rubbing the space between his eyebrows with his forefinger. Then he sat up again. 'No, I'm not a creative person. I just – I need occupation. I'm unhappy,' he said, simply. 'I imagine Oscar told you.'

'Yes.' They exchanged a glance. He nodded, briefly grimacing.

'Well, then. You see, I need a task. I need to be told what to do. It's the only thing for it, at the moment. I could do research,' he offered. 'Couldn't you put me to work on something? Anything?'

'You mean, like a consultant?'

'Oh God no; an assistant!'

The waiter materialised at their table, and there was a diversion while they organised their meal.

'I don't know what to say,' she said, when they were alone again. 'An assistant…' She shook her head. 'I feel embarrassed.'

'Why not just tell me what you're doing,' he asked encouragingly. 'Maybe something will occur to us.'

It was like that, from the beginning – it was *us*, right from the beginning, as though they were only continuing a long-established, accidentally interrupted friendship. It took her off-guard, how it developed like a friendship. In those days, she seldom saw people like the Goldmans, the Seymours. It seemed a long time since she'd had a friend.

'Shall we meet again?' he said, when they found the waiter hovering with the bill. 'Would that be a good idea?' But when she hesitated, he said, 'I think we should talk again. Don't worry,' he added, as she got out her wallet. 'The next one's on me.' So it was settled.

She thought she was just enjoying his company. It was pleasant to walk through Covent Garden with him, while he told her anecdotes about its history, pointed out quirks of its architecture. The next time they met, he took her to a wonderfully grubby little café, run by an embattled Italian couple whose idiosyncrasies included a surprisingly good soup which depended heavily on salad scraps, and a counter along one wall with a badly hand-lettered sign warning: 'Dancers Only!'

She and Tony obediently sat themselves well to the back,

with their soup and sandwiches, and eventually forgot to look for the dancers, who never appeared.

He seemed determined to draw her out. How was it she'd come to work with Oscar, anyway? She seemed so different from the others.

'You mean older,' she said. She was highly aware of how much older she was than Peta, and Annabelle, and the girls now arriving from more established publishers – young girls, just in their twenties but so much more knowledgeable, so much more knowing, drawn by Otford's rapid expansion. But he shook his head.

'No, no,' he said. 'Just – perhaps just not very English, I don't know. But tell me the story, anyway. You said there weren't even any books, then. He was flying a kite, I think.'

It was very pleasant, and it was flattering – of course it was flattering.

At first she didn't mention him to Danny. Over the summer, while she was so depressed, she had found herself speaking less and less – to anyone, really, even to Ben and Ella, though she tried, with them, stiff and stupid as she often felt. She was painfully conscious of how dull she was. She sometimes wondered why Danny never seemed to notice. Then, though the depression lifted, she had continued to feel awkward and self-conscious with him; she seemed to be out of practice. They seemed to have stopped telling each other things about their lives.

A little later, as their marriage seemed to revive, she began to drop the occasional reference to this friend of Oscar's she was trying to find a role for, and the joke of the meetings and lunches they kept having, on this tenuous pretext.

She did this to pique his interest and to let him know she had a separate life. He had wanted her to have a separate life. It had been an issue.

After all, it was scarcely more than a handful or two of meetings, this interlude with Tony. And at first, it was just so light, so gentle. But after a while, he'd had to say to her, that he supposed she really wasn't going to find a project for him, and she'd had to admit that no, she probably wasn't, at the moment.

He'd done his best to keep her talking. Oh, this was the way to do it, he insisted. He'd never worked for a children's publisher before; he'd never considered writing books for children, let alone these little fact books they were doing. He needed to learn from her. What did she think about how children learn, how children use books? He had so nicely put her at ease, with a friendliness that inspired her gratitude.

'No, this is good,' he'd say, when she tried to divert the conversation back to him. 'I'll get my turn. Don't worry. This is all very interesting; I want to know. But tell me…'

He was one of those people who always has the right question; the sort of listener who endows you with eloquence. And of course, it was wonderful to be actually urged to tell her stories. It was exhilarating. And she did have ideas about how children learn, and what you might do with books – she found she was bursting with pent-up theories and notions about children, and about learning, and about how you could communicate through books. Not to mention discoveries made along the way, to do with graphics and comics and dealing with so-called educators.

In the warmth of his attention, she expanded. She even found herself, sometimes, being funny; she'd forgotten that she could be funny. Twice, she made him laugh outright. She found herself sharing her old enthusiasms: *This is what I saw. This is what I wanted. This is what we were up against.*

The problems of Otford's first winter readily lent themselves to a tale of comic horror: not just the usual winter flus and colds, the sudden departure of the first production manager, various predictable financial crises, and the storm lanterns and unheated office (remember? the three-day week, the coal strike!), but also the entirely wayward course taken by each of the first two projects – that cherished dinosaur of Oscar's (as she called it, scathingly), for which the budgets and schedules had to be extended by a factor of three, but even her own books, which she insisted that she herself (and then that burgeoning number of assistants) should personally write and visualise, while Oscar stomped and raged and insisted that nobody, nobody did books like this; no publisher had people designing and writing the books in-house; you couldn't survive.

It was delightful to make him laugh, with her mimicry of Oscar, and her own passionate stubbornness about the books, which had included making every item in a how-to book herself. She began to confide in him what it had cost her – the troubles with Marjorie, her increasing isolation, even the depressions that began to hit her, the emotional depths she found herself plunging into, at the end of a project.

But eventually, he shook his head. 'You care so much. I can't imagine caring as much as that,' he said.

'Oh, Oscar does.'

'That's different. Oscar wants to conquer the world.'

'I guess,' she said. She wasn't sure she could tell, with Oscar.

'I wish I could even care about that,' he said, and she was struck by a note of bitterness in his voice. 'I have no ambition whatsoever.'

'I suppose you don't have to. You have money, don't you.'

This made him laugh again, and suddenly – they were back in the Spaghetti House when this happened, lingering over coffee – he put his arm round her shoulders in a quick, friendly squeeze that cancelled the sudden intimacy of his confession with a different, altogether lighter intimacy.

'Meet me again,' he said, when he'd paid the bill. 'I'm sure it's helping.'

24

Summer, 1976

'But he sounds like a nice guy,' Arlis had said, when Jessie began, one night, to talk about Tony during one of the late-night bouts of girlish confidences they drifted into when she stayed over, while Ben and Ella were spending their first nights with Danny.

Arlis was impressed by Tony's background. 'I don't think Danny would like that very much,' she remarked with relish, though Danny hadn't minded; he was not displeased by the pedigree of a wife's presumed admirer.

They had a pattern, those evenings. Marty would wander off after supper to do some work and Arlis would bring out the whisky again, and she and Jessie would talk and smoke, while the golden level in the bottle dropped and dropped, until the small hours – focusing mostly on the marriage and its wreckage; sometimes on the children; sometimes touching on Jessie's prospects; eventually lapsing into stories of their respective pasts, their childhoods, Arlis's life and times as a single woman – a subject of great curiosity to Jessie, who was pleased when she could offer the Tony story in exchange.

But as time went on, Arlis pursued the subject. Why shouldn't Jessie get in touch with him – shouldn't she make the effort? Here was a man who seemed to have been quite interested; a man on his own; why didn't she try to contact him? Why not just ring him up?

She became impatient with Jessie, sometimes. What was the problem? She'd only stopped seeing Tony when it became too serious, hadn't she? Because she wanted to keep her marriage? And now the marriage was over, so why not?

As for Jessie, even when she'd finally made the contact, she found it hard to explain – hard to remember, even – her own reluctance. At last she said, self-consciously, 'Maybe it was his politics. I did feel uneasy about his politics.'

'His politics,' said Arlis. 'Right-wing? Left-wing?'

'Oh, left-wing. Pretty left, I think.'

'Oh, that's too much,' said Arlis. 'Danny would hate that. A rich, woolly liberal?'

'Oh, no,' said Jessie. She knew what was meant by woolly liberals. Woolly liberals were earnest, sentimental people, usually Labour supporters, burdened with pieties about trade unions (however vast, entrenched and bureaucratic) and other questionably opaque power-blocs. What she referred to as Tony's politics entailed no pieties.

'I don't know; maybe I'm giving you the wrong idea. It's not that he talked about social policies; he was just angry. Places like India, for example; he's been to India.'

'Of course,' said Arlis, knowingly. 'The hippy trail.'

'Well yes, except the poverty bothered him so much he had to leave. But he doesn't have any idea what to do about it.

But I think he thinks there ought to be some political answer. Or some answer. I don't think it's guilt. He just feels useless.'

'Jessie,' said Arlis tentatively, after a moment. Jessie looked up to meet a long, thoughtful stare from those hazel eyes. 'Are you afraid of kindness?'

'What?' said Jessie. 'What do you mean?' she asked. These talks were taking a turn she didn't like. It had been bad enough, back at the beginning, seeing the analyst's knife go into Danny.

'Tony sounds like a man who's got a conscience – a man with kindness. Are you sure you're just not used to a man with kindness? Jessie, you need a kind man.'

She didn't think she liked the sound of that.

This question of Tony's politics, however – she'd been relieved that he wasn't party-political; that he had no programme. She'd been afraid that he would, and that this would have been a barrier; but not because she had any of her own, not in that sense of judgement and allegiance and a programme. She felt awkward mentioning politics to Arlis, the one-time socialist, whose casual command of political gossip and minutiae quite defeated her.

She thought perhaps Marty might have understood. With Marty she still felt, sometimes, that you might explore that elusive connection between private and public which had once haunted her. He would probably make some joke, and she understood the jokes: 'Should the government be our conscience? Isn't that usually somebody else's business?'

They had often discussed this kind of thing in the abstract. It was the kind of topic that might exercise the three of them – she and Danny and Marty – in the early days, before Arlis, that far-off period of passionate late-night conversations: problems of the individual conscience and the state, the difference between morality and law; the emotional resonance of political attitudes. She still remembered the exhilaration of it, the occasional, breath-taking glimpse of large questions to be examined; the tantalising possibility of making some contribution. Surely you could use this apparatus of clear thinking to strip away the vagueness and hypocrisy, the false claims and the pieties, without cutting off every vision, every hope.

And yet, those sensible, humane, wry voices – people like Danny and Marty – supported a status quo which seemed to require an unstoppable industrial juggernaut, a remorseless flattening and emptying of the natural world, not to mention a social structure in which human possibility seemed, after all, so very narrowly defined. If your only business was business – as it seemed – where was your life?

As for imagining there was some simple answer to all the woe – to poverty, inequity, injustice – some way to make common cause against the evils… It seemed it was this that led to the worst excesses: the guillotines, the gulags – well, Vietnam, to bring it close to home. You had to resist the idea that you could help. It was as though compassion was potentially contaminating. You had to resist it.

As for Vietnam… she seemed to remember times when you heard voices urging rescue, urging intervention to save a threatened and beleaguered people; but then, only a few years later, who was it who had thrust on her that terrible photograph of the naked girl, running towards the empty gaze of the camera – that screaming girl, her little body encased in flames – and the flaming bombs were dropped by her own country in that, apparently, perverted and doomed campaign on behalf of the supposedly beleaguered people…

There was no point giving way to pity, or indignation.

It sometimes seemed that there was no way, morally, *to be*, in the public sphere. There was no way to be that wasn't wrong. You could be destructive or inert: those were the choices.

Danny and Marty hadn't discussed rights and wrongs over Vietnam. Their questions had been about strategy; they argued about threat, containment, the domino theory. And Danny had said to Marty (as the American he still was, then): 'Listen; this place is just too far away; surely it isn't part of your sphere of interest. The US has no strategic interest in this area; you should mind your own business.'

So limited, cold, self-interested. And how much blood could this cool assessment have avoided?

It was maybe the fourth or fifth time she'd met Tony that he took her to a place that was almost a proper restaurant, where they served these delicate vegetarian dishes that he'd first come across in India – street food there, he said. There were crisp little triangles of deep-fried pastry, filled with fragrant, succulent vegetables, and a dish of puffed-wheat shells, each sitting in its own depression in the dish, and you filled them with savoury beans and a fine, light sauce; but Tony said that on the streets, in India, they were handed to you folded up in a big green leaf. And then there arrived an incredible sculptured pancake stuffed with something so aromatic that her eyes widened as she bit into it, and he laughed and said, 'Potato,' and at her exclamations, laughed again, and they smiled at each other with delight.

She told him how she had always imagined India as a hot, miserable plain, poor and crowded, and he said, oh, there were mountains in the north, and it was staggeringly beautiful. But after a while he said that yes, across large areas it was like that. Miles and miles of it were like that. And it got to you.

Then she said, 'All the same, it makes such a different picture, street vendors selling such delightful things, and made from such – well, to be so inventive, with so little.'

'Yes,' he said. But he looked absent. He was playing with the cutlery beside his plate. He was trying to balance the end of the fork on the end of the knife, which rested on his empty plate, and it kept slipping off. Then he said, 'Do you know the worst thing? So many places, they don't even have clean water.' He caught her glance, and then looked down again at his cutlery. He put it down and rested his face on one hand, the way he did, sometimes, gazing into the plate.

'The first time I saw it – we'd ended up at a tiny little village once, off the beaten track. We were heading for some monuments, but we took a detour; we were taking our time. We thought we were having an adventure. We got to a place where we wanted to take some photographs, so we just got the bus driver to make an unscheduled stop and let us off. We had a map. We could see there was a village further along, so we just walked there.'

'Ah,' she sighed. How she longed, sometimes, to have had adventures. At home with the children, when they were little, she would sometimes take them off with sandwiches to the far edge of the common, to pretend. Sometimes she took them wandering through historic bits of London (obscured by traffic, as it often was), or to the British Museum, where they had crisps and orange squash in a dreary basement café, memorably glared at by the occasional wild-haired, muttering scholar.

'Oh, we were lucky,' he said. 'I know we were. And when we got there, and there was no place to stay, no guest house – it was so tiny! – we weren't even surprised when somebody took us in. And people brought us food, and we went to sleep that night thinking the world was a wonderful, easy place. But in the morning, everyone was gone.'

He lifted his head and fixed her with his blue, light eyes. 'There was nobody there but babies and toddlers, and an old, old man, and a couple of old women. All the able-bodied men had gone off to some big project; but it turned out that the women had to spend half the day just getting water, because they didn't have a well. Could you believe it? You saw these women with the water jugs, and they were walking miles every day – every day – and all they needed was a well. Fifty pounds and a couple of days to dig it. And I'd just spent two hundred pounds on the camera.' He shook his head. 'I wanted to give them a well.'

'Couldn't you do that?' she said.

'It would be disgusting,' he said. 'It would be the worst thing. To put them in debt to somebody like me? It shouldn't be a gift, it should be a right. Shouldn't it be a right? It should be like air.'

She didn't know what to say to this, because of course,

it should. But where does *should* fit, where does *ought to* fit, in how things are, or can be?

When she didn't answer, he said, 'The world is a bloody nightmare, isn't it.'

She shook her head. She felt embarrassed to say such things as they sat in this clean, quiet place, her eyes fixed on the fresh, pink-edged carnations in the glass in the middle of the table. She said, 'I don't know how to think about it. I don't know how to put it together. What can we do? We can't do anything directly – can we?'

It was strange that with all his money, his education and background and connections, he seemed to feel more helpless than she did. For at that moment, she didn't feel quite helpless. She'd started work on something that seemed worthwhile, but he had no work. How terrible it was, to have no work.

And she was thinking of Danny, of asking him similar questions in the past, at times when she felt particularly oppressed by a sense of that vast weight of misery in so much of the world – a tenth? *A fifth?* Proportions she couldn't, in any case, imagine. Like a huge tide of mud or shit on which we in the west are perched, in the fragile little craft of our unsatisfying hedonism; and she and Danny would have these talks about freedom, and about what makes for happiness; and once when she protested, angrily, 'But surely, you can't be happy when you're actually hungry,' he had said, 'How do we know?'

He could say things like that. He could remind her of herself – what she knew; what she didn't know.

She said now to Tony, 'I don't know if I'm that concerned about human misery. Not when I can't do anything about it.' She hesitated a moment, and then she said, 'I've read stories of people in Soviet prison camps who seemed so alive, I envied them.'

She glanced at him, but he was playing with the cutlery again.

She said, 'You know, when I think about all this – I don't really think it's guilt; it's something else.'

Now he looked up, and when they met each other's eyes, there was a degree of understanding that alarmed her. It was a level of intimacy she had not expected.

'No,' he said, slowly. 'No, it isn't.' She felt relieved when he simply shook his head, and looked away again, saying only, 'No – it's not just guilt.'

25

August, 1976

As Jessie reached the office door, Annabelle was trying to identify a would-be consultant for Marjorie's benefit. 'You'd remember if you saw him – brown nylon stretch trousers, black short socks, Jesus sandals, and no hair on his legs.'

'I think I know the one you mean. Didn't he come in on the same day as that terrible man with the yellow shoes?'

Jessie waited as unobtrusively as possible for a break in the conversation, not wanting to draw attention to her late arrival back from lunch. As ever, she felt relieved to have made her escape from all this chat.

Peta and Henry could work right through such gossipy interludes. Henry could actually join in – looking up, sometimes, with an apposite quip or comment – even as he continued to plough on with his current task, though perhaps because of the nature of the tasks he set himself. Once, indeed, he had spent several days carefully copying a cutaway diagram of a diving-bell from the *Ladybird Book of Deep-Sea*

Diving to present as a part of a proposal for a new series on First Tales of Adventure.

Henry's pedestrian approach – which embraced a lack of originality amounting to simple, straightforward plagiarism – excited no criticism; was even greeted by Marjorie with respectful attention, though Oscar's response was perhaps more ambiguous. Still, all that was asked was, did it do the job? (What job? What were they all trying to do, now?) And the fact that it seldom did, seemed never to harm Henry's curiously secure position.

Why was this? Because he was a man? Because he had been to a school they knew, and was a friend of a friend of Marjorie's? Or simply because of that bluff, hearty energy? He failed and failed and failed, but he did it so unapologetically and sturdily – crying, back to the drawing board! – that he was indulgently smiled upon.

Yet with Jessie, even success always seemed to put someone out. Or else it came too late, after too much struggle and delay, somehow nullifying even the sales figures finally rolling in, even the splendid reviews she got, which seemed now to belong to work from a distant past, another era – possibly suggesting that such work (or any attempt to rise to it again) smacked of showing off, attention-seeking – trying to be different (as they'd have said, back home).

Yet she could not help wanting to do something fresh again.

Not long into the second year, when she'd become engaged in a new series and had to battle all over for a new approach, Danny had said to her, 'Look, you don't understand what Oscar wants. He's a businessman; he wants a product. You keep trying to complicate things. Maybe that's what poets do,' he'd said. 'Maybe that's why they're so poor at actually living.'

Even Tony had finally said to her, eventually, that he thought she'd probably become expendable to Oscar. She had protested: No, that couldn't be; she was a prototype maker, the one who could create new formats.

But Tony said, 'He doesn't need new formats, Jessie; he's got what he needs. Don't you see, you gave him his soup tin, you set up the first production line; but now it's done. All he needs now is an overseer, and you're not an overseer.'

'But it shouldn't be a production line. Ideally, once you've got a prototype you could train people; you could give them proper guidelines—'

'Oh, Jessie,' he said. 'You're a poet. Why are you doing this?'

'No,' she said. 'I'm not a poet.'

What was he doing? Evicting her from that warm, busy world, the real world, full of energy and jokes, where people like Oscar lived; people like Danny. People who got things done.

Well, now she was committed to that world. She had to be.

'…that terrible man with the yellow shoes?'

It was in the midst of just such a conversation, not long after the split with Danny, not many weeks after the appointment with Henry's acquaintance, the solicitor, that Jessie had, one morning, picked up her typewriter and the pages for the current layout and escaped upstairs to an empty desk in the design department. At that particular moment, she had felt so driven by the idea she was trying to pin down that it seemed to pick her up and propel her into action; it shielded her so thoroughly that over the rest of the day she was able to nip down several times to pick up one after another necessary belonging until the entire contents of her desk had been transferred; and Marjorie had never made a comment.

...with the yellow shoes?

It was so much easier to work upstairs, where she never felt left out because she wasn't expected to understand the references, which (there) were about things like speed and degrees and weight (the guys being mainly focused on topics of interest to young males, such as comets and motorbikes), and in any case, they didn't usually talk that much, except for the odd joke, or tranquil mutter between two heads bent over a layout.

...the yellow shoes?

And freed from a distraction half-composed of sheer, helpless irritation and antagonism, it seemed for a time that she really was more productive, despite her own obdurate perfectionism.

... and no hair on his legs...

... that terrible man...

But she still had to enter the lion's den several times a week for briefings, and at various stages of completion, and from the beginning of this new regime she had simply submitted herself (perhaps even brazenly) at Marjorie's desk, without comment or explanation, which miraculously, hadn't been required.

... that terrible man...

But today was different. She was all too conscious that it was now three-thirty, and that she was flushed from the stairs and her lateness and the heat outside, not to mention the wine she'd had with Danny, at that terrible, mistaken lunch: the wine she'd kept on drinking while the afternoon was lost. Now Marjorie, catching sight of her, broke off suddenly and sat back in her chair and for a moment, simply scrutinised her approach.

Annabelle turned on her a blank, bright smile before bending her golden head over her work again; Henry, too, looked down again at his diligent copying, and Peta rattled with renewed officiousness at her typewriter.

Jessie had got a few paces into the room, just taking breath to ask for the familiar folder, which she could see waiting on Marjorie's desk, when Marjorie said, 'Someone rang about Ben, when you were out. The master of the middle school, I believe. Johnny came down, looking for you – he didn't seem to know where you'd got to. He said they seemed quite anxious to get hold of you.'

'Ben?'

'Nothing serious,' said Marjorie, dryly. 'Well, nothing physically serious; he isn't ill. But they do want to hear from you as soon as possible. It seems to be some sort of disciplinary matter.'

Disoriented, Jessie turned towards the stairs to the design department, but Marjorie called her back. 'You might want to take this, mightn't you? While you're here,' and handed her the folder.

'Oh, thanks,' she said, automatically, turning away again.

Marjorie said, 'Perhaps you'll have time to see me tomorrow to discuss your schedules.'

'Ah, there you are,' said Johnny, when she reached the upstairs office. 'Your Ben seems to have hit a spot of trouble.' He looked up, and saw her face. 'Not to worry, kiddo. Boys will be boys, and all that. Still, you'd better get on the blower straight away; they didn't half make a fuss about having a word with you.'

But when she rang the number she was given, at Mr Faithcourt's office, his secretary seemed unable to enlighten her. Yes, she understood that a disciplinary problem had arisen, concerning Ben, but she really had no authority to divulge the details, and Mr Faithcourt was now in a meeting with the housemasters; he had a busy schedule, as Jessie must be aware, and had already tried to contact her more than once.

'Yes, I'm returning his call; I was hoping to speak to him.'

'I'm afraid that won't be possible this afternoon, now. I believe he tried to catch you on your return from lunch.'

Yes. 'So can you tell me when I can hope to find him? Shall I ring again in the morning?'

'I'll check the diary. Yes, I can make an appointment for the quarter-hour before lessons, eight forty-five? If that would be convenient.'

'An appointment?'

'Mr Faithcourt thinks it would be best to discuss the matter personally. In person. If you could.'

'Is it that serious?' asked Jessie, who realised she had begun to tremble.

'A certain amount of personal liaison isn't a bad thing, surely?'

'No, of course not, only—'

The voice seemed ever so slightly to relent. 'I'm sure it will be possible to smooth things over. In time. With some discussion.'

26

A problem with Ben. A disciplinary problem with Ben What new threat could this be?

The day had started off so differently! She had felt unusually brave and strong, that very morning. She'd been pleased with herself; she had been – so childishly! – hopeful and excited and almost happy.

For one thing, she was pleased with how she looked.

Despite what Arlis thought, despite the predictable result of her own long periods of absentmindedness and neglect of this area (not to mention lack of opportunity and money), there were times when Jessie was good with clothes.

When they were first in London, back in those halcyon days when there were parties, she discovered a gift for it that delighted Danny. At certain points since then she'd achieved a similar success; then yet again, this summer – on recovering from that terrible, mistaken wobble into dependence on what Arlis judged a grown-up style – she'd finally summoned the state of mind (a particular fusion of determination, decisiveness, and a degree of self-belief almost amounting to self-hypnosis) that allowed her to exercise this capricious talent. It was in this state that she'd bought the shirt she wore to meet Danny for this lunch, and those particularly successful shoes, and thus – bravely tricked out, after a week of setbacks – she recovered an image of herself as a successful person, someone who made life work.

She'd been thrilled by the smart little restaurant. She had felt that, after all, she was up to it. And then, when she saw him waiting there... Just to see him, waiting. She felt that old, irrepressible lurch of the heart: excitement, tenderness, defiance – apprehension…

He, too, had dressed up for this meeting. She was touched by a note of formality in his bearing, perhaps even nervousness. He had got very thin and brown; she thought he looked beautiful.

The initial, gentle courtesy with which they greeted each other seemed to develop into something warmer. It was as though, finally released from some deforming pressure (perhaps just the endless attrition of the everyday), the attraction between them sprang into life again.

They began to show off a little, to each other. They smiled at each other. They entertained each other.

And then, inevitably, there emerged some reference to Jessie's problems – the recent setback on the house front – and at this, Danny nodded, and looked thoughtful. The conversation lapsed. A pause developed. She found herself thinking, with a pang of hope, that he looked sad. And then he said, at last, 'Why did you do it, Jessie?'

He said, 'Why are you so determined to be a loser?'

At some point, a second bottle had arrived; a waiter was filling their glasses once again. Danny was saying, 'Sometimes, it seems just unbelievable – what you've managed to do, with all your talent. How you managed to get yourself in this position. It's like you have your pockets full of gold, and you just scatter it around, like, I don't know – like bird food.'

She gave a laugh; his eyes flashed with hostility.

'It's beyond a joke,' he said. 'You snatch defeat from the jaws of victory.'

This had gone on too long. Her throat swelled with a lump of tears and anger. She reached for her bag.

'You're leaving?'

'I should get back,' she said, almost steadily. 'It's two-thirty. Nearly.'

'So?'

'Well, I've got work to do. I should be back.'

'You don't work late any more?'

'Sometimes…'

He lifted his eyebrows. 'And you still have to punch a time-clock?'

She gazed past him for a moment, washed through with a surge of pure resentment at her position.

'Well.' He was leaning forward, now, his folded arms at rest on the table; he glanced at the bottle, at their glasses.

'I shouldn't have let you order that,' she said.

'Oh, that was my decision.' He made a wry face. 'I took the risk.'

She hesitated.

He added, 'You really don't like this conversation, do you.'

She put down her bag and it continued, for nearly an hour.

What could Ben have done? she wondered, staring out through the grimy glare of the carriage windows, later, as she travelled home through the exhausted summer sunshine. What could he possibly have done? How could they ring her at work and summon her for this interview, calling her in with no explanation, like a naughty child, even now, in the last week of term? They knew he was leaving the College; she'd already settled it that he was leaving.

She couldn't imagine what Ben could possibly be accused of. His problem was dreaminess, a certain lonely absence, a lack of attention – disciplinary problem? Ben was no troublemaker; he was no rebel… Was he?

She expected little enlightenment from Mr Faithcourt. The other ones – Ben's form master and his tutor, with whom she'd discussed the change of schools – had been only unencouragingly lackadaisical, uninclined to take any particular interest, but from Faithcourt, she feared much worse: a last quiverful of those fine barbs that make their way under your skin and begin their poisoning before you've even identified their points of entry.

On one occasion during Ben's first year, while Danny was away in West Berlin and Jessie was struggling with the opacities of her son's brief tenure as a boarder, this remote, important person had found the time to compose a long, elaborately snide letter protesting her requests for assistance from the matron: not only had Jessie's arrangements been quite unreasonable, but, he suggested, it was due in part to her delinquencies (she had failed to get Ben's spectacles replaced during a holiday) that Ben's eyesight had markedly deteriorated.

She was unconvinced that concern for her son paid any real part in his motivation; she even doubted the accuracy of what he said. Yet her sense of its spitefulness added to her remorse. They were not interested in Ben – his instincts, his idiosyncrasies, his musicality. They were interested in something to throw at you. Like a hand grenade.

She remembered the initial interview, at the College: the sense of almost palpable rivalry that had developed between Danny and Faithcourt. Danny believed that as an academic he trumped a master of Faithcourt's standing. Faithcourt, she could see, disputed this. And Jessie couldn't understand why this was relevant, why either should have allowed himself to engage in this pitiful sideshow.

As she made her way home, up the long, shallow hill from the railway station, she realised with some fear how tired she was. Of course, she was also, by now, hung over. And now, once again, there was the house question.

27

Oh, the house question.

Only a few weeks earlier, she was still managing to maintain the fiction that she could handle the financing and restoration of that big, handsome ruin of a house, for which she and her friends had entertained such delightful visions. There had been a happy lull, after she'd done all the necessary groundwork (the survey, the mortgage application, the first meetings with builder, plumber, etc.); at the same time, by dint of the enthusiastic first responses to her ideas for the new Otford project (though only from Marty, and the people she'd rung up unofficially), she was basking in a rare sense of professional self-confidence. During that time, it had seemed her energy was limitless.

You had to keep taking initiatives; that was the key; you had to keep taking risks.

There was the phone call to Tony: his voice like a shot of adrenaline.

There was the great success of the Beatles songbook: Ben looking happy and alive again, as he hadn't, it seemed, in years; running upstairs to practise, the moment his homework and chores were finished.

She went shopping for clothes; she got an extension to her overdraft.

Adventurously, she took Ben and Ella boating, one weekend, on the Serpentine in central London – all those outings that they'd never had, before! – and the weather briefly clouded and cooled and threatened rain.

She took them for Sunday lunch with distant friends, and they returned exhausted, late, a little frightened by their misadventures with transport connections.

A letter arrived from her father, saying that he and her small brother had, after all, gone back to Jessie's mother, who had come to her senses – missed him so much – but who was now, unfortunately, in the depths of an extreme depression.

Peter the guinea pig was behaving erratically. One night, he began chewing the cardboard of his sleeping box.

Everything began to fall apart.

There'd been the strange good news that Danny was handing her the equity in the house; there was then the bad news, almost immediately afterwards, of how little was left of it.

There'd been the surveyor's report, adding two major reconstruction jobs to the list, and some half-dozen apparently minor problems, though since she hadn't yet had a chance to consult on these, she could not be sure. Don't worry, said Marty, on the phone; but Maggie (who would have known) was marking exams and hadn't time to talk.

Then, several of the people with whom she'd talked about the new Otford project began to get back to her.

It hadn't occurred to her that this would happen.

One (the most experienced) rang to pull out, having taken on other work. Another was in need of extensive persuasion and further discussion as well as firmer notions of pay and schedule – reasonable requests she was in no position to fulfil. From a third, she received an entirely unexpected, detailed, four-page summary of ideas and suggestions (fully referenced), much of which appeared, at first glance, ominously academic and wrong-headed.

New problems arose in her current work and yet again, she had to delay her proposal to Oscar. Notwithstanding which, a package arrived from Jim, the illustrator, who'd not been able to resist some preliminary sketches.

Oscar stopped her in the corridor one day, and rather hastily asked if she could possibly meet him for a drink one night, the following week.

Maggie's pet builder, the burly Welshman who'd been so confident and enthusiastic when they met – strolling through the romantic rooms one Saturday morning, with sunshine lighting the cobwebs in the gothic bathroom – could not be reached for the next two weeks, and was found to have eloped with his wife's au pair.

His successor was just going off on holiday, and could meet her only on a midweek evening.

Ella's babysitter, having agreed to give Ella her supper on that evening, came round with apologies the night before.

That morning, Peter the guinea pig (for whom Jessie had not yet managed to find a vet) had been discovered dead, stretched out flat and rigid as a cartoon cat, within his sagging, chewed-up cardboard box.

It hadn't been easy to get to the meeting in north London with this new builder. She didn't like to ask Ben to take charge for the whole afternoon and evening, but no sitters were available, and the neighbour she sometimes called on was away. At last Jessie convinced herself and Ben and Ella that after all, Ben could see Ella onto the train, and she (Jessie) could leave work early to be at the barrier to greet her, and then, if they changed immediately to the Tube and kept a brisk pace, they could collect the keys from the estate agent before the office closed and get to Mountfield Road by seven o'clock. Mr McDowell had insisted that this was the only possible opening until after his holiday, midway into August, and Jessie clung to the hope that they might be able to move in – at least, to camp there, somehow – in time for the children to start the term at their new schools.

At the cost of considerable nervous tension, she managed to get to the house with Ella some five minutes before the builder was due. She looked forward to showing the house to Ella, hearing her decide which room she'd like, the two of them picturing how it could be set up. She thought that, with luck, her interview with Mr McDowell needn't take that long; by now, she was well briefed on the essential questions. She vaguely imagined sitting afterwards with Ella in the nearby park, eating the crisps and sandwiches she'd brought, discussing how the rooms would be arranged, talking about the fun they'd have there, agreeing how well worth all the trouble it would be.

An hour later they were still alone, camped on a newspaper on the floor of the big front room, among the crumbs of their picnic. They were thirsty by now, but all the utilities had been turned off: no water, no electricity, no gas.

The house looked different in the evening, with the sun moved round.

Ella hadn't been impressed. She looked up apprehensively at the tall, cracked ceilings, the cobwebs in the shadowed corners; she remarked how big it was, how many rooms. She seemed doubtful about the reason for all these rooms.

They waited and waited. A pallid gloom developed in the sunless rooms; a chill stole into the heavy, humid atmosphere.

Jessie shivered, rubbing her bare arms. She began to dread the homeward journey: the walk and the Tube and the walk; then the long, rattling journey on the train; then the last long walk. Ella was tired already: the night before, it had been nearly ten by the time they'd finished the improvised burial service for Peter Pig, and by now it had got so late that even if McDowell showed up immediately – even were they to get through the most cursory inspection (and how much could they see, in this half-light?) – they wouldn't be back till half-past ten, possibly eleven – hours past Ella's bedtime.

How could he have done this? How could he have allowed her to travel all this way, and not show up?

But of course, this was only the beginning. This meeting – difficult as it had been to set it up – was only the first in what, if she were honest, she must expect to be a whole great chain of discussions and decisions and negotiations. There would be further breakdowns, further disappointments, more false starts. They were just at the bottom of the mountain, and she felt it loom.

Several times, Maggie had intimated that there should really be some input from an architect, and Horst had muttered about planning regulations; she should have listened; she should have enquired more closely. Then, there were those new problems mentioned in the survey, which meant that difficulties might arise about the mortgage. There'd be the plumber, the carpenter, the electrician…

Ella asked, 'Do you really think he's coming?'

'No,' said Jessie. 'Not any more.' She could feel Ella's questioning eyes, looking up at her. After a while, she said, 'He's let us down.'

'Mum,' said Ella, 'do we have to live here?'

'No,' said Jessie.

'Really? We really don't?'

'No,' she said, with sudden decision, shaking her head; and she got up and began rapidly to gather together the newspaper, the paper bag, the napkins. 'Come on,' she said. 'We're going home.' She felt a lurch of shame at having put Ella through all this – at having even considered putting her through any more of it. 'I'm sorry,' she said. 'Ella, you're right; this is ridiculous. We'll find another house. We'll find a better house.'

It was the lifting of a burden. The next day she'd rung the estate agent to pull out, and made plans to see other properties on his list.

She hadn't even mentioned it when Danny rang, suggesting lunch. Who knew – by the time she met him, she might have found another prospect.

She promised Ella they'd get a kitten when they moved. And Ben, of course, had his music, now; Ben was all right, now…

28

In any case, she was right about the house. It wasn't really all that long before a better possibility turned up; in fact, the very Saturday following her lunch with Danny and its painful aftermath.

By then, she'd got herself together, and was back in north London on the house hunt; but the house appeared before she'd even started. She hadn't even checked out the stack of property details she'd picked up from the agent. She was dropping off Ella with the Buchardt children before she made the first rounds of inspection, when Maggie noticed the 'For Sale' sign in front of the small house across the street.

'Jessie, look, just over there – that's what you want; look. Why didn't we notice it before? That place on Mountfield Road was far too ambitious for you. This looks like a nice little house; I wonder if it's just gone on the market? Go on, have a look; get the agent's name.'

It was a different agent, but within an hour, Jessie had the key and was looking round it, and this time, Ella came along, as well as Maggie. Ella said, 'Why don't we live here, Mum?

The garden's nice. Look, Mum – the back door already has a cat flap!'

There was an apple tree, and the unkempt garden was full of summer. The rooms were small and low, the stair and hallway narrow – almost pinched; there was a dubious and cumbersome complex of doors between the entrance hall and the scullery (straight ahead) and (to the left) the back room that seemed to serve as a dining room.

But the back room was a good room. It had white walls, brightened by a blaze of sunlight; long, low windows and a door straight into the garden; it had a moss-coloured, close-napped carpet, a small, pretty fireplace – even, Jessie noticed, a picture-rail. The squares of old carpet in the remaining rooms had rather obtrusively swirly designs; the rooms themselves were covered with plasticised wallpaper in tones of brown and beige, mauve and olive, with notes of ochre and in patterns of dedicated hideousness, except for the scullery, which had been painted floor to ceiling in a deep, egg-yolk yellow; but did it matter?

'Look, it's got central heating,' Maggie observed, to Jessie's alarm – she hadn't even imagined it might not. 'A perfectly nice little house,' continued Maggie. 'Just what you want, hmm? Just move straight in – a lick of paint, later on – no bother.'

Certainly, it looked manageable. It was modest; it was affordable; it had no obvious, glaring defects – it seemed it might even leave Jessie with a margin, though then again, the mortgage survey might throw up who knows how many problems, and of course, it did.

Meanwhile, it seemed once again that perhaps things would all work out.

It had been arranged for her and Ben to go together to meet the headmaster, Mr Faithcourt.

It had been a lovely morning. It was unexpectedly pleasant to be walking through the grounds of the College, under the great bells of the horse chestnut trees, in the morning freshness – she was so seldom out in such surroundings, at such an hour. Boys were practising their bowling at the nets in the playing fields nearby, where there still lingered the smell of new-cut grass, and roses glowed in the small formal garden fronting the hall. As they passed the music room, a pure young treble essayed a complicated passage; when it broke off, Jessie heard the murmur of a good-natured adult voice, and the boy's relieved, cheerful laugh, and she felt a pang at the thought of losing access to a place with so much beauty and apparent civility – wrenched, unexpectedly, by the fact that they did not belong here; but had they ever?

Ben had loved the choir. She remembered a moment after his first concert, when, as she discovered him among the boys and came to greet him, the choirmaster spotted her and slipped across to shake her hand, warm and smiling, saying, 'Ben's mum? Very nice voice, very nice – so glad to have him.'

Naturally, the interview with Mr Faithcourt wasn't like this. He kept them waiting several minutes, and the brief time he then allowed them seemed dense with unnecessary malice. There was first the implied threat of a black mark on Ben's school record. 'So glad we could have a word to smooth things over, before you leave us,' he had murmured, by way of introduction to this possibility, mentioning great pities, and transfers of responsibility, and the natural distress at difficult home lives, and then of course, the awkward fact that there'd been younger boys involved in the incident…

'And several older boys,' added Jessie, stung into reaction.

'I don't wish to quibble.' Faithcourt spread his hands magnanimously. 'If Ben should wish to claim that someone else was responsible for—'

'I'm responsible,' Ben interrupted, as she might have expected – though it wasn't true; he'd told her the story and this hardly covered it – adding, belatedly, 'sir.'

Faithcourt directed at Jessie a gaze of silent, confident reprimand.

Nevertheless (he then gave her to understand), in view of the very unfortunate circumstances her family was struggling with – and Ben, no doubt, was learning he must deal with – he considered that the necessary lessons had been learned, and the good name of the College would not be allowed to suffer if this lapse were, after all, to remain unrecorded.

'I'm sure,' said Jessie. But despite her relief – or even because of it, because of a brief illusion of mutual confidence – she could not refrain from adding, 'And after all, it can't be that uncommon for boys this age to occasionally experiment with – I mean – smoking.'

'You consider this a minor infringement, possibly?'

'Oh, a rule is a rule,' she said, recovering herself.

He shrugged. 'Your own household may be – more relaxed, shall we say, than—'

'Not at all,' she said, 'no, no.'

'Of course,' he said, unconvincingly, with a glance at his watch, for after all, it really had been a matter, to these people, of following certain necessary forms; and very soon, swiftly and smoothly, he was giving her a cursory handshake and it was over, though Jessie was still flushed with the certainty that he realised that she, too, was a smoker, in addition to all her other less than entirely reputable characteristics.

The night before, when she'd learned from Ben what the problem was – this serious problem that had led to such an uproar – her main reaction was fury, not with him, but with these uncaring, rule-bound authorities, though she could not quite bring herself to tell him so. In any case, she was struggling with other reactions, too: shock, self-questioning, the problem of what line to take.

'Smoking,' she repeated, when he told her, and managed to stop herself from adding, 'Is that all?' – though in a moment, she almost wished she had.

He'd been looking out for her when she got home with Ella. The sparkle and energy of recent days, which had had the effect of making him seem actually larger, a visibly more expansive self, as though entitled to claim a bigger space – this had gone out, shut down; he had the subdued, white look she'd begun to see some years before, during all the anxieties about his schooling.

He hadn't done it all that often, he told her. There was a little gang who met sometimes behind the changing rooms, at the edge of the playing field, and it was just bad luck that he was holding the packet, this time. Well, in fact, this time he'd gone and bought it for them, as he was tall for his age and they really begged him, and he'd just lit one and was starting to hand them round...

'You had a lighted cigarette when they caught you?'

'And the packet,' he said, punctiliously. And seeing her face (she didn't like that picture, Ben with a lighted cigarette in his mouth, but more than anything it was just the problem of absorbing it), he cried out, 'Oh, I'm sorry, Mum – I'm so sorry!'

His face was pink, now; he dashed his hand against a sudden wetness in his eyes, half-rising from his chair; then sat again and turned to face her. 'After all the times I've pestered you and Dad,' he broke out. 'Tried to get you and Dad to give up smoking.'

'Oh…' She tried to shrug away this depth of worry. 'Well, I really was surprised – I was surprised. You certainly knew all the arguments.' She offered a smile, but he gave his head a dismissive shake. He'd always hated lies; he'd be railing inside, now, at his own hypocrisy. After a moment, she said, 'I suppose maybe you wanted to look big.'

'Not big.' He gave a helpless little laugh, as though this idea was quite preposterous. 'Just…' He shrugged.

'Part of things,' she said, then.

'Yeah,' he said.

At lunch with Danny, that afternoon, they'd talked very little about Ben or Ella. They hadn't talked about anything of substance, really, any of the material points they might have been expected to get straightened out. They'd been flirting – at any rate, to begin with.

To begin with, this had seemed benign. It seemed like an opening, a little holiday of goodwill. Wouldn't it do them good to revive what had brought them together in the first place? Her first glimpse of him, waiting in the restaurant with that look of expectancy, had touched her to the quick. For a moment she had felt that, after all, perhaps, perhaps…They had liked to believe (from time to time) that they were rare, unconventional creatures who could take their own wayward routes to emotional resolution.

So it began again, as it so often had: the looks, the smiles, the breath of exhilaration. For that first while, she basked in the luxury of his attention and regard; and it seemed that the avoidance of any mention of serious concerns was like the delicacy contingent on an unhealed wound. Somewhere, there was this assumption that such a project was by its nature generous and expansive. It was this that would enfold a family; the children would be enfolded in their rediscovery of each other.

But the mood had shifted, the course of things had turned, and once again she was struggling to defend – what? Her stance, her past, herself? Any chance of seriousness was lost: any chance of meeting on that ground – their family – that they should have held in common.

Now, food restored her. She defrosted some spaghetti sauce she'd providently made lots of the previous weekend, and she let Ella make garlic bread, diligently mashing and mashing the butter, to soften it, after Jessie had chopped the garlic into the bowl, then thickly, laboriously spreading it out to the very edge of every slice of bread (not a French loaf, but they didn't mind; it was the garlicky butteriness they loved, and of course the smell, when they toasted it). Ben made the salad, moving about, now, with a relieved, easy lightness that shifted Jessie's spirits, too.

Afterwards, she got him to bring down his guitar. He'd recently mastered the chords of a new Beatles song, and by the end of the first verse, Jessie was so cheered up that she started to sing along. She couldn't resist attempting a harmony, the way she'd always done – with siblings, with friends at university – but Ella forcefully objected: she had a highly developed sense of the proprieties, and this was not how the Beatles did it, and there were four of them, after all, and they were boys. Even Ben, amiable Ben, admitted that Ella was right; this was the wrong harmonic line; it didn't work, really.

'You could sing the lead,' he said, 'only I'm sorry, I can't harmonise it either; I still have to concentrate on playing it; I can't do both.'

They began again. She sang along with Ben in unison, really pleased that he got through it at one go, almost without faltering. But she had to fight down a disproportionate sense of hurt, and she was angry at the flimsiness of her own self-confidence. This was how it was with her, wasn't it: self-belief washed through and ebbed away again like a capricious tide, entirely dependent on a surge of love, or even anger, or enthusiasm, or a new idea; so what did she have to offer Ben and Ella? What sort of grown-up was she; what kind of example was that?

And how much longer would these demons of self-doubt continue to resurface and torment her?

29

Arlis had promised her a brighter life. Almost from the beginning of those consultations in the Bloomsbury flat, this had been a theme.

Back in April, on the night when she first found herself with the Goldmans, excited and frightened by her own daring, this had disconcerted her. She had expected a certain grim regard for the precipice she believed she faced. Without being quite aware of it, she'd assumed they'd recognise how difficult her situation was – they'd stress the hardships; they'd be trying to dissuade her.

But underlying her own pictures of the future (though so deep that it wasn't until long afterwards that she recognised the force it had held for her) was a particular childish fantasy of redemption. It would be terrible, but then there would be miracles of friendship. A sisterhood of single parents, for example. Neighbourhoods of colourful, off-beat characters, perhaps, released from the insularity of suburban households. A camaraderie of the dispossessed.

She'd had a number of unconscious expectations of the

Goldmans. Pressed, they'd realise they had leads to this new territory. Marty told such stories, after all. In Notting Hill, years before, and then in Highgate, later, he'd had a local, a local pub, that enviable British institution, available only to the undomesticated (as it seemed to her); and from their conversation, it seemed as though they knew so many people…

Oddly, the very bleakest image (a furnished flat in some especially gritty area of London) was linked so tightly to these consoling fantasies that when Arlis dismissed it, an important sweetness seemed to have evaporated.

For instead, Arlis ridiculed her fears. A social worker for many years, she knew the poor; Jessie would not be poor. Jessie by comparison would have it easy. Liberated from her bad marriage, she would surprise herself. She'd find unsuspected energy, new levels of confidence and competence; doors would open – life would open up.

Meanwhile, Jessie's problem was just herself: a view which Arlis shared, in a sense, with Danny. It was just that Jessie didn't see her opportunities; she was far too isolated, introverted – she was so intense. It wasn't good to be that intense! She should be getting out more; she should have more clothes. She should have more fun, Arlis insisted; almost as though all this was in her gift.

The topic of clothes had for Arlis a peculiarly compelling interest: it seemed to illustrate so many significant themes: assertion, aspiration, social competence and drive; you dressed to advertise your self-belief. Look at Danny, and that jacket he brought back from West Berlin! (Jessie loved that jacket; she knew what a deeply considered purchase it had been. They had even discussed it, together, in one of those last, sweet periods when they still discussed such things; and then, he looked so handsome in it…)

'And you in the same old duffle!'

But it wasn't just some old duffle; it was, in fact, a designer greatcoat, Finnish, and that, too, had once been a happy topic; Danny had applauded the gesture of that coat – even the expense of it; and that she had brought it off, back then, at the end of sixties London, when it was all about costume and performance.

'Arlis, that coat's a classic; it was terribly expensive!' she insisted, but Arlis scoffed, 'All right, so when you bought it, it was good, but when was that? How many years ago?'

Arlis herself was still newly proud of her own personal metamorphosis, as Marty's partner. She seemed to regard this new affluence and committed acquisitiveness as a mark of maturity, and winced to remember her green years of socialist feminism – as though to discard ideals or dogmas (it was not clear that a distinction was made) was a necessary rite of passage. She jeered at the old banner-waving days; she was keen to promote, now, the more secure and solid joys of trade and barter.

As a trainee therapist, however, she retained many of the old, romantic certainties, in particular the notion that the good life was only tangentially concerned with bourgeois considerations of money, status, housing, but had much more to do with a spirit of liberation, a sense of emotional entitlement. In this light, she insisted that Jessie's situation held great numbers of unexplored possibilities. It was not a question of money! There were women on benefit who had more fun than Jessie. Oh, all kinds of ways – for instance, auctions: an entertainment in themselves. Concerts in the parks, in summer. Jazz on Sunday lunchtimes, in the pubs; you just had to look around you. Had Jessie ever been to the Royal Academy's Summer Exhibition – all for free? Then, there were sales, the Soho street market… there were jumble sales, as Ella had so successfully demonstrated.

But even had Jessie enjoyed the leisure to explore these occasions, the new social world she had hazily presumed on, to enliven them, did not materialise. The Goldmans' contacts were not, after all, as extensive or enriching as she'd imagined. There was the occasional interesting new face, but as often as not, it belonged to someone who lived in some distant hinterland (London was so incredibly vast and sprawling), or turned out to be a visiting academic, or was already too thoroughly enmeshed in relationships and projects to hold out the promise of any but the most occasional companionship.

A more enduring residue was Arlis's single women friends, but they did not provide the hoped-for inspiration – rather the opposite. As the summer progressed, Arlis began to offer Jessie a series of more or less desperate and angry single women: former wives, lone parents, all with alarmingly obvious axes to grind.

A phone call would come, on a Saturday morning, for example: 'Jessie? A friend of mine's come round; you ought to meet her. She's just left her husband – very controlling man, spoiled child, threw her down the stairs when she was pregnant; completely suppressed her talent. She's wanting out. Out!'

'But the baby… is she all right, now?'

'Baby?'

'You said she's pregnant. And he threw her—'

'Oh, the child's nine years old now… Well in fact, she's been doing most of his work for the last nine years, and he puts his name on the cards – you know, the name on the cards is his name on its own, and she prints the fucking cards! She's very talented. Really, you two ought to get together.'

Jessie became increasingly apprehensive about these summons. Did it really seem she would want a sisterhood of victims?

It was like the Bible stories of the man who threw out a devil from his soul, only to create space for seven more to enter it. She had hoped to stop being angry, but it began to seem that this was all that was being offered.

Indeed, for a while it seemed that whatever piece of writing she picked up was focused through the lens of a special grievance. You couldn't just be human. You were black or female or working class or gay, and thus endowed with an evangelising glamour; but she didn't want to define herself that way: a person with a grievance. What a grey, flat desert stretched before her now, if this was to be the largest meaning of her life.

She was angry now, of course. She was angry enough, already; she didn't need any help with being angry. Sometimes, the fervour of her anger, and its sheer futility, seemed almost to choke her. Sometimes, it kept her awake at night. She itched with it.

30

All the same, as the last hot nub-end of July melted into August, she managed to cling to a degree of optimism, though the meeting with Marjorie had been awkward.

It wasn't surprising that it should be awkward; she knew how much her schedules had been slipping. She'd been late several times with rewrites and corrections; she'd had to put off the designer; she'd had to apologise to Marjorie, whose own work might reasonably be considered to be affected. Partly because of this increasing backlog, she'd lost impetus on the remaining section of the draft. She'd got slower at it, as you often do, at this point (as she did, herself, at any rate), and then you faced Marjorie's dreary inquisitions.

'Are you sure?' Marjorie would ask, in response to Jessie's latest promises, and in a tone that suggested unfathomable vistas of uncertainty where Jessie was concerned; 'Do you really think so?' – with the implication that Jessie couldn't, possibly.

If, as sometimes happened, Jessie faltered, or paused to

reconsider, drawn in by the notion that this was a genuine question – an invitation to a mutually helpful reassessment – Marjorie would invariably add, with a meaningful look, something along the lines of: 'You do realise, you've never worked that fast before.' And then, 'I assume you realise, everyone else has kept the schedule. Annabelle' – or Peta, or, for God's sake, Henry – 'has nearly finished the first set of briefs.'

The fact that Jessie had often rushed to supply them with the groundwork, the initial concept – well, she couldn't help herself, she loved that bit, had even, sometimes, planned out their books, in the first flush of enthusiasm – this now seemed so long ago that even Jessie forgot about it.

Meanwhile, her punctiliousness at the completion stage was sighed over ('Jessie, you're so intense – so over-complicated!') and the little graces over which she laboured drew no comment, except when a reviewer picked them up, so many months later that it hardly mattered, or when – dangerously – Oscar used her as a stick to beat the others. (He had once wandered in, waving a handful of pages, and proclaimed disgustedly, 'Jessie is the only one in this office who can write!' – after which he walked out again, leaving her alone with a roomful of offence).

To her relief, however, when she finally made it to work that morning, after the appointment at Ben's school, Marjorie's manner was distinctly lenient.

Unusually, she found Marjorie on her own. Henry, it appeared, was at the dentist, Peta and Annabelle out together for an early lunch. Marjorie enquired about the morning's interview in an almost friendly manner.

'Ah, smoking,' she remarked, when Jessie told her, and gave a laugh as she offered her pack of Marlboros. 'Well, we all know what that can lead to.'

She held out her hand for Jessie's folder, and began to study its contents.

At last they'd more or less finished. Marjorie was sorting through the papers one more time. Jessie watched as she thumbed through a stack of rewrites, pausing to remove the cigarette from between her lips to point out the occasional red tick that still hadn't been attended to, raising her eyebrows as she did so. Finally she mashed out the cigarette and squared up the last set of pages, handing them to Jessie with the folder.

'Could be worse,' she said. But before Jessie could rise to leave, she continued, 'Well, you've had quite a morning, then… Smoking,' she prompted.

'Oh,' said Jessie. 'Oh, there was a group of them,' she said. 'They were hiding behind the changing rooms at the sports ground.'

'How very traditional,' said Marjorie, folding her arms, leaning comfortably back. She laughed again, and was soon embarked on her own story of first adolescent cigarettes.

At the end of it, an awkward pause ensued. Marjorie seemed to expect a reciprocal anecdote and Jessie eventually supplied one, but she was beginning to feel trapped and restless. This was the other problem that she had with Marjorie: the chatting. If her own great flaw was supposed to be her slowness, her lateness, why was she expected to do this chatting… this empty, silly waffling… the trivial jokes, the pointless reminiscing…

'What about some lunch, then?' Marjorie looked at her watch. 'Look what the time is!'

Jessie rose, in some alarm. 'Oh, no thanks,' she said, gathering up her papers, 'I need to get on with things.'

'Go on,' said Marjorie, 'give yourself a break. You have to eat.'

'No, really,' Jessie said, again. 'I'll get a sandwich from across the road. I need to get back to work.' She was aghast at how prim she sounded; but it was too late.

'Suit yourself,' said Marjorie. And then, as Jessie began to leave, 'At some point we should talk about new projects.'

Jessie turned back.

'I'm thinking of history,' said Marjorie, in a leisurely, speculative tone of voice, settling back again, arms folded.

'History,' Jessie repeated. History? But her own beloved, private project...

'Oh, we've talked about it before; don't you remember? I thought you rather liked the idea – everyday life in different periods? Tudor times...Victorian times... I'm thinking we should bring in Maynard Godley.'

'Ah.'

'Well, you know I've wanted to do that for a long time. Proper research.'

To her dismay, Jessie was beginning to remember, now. Marjorie had mentioned something like this, in passing, but since, at the time, the idea hadn't really caught her interest... But, Maynard Godley! 'Maynard Godley?' she repeated. 'But he's not a historian,' she said. 'He's just...' She barely managed to stop herself from saying just a hack. 'Well, he's more just an educationist, isn't he?'

'Always useful,' said Marjorie. 'He has a lot to teach us.' She held Jessie's glance for a long, unfortunate moment, as though she guessed, and Jessie lingered, frozen.

'Anyway. Think about it,' commanded Marjorie, and waved her away. 'Enjoy your sandwich,' she called out, as Jessie left.

Jessie reassured herself that on the whole, she'd done all right. The deadlines she'd agreed to were not too stringent – not, at any rate, impossible – and she hadn't had to surrender anything crucial. She'd kept the glossary, for example, safe from the deadly helping hands of Henry. She had such a good idea for the glossary; it could be an ingenious teaching instrument, though of course, that would require a lot of input; there'd be another struggle about extending the schedule to accommodate it.

And the next day, she found the house on Greenlea Avenue – the one that worked.

After all, she was going to pull it off. She wasn't a loser; she was a going concern. There were plenty of reasons to be hopeful.

She tried to focus on the good things. Some people liked her – the people she most respected seemed to like her. Lucy did (though she rarely got to see her), and of course Marty, though she had less time to spend with him these days, and the long, splendid talks they used to have had lapsed, as though Jessie had somehow turned into Arlis's friend, or even (as it increasingly seemed) her project.

But then, the house had turned up so opportunely, and she was confident that her offer would be accepted. She'd survived the meeting with Marjorie. There'd been that overture from Oscar... Men seemed to like her. Surely that was something? And her work was good; it was fresh; it was original. Oscar, of all people, surely knew that. He must realise, now, that it was worth the time she spent on it. Perhaps he finally realised how much they needed her...

Perhaps, even without having heard her new proposals, he'd seen some interesting new future for her, in the company.

And in just a week, Tony would be back. She was barely conscious that she thought of this, but the thought was there, now, in the back of her mind: an unexamined warmth.

31

What she'd forgotten about Tony was that element she haphazardly referred to as his politics, though of course it wasn't – it was not quite that. During the weeks after reconnecting with him, after she'd finally picked up the phone to ring him from the Otford offices, the memory sometimes recurred of an emotional awkwardness, but she didn't dwell on it. It was like a cloud-shadow on a sunny day; she let it pass.

Sharing her memories of him with Arlis, back in the spring, had reminded her of all the good things. Starting to think of him again in the changing light of her new situation, what she found herself remembering was just the sense of uncomplicated liking, the nice times she'd had with him, the pleasant discoveries of things and places.

Those memories had developed a more intriguing aspect. At Arlis's probing, she remembered realising he was attracted to her. How do you know these things? It was such tiny signs. A certain deliberation in the way he moved within her physical territory – pointing out an item on the dingy menu of the Spaghetti House (for example), the way his hand almost touched her own hand, but not quite; and she felt suddenly aware of how close he was… Or, just the way his eyes roved over her face, another time, as he sat across from her, and his gaze moved up to her hairline and then down again to her mouth, as though he was trying to memorise this face.

The more she and Arlis discussed the implications of various episodes, the more promising they seemed.

She didn't tell Arlis about the background to all this: the abject misery of the summer that preceded it, and what was going on between her and Danny. That belonged to a different conversation – much of it she'd have hardly known how to share.

She'd had plenty to say already about Danny. She'd been ready to confess to a long list of indignities, sorrows, frustrations, disappointments. For years she'd struggled with his wilfulness, the cold, keen sarcasms that so often seemed just the sharp edge of that buccaneering style of his. For years, she'd tried to rise to the outrageous demands he made, which could also be so exhilarating; she'd tried to find some imaginative way to deal with his capriciousness. It was hard to abandon that enterprise. But then, again, what a relief it was, in the early days, to give way at last to outpourings of protest and indignation.

At times there'd been bursts of sheer hilarity among the three of them, at the absurdity of what she'd been willing to endure, what Danny had managed to persuade her into. And then, they each had stories of quips that had crossed the line into cruelty, jokes gone too far, moments of arrogance they'd witnessed – long-concealed opinions and private judgements to shore up this decision that it must end; that she mustn't be asked to deal with it any longer.

For some time, Marty continued to believe that it would be possible to take a critical view of Danny and remain his friend; eventually, he tried to convey this belief to Danny. However, he had unconsciously become infected with Arlis's therapeutic lingo, to which Danny was so powerfully allergic that, at first contact, it created an immediate and final severance.

Jessie had her sympathies with Danny; she'd endured certain struggles of her own over Arlis's happy references to bad breast, object choice, controlling narcissist, etc. Glad as she'd been of the support she was being offered, she was sometimes uneasy at its terms, at the caricatures they presented – the strangely flattened, black-and-white rendering of the long, complicated, many-coloured history of her attachment. After all, she'd loved him. She still loved him. At some level she was still confused, and torn.

She was haunted by the sense that there was an emotional dynamic beyond these questions of who was right, who was wrong. There were possibilities Arlis would never understand; there were also territories so bleak and private that Jessie hesitated to broach them with Arlis. There was no way to give her the whole story, in part because Jessie herself couldn't make up her mind what the story was.

She knew that she had to do what she was doing, but she was not sure why.

There'd been a period, a few years back, before she went out and got the job with Oscar, when she wondered if Danny was beginning to have some kind of breakdown.

He wanted change, action. There was something stagnant about their lives, he said; it was one of the times when he began to talk again about North America, or perhaps West Berlin. He liked to do this; he liked to flash before her eyes an array of possible futures they might select from, but at this time he was particularly insistent, particularly impatient.

It was summer and there was a paper he was trying to write, but it wasn't working; he kept throwing it down and trying to draw her into talk with him. Sometimes it would be this talk about different futures; other times, just trying to provoke or engage her into a kind of exchange that so easily verged on quarrelling, and yet it wasn't; what he wanted was more like a debate, a chance to exercise some particular muscle of communication.

This was not a new thing. It was part of his style: he liked to throw some large, challenging statement onto the table, or even a stupidly blunt one on which he would insist and insist, until he himself had to take it up and show how splendidly it could be defended unless you were really determined to be inept and uncooperative and dull.

This game could have its rewards – privileged glimpses of how the world might be seen by a particularly active imagination (or just a profoundly different one); provocations that yielded to a brilliant sense of mutual discovery; imminent insult transformed into delight by a lucky return on her side. It sometimes worked like that, in the past. But it wasn't like that, now; there was something frantic in it.

She was aware that he was in some kind of nervous pain. However, she couldn't understand it, or understand how to address it, and when she tried, her tentativeness made him angry. Her flashes of self-assurance made him angry, too. In fact, at times her existence seemed an almost limitless source of irritation to him. There were times when he seemed to be poking at her, shaking and poking at her, like a gadget that refused to do what it said on the box: 'Why don't you defend yourself?' he cried. 'I can't do it for you; it's like playing chess against myself. I need something to react to; I'm in a vacuum, with you. Say something interesting – challenge me, why don't you!' At other times, it was as though he had decided to make some whole, new attempt at fostering their marriage, but these decisions originated in a realm to which she had no access. It was as though he was in conversation with some unknown version of herself, a doppelganger who rather maliciously misled him – the angry flash of his eyes showed clearly how he felt misled.

He attempted to teach her to play chess, to learn the elements of bridge; he started to try to buy things for the house – various household gadgets and small appliances which she'd never wanted; he pressed on her, one day, a whole new pricey set of stacking saucepans, though the kitchen itself (they still lived, then, in that tacky little development) hadn't been repainted since they first arrived, and he'd broken the backs of nearly all the kitchen chairs (leaning back, tilting them back on their hind legs, stretching his muscular, long back) and he didn't mind. He didn't mind that they could never ask people round these days; he didn't mind that they still weren't living a real life, there, because he could never be sure if they'd really be staying there in that house, in that neighbourhood, in this country, even…

But when she objected to the saucepans, he said bitterly, 'You can't accept things from me, can you. I'm not offering chairs; this is what I'm offering. Why can't you accept what I have to offer?'

When he forgave her, it was to raise again those questions about the future, saying how he had heard of an interesting post that might be going in Virginia, and he was still toying with the idea of West Berlin: well, it would be a change, at least – and she hardly knew how to tell him how much she hated the idea of so much change, so abrupt and total. There was so little in their lives that seemed to be about now, how it is right now, right here.

On their rare holidays, it had been like that, sometimes. In particular, on that one special holiday in France, driving along the foothills of the Pyrenees and then across to stay for a week in a rocky cove in Spain – during those three precious weeks, it had been like that, thy had all just been there, all of them in that place together, on that adventure.

Everything they encountered on that trip was an adventure: the landscape itself, the names of places, links with the books they'd read (together or in childhood), childhood fantasies, crumbs of history, the relaxed, warm liveliness of the public squares in the evenings – the huge pleasure of companionably watching the gentle choreography of other humans, and above them, the flat, classic planes of very old stone buildings and then the deep, star-filled sky. Just the companionship, really: looking, noticing, pointing things out to the children, sharing impressions. She remembered one moment in particular, crossing a great field of tobacco just coming into flower, a distinctive, glowing, purplish-brown, and how it suddenly occurred to her that the colour was actually intensified by the grey of the sky that day, the only day, in a week of lucky weather, that the sky was dark with cloud; but when she turned towards him to say so, she found him turning to her with the same observation, and they both laughed with delight at this unconscious harmony.

Ben and Ella, thrilled by the unusual presence and attention of both parents, seemed to glow with happiness and importance. They adored eating out, in the cafés and modest restaurants, and gamely tried any food, in every region, though with an unexpected, very expensive taste for snails, which Danny – having offered them as a tease – liked to tell about afterwards as a great joke on himself.

Danny had mourned their return to London. Increasingly, he hated England.

He hadn't really wanted to come back. They'd come to live in England almost by default, drawn by the prestige of the university (though the money was so poor) and, for Jessie, the yearning for a more vivid, urban life; but Danny hated it. He was scornful of the neighbourhood they lived in (the precious, picture-book village down the road, the tawdry shopping precinct up the way); he hated his commute; he found the actual country cramped and hampering – physically cramped and small, its public life clogged by bureaucracy. It hadn't helped that after a brief upward swing, university salaries had dropped again.

But to Jessie, the thought of West Berlin was chilling. To be so isolated, trapped in a divided city, a fortified city in a sea of hostility; to be rootless, friendless, without function, in a place where they didn't even speak the language – 'Danny, what kind of life could we have there?' she finally protested.

'God, what kind of life do we have here?' he flashed out, gesturing at the run-down, under-furnished room, at the characterless neighbourhood visible beyond its windows, and she hadn't known how to answer him.

He was restless, desperate; he felt crippled by a lack of scope. Having found, in his profession, a passion for methodology that more or less filled the place of dogma or belief, he'd become dependent on a source of material which still eluded him; it left him, sometimes, raging with frustration. He needed something to work with. Not those bloody students, who gathered round like sheep, like calves around a milch cow – he needed problems to solve, adversaries to battle with.

'I react,' he told her, once, almost despairingly. 'I respond; that's what I'm good at. I need to use myself; what can I do, here?' What place was there for him, he demanded, in the current smothering atmosphere of British public life, so hampered by tedious bureaucrats and crippling red tape, so deformed by this wrong-headed, self-righteous sentimentality about the claims of worker power blocs.

He rebelled against any authority, certainly against any dogma, any party, and this Jessie understood. It was one of the reasons she found politics so impenetrable: these programmes in which objectives she'd have liked to champion seemed embedded in belief systems which – even at a glance – seemed to involve insupportable claims.

But as for Danny – what exactly was it that he believed, or wanted? The remnants of inherited privilege enraged him, yet he had only contempt for the spite and grievances of British socialism – well, he'd observe, of every kind of socialism he'd encountered – and that seemed the only alternative that was offered.

'The state is nobody,' he'd said to Ben, once, who from early on had begun to be troubled about inequity, about injustice, and how can these things be resolved. Can't the state…

'But the state is just a great big blob of bureaucrats,' said Danny, 'unless it's a dictator. Who do you think the state is? They go on believing in this omniscient and benevolent government,' he went on, to Jessie, forgetting Ben in his ire against that constituency of wishful thinking. 'Have they forgotten Stalin?'

'Have you forgotten Hitler?' he said, turning again to Ben, who had heard rather more about Hitler, because of the war films. 'Hitler is what the state does.'

'But Hitler was a fascist,' Ben objected, worried and frowning.

'Hitler was elected,' said Danny, scathingly.

Jessie would remember for years the helplessness she felt, at this exchange, and the sense of shame. She hadn't known this – let alone how it had happened or how to deal with this odd, terrible information. Hitler had been elected?

Worse, she knew that any response of hers would seem

to Danny even more offensively naïve than the questions of ten-year-old Ben, who could clearly see, now, that he was being snubbed… the two of them left floundering in a moral morass for which she felt painfully responsible.

She was unequipped to challenge Danny at this level. She couldn't offer him anything like a proper game. She couldn't, actually, even imagine acquiring enough information about such things as historic parallels or differing social conditions to ever confront him as an equal partner.

Oh, she knew she had a good analytical brain, and imagination, and certain emotional insights that Danny had once recognised as valuable. Once it had been assumed that they would think together; this was to be the basis of their project.

But Danny refused to see any future in these ideas, now. He was increasingly impatient with conversations about moral values, conversations that transcended (or, as he thought, evaded) the conventional divisions of his profession. There were rules of discourse, rules of presentation. Jessie's kind of thinking wasn't serious; she wasn't serious; if she was, she should go ahead and do something on her own.

He believed she was holding out on him. She knew this.

It was an unspoken element of his bitterness: that she hadn't found a profession of her own, some practical way to use her intelligence; that she still allowed herself to be – like Ben – distracted by unanswerable questions.

32

Autumn, 1959

Yet there'd been a time when Danny had done that, too. There'd been a time when he wanted to be good.

He'd been surprised to find himself in love with her. He'd always assumed (he told her) that he was looking for a different sort of woman, someone older, cool, experienced – even, possibly, a little hard. That was what he liked, or so he'd thought. He liked people who knew what they wanted, and how to get it; he valued realism. He didn't believe in sentiment. He'd never meant to choose someone like Jessie.

During that time, he became much exercised by the question of altruism. He found that he wanted to do it; but how do you? How could you know what was best for someone else? And in any case – did you have the right?

For weeks, he drew her into this debate, all through the autumn they were first together: Look at what people did, when they thought they knew what was best for other people – when they thought they knew what was best for the greater good. Look at Stalin – look at the Inquisition…

Already he had read and thought about these things: about empires, about institutions, about whole cultures. Jessie was much affected by his intensity, though almost disturbed that it was she who seemed to have raised such questions in this, apparently, tormenting fashion. In those first weeks, when they were on the verge of becoming lovers, he really did seem tormented by introspection. He'd never done it; he wasn't used to it, he told her. It wasn't something he did; it was like dancing… Which also he'd done, so uncharacteristically, just that summer, when he was with her out in California.

She'd thought she could release him from these unsatisfying speculations. She believed in his goodness; she thought she had always seen it, beneath the surface. She believed in his passion for clarity, his indignation at sloppy thinking, his alarm at the treacherous marshes of good intentions insufficiently examined. This was a big part of what had drawn her to him. She wanted to learn that rigour. This was goodness, wasn't it, this commitment to honesty?

It had seemed, then, for a while, that she had only to make him see this – to see that there was no contradiction, here – and just allow himself (and the two of them) to be happy.

It had seemed a miracle, him turning up at her door in search of work that summer, after the steel strike in Chicago had ended his prospects there.

As it happened, when he arrived, Jessie's dad was away on a field trip with his company, but her mother welcomed him. A bunk was found for him in their crowded, jumbled little house, alive with young children and small animals, where something was always happening, and someone was always dropping round, and music was always playing, and the Californian sunshine poured in through the big, light windows, with the gentle, mottled hills in one direction, and in the other, a plot of land in which you could pick a breakfast of plums and apricots straight from the tree.

Danny had been enchanted – he was charmed by everything he found there.

He thought he had discovered it himself. During that time, he wore a look of joyous triumph: he seemed to open out. He seemed suddenly much younger, softened by pleasure and by that atmosphere of undemanding interest and affection, for of course, they all thought (then) that he was wonderful: all the little sisters and Jessie's brother, and above all, her mother, in whom he brought out a streak of queenly wit and gaiety that appeared too rarely.

He told them his air force stories and did his Englishman act, which merged seamlessly into the weave of his own personal style.

He did the Englishman with great panache, the way he could, and they were dazzled and entertained – him telling the outrageous stories, singing the songs – having that big, exotic, masculine presence right there in their kitchen, being interested in things like French toast and curly American bacon strips and in Jessie's mother (who lit up with pleasure and became young and pretty again). It was a dream come true.

For almost the whole of the academic year, Jessie had longed for him, and here he was, teasing her and claiming her attention and in fact rapidly, unbelievably, falling in love with her.

Years afterwards (and though so much bitterness and turbulence had happened since, so much estrangement), Jessie's mother remembered them dancing in the kitchen. And Danny didn't dance – as a rule, he didn't dance, and couldn't really dance, but in a burst of high spirits, with Jessie at the sink and him with a cloth in his hand, and the radio beginning one of those songs that call you to your feet, if you're at all susceptible that way (and briefly, he was susceptible), he put his arms around her and pulled her into the centre of the kitchen, and with Jessie's mother beaming from the doorway, whirled her away, singing along until the song was ended.

He got himself a job for the rest of the summer, and a place to stay, and the use of a car now and then, and he and Jessie had small-town, summertime adventures – the beaches, a couple of bars he found (so delectably grown-up), even the drive-in, once.

Jessie's dad, when he got home again, was doubtless aware of something missing in the usual hero's welcome. At any rate, there was a sense of mutual bristling when the two men met each other, which turned out to be a taste of things to come. Suddenly, there were judgements going on – assessments being made, a critical eye being cast – and if that was the game, Danny was always ready; you could almost see the spark of it in his eyes.

And in a way, that's when the good times ended, when Jessie's dad came back, with a challenge in every muscle of his body.

It wasn't the end of all the happy times, but of a period of trust, and maybe even hope. It was hard not to blame both sides, when they began their murmuring against each other. Selfish, her mother said now, relaying (as Jessie knew) her father's judgement; and Danny – tall, rangy Danny – said of her father, with withering finality, 'Well, of course, he's short.'

When the niggling began, Danny reacted as you'd expect him to react. He wasn't used to being vulnerable. Conflict was his more familiar territory.

It still hurt, remembering that time. He'd been ready to embrace that big, warm, giggly family – it was perhaps what had opened his heart to her. He was suddenly vulnerable, and then bewildered to find himself so vulnerable.

He wasn't used to being vulnerable. She should have realised.

It hadn't quite ended there. The really deep rift didn't happen for another three years – not until the summer Jessie returned with infant Ben, to take up a job at the local summer school, fifteen months after an unplanned wedding in far-away Chicago.

Danny came later. In the meanwhile, he'd spent eight weeks' hard slog at his thesis, gathering data in the dusty bowels of the university library in the exhausting humidity of a Chicago summer, living alone in a rented room so that he and Jessie could sublet their own place. When he finally joined her, it was in the happy expectation of starting a hard-earned break by a promised backpacking trip in the Sierras with his new father-in-law.

However, he was in for a surprise. Jessie's father had

instead taken up an unexpected opportunity to book Danny for a job with his company, excavating a hole to bury some debris from the company's operations. Instead of exploring the cool, scented highlands of the Sierras, Danny would be employed with a digger and shovel, for the last month of the summer, in the chalky, dusty brush of the local hills.

'Got some good news!' Jessie's dad had greeted him, on arrival – with the slap on the back and the look on the face that clearly conveyed how this news was to be received. That's how he did things. And thus, the last chance for bonding between the two went gurgling with all rapidity down the plughole.

Jessie couldn't understand how it had happened. There was a sick, familiar sense of insecurity, as though the ground was suddenly slippery underfoot. What was it her dad had said? Maybe. Hadn't he said, maybe? Maybe Danny'd prefer to get some cash together… Hadn't he meant to ask Danny?

Now it was implied that Danny should be glad to take any opportunity to support his little family. She should have stood up for Danny, and she had not known how; she, too, had been entangled in the pretending, for which her dad had a considerable knack. As for Danny, he had a long memory for slights; there was never a next year. There was never another light-hearted summer in California for him and Jessie.

Remembering, there were times when Jessie was stricken with remorse. This was the hardest part: those simple, tormenting memories of happiness. Much as she inwardly railed and raged at him, now, when it was all over and so long ago, there were times it could still hit her, out of nowhere – in the midst of all the anger and confusion – a sudden flash of his face, his dark eyes lost and angry, seducing her with a look which was at once an accusation and a plea: You could have made me happy.

33

Summer, 1976

When she confided this to Arlis, Arlis said, 'But what about Jessie being happy? Jessie, what do you want? For yourself?'

What did she want? Well, she wanted to succeed – didn't she? And after all, wasn't that what Danny wanted from her? She was a grown-up, now; she was at last committed to simple, practical objectives.

How had it become so complicated?

In many ways, Arlis was just so wrong. Danny had never wanted to suppress her. He loved it when she dressed up; he liked her to buy nice clothes – he wanted her to make a splash. He wanted her to play his game. He wanted her to be independent and purposeful and strong, and so did she; she longed to have some weight in the world, to engage with it, like Danny. He would release her from nun-like abstractions, thin, poetic fantasies, into that real world, where people sparred and struggled.

And yet, when Oscar had first tried to promote her, she'd done her best to try to talk him out of it.

And Danny would never understand.

It had happened so fast! She hadn't even started the first Otford project when Danny left for his sabbatical in West Berlin. Then, less than six months later, the project had grown so much that there was a staff to manage, and Oscar had decided she should manage it.

How could she do that? She was still struggling to develop a series of prototypes – how could she possibly manage a team as well? It wasn't that she lacked ambition. She was devoted to making the project work. In fact, when she first took it over, she'd demanded a payrise that made Oscar blench. Oh, what a moment that had been! She'd felt so confident, then, so sure of what she was worth and what she wanted. She felt resolute, standing up to him with that demand, but she hadn't expected him to look so grim next morning, when he'd realised that she meant it. And she hadn't expected that Danny, when she wrote to him, would respond with such alarm at her temerity. Wasn't this exactly what he'd have wanted?

But, those first days had been exhilarating.

At the beginning, she'd been pretty much left alone. Oscar and Alison were absorbed in other aspects of the business: putting together a production department, giving presentations to bankers and backers, and of course, hiring the staff for Oscar's other project, the one he expected to be his flagship series – a number of worthy, illustrated tomes on scientific topics, aimed at older children. Jessie was pleased to be left to her own devices.

Then she discovered that what they'd asked for wasn't possible.

It had seemed such a simple task. It was to be the first of a series of children's practical books – a book of projects explained in comic-strip format, step-by-step – much like other books already out there, on the market, but with flair, and freshness, and of course, unlike those other books, it would work.

Everyone had liked the book-plan she'd put together, drawing on possibilities suggested by the potential author; it was part of how Oscar pre-sold the series. Now the author, an origami expert, had submitted her text, accompanied by diagrams and a box of finished items. All that was needed, supposedly, was for Jessie to organise this material, breaking the text into short, informative captions and pasting these bits of text on a double-page grid in a sequence to which the designer could match the diagrams, after which he'd hand the pages over to the illustrator. This had seemed, as described to her, so straightforward.

But to begin with, there weren't enough diagrams – not nearly enough, barely a handful – and, on examination, these few were dull, inscrutable, and all but unrelated to the typed instructions.

Worst of all, even the typed instructions made no sense.

After struggling for some time with these offerings, Jessie telephoned the author for enlightenment.

'Well,' said the author, exasperated, 'Naturally, you have to score the paper, first.'

'I have to… what?' asked Jessie.

She soon learned how problematic experts are: they

rarely understand how very little other people know of what obsesses them. Though they might write at length about the obvious, they tend to be abruptly cryptic about their mysteries, and rarely know how you could use images to explain a process – rarely appreciate the power of a caption that simply says, like this.

In the end, Jessie paid numbers of visits to her 'author'. Oh, this person would be credited as an author, she reassured her, only you see, Jessie would have to write new words, to go with the visual material, because they needed to be necessary words – the words and pictures should be closely integrated; they should work together as a whole, as in good magazines. So you couldn't quite know what was needed from the text until you'd worked out what you were showing in the pictures – and then, you needed some way to dramatise the thing. And you needed to include a few surprises, too: surprising facts and jokes to brighten up the layout.

The vision that unfolded of these integrated pages was like a whole new playground of possibilities to Jessie. She was excited by how much value each page could hold, if you really used both the images and the words, with one central person pulling it together, writing and sketching out the images to work together. And what fun to use the visual impact of the type itself: its size, position, density…

After her first visit to the origami expert, she got permission to buy a camera, but quickly realised it was better to draw simple diagrams – very simple diagrams, they were. After all, she realised, it's just not possible to create instructions 'any child' could follow, but what if your default objective was the parent? A parent just giving a hand from time to time? If you could just make it simple enough for the average parent, a busy parent glancing at the page…

Then, the next trick was providing enough visual variety on each two pages; you had to brief the designer carefully on what would work. And then, there was the challenge of the words: how to create the most succinct of friendly captions, like writing a poem… It almost seemed to her as exacting and satisfying as writing poems, but unlike her poems, it would be read, and it would work, and sometimes, it might even raise a laugh.

During this time, she was entirely happy. Once in a while, Alison might just glance absentmindedly over her shoulder, or Oscar might stop by with a word or two. They'd ask how it was going, and she'd say fine; she'd say wonderful; occasionally she might say, oh, a couple of problems, but it's getting there.

Then, when at last the designer brought some finished layouts, and the time came to finally show the first results, to spread out in front of them those first six pages, she enjoyed a moment of true vindication. How they exclaimed! How delighted they both were!

Then they realised this was all there was.

She'd been expected to have the first book finished in three weeks, but that was how long it took her to get these pages right.

Oscar really did tear his hair.

Jessie never forgot the sight of him, pacing the floor and pulling at his hair, flinging his arms up, in gestures of abandon. She was frightened at what she was doing – what she was asking of him. What if she couldn't actually pull it off? What would happen to the company if she didn't?

She felt enormously responsible for the company.

But by now, she had a vision, and it had captured her. She insisted, doggedly, but we have to, Oscar; they'll be classics; they'll be well worth it; really, they'll sell for years...

She won the battle, but it really was a battle, and it wore her out. By the time he capitulated, she had given way so much, in terms of wildly improbable schedules, that perhaps it couldn't be called a win at all. And by the time he decided to promote her, things had changed.

By then it was early March, 1974. The terrible winter of strikes and shortages was ending, but it had taken its toll, and as for Jessie, her life was coming apart at the seams. The arrangements for Ella were continually disintegrating, and there was no back-up – the friendly young student who had lodged with them during Danny's absence was now entirely absorbed in a love affair, leaving Ella bereft. Ben's first term at the expensive boarding school had ended with a disastrous school report, which had cast its chill; and Danny was angry. There'd been a frightening quarrel when he flew home from Berlin in January, for an interview; since then, his letters had grown impersonal and infrequent.

As for the office, it was no longer a source of comradeship. Oscar had hired one after another new 'editor' to work with her, but they were bemused to find that they were actually expected to write the copy, to sketch the visuals, to make every one of these how-to projects themselves (themselves!), to take on the half-finished books that Jessie couldn't manage on her own, and to follow her lead, to be guided by her – this inexperienced person!

Jessie could usually create some initial enthusiasm for the process. It could be fun, sometimes, sharing ideas, working as a team. But at other times, it took them a while to get it – to get what she was aiming at, in the books – and she was uneasy at having to criticise their work. She'd had no chance to work out guidelines for what she was doing; it remained largely a matter of improvisation; and there was no support, because of course, she was still proving herself to Oscar.

In any case, he and Alison had no time to give her, distracted as they were by competing pressures, up to their eyes in business plans, production schedules, and the burgeoning problems of Oscar's other series, which seemed to be in a state of continual breakdown. The happy, sociable buzz of those first months had begun to flatten into a dull, grinding panic. To Jessie, it seemed she'd been trailing a baggage of missed deadlines and broken schedules for weeks and months, like almost visible evidence of impairment – suffering from a constant cloud of anxiety – and when Oscar asked her to have a word with him over lunch, she suspected the worst.

To her astonishment, she found he was taking her to Mario's. She was jarred. Always before it had been pubs, or workmen's cafés, and she wasn't prepared – for months now, she'd been turning up in jeans.

She felt tremendously self-conscious, walking beside him through the drizzly, miserable March afternoon. She was sure he felt self-conscious, too. It was most peculiar to hear him attempting small talk – to have him talking about anything but work. He led her down a turning she'd never noticed, into a hidden alleyway of small, dark buildings, including one that turned out to be a restaurant – you'd hardly have noticed it, if you hadn't known where to look.

Once seated, he picked up the wine list, and after a moment, turned to the hovering waiter and ordered a bottle. Jessie was baffled. Why were they doing this? What was there to celebrate? Surely they were all still up against it – surely the whole company was still at risk…

Oscar gestured to the menu, telling her to go on, pick something good, and she was alarmed to find, when she picked up this heavy folder, that there weren't any prices listed. She had no idea what to choose. She wasn't hungry. To be eating fancy food like this, at lunchtime, in this tiny, tucked-away place with its mullioned windows, in the hushed, carpeted silence… At last she hazarded an order, and the waiter left. Oscar folded his arms on the table; gave her a big, bland smile. He'd come to a decision, he said; he was making her managing editor of the project.

'It means a payrise, Jess,' he said, with a self-satisfied look. He mentioned the figure. After a moment, he asked, 'So?'

'Managing editor,' repeated Jessie.

He favoured her again with that official smile.

She took a long, deep breath.

'What's the matter? It's another payrise. It's a very decent payrise.' Though of course it wasn't; it never was. But that wasn't the point.

'Oh, Oscar,' she said. 'How can I? Bubsie and Annabelle? Marjorie?'

'Why not?' The smile had faded; his brow had furrowed slightly.

Well, but there was no need for it, she protested. They were a team, she said; it was fine the way it was.

'A team,' he said.

'Why not? Why do we have to have a hierarchy? Why do we need to have a boss,' she said, with perhaps more emphasis than was quite welcome; but she hardly noticed. 'Different people are better at different things, and they take the lead; there's a kind of natural hierarchy; don't you see?'

'And who's responsible for seeing the schedules are met?'

'Well, but we're all responsible.'

'You are?'

She knew it would come to this. She sighed and looked down at her plate.

'Jess, I can't give you any more time. And you can't keep trying to take up the slack, yourself. You'll just have to learn to manage them. Dominate them, Jess. You've got to dominate them!'

Dominate them?

Oscar was adamant. He had to have a manager, he said at last. He had to delegate; he had to protect himself. If Jessie wouldn't do it, he'd have Marjorie.

Marjorie.

'Sorry, Jess,' he said, perfunctorily.

It came to her that he really had no idea what Marjorie was capable of doing to this first child of theirs.

'Well,' she said, finally, 'if that's the alternative.'

Of course, she couldn't do both jobs at once – establish the prototype and do the managing. The truth was, she didn't know how to do the managing; it required so much more than helping the others get the content right.

She didn't have the basic technical skills. She didn't know how to correct the printer's copy; she didn't know how to produce editorial schedules or production schedules; she'd never before had to talk to typesetters and repro people and photographers.

It was an uphill struggle to try to solve the inevitable problems in these areas, and to rectify the inevitable mistakes (which indeed the capable Marjorie handled with the smiling, passionless ease of a good-humoured housewife), while continuing, in a parallel process, to agonise over ideas about how the pages should look and what the words could do. And although in the end she did that (finding the look and the words), it was Marjorie who ran the salvage operation and ensured that, as a product, it all came together in the end, and met the deadlines.

After which, publication was delayed for a year in any case, because it was decided to wait for Oscar's other series, which was a good eight months overdue; so all that panic and agony had been for nothing, and when it was over, Marjorie became her boss.

That's what she'd found when she came home alone that summer, leaving Danny with his mother and the children, back among the German lakes and forests.

34

Autumn, 1974

She refused to acknowledge that she'd had a knock. She refused to consider that she'd been beaten. Refused to acknowledge that this could make any difference.

After all, she didn't see why it should. She'd never wanted this manager role; now she was free of it. Released, she'd make something new and wonderful again. She would come through; she'd prove herself a winner.

Of course, she had to. Given what had been happening with Danny – given how things had developed between the two of them, how they had changed and hardened – she had to show herself successful and self-sufficient. Now, she really had to prove herself.

Over the next two years, she devised a number of new looks for this integrated visual approach. In the first flush of inspiration, she often found she could lay the groundwork for a whole new series, mapping out the content and guidelines for her colleagues, arguing the case for its adoption; and at some point, each new project seemed to hold out the promise of vindication. She'd be so sure she'd got it: an idea at once worthwhile, commercial, and readily implemented – or at least, implemented without too high a surcharge of goodwill, enthusiasm, flexibility – because oddly, this was necessary every time. She found herself battling, every time, just for a chance to show how this new idea would work.

She couldn't help falling in love with it, herself, while the others stood back (metaphorically) to see it proved. And then inevitably a time would come when it would turn out that there was no way this thing could be brought off without special concessions of the systems now in place – the systems established for the last project – or without (in Jessie's eyes) fatally compromising the idea. In the ensuing struggle, she'd find herself once again harassed and in trouble, fallen into pits of obloquy and despair; and, at last, by the end, utterly burnt out and under a cloud.

At the beginning, she could often rekindle the old enthusiasm among her colleagues. Marjorie might even sit back and allow it, with an amused and tolerant air, like a benign headmistress. As soon as any obstacle arose, however, or the schedules pressed, Marjorie stepped in, pulled rank, took over. And the truth was, the others were more comfortable with Marjorie. She was less exacting; she told jokes; she brought out – to their delight – all the journalist tricks and hoary clichés that Jessie so assiduously avoided. She spoke their language.

Jessie had never been able to come to terms with Marjorie. She wouldn't accept Marjorie's easy-going approach, her tendency to create routines and shortcuts – she wasn't even sure she could have, if she were willing, and she wasn't willing – no, she wasn't. In fact, it sometimes seemed to her that she would die if she couldn't aspire to a certain freshness in what she did, a dash of colour and sparkle, a touch of wit. Time and again, in the months that followed, she had to suppress the nagging sense that there should be some way to do this, to get to achieve what she wanted without creating rivalries and problems and offence and trouble.

It was during the adrenaline-fired creative burst that followed her split with Danny that it came to her: if only she had a team of outside writers, it could work – her own team, answerable just to her. Once she had thought of it – why ever not?

After all, this was exactly what had been expected of her, back at the beginning. She'd been expected to be a conventional editor, guiding and managing freelance authors and consultants. It was just that the authors assigned to her had no idea of what she wanted, because the books she was imagining did not exist yet. She also had none of the technical skills, then, and no experience, either; but most importantly, at the time, there were no examples to show them, and now there were. At last, all those terrible birth-pangs would prove worthwhile. The books were made; they'd even, finally, been published (to glowing reviews and excellent sales, too); now you could point to them. Now you could say, like this.

As this revelation opened out, she found herself almost flooded with ideas for the project that had caught her interest. Titles, topics, angles, images, whole flocks of delicious detail came crowding in on her, and during that brief, halcyon springtime period, when the future was so unformed and promising, Jessie was filled with that degree of hope that she inevitably took for confidence.

Of course, the confidence, or hope, came and went as the weeks and months wore on – as practical difficulties and problems pressed ever harder, and the emotional landscape continued to unfold (revealing new, painful dips and swamps and treacherous currents). Yet there would still occur, now and then, spells of tranquillity when her spirits lifted and her thoughts expanded, and later on, even as the summer days grew shorter – even as the season sank towards a hot, tired August – a morsel of real good news could revive those visions.

On the day she put in her offer for the Greenlea Avenue house, which she'd done as soon as she got to the office the following Monday, she experienced just that sort of rally. Finding the little house cheered her so much. She was proud of pulling out of the Mountfield scheme. By contrast, this prospect seemed modest and practical; it seemed sensible. She was proud of being sensible. The way it showed up seemed a reward for virtue.

At this, it seemed her mind came alive again, regained its appetite; and now, she found herself longing to talk about her plans and visions – longing to talk to someone who would see what she saw, appreciate the possibilities. On an impulse, after supper that evening, she hunted up the phone number of someone Oscar had introduced to the staff as a consultant: Liz Trevor, the woman who'd started the children's book groups.

Jessie had no real excuse for ringing her, just that she liked her, and knew this woman liked her work, and thought she'd be interested – someone with no political investment, who could be counted on to respond whole-heartedly. Well, if she was there, if she picked up the phone, if, then, she liked it…

And she was there, and she did answer the phone. She was surprised by the phone call, but she was ready to accept an appeal to friendship and like-mindedness. Coincidentally, she said, she was actually expecting to drop in at Otford's in a few days' time; Oscar had asked her to come in to lunch. But as Jessie had guessed, she was delighted by the project.

'It's a wonderful idea. Wonderful,' she said, eventually. 'And you could do it. If anybody could, you could; you know you could. Make sure it happens. Make Oscar do it,' she cried, briefly exalting Jessie with ideas way above her station. Then she added, that after all there was nothing whatever out there, at the moment, nothing at all in that area. Well, of course, except for those deadly little books by Maynard Godley.

'You don't think much of him?' asked Jessie.

'Ha!'

Ella was calling.

As Jessie went up to her, Ben (in the room across the landing) began again on the hard bit of guitaring he was getting hold of: '*Lucy in the sky-eye with…*' clunk… '*Lucy in the sky-eye with…*' clunk...

Ben was enormously persistent. He'd continue working on this phrase, she knew, until he mastered it, or as long as she and Ella could put up with it. Jessie looked into his room and gave him just five minutes more. It was Ella's bedtime, now – well, past her bedtime, really – time for the story, and cuddles, and last confidences, and friendly chat. It was always a particularly cosy time, and tonight, feeling cheered and optimistic, Jessie allowed it to be prolonged by a lengthy discussion of breeds of cats, and which of them might be most fun to own, when they got this long-awaited kitten.

Then, as usual, a heap of chores still waited. There was a rip to mend in Ella's favourite shirt, and the chilli beans for tomorrow's supper to get started, and she'd better manage a quick tidy-up, as well, since tomorrow evening a potential buyer for the house would be more or less waiting at the door when she got home.

Of course, this was a good development. Giving up at last on the estate agent, she'd recently put her own ads in the local papers and got some interest, which could potentially save a lot in agent's fees, as well as time. Yet at the thought, she felt her energy falter. After all, it seemed you had only to glance in this direction and other concerns leapt at you from the shadows: all those bills to pay, and the bank balance and her credit card to check, and then, oh God, the reminder about Ben's next appointment with the optician…

At the thought of which, the question arose of just how angry she ought to be about Ben losing the garage key. Which meant that until they'd somehow organised a new one (and how did you do that? They'd been here such a short time, she'd never found out who ran the residents' association), he couldn't get at his bike. Which meant he couldn't cycle to the appointment; he'd have to take two buses, which meant he'd have to leave too early to meet Ella after school, if that was the day he was booked to take her to her sitter – which meant that Jessie had better check those dates in her diary before she even thought about anything else.

Luckily, the dates worked out all right.

Then it occurred to her that if Ben had to spend an hour each way on travelling, including the long, boring waits for buses, this, together with the cost of the new key, might be counted as penalty enough.

Relieved, she lit a cigarette and went out to the little balcony to enjoy the respite. She leaned back on the door frame, looking across at the shadowed wood, and indulged in a moment of hope.

The support from Liz Trevor was a tonic. How wonderful if she could work with her, some day – suppose Liz Trevor could be an advisor on the project? But no, that was getting too far ahead; she needed to stay calm; she needed to concentrate.

So she began by tackling the living room, to get through the most challenging bit of the evening's programme – gathering up the papers and felt-tips from Ella's latest art project, straightening magazines, collecting an ashtray, a couple of coffee cups, a plate with crumbs, an empty biscuit wrapper. Then, with a flash of decisiveness, she got out the little broom and dustpan instead of the vacuum cleaner, and in just a few minutes, working quickly, brushed up the most obvious bits of debris from here and there on the pale, thick carpet.

Back in the kitchen, as she chopped and fried the onions for the chilli, she could still feel the glow of this future she was now creating – a plausible, practical, interesting and satisfying future.

35

If only Danny had believed in her.

It could have worked. At times like this, she felt so sure of it. She could have been the sort of person that he wanted, the sort of calm, independent, realistic person they both admired.

But on his return from West Berlin, the second year of her job at Otfords, he'd begun playing rougher. He began using threats, throwing his financial weight around, having affairs.

It wasn't supposed to be like that. Her job was supposed to re-balance their relationship, so that they'd be more equal, more like comrades. He wasn't supposed to start talking about 'my money' and 'my house' the way he did, to other people.

It had started so sweetly, when he first went off on that sabbatical. It started so sweetly, and then it ended so frighteningly badly.

'My little love,' he'd called her, when he came home to them, that Christmas. 'My little honey,' he said affectionately, using that familiar American endearment in his own touchingly peculiar manner.

Ella was staying with neighbours for the night, Ben was still at his boarding school, the lodger had already left for the holiday. Jessie went to the airport on her own, to meet him. For that first night, they had the house all to themselves, and Jessie had prepared a little feast.

Danny paid no attention to her feast; all he wanted was to have his hands on her again. As she tried to bring out the dishes from the fridge, he kept trying to catch hold of her, trying to get his arms round her, sliding his hand up underneath her skirt. Excited as she was, she was flustered, too, and even a little disappointed: she had been so proud of all the treats she'd got for him. She had looked forward to enjoying it all together – enjoying these good things, alone together, at their leisure, in the candlelight – gradually getting to know each other again.

For it was strange: after ten weeks, they were almost like strangers. Their positions had altered. Now it was Jessie whose days were full and busy (even too full, and increasingly too busy), while Danny, more isolated than he had expected, had found himself, in Berlin, surprisingly at a loss, and he had missed her. He often wrote about how much he missed her; but also, disconcertingly, about how curiously empty life began to seem, and even, as the winter darkened and closed in, how meaningless. What was he doing with his life, he asked? And even: what – after all – was a life about?

She was moved by this, especially at first, but it disturbed her. At last she'd released herself from just those questions, as Danny had long wanted her to do – she'd given up those longings for a larger purpose. She'd found, instead, a job she loved, a satisfying task; she'd begun to taste ambition and the lure of success. She didn't want to be drawn back into introspection.

And yet, to see him so vulnerable, so tender; to find herself so important to him…

In the morning, after collecting a delighted Ella, the three of them had gone for a walk together. It wasn't their usual walk, down through the village and straight across the common. Instead, they actually poked about among the neighbouring streets; they wandered.

They came across a churchyard, and circulated among the mossy, hummocky gravesides. She and Danny held hands with each other, and sometimes with Ella. Sometimes, Ella would go off to investigate – there was a cat, at one point, a white cat with one black eye, winding among the gravestones, and the cat allowed Ella to stroke it for several blissful moments, and then she came back and, looking up at them, smiling wordlessly, inserted herself again between them, taking their hands again.

And they hardly spoke at all.

The slanting winter sunlight glowed in the berries of an enormous yew. It fluoresced on the greeny flagstones, and where it struck through the cushion of the moss, at eye level on the churchyard wall, it lit up the tiny, folded parasols of a miniature moss-forest rising from it – a fairy forest.

It was wonderful how you didn't need to speak, when you were most content. How free you were to notice things, just notice them, and enjoy.

For years, she would remember that perfect moment.

Over Christmas, they were almost entirely happy. It felt as though they were finally a real family; they were a going concern; they were going places – you could use such terms about them.

It was such a short time.

They spent hours entertaining each other, doing things together, like a real family.

On the train going up to the Midlands for the Christmas break, Danny and Jessie regaled Ben and Ella with a recap of the notoriously ribald pantomime they'd seen the night before, at Oscar's first works' outing. To the children's delight, they treated them to uncensored versions of some of the most outrageous skits and jokes; the four of them laughed till they ached, in the friendly, stuffy confines of the train compartment.

Up in Leicester, they were greeted by Gran as heroes. They were welcomed into a haven of comfort and Christmas cheer, Gran listening with rapt enthusiasm to the tales of all the new adventures: Danny's sojourn in West Berlin, Ben's school, Jessie's job.

It was all going to be so different, now.

Danny was very happy. Soon after his arrival, he'd heard that a close colleague had been promoted, despite a publications record even lighter than his own. Josif, the colleague, was sure there'd be similar good news for Danny after Christmas, when he, too, met the committee. Danny would at last get the recognition he had long thought he deserved. And now, of course, his marriage was going to work, too, with Jessie so much more confident and strong and happy; and of course, an extra salary didn't hurt.

That was the best of it, that comfortable, indulged, uxorious Christmas.

Almost as soon as they got back to London, it was over, as the blows of a mean fate began to hit.

She hadn't realised it would affect him the way it did. That not getting this particular promotion would mean so much to him – would make him ready to tear up their whole new way of life: the great surprise of a real career for her, this partnership that was going to save their marriage…

But yes, immediately, he was talking about leaving London, He would look for a permanent post at the institute in Berlin; he would check out possibilities in the States; he'd be taking them all away as soon as possible; and why?

He was contemptuous of those people at the university who had passed him over. He seemed to despise them. And yet he was prepared to deform his family's life in order to, somehow, affront them, but how would they know this? Why would they care? Who was this *they*, to matter so much – to, in fact, in this negative, defaulting way, rule his life, and hers, to change the shape of their whole world?

The last days of the Christmas visit were an ordeal, but for Jessie, worse would follow, even as the rigours of the heatless office and the three-day week continued: the bitter, bleak, unanswerable letters from him, just while her own life grew so very bleak and solitary. And then that terrible flying visit, when he came back demanding her enthusiasm for a job that would rip them away from everything they knew: and she refused it. She wasn't able to supply it.

He'd probably never have taken that particular job, she realised later. However, it had thrown her to see how much it flattered and excited him to be approached. They'd paid his expenses to fly to London for an interview, and he'd rung in high spirits to announce this rendezvous – an emotion she'd struggled to share, given the reason for it. In her panic, she failed to cancel a meeting with an author on the day of their reunion, thinking that anyhow, she must somehow impress on him the fact that she had a life; she, too. For he seemed unaware that she herself, now, might have a stake in these future plans.

Of course, it wasn't as though this feeble sprig of a career of hers was such a great thing. It was a shaky, unsupported little plant. She was beginning to be attacked from every side: Oscar shouting from above, colleagues sniping from below; almost all the excitement and fun had drained away. It was only with real effort that she still managed to cling to the hopes she'd had for her work; it was partly in order to reassure herself of this that she'd insisted on going back, that day, to the office.

And yet, how could she? How could she have been so clumsy? She remembered the surprise among her colleagues, seeing her arrive for that unnecessary meeting; hadn't she been greeting her husband at the airport?

She remembered the look on Danny's face, when she finally returned to the car he'd rented for the occasion.

Then, to have compounded the damage the way she did, when he had left. Alone again with all the problems, seared by the memory of the implacable and icy fury with which he'd treated her failure to give him a proper welcome, she gave way to a surge of indignation of her own, and wrote to him about it. To have been indignant with him, on paper. On paper! With him! She might have known she'd never be forgiven that.

This became one of the sequences that continued to play out in her mind, over the years, again and again: those painful mental dramas of remembered hope and loss and sheer confusion.

Because surely she should have had some rights in that situation – surely he ought to have understood.

But as for her, she ought to have been able to just stand up for herself. Yes! To simply and calmly stand up for herself. Why couldn't she do that? Why was she always so needy, so embattled; why did she always end up being the loser?

After all, what was it? *What was wrong with her?*

36

She couldn't sleep. By 2am she'd given up the attempt, and gone upstairs again, to the newly tidy, empty living room, to get the whisky bottle from the smart new drinks cabinet that Danny had been so proud of.

She took a drink and her cigarettes onto the balcony, to the stair leading down to the little sterile patch of garden; she sat there smoking and looking out again at the wood, now just a mass of darkness under the purplish pall of the city sky.

It was going to be one of those nights.

'Why is it?' Danny had asked her, at the fancy lunch she had so foolishly looked forward to. 'Jessie, why do you do it? Do you know?'

Sometimes, it seemed as though he might explain.

'Is that what happened with Oscar?' he had said. 'Jessie, you gave him his first winning series; why is it you couldn't make something out of that? Why are you at the bottom of the heap, now? It's like you forge your way through some great thicket of opportunities – like that's your quest! Like that's your aim in life! It's like you have your pockets full of gold and you just scatter it around, like, I don't know – like bird food.'

And in the midst of everything, she was softened by his saying bird food, not birdseed. This beautiful man, his face alive with communication – once again, she was ensnared by his attention, and the truth was, she was dazzled by this vision of herself, and her opportunities. He gave her these pictures of herself that confused and excited her.

'God,' he'd said, 'How could you get yourself in that position. You can see why I didn't want you to have the kids.'

Oh, this had rattled her. She had actually forgotten this. She had buried this memory: as though of his knife against her throat.

'You seem to have this gift for screwing up. This instinct towards failure. Is it your background? Is it your family? Are you afraid you'll owe them, if you ever make it?'

He knew her so well – her past, her secrets, her weaknesses, her regrets and fears. She could always be sucked back into this conversation, which had her own vexed psychology as its axis of energy.

He said, 'Did you know, there are tribes in Africa that do that. All the successful people hide their wealth and go around in specially dirty, ragged clothes—' Seeing her look, he gave a laugh and said, 'Oh, you look very nice today – you know I'm not referring to your clothes, but that's what you do; you seem to hide behind incompetence. It's as though all those needy people are still making claims on you, and you're still trying to avoid that responsibility.'

Was it just that he made her interesting to herself, with these elaborate analyses of her situation, her history, her problems?

Ah, but sometimes, at least, it was the conversation itself that hooked her.

It was a game that had gone on so long. Even from the unpromising starting-point of her personal failings, it could flower into such tantalising theories, such interesting speculations about communication, about expectation, about the many hidden assumptions that we live by – men and women, Americans and Europeans, innovators and traditionalists – left and right… Soon she would be unable to resist the temptation to float some notion of her own; and then it became, after all, part of the ongoing conversation of their lives together, for which she had once had such extravagant expectations, though it had never developed – never resolved itself into a line of enquiry that either of them pursued with diligence; or a path to follow.

Personal responsibility, honesty, clarity, truth…

With Tony, she'd almost never talked like this.

How good it had been, to spend that time with Tony! For a moment, rebelliously, she allowed herself to indulge in daydreams.

With Tony, it had just been easy, hadn't it. They had just enjoyed each other's company. There was talk – they shared their stories – but they did things, too. Even in the short space of a lunch hour, they had adventures. They looked in at the Photographers' Gallery around the corner from Jessie's office;

they bought cockles and whelks from a street stall, once, and ate them on a bench in a quiet churchyard; another time, they took a picnic of delicatessen to Trafalgar Square.

Yes, and while they sat on the edge of the fountain, gazing up at the great stone lions, he told her how, when the lions were finally installed there, after years of delay, the public were so annoyed that somebody said that the lion on top of Northumberland House would probably not acknowledge these new lions as its relations…

He had a fund of anecdotes like this, and he seemed to like nothing better than to amuse her with them. He seemed – at least, at first – so easy with himself, so gentle and droll and tolerant. He just wanted (he said) something to do. He wanted a project, a purpose.

But even as she dwelt on these reminiscences, the placid surface began to break up into a disturbing mix of more troubling emotion, like brightness and shadow. She poured another drink, lit another cigarette, found herself trying to cling to certain memories of those good times – certain light-hearted, simple times. But it was like clutching the dissolving fabric of a dream.

There were other memories, too. Unlike Danny, he had seemed genuinely interested when she described the ideas she'd had, of what she could do, at Otford, and her troubles there. When she showed him her work, his response was everything she could have wished. He got all the jokes; he caught all the subtleties; his appreciation was balm to her beleaguered soul. But he couldn't seem to understand why she cared so much. He couldn't grasp how a success in this field could matter to her. How to explain that it was just the idea of mass-market quality that enthralled her – the possibility that you could make something original and distinctive, and it would sell.

'Jessie, you're a poet!' he'd insisted – as though this was an accolade, and not a curse.

When, as always, she protested, he finally shrugged, and said, 'Well, an inventor, shall we say,' which cheered her up. But then he added, 'You do realise, inventors always end up penniless. You know that, don't you? You don't get rich by inventing something wonderful. You get rich by erecting a turnstile.'

She didn't want to remember him saying things like this. She hadn't wanted to hear such doubts of her hopes and plans, but particularly not from Tony, whom she'd counted on (really, despite what she could have known of him) to be at ease with life, the way she wanted to be, herself. It was a counsel of despair, of romantic futility. It was not what she'd ever meant to be about.

But after all, it was only too probable that – non-aligned and fastidious as he had seemed to be – he was tempted, at some level, by some such vaguely political attitude, some such broad, slack, self-excusing slur… It was so common, with people like him. It was so fashionable.

One day, after referring idly to his own uselessness (as he did), and the frustration he sometimes felt, he broke out, suddenly, 'Well, I could work for the end of the whole rotten system…' He managed to salvage the moment; he widened his eyes at her, almost immediately, with a look of self-mockery, but she had heard that note of personal bitterness.

The system... Oh, that was so familiar, and so unwanted. Hearing this outburst, there had flashed on her a disturbing memory of the political radicals of her student days, in the sixties, the casual violence of their slogans: *Kill the Pigs*, *Let it Burn*, *Death to the Man* – posturing, grandiose, vindictive.

By comparison, Danny's cool non-interventionism had seemed so modest. Till your own garden, in effect. It seemed clear-sighted; it seemed punctilious in its respect for particulars and individuals; it seemed benign. It seemed realistic and responsible. It seemed grown-up.

She wasn't like that. After all, she was not one of those cool, self-sufficient beings; she didn't have those qualities. She only, rather pathetically, aspired to them. Now she felt inadequate and small, like a child unable to clean up after itself, forever liable to be tripped up by such unreasonable longings – forever trapped in the squalor of emotions she could not make sense or use of.

The sky was white by the time she finally got to sleep.

37

Oscar gave a deep, exhausted sigh. 'Be reasonable,' he said, in tones that suggested that this was perhaps almost more than he could expect of her. 'How could I put you in charge of anything? You can't manage people. You're hopeless with people, Jess.'

He paused, but for a moment, she couldn't speak.

'You're a nice person,' he said, as though relenting. 'At least, I think so. I don't think there's anything evil about you,' he explained, as though this were a possibility it was necessary to discount. 'It's just that you're so desperately insensitive.'

It was the end of a difficult and painful week.

On Tuesday morning, she'd been half an hour late for work. Unsurprisingly, after her late night on the back stairs with the whisky, she'd overslept. She'd set the alarm for a quarter past seven, a good half-hour earlier than would have been absolutely necessary, and then she'd turned it off in her sleep, almost reflexively. It was Ella who woke her up. Jessie had to tell her to grab a banana for her breakfast, while she herself pulled on her jeans and ran outside in her bare feet, calling out to the neighbour in the waiting car, who was giving Ella a lift to the summer day-care place. Of course, she was also late with the promised wake-up call to Ben, who was hoping to meet with a friend from their old neighbourhood, and who was now still deep in the usual adolescent coma. And she'd missed the train she should have taken.

How very grotesque it was, to have got over-excited by the idea that she might have the capacity to be calm.

By the time she got to work that day, she'd already missed two phone calls, and it seemed that Oscar had been looking for her.

'You're popular, today,' said Johnny, who'd taken the messages.

'Popular?'

'In a manner of speaking,' he said, raising an eyebrow.

Oscar sounded extremely irritated, when she got hold of him, though of course, you could never be sure why that might be. 'Where have you been? Where are you, anyway? Nobody seems to know.'

'I'm very sorry; I was late this morning.'

'But I mean, where are you? You're supposed to be in Marjorie's department.'

'I'm just using a desk up here. There's plenty of room. It's—'

'Never mind. Look – can you stick around for an hour on Friday? We were going to have a chat; I'll buy you a drink. Can you sort out your family? Will that be possible? Right.'

So at last this meeting was going to come about, but after all, it didn't sound much like good news.

The phone calls were from the agent for the Greenlea house, and Tony Wentworth; both numbers gave busy signals when she dialled them. When she put the phone down the second time, Johnny spoke up: 'Jess, this Wentworth chap. He said he might be difficult to reach; he'll try tomorrow. Or was it Thursday? Anyway, he said he'll ring again, soon; never fear.'

The tiny kitchenette with the coffee machine, beneath the stair that led to the design department, stood just between Marjorie's domain and the entrance to the large main room that opened out to the rest of the offices. When Jessie went down for a second cup that morning, she found the machine just chuckling through the final stages of its performance, while Marjorie watched it.

'Ah, Jessie,' said Marjorie, 'has Oscar managed to get hold of you?'

Jessie said yes, he had.

'He's been wanting to have a chat with you, hasn't he.'

'That's right,' said Jessie.

'I know he's been meaning to arrange it,' continued Marjorie, relentlessly proprietorial, 'but he's got a lot on his mind, just now.'

Jessie looked over at her. The coffee-making noise had stopped; Marjorie, her lips now crimped on her cigarette, was reaching to lift out the coffee pot. 'Otford's expanding very fast,' she said, in the tight diction imposed by the cigarette. 'It's a strain on him.'

She looked up, squinting over the smoke, her face unreadable, and offered the coffee pot. Jessie held out her mug.

'But he is worried about you,' continued Marjorie, removing the cigarette, for a moment, as she poured out. 'He's very kind, you know. He may act like a bear with a sore head, but he's soft as butter, really. And he's truly worried.' She paused, her head a little on one side. 'He just doesn't know how to handle you.' Then, before Jessie could respond, she added – with a smile, a shrug, a note of mock duress – 'None of us do.'

She turned and left, holding high the coffee pot, calling out to the room beyond, 'Here it comes!'

Jessie had to leave on the dot, that afternoon, to meet the prospective buyers for Albion Grove. Tony still hadn't rung, but she'd caught up with the agent for Greenlea and learned that her offer had been accepted. That was good – she should have felt good about that.

Passing the open door to Marjorie's office, as she left, she heard them laughing. She heard the familiar bubbling noise of Annabelle light-heartedly sending herself up, the way she did, and Marjorie's sardonic murmur, and the tones of Henry's cheerful jocularity, and then she heard Oscar, too – that theatrically forced guffaw of his.

She'd sometimes wondered if that loud, forced laugh derived from some forlorn hope of joining in, at times when he didn't actually enjoy the joke at all. She knew what his laugh was like when he was genuinely amused. Yet, all the same…

How friendly it sounded, in there. She could just imagine one of Marjorie's broad jokes, and Annabelle elaborating on it with such glee that if you were Oscar, you would want to find it funny. You'd want to join the party in that room.

It was time she got her proposals down on paper. Before she got home that night, this thought had begun to dominate her. The exchange with Marjorie was unsettling; it seemed to suggest some indeterminate shift in the situation – in attitudes, or allegiances, or direction… It had happened before. What could she do, but set out to prove herself, again?

Meanwhile, however, here were Mr and Mrs Ferguson just coming up the walk to the front door, and they stayed an hour. They checked out the garages (though only from the outside, since Jessie still had no key), and they went down into the tiny garden at the back and paced it out. They did not seem charmed by the little wood, just over the fence – indeed, the wood seemed somehow smaller, even rather pointless, under the impassive gaze they directed at it. The wife actually measured up the cupboards, to double-check the dimensions, and the husband asked difficult and detailed questions about the utilities bills. They seemed intent on demonstrating that they would not be fooled.

There was no let-up. She'd looked forward to telling the kids about Greenlea Avenue, but once she began, she felt embarrassingly inadequate: after all, she had no idea how long it would take to complete the sale, no idea how long before they could move there – nor even if they could start the term at their new schools.

She'd have liked, at least, to tell her news to Marty, who

was invariably upbeat and approving, but he and Arlis were away on holiday. Maggie, on the other hand, was dismayingly cautious, insisting on the need for a thorough survey before anybody should be allowed to get excited. 'Don't forget what happened with Mountfield,' she said, warningly. She even muttered, 'They must have been desperate for a sale.'

On which note, Jessie took herself off to bed.

The following night she worked till dawn on the proposal, and by the time she'd finished it, she felt much stronger. Just looking back through her notes brought a surge of hope, and a burst of adrenaline that seemed to generate more and more possibilities from the outline, even as it fell into place. What a lively, exciting approach it was; what numbers of visual opportunities it opened up. And then, reading over the responses from the people that she'd talked to, her notes of the more interesting conversations – most were enthusiastic; a few seemed genuinely promising.

How wonderful it would be, to be working like that again! How wonderful to be part of a team again, doing something that you all believed in.

She got to the office early the next morning, in order to get the photocopier to herself. Then, back at her desk, she read through the whole thing once again.

She'd outlined a rough schedule for producing a selling pack for the big sales fair in October, and at the last moment, she even added Jim Collins' flurry of sketches. In a cover note to Oscar, she mentioned the names of some of the people that she'd talked to, and how the work for the project might be organised: the advantages of using freelancers, doing it out of house.

Downstairs, several people had gathered outside the opened door to Oscar's office. She noticed Marjorie, first; then Henry. Maynard Godley was there; once again he had pinned Liz Trevor in chat; she stood beside him leaning against a desk, with folded arms and a look of glazed politeness. Behind them, in Oscar's office, Jessie caught sight of a slender woman with a lot of very fine, long hair looking somehow extremely elegant in faded blue jeans and an embroidered jacket, and the man just beyond her – was it Tony?

Oscar emerged, casting a bland look round at the assembled others.

Jessie hesitated. She'd meant to slip in and hand the package to him, or leave it on his desk, but not in such a blaze of publicity. She wondered if she might pretend to be heading past them, towards the post-box or the lavatory.

But at that moment, Liz Trevor looked up and spotted her; she straightened up and smiled, her whole face brightening. 'Oh, here she is!' she cried, her arm flung out in greeting, towards Jessie. 'Your prodigy!' she said happily, looking round.

Marjorie gave Jessie a brief, sardonic glance; Oscar simply, brightly ignored the comment entirely.

'I think we're all here,' said Oscar. 'Let's make a start.' And with wide, welcoming arms he ushered them all – Marjorie, Henry, Maynard Godley and Liz Trevor (she looking back with a puzzled frown) – into his office, and closed the door behind him.

38

By the end of the next day, it was clear her hopes were lost.

She'd finally left the proposal on Oscar's desk, when she found him away from his office, mid-afternoon, having presumably taken the others off to lunch. The desk was strewn with papers, including numbers of abandoned copies of some duplicated set of production specs (defaced with varieties of doodle), and samples of a Maynard Godley series, bearing his trademark cover of a strikingly dull and obvious single item, such as a clock or antique stereoscope, photographed against a solid background colour and entitled something like *Tudor Times*, or *Victorian Views*.

She cleared off a space just in front of Oscar's chair, and laid her folder there, where it would be impossible for him to miss. Then she went back upstairs and got out the pile of briefs overdue, by now, for correction, and began to make her way through them.

What with one thing and another, it was a long, long day.

The call from Oscar came shortly before five-thirty, on Friday, the following afternoon. She'd been waiting, but she could read nothing in his voice. 'Jess? Any time you're ready.' It sounded friendly enough; but then, why wouldn't it?

When she met him, she noticed he was carrying her folder. However, there was something about the blankness of his expression that seemed to preclude any mention of it, as though he himself was unaware he had something hanging from his hand. As they made their way outside and down the street, he enquired in a bland, impersonally hearty tone of voice about the children, about her projected house move.

Once in the pub, he dropped the folder on the table next to her with such casual disregard that Jessie wondered fleetingly if perhaps it was really not her proposal, after all, but something else entirely; when he went off to the bar, she peered more closely at it, almost surreptitiously – almost surprised to discover what it was.

But when he returned, he again ignored it. He set their beers down carefully beside it, but then, seating himself, rested his arm on it obliviously.

'Well, where to start,' he said, offering her a cigarette. 'I'm sure you realise, Marjorie's very worried about you. You need help, Jess.'

Help?

'Why do you isolate yourself? You need people.'

She looked away, trying to reassemble her composure.

He said, 'I gather Henry's perfectly willing to help you out. Why not use Henry?'

'I can't,' she said. Her heart began to thump.

'Oh no? I believe he's actually ahead of schedule. All the

rest of them are up to schedule. And you're, what – two weeks behind? Or more?'

'You realise why?' she said.

'Jessie, I do know about your problems. I'm sure the difficulties you're faced with are appalling.' He began a brief performance of concern: the lifted eyes, the lifted hands. 'I'm sure—'

'I didn't mean that,' she said.

'Oh, well.' Now he did pull out the folder. 'I'm sorry, Jessie, but if you mean—'

'I meant the schedules, the others being ahead of me. Has Marjorie ever mentioned the work I've done for them? All the work I did for them, early on? Why does it matter if I'm a bit behind, now? Why shouldn't I have some extra time? I've earned it.' She thought she had his attention for a moment, and indignation overtook her. 'If they'd let me alone—'

'Oh no, oh no,' he said. 'Let you alone? You know what happens; you go chasing all over the place.' Now he picked up the folder and waved it, dismissively. 'Look at this. How much time did you spend on this?'

'I did it at weekends. It was weekends. And after work. Sitting on the train—'

'You're out of your mind,' he said. 'You have a family to look after; you can't afford it. You ought to be keeping your head down, keeping yourself on track. Not dreaming up yet more grandiose new schemes, more projects—'

'But it's good,' she said. 'Haven't you even looked at it? It's good.'

'Of course it's good,' he said. 'You're very bright, Jess.

Everyone knows you're bright. But – you make messes. You alienate your allies. Look at Marjorie. Your manager should be your friend; she's there to help you. But what do you do? You simply pick up and leave; you pick up and move out of Marjorie's office.'

Oh, for God's sake.

'How could you do it?' Oscar pursued. 'Marjorie was extremely upset; did that occur to you? Don't you realise how much you upset people?'

'Listen. Listen,' she said, but she hardly knew where to start. 'I planned their books for them; I gave them their ideas. Why can't I concentrate on doing that? That's what I'm good at. I could be – I don't know – in charge of development, an ideas department; don't people do that?'

'Oh no,' he said, sitting back and folding his arms implacably. 'Ideas are cheap, Jess. Anyone can have ideas. I worked in a company that had these special people, the ideas people.' He pronounced the phrase with scorn, almost the way people in high school, long ago, had said the word intellectual, as though savouring its distinct, repellent flavour. 'I'm not going to have that, in this company. What we do here is teamwork. I don't have hierarchies.'

'Yes you do,' she said. 'You have managers. You insisted on having managers. That's a hierarchy.'

'No, no, no,' he said. 'Those are people who take responsibility. That's what I pay them for.'

She nodded; for a moment she thought she could understand.

But he continued. 'I pay people,' he said, 'for getting things done.'

Now she straightened up, alert with protest – struck by thoughts of that first series of his, the one she privately thought of as Oscar's dinosaur; how after all its lateness and overspend, it subsequently sank without a trace, while its manager moved seamlessly on to something new. For getting things done?

From the crackle in his eyes, she knew he read these thoughts. Or something like them.

'Don't fight me. You can't win,' he said. 'I wouldn't stand for it; I'm a terrible loser.'

What must it be like, to be able to say this of yourself? To be able to get what you want, this way? And not to mind?

'Cheer up,' he said. 'I won't say your job is on the line; we're not that heartless. But you need to pull up your socks.'

This was too much. She reached for the folder and pulled out her proposal, fanning out the pages across the table.

'Oscar, just look at this,' she said. 'Just look.'

He looked. His eyes were hooded, his arms still shielding his body – one hand cupping an elbow, thumb and finger of the other pinching his lips.

Within moments his posture loosened, his attention captured.

'Everybody I've talked to really loves it,' she said. 'I've talked to a lot of people, and they love it.' She riffled through the pages. 'Did you see these sketches? Jim got carried away by the idea. I didn't ask him to do all this; I didn't want him to. But look.'

She fished out the page of sketches, a page alive with images of busy little people, evocative scenic fragments, and random artefacts – each so full of character it almost seemed like a little personage itself.

He took it from her, holding it in both hands to examine it.

'They're wonderful, aren't they. Don't you think they're wonderful?'

'Jim was a find,' he said.

He put it down, thoughtfully tapping a corner as he gazed at it.

'It could be so nice,' she said.

Now he began to flip through the little document, stopping to read a paragraph here, a paragraph there. He said, 'We may be able to use this. Some of it.'

Well, this was something. 'It is good, isn't it,' she said.

He looked up, turning his full attention on her, for a moment. He said, 'Of course you realise, this is Marjorie's territory.'

'Marjorie?'

'Surely you knew that, Jessie. Didn't you know she's started talks with Maynard Godley?'

'Oh, Maynard Godley,' she said, dismissively.

He gave her a peculiar look. 'Marjorie's wanted to tackle history for a long time. You must have known that. Don't you ever talk to her at all?'

'Well, she did mention,' Jessie began, but then she stopped. She thought of Marjorie circling ads in situations vacant, Marjorie, her head bent over the crossword. 'I thought it was just a hobby. Like the crossword.'

'Sorry?'

'I didn't realise she was serious.'

'Well,' he said, 'I'm afraid you've missed a trick, there. Marjorie's already made her claim.'

'Oh, but you can't,' she said, unbelievingly. 'You can't

give this to Marjorie. Marjorie?' she cried, bursting out, irresistibly. 'She has no ambition whatsoever!'

Oscar stared at her. 'You must be joking.'

'But she doesn't care about anything!'

'I can't think what you mean. What do you mean? Marjorie is enormously experienced. She's extremely professional. We're terribly lucky to have someone like Marjorie.'

Desperately, she tried to backtrack. 'Oh, I know. Of course we are,' she said. 'I didn't mean – I'm sorry; of course she is. But the thing is, I've already laid the groundwork. I've got people interested. I've roughed it out. And the point is, I could do it out of house. Did you read what I said about freelancers? Think of the overheads it would save,' she continued, pleadingly. This was her big card; how could it not matter?

'Oh.' He'd gone back to examining the proposal; now he looked up, as though she'd surprisingly changed the subject. 'You mean you managing a freelance team?'

'That's right.'

'Oh, that.' He shook his head. 'Oh no.'

'But—'

'No,' he said, in a tone of finality. 'That's simply not an option.'

'But why not, Oscar? Won't you even consider it?'

'Oh, Jessie,' he said.

'I don't see why. It's just what you used to want. It just makes sense. And now that we've got some prototypes, I could—'

'Jessie.' It was then that he simply sighed that deep, deep sigh. He closed his eyes. 'Oh no,' he said. 'Be reasonable,' he said.

39

It was Tony who explained things, when they finally met for lunch, the following week.

She'd connected with him at last before seeing Oscar, but it had been a brief call, almost rushed; he'd been about to leave town again – just for the weekend, he said, but he'd wanted to make sure to confirm their lunch arrangement. It was still going to be all right? Oh, that was good; it would be good to see her; he was looking forward to it.

She should have been glad to hear from him. However, the phone had rung just after she'd taken a call from Marjorie, and as soon as she put down the receiver, she'd had to gather the requisite paperwork and head downstairs for this – as ever – lengthy, chatty, ruminative exercise; so she was too distracted to appreciate it.

More phone calls ensued, more interruptions and demands; the momentum of the day took over. It did not seem long before she began to be aware that she was watching the clock, conscious of waiting for the call from Oscar that she'd been so stupidly looking forward to. And then, by the time she and Oscar parted, among the last, late commuters in the emptying Tube station, her mind was elsewhere.

Finding herself in the train at Victoria, she realised she was not altogether sure how she'd come to be there. She sat in a corner of the carriage, smoking and staring unseeing out of the window, very upright, energised by what she thought was resolution, as though all the emotions stirred up in the last hour or so had combined to crystallise in that particular physical attitude.

She wasn't aware of going over what had happened between her and Oscar. She didn't seem to be thinking of anything in particular. It almost seemed as though thoughts of any kind would have some sort of weakening effect. What was necessary was to just keep going.

It was a busy weekend, with several more potential buyers coming to view the house, as well as the big, fortnightly shop with the neighbour who had the estate car. Ben and Ella were with her, since Danny was preparing to go abroad at some point – he hadn't been sure exactly when – for one of the new consultancies that had been cropping up. And there was paperwork to get through – there was always paperwork: a survey to arrange for the Greenlea house, enquiries about movers.

She heard herself being unusually brisk with Ben and Ella – even brusque – and wondered whether she was being decisive; she heard herself talking and talking to the potential buyers, with an oddly glib flow of words, and wondered if perhaps, now, she finally sounded self-assured. The truth was, she didn't know what that was.

On Saturday, there was a blow from a different direction.

For several days, she'd been nagging Ben to get in touch with Danny before he left. Some while back, Danny had offered to hire him to decorate his flat; Ben had been delighted, but, with his usual diffidence, reluctant to press Danny as to how this operation would be organised. The time wore on; the summer was slipping away. Clearly, this trip of Danny's would provide the best opportunity, but various arrangements were needed; Ben and Danny would have to consult about it.

And no, she had no idea when Danny was leaving; that was for Ben to find out; and no, he shouldn't worry so much about bothering Danny, this was his dad, they had a project together; it was important.

At last, to her relief, Ben made the call; but he returned with an odd look on his face.

It seemed that Danny was already gone; he had left on Friday. The phone had been answered by a stranger, someone who apparently thought it might be a call from the people he worked for, a firm called Gentle Ghosts. Jessie had heard of these people with the charming name; they were a trendy bunch of resting actors and underemployed musicians who hired themselves out for miscellaneous household tasks: for odd jobs, removals, the occasional bit of plumbing – and of course, painting and decorating.

She phoned Danny's number to confirm it. Yes, the young man had been hired to decorate the flat while Danny was gone.

'He's hired somebody else to paint his flat,' she said to Ben, as she hung up the phone.

'I thought that might be it,' said Ben.

They stared at each other.

'I suppose he forgot,' said Ben. 'He's very busy,' he added, after a moment.

It seemed as though these blows could make you tough. Yes, she felt as though she was becoming tougher, as well as faster. She seemed to be getting through things very quickly. She was doing everything very quickly. She noticed that she even smoked more quickly.

She made a conscious effort to slow down for the bedtime story. She found that it helped to throw herself into the drama of it, and she'd have thought she was doing it particularly well, with special verve and feeling, except that Ella didn't seem to appreciate it – she seemed unusually subdued, and Jessie caught on her face a puzzled and uneasy look.

She rang Tony on Monday, to let him know what had happened with Oscar.

He said, 'But we're still having lunch? I think we should. I think we should meet.'

At the urgency in his voice, her spirits lightened. He'd be indignant when he heard what was happening. Perhaps he did know – perhaps that was why he was so concerned that they should meet. She was important to him.

Yes, of course. She was important to him. The thought sustained her, over the next few days.

But from the start, nothing about their meeting was quite right.

The restaurant was much busier than it used to be; the corner table to which they had always gravitated had been taken. Tony had arrived before her, and she found him at a small, central table, looking somehow temporary and ill at ease, even as he smiled and rose at her approach.

It was a shock to see him. She'd forgotten what an elegant man he was, even wearing an old jumper and a shabby coat: that long, fine-boned face, and those high, narrow, very light, bright eyes. And then, his hands on her arms, the quick, social kiss on the cheek, and his face bent down towards her: alert, affectionate, but somehow, at the same time, too enquiring, almost too kind – and anxiously enquiring.

'You look well,' he said, when they were seated. Now his hand had slipped onto hers, and held it tightly, for a moment; his look was warm. 'You're all right?' he said.

'I'm fine.'

'I'm so sorry,' he said. 'You must have been counting on that project. What rotten timing.' He took a deep breath, sat up, let go of her hand.

The waitress was already at their table. She was a small, elderly woman with dark eyes, scraped-back hair and an attractively ironic face; they knew her from the old days. He looked up, now, with an expression of acknowledgement that Jessie realised was part of his charm, and which was immediately answered by the tiniest nod of gratified response.

'Shall we just get this organised straight away?' he said to Jessie. 'Then we can relax.' But when the waitress left, he said, 'So you really didn't know about Maynard Godley?'

It seemed that, in fact, the key to it all was Godley, who'd recently been honoured for his services to education – and whose influence on the educational establishment would thus be sealed.

'His services to education?'

'I suppose Marjorie knew,' said Tony. 'I suppose that's why she's so interested in this project.'

'Not necessarily,' said Jessie. 'I think she's impressed by people like him. And I think that's worse,' she added, fiercely.

'I don't know,' he said. 'I really don't know this area at all. But I gather he has a lot of clout in the educational market, and it's a huge, important market.'

'But Oscar's a mass-market publisher – he's a funny man!' Jessie clung to her belief in Oscar's innate discernment, however opportunistically concealed. 'Why should he care?'

'But my God, Jessie, the schools market must be vast.'

'It isn't Oscar's,' she said. 'It's a completely different market.'

'If there's any way to combine the two, he'll find it. He's an enormously clever businessman.'

'Ah, no,' she said. 'Is that all it's about?'

'What else,' he said, sombrely.

She sat back, temporarily subdued. Their waitress had reappeared, bringing their orders and setting them down with that air of elegant precision she employed. Once again, Jessie caught the flicker of appreciation in Tony's eyes, the glint it brought to the woman's face – a glimmer of light just short of a smile.

But as soon as she left, he returned to the Otford meeting. He said, 'I was surprised when Oscar rang me. The project he mentioned – it sounded so much like what you described to me. Well, no,' he amended, 'not the way you described it; nothing like that, but the same sort of area – history, daily life – and of course, that period, in particular. He knows it was an interest of mine, at one time. But didn't you even know about this meeting? Didn't you realise something was afoot?'

'I suppose I should have,' said Jessie, slowly. 'I haven't spent much time with Marjorie, lately.'

He waited, looking puzzled.

'Well, I've just been keeping to myself,' she said

'Well, anyway,' he said, after a moment. 'You should have been told, surely. You should have been in on it.'

She nodded. That sounded reasonable. It could have been like that.

'I couldn't understand why you weren't there,' he said. 'Actually, I couldn't understand why I was there; I should have explained to him… But you know what he's like, he likes to gather people round, from time to time. And when he rang, it was such a brief conversation; he's so brusque, sometimes. But then that day – Jessie, he practically shut the door on you.'

'I know,' she said.

'I didn't know what to think,' he said. After a moment, he said, 'It was Liz who mentioned you.'

'Liz Trevor?'

'She said it sounded like just your sort of thing. She said she was surprised you weren't included.'

'She did?' said Jessie, with a brief rush of pleasure.

'She says what she likes,' said Tony.

'And what did he say to that?'

It took him a moment to reply; he looked at his hands. 'Oh, Jessie, he just doesn't need you, now,' he said, eventually. 'He wants to streamline his operation, and you keep complicating things. It's not that your ideas aren't good; it's just—'

'Just tell me,' she said. She didn't need to hear yet again about how intense she was, and over-complicated and demanding.

'Well, he said what you'd imagine. He'd love to have included you, but it wouldn't be right, given your situation.'

'My situation,' she repeated.

'With you under pressure at home, struggling to keep your head up…' He shrugged. 'How could he put more pressure on you?'

'That's what he said?'

'That's what he said.'

She nodded.

'I'm sorry,' he said. 'Oh, Jessie, I'm so sorry.'

She took a long, deep breath.

After a while, he said, 'You're not eating anything. I should have taken you somewhere nicer. Only—'

'This is our place,' she said.

He nodded.

'It was our place,' he said, with an affectionate smile, and she smiled back, trying to discount the change of tense.

She managed to make some inroads into the pasta, but after a few mouthfuls, gave it up. 'I think I could use a drink,' she said.

'A glass of wine? Excellent idea.'

He'd always been such an unsplashy man; she liked that in him. And she liked how he seemed to know what to do, when it was wanted. When their glasses arrived, he raised his own and said, 'To brighter futures.'

'Brighter futures,' she said. But then, she gave her head a shake. 'Oh shit,' she said, 'Oh, Tony. It would have been good.'

'You'd have done it brilliantly,' he said. 'I know. I'm sorry.'

But she went on, suddenly filled with longing. 'We'd have had so much fun.'

At this, he drew back; he gave his head a shake. 'I don't know,' he said. 'In fact, for me – I'm afraid, for me, it's probably for the best. I've actually got quite heavily involved in something. I don't know… It was all just beginning when you rang, and then… Although you're right, of course; I would have loved to work on those books with you.' Now he was staring at his hands, clasped on the table. 'I enjoyed those meetings with you.' He looked up, as though he'd come to a decision. 'I think they kept me alive,' he said.

'I'm glad,' said Jessie.

But this was wrong. It was not how she'd expected. Or maybe hoped.

He said, 'I think I was a bit in love with you.'

Was. For a moment, he held her gaze.

'You're very loveable – you know?' Impulsively, he took her hand again, his fingers tightening on hers, and for that moment, it seemed impossible that something was not going to happen for them.

Then, just as suddenly, he let it go, and bent his forehead to his steepled fingers. 'Oh, lord,' he said.

'What is it?'

'Well, I suppose you know that – no, of course not; how would you know? The thing is, I've patched it up with Marianne. My wife.' Now he looked back at her. 'So you see…'

'Oh,' she said, with a meaningless nod; and looked away.

After a while, she said, 'So what's this project that you've got involved with?'

'It's not my project, actually; it's Marianne's. She's a passionate feminist; we're starting a magazine. I love enthusiasm, somebody else's passion. I don't have a drop of my own,' he said, almost apologetically. 'I'll be the money man. I'll be the organiser.'

'Oh, but Tony,' she broke out, watching him, 'that's not enough. You do have enthusiasms – you have passions – it's not enough,' she cried, in a last burst of protest.

He made a grimace of acknowledgement, but then he shrugged. 'It's something,' he said, decisively.

Eventually, he began to play with the cutlery again, the way he did. He said, 'I wanted at least to see you. It was quite recent, really. It's been such extraordinary timing. When we spoke, last month, I was just going off with her on one of those trips – you know – to see if we could make things work.' She thought he was going to add something, but he didn't.

'I'm glad we met,' she said, finally. 'It's been good to see you. Especially with – oh –' she made a gesture with her hands, intended to include it all – 'everything that's happening. You know.'

'Thanks.'

She picked up her glass again. 'To brighter futures.'

And now, he straightened up, raising his own glass, and his face cleared into that smile she'd always liked – a look of warmth and openness – with only the faintest shadow of regret. 'To brighter futures,' he said.

40

She hadn't realised how much it would matter. She began to wonder what it was she'd expected of him, what grounds she'd had for such huge expectations – realising only now how overblown they must have been, given the depth of let-down as she walked away from him that afternoon, back to the office where nothing better would be waiting.

She was angry with Arlis, for having drawn her into such foolish hopes. She was very angry with herself, for her weakness in entertaining them.

It seemed a huge mistake to have risked that meeting. She seemed to have forgotten how likeable he was, how endearing, and what good company – how cared-for you could feel, with him. How safe.

Yet in the beginning, she'd almost rejected his friendly overtures. Meeting him, the year before, she'd hardly noticed the sort of person he was. She was so anxious, then. She'd almost refused to allow herself to respond to him.

Meeting Tony had come at the end of a very bad time.

Something had happened to her: something that seemed to keep on happening, despite her best efforts. The summers had become the worst, and particularly that summer, the last, bleak summer of her marriage, as it happened, and the end of the second wave of projects.

It was as though, finally emerging from a project (they always seemed to wind up in the summer, and everyone had a hard time, everyone panicked, Oscar had tantrums, people became, briefly, hysterical), what happened to Jessie was she would realise that she didn't know how to live.

She couldn't even join in the hysterics. What was the point of it? Why did you bother?

It was as though the pressure to deliver had disguised the fact that she didn't know what any of it meant. She could no longer find in herself any genuine interest in anything – not in anything at all; she'd lost her taste for life; lost appetite, affection, hope. She found herself trudging through the days with an increasing sense of hopelessness. She despised the emptiness she carried home with her.

More than once, on the nights when Danny was away (he was away a lot, during that period), she tried going to sleep in Ella's bed with her, after reading the bedtime story. By now, Ella had been an avid reader for over a year; it was Jessie who clung to the ritual of the story. She would seek out, by preference, one of the few old clothbound books that had come as gifts for Ben, the first-born – tales of an alien Edwardian childhood whose images of the good and wholesome were now (if ever they'd been at all realistic or even entirely desirable) quite irrecoverable.

It seemed like the pornography of sentiment; she was

half-ashamed of her longing for its shelter. Stories of owls and moles and water rats. She'd only ever seen an owl once, in the distance, in the bole of a eucalyptus, across the dry gold of a Californian valley. She'd never seen a water rat, or water vole, as she found out they were really called, or even a mole; never seen such woods and rivers as in these stories. She wasn't sure they even existed, any more. None of it was hers to be wistful about. Yet there she'd be, curtains drawn against the long midsummer light, wondering how much Ella suspected of her neediness. How much she minded.

It had happened before. It had been happening, now and again, since she was eighteen, the year she and Danny began their love affair. She'd thought that the job at Otford's would release her, but after barely a year, it began again, intensified by the phenomenon of burnout, by working nights and weekends, that terrible winter, with Ella increasingly lonely, Ben in difficulties at the College, and Danny on another continent, writing less and less…

Things had gone so wrong with Danny, in the wake of the missed promotion and terrible quarrel, and after this, it was more than miles that separated them. It wasn't even the girl he started seeing, in Berlin. In fact, Jessie hadn't found out about her till afterwards, and when she did, what sank her spirits wasn't jealousy – it wasn't even resentment. It was something more nearly like despair.

Hilde sounded so gay and sunny, so light-hearted. In her company, it seemed he'd allowed himself to play. Jessie had forgotten how to play.

Of course, by the time Danny's year in Berlin was over, she had recovered herself; indeed, she had made a number of resolutions. She had resolved that she would be cooler, more effective, more independent. She would stop caring about things so much. She would be less emotional. She would look out for herself; she would remember about clothes; she would be, after all, a success…

Within less than a year, she'd begun to descend again into that pit of emptiness; and this time, it was even worse. Finishing the first lot of books, there'd at least been the impetus of terror, but having finished another risky project, gone through another cycle of flaring hope and struggle and grind, there she was again, for many months, just a machine, a sham, a shell, until, again, she'd begun at last, miraculously, to revive.

By that time, it was August, and the end of that long, lonely summer was in sight. The last bundle of patched-up, bodged-together, sweated-over galleys and colour proofs had been despatched. After a tedious week or so, surveying possibilities for the next big Otford series, there came a day when she glimpsed the fragile shoot of a new idea. She began cautiously to gather materials to support it. She realised she'd recovered the ability to concentrate. Gradually, it seemed as though the world came back to her, with all its tastes and fragrances and colour. And it was during this sensitive period that Oscar had called on her to meet this friend of his, and Tony began to figure in her life.

Of course she was wary of him and his effect on her. She was so grateful to have rediscovered how to work, to get her work done, be alive again. She was afraid of anything that might threaten this new beginning. And yet, it had seemed so harmless. He was interested in what she had to say; he bent himself to entertain her. He was kind and funny.

She found that it helped to drop the occasional mention of him to Danny, as indications that she could create a life of her own. He wanted to know she had her own life. He didn't want to be responsible for her happiness. People should be responsible for their own wellbeing. She made a game of it, establishing an image of herself for Danny. She knew he liked the idea of his wife being on those terms with a member of that class. He liked its style. He took a sort of connoisseur's delight in the curious magic of that assumption of a right, how it allowed the flourishing of a distinctive manner. How it worked; how it even created value; how it not only smoothed a passage, but spread a glow…

As for Jessie, he began to pay her more attention, for a time. He began to take her a little more seriously, again. For months, he'd been so cool, so remote. Often, he'd been simply absent. But in the meantime, as she slowly came back to herself, she thought she was learning a new way to be. She thought that now she could control her own reactions. She was in less danger of those eruptions of tears and rage; she had stopped blaming him for blaming her for what had happened between them, and at last, it seemed she'd become less anxious.

For a while, their lives acquired a more cheerful aspect. He began to suggest an occasional walk, with her and the children; sometimes, he and Ben threw a ball around.

The trouble was that even as this was happening at home, the feeling between her and Tony had begun to change.

Sometimes she thought she was just imagining it; sometimes she was sure she wasn't. Their meetings were happening with increasing frequency. He seemed to find many reasons to be in the neighbourhood, checking out some vague business possibility, chasing a hunch about some rare book. Once, when he rang, he admitted that he had no excuse at all except the fancy to show her this funny place that she might like. He began to call her as often as twice a week. At the beginning, his approach was carefree: 'Lunch, then?' But soon, she began to hear a more vulnerable note, a hesitation. There were those looks. There began to be more thoughtful conversations. There was a change of tone that worried her, and she was relieved when a spell of good weather meant she could divert him by asking for a walk, asking to get fish and chips and stroll round the neighbourhood again, and hear his stories.

And then it happened.

One bright, windy afternoon, as they were returning from a look round Chinatown, they drew near a couple of young men scuffling in the doorway of a shop. They were hardly more than adolescents, and they seemed to be laughing, but suddenly one of them broke free, heading straight towards them, the other chasing him. Jessie jumped back, reflexively, straight into Tony's arms. The movement had thrown her against him with some force. His arm whipped round to steady her, and she laughed – but the readiness of that arm, the tender, instant tightening of the fingers, was like a message she'd been waiting for. She looked up at him, and he looked down at her. A moment passed before he let her go, and in that moment, the smile left her face. There was a look in his eyes – a serious and steady look – that seemed to go straight through her. He dropped his arm and looked away, and they walked on, but she felt dazed, and neither of them spoke.

A short distance from the door to her office, he stopped and looked at her again.

He said, 'Shall we meet again, soon?'

She met his eyes with the same helpless responsiveness. She didn't want to look away. She didn't have any idea how to answer. At last she said, clumsily, 'I love my husband.'

Something in his face seemed to relax and loosen, and withdraw. 'Of course you do,' he said. He bent and lightly kissed her cheek; straightened and gave a little nod.

'See you,' she said.

But he only smiled, and nodded again, raised his hand in a little wave, and turned away.

41

The woman Danny had been seeing, during the time he was away so much that spring and summer, was someone from Tony's class. However, in crucial ways, she was more impressive.

She was crushingly impressive.

Karen was younger than Jessie by a year or so, yet her children were slightly older. Daringly, romantically, she had eloped as a teenager with the interesting older man from whom she was now divorced. It seemed she had always been independent and adventurous. 'Had to be. She was shipped off to boarding school when she was four,' said Danny, compassionately. She was beautiful and wealthy, free to pursue her own projects and passions, her children having also been sent to boarding schools. ('What else would she know?' asked Danny.) A high-powered anthropologist, she had at one time lived in a tree, in Africa.

'And she probably had a little bottle of Chanel perfume in the tree with her,' said Danny, with satisfaction. 'In her rucksack. Or even in her pocket.' Because she was also a person of considerable style, dash, and imagination; seldom wore anything but blue jeans and shirts, but they were silk shirts, Gucci, he specified. Or maybe Pucci.

The burden of all this, which emerged only later, was how one evening, at a party with her, he had found himself thinking, 'But I love Jessie.' And had left the party, thereby ending the affair, and come back home.

Jessie remembered that night very well. She remembered his unaccustomed tenderness, sitting beside her on the bed when she woke up at his entrance to their room. 'It's all right,' he said, gently, and he stroked her face, and she said, 'What time is it?' and then she said, 'Where have you been?' and he wouldn't tell her. She could see the clock: it was twenty past four.

She remembered feeling dazed and sleepy – so deeply sunk in sleep that she couldn't wake, or didn't want to wake – and him not telling her, because this was the period when he refused to say where he was, when he was away in the evening or at weekends, and she was not supposed to ask.

When he was finally free to do so, he was eager to share the story. Karen was a colleague, of course; he had encountered her at a seminar he'd looked in on in an experimental mood and never attended afterwards – 'Fuzzy,' he said, of the seminar: not his sort of thing – but the spark was struck, and they'd met again for coffee, and then again. And so forth.

Karen had taken him to some wonderful places, including a cottage she had, in the Cotswolds; remember that weekend in April he was away? Jessie remembered. She recalled in particular the stunning hostility in his face when he walked in, late on the Sunday evening, and found her engrossed in working on her current book with someone: a young biology teacher, who'd come to the house to demonstrate to Jessie the beauties of dissecting a white rat.

At the time Danny had said only that he needed to get away; possibly he might go walking, with a colleague. Now he could tell her more: Karen had taken him to a bluebell wood. Could Jessie even imagine it? A lake of bluebells, as far as you could see – astonishing, a simply amazing sight; a lake of astonishing colour, astonishing perfume.

This was the sort of thing he wanted to tell her. He wanted to tell her about the experiences he'd had, the way he'd wanted to tell her about experiences he'd had with Hilde (the energy and affluence of West Berlin, the shops, the coffee houses, and then, the atmosphere of watchfulness and tension when they visited East Berlin) – not really about the affair itself, or even about the woman: not about her as a person, only as, rather, a marvellous phenomenon he'd encountered, an experience. He wanted to share it. And of course, she could understand him wanting to share such things. When they talked, those times when they talked and talked, it was what they did; and this was a further, almost indigestible element in the odd mix of her feelings. The stories of Karen tore her apart in so many directions that she was utterly confused.

To begin with, she was abashed by the extraordinary and unfair glamour of her rival. To be beautiful and wealthy, accomplished and adventurous, and (as well) so poignantly young a mother – so much so that Jessie's own one-time achievement as a student mother seemed comparatively ordinary, even as Jessie herself seemed ordinary – this was so corrosively unfair that somehow it was no solace that Jessie had, in effect, apparently won the contest.

She burned at remembering, in particular, a certain evening during the Easter break she'd spent sewing name tags, by hand, on Ben's summer uniform. She had almost wept with furious self-pity – stuck with this hated task, so lonely, at the end of a working day, while the children played for a last half-hour outside, in the long, spring light, and Danny was – who knew where?

Danny hadn't come home that evening; he had mentioned not long before that he might possibly go walking with this colleague. She hadn't thought to suspect that the colleague might be a woman. It was enough to enrage her that he was going off walking, somewhere, going off on his own, without her. This was all he'd say, and the subject was under a special prohibition since it had been, in the past, so bitterly contested. For years, Jessie had yearned to go out walking in this fabled English countryside, that you still read about, or caught rare glimpses of, on television, like that man in the programme striding across the grassy uplands (which were, oddly, called downs) under the great, sailing English clouds. She wanted them to take the children walking, or to have been the sort of family who went camping… but even just for the two of them, for her and Danny, to go out walking in the countryside; and he refused. It would be utterly unsatisfying for him, he said; she would amble, she wouldn't walk; she'd be always stopping to look at things; he knew her. He wouldn't consider it.

So it was painful to hear about these bluebells that she hadn't got to see, now that she and Danny were reconciled. She didn't want to be angry with him. She was so grateful to be close, again.

It had begun with an incidental, unimportant quarrel, late one evening, one Friday when the children were in bed.

Jessie wasn't sure how the quarrel started. Maybe it was some grumble of her own, some bitter little discontented mutter. Maybe Danny had snapped at a remark she'd made, annoyed by its imprecision, and she'd fired back, and he'd responded with a yet more scathing quip, the way he could, sometimes. One of them went off and got a whisky; the other followed; soon, across the room, they had faced off, almost like partners in the ring.

'Were you hoping to start a quarrel?' he said at one point, and she said, challengingly, 'I don't mind.'

She was interested that he seemed so ready to engage with her. It seemed the most lively exchange there'd been with him in weeks, or months. She made some comment to this effect.

This sense of electricity between them, even of a hostile kind, showed up with particular clarity its recent absence. It was long since the end of Danny's affair, though of course, she didn't know about that, yet. It was long since her own depression had finally lifted (a state she'd been preoccupied with concealing). She'd stopped hearing from Tony (as she'd known she would), but this, too, she had never mentioned – the fact that she'd funked it there, and could no longer lay claim to any regard on that account.

She and Danny had gone on sleeping together. They even slept entwined, as though their two bodies had their own different, separate relationship; they even continued to have sex together, as frequently as ever, as physically avid, but in a strangely hidden and desultory way.

Yet it suddenly came to her that she could hardly remember when they last had any connection that seemed quite real.

'I suppose that's right,' he said. 'Have you ever wondered why?'

'I suppose you get your excitement somewhere else,' she said, 'the way you did with Hilde.'

He stared at her, with amusement. She knew it was a foolish thing to say. He was heavily involved in some piece of work; he was rarely away, these days; where would he have found the time? It was a random shot, just an expression of bitterness, but she was inflamed by his amused composure, and frustrated by her lack of ammunition. 'Or maybe you're saving yourself,' she said. 'Or maybe you're resting up?'

He gave a shrug and took a sip of his drink; she jumped up and splashed more whisky in her own glass. She stood with it in her hands, so angry she wanted to pace or throw things. She was furious at having indulged in these cheap shots: he must be gratified to see her so wildly off the mark.

But he said, 'It took you a while to work it out.'

'To work it out,' she repeated. Now she sat down on the sofa again, opposite him. Her breath came short. She hadn't really expected this at all. 'To work what out,' she said.

It must have been easier for him to tell her, when she'd been so foolish. However, even awareness of her own foolishness couldn't dampen the grief and outrage that blazed up when she understood. Also, she was beginning to be drunk; she hardly minded how she screamed, or how she looked, or what he thought; and of course, she kept on drinking, too; they both did.

Hilde was one thing; it had always been understood between them that if they were parted for any length of time, it would be forgivable to look for company; all she'd minded was that it had been, in some ways, used against her – and perhaps it was she who'd done that; perhaps she'd used it against herself…

But this was different. This was here, in London, with his family; and she'd accepted that whole separate life crap; what a fool he'd made her; what a fool she felt!

But if she was a fool, was that his fault? he cried. Yes, she was a fool; why not accept it? He could live with it, if she could; he could live with having a wife who was a fool. Surely that should be enough for her. Surely, that was enough to ask of him! He wouldn't have chosen it, but he could live with it; yes he could live with that; it was this emotionalism he couldn't handle, and why should he?

She continued to weep; she continued just to cry: how could he – oh, how could he!

How could he not? she heard him demanding.

To disregarded passion, disregarded sobs from Jessie, he continued, how could he not go looking for some comfort, some relief from the bloody rat-run he was trapped in, bouncing like a bloody ping-pong ball between it and his needy wife, with her endless dissatisfactions, and anxieties; her long, long memory for slights and grudges, her total lack of capacity for simple calm! For calm, for peace!

She wept straight through this infuriated plea for calm; she continued to sob, huddled at last into a drunken, sodden ball, curled on the sofa, until he finally ran down and she was vaguely aware that he'd stood up, that he'd come over to her; she felt his hand on her shoulder and she shrugged it off, not looking at him, only screaming, in a harsh, deep voice she hardly recognised, 'Don't touch me! Go away! Just go away!' And then at last, he did.

She woke at dawn, on the far side of their bed, to which she dimly remembered having found her way, some time in the night.

She woke from the saddest dream she'd ever had.

In the dream, she was marooned on a tiny island, hardly more than a rock, looming out of the sea. She was backed up against the rock, her arms outstretched against it, feeling for footholds, cautiously working her way around it, to get to Ella. She could hear her crying. She knew that Ella was stranded, alone and frightened, somewhere on the other side of the rock. She was trying to call to Ella, but the desolate, lonely noise went on and on, and even as Jessie woke, desperate to reach her, she was conscious that if she did, she'd have no idea what to do.

She woke up knowing her marriage had ended; her family was finished.

When she confided this dream to Arlis, the following year, Arlis said, 'Of course, that wasn't Ella in your dream. It was Jessie.'

You couldn't argue with Arlis, when she said things like this, but she was wrong. It was Ella's voice she heard. It was Ella she found herself most aware of, when she woke up that morning; how could she bereave her of her home, her father? What would it be like, for Ella? To be left with a mother who didn't know her way around such a bleak and terrifying place – a mother who didn't know her way around...

She went off to the bathroom, for a pee. When she came back, she found Danny sitting up in bed. She didn't know what to do. She picked up her bathrobe and pulled it on, slowly tying the belt, and then stood for a moment, holding the ties, looking at nothing. There didn't seem to be anything to say.

Danny said, 'What are you going to do?'

'What? Now?' she asked. But she knew he didn't mean that. 'I don't know,' she said. She looked at him.

He said, 'You don't understand, do you.'

She didn't know if she did or not, or if it mattered.

She waited.

'I wish I could explain,' he said. 'It wasn't the way you think. Truly it wasn't. It wasn't that I was looking for someone else. It was—' He broke off, bringing his hands up to his face, in an uncharacteristic gesture of distress.

'You said you wanted to get a sense of yourself, again,' she said. 'You wanted to feel yourself as an independent person. You wanted to remember who you were.'

'I wanted to move,' he cried. He took his hands away from his face. 'I need some freedom to act – I need to move.'

She nodded, dumbly.

'Only I feel like if I move – like if I move –' suddenly his face wrenched into tears – 'I feel like, if I move, I'll hurt you!'

In moments she was with him, her arms around him, holding in her arms this sobbing man, whose arms whipped round her in response, as she pressed her face to his wet, weeping face, rocking and murmuring, oh, Danny, oh love, oh sweetheart, don't cry; oh Danny.

It had been so long since they made love like this, when it was really love you made, together.

42

And a year later, she was dismantling the last home they shared.

It had felt so powerful: when he broke down like that, and let her in. Lying there afterwards, wrapped in each other's arms, brushing the wetness from each other's faces… you forget what it feels like, don't you. Like something being born.

After the storm of tears and tenderness and lovemaking, they lay together for a long time, smiling at each other, absorbed in each other's faces.

Then, of course, the day began, the usual Saturday – with sounds of Ben and Ella stirring, a cry for help from Ella, Ben tapping their door to announce the milkman wanting payment. But even as they greeted the children, opened the jar for Ella, got out the cash for Ben to take down to the milkman; even as they began to dress and move about; the sense remained of a new, poignant bond.

It felt like a convalescence. It had that sense of a slight

feverishness and weakness, a heightened sensibility, unsettling intimations of new beginnings.

All that morning, they were tenderly awkward with each other; stopping to smile or touch – stumbling at the continuation of routines which seemed suddenly divisive or unnecessary. They made the breakfast together. He asked her what he could do.

He was as quiet as a pacified child. She watched him, at one point, stop and gaze out of the kitchen window at the barren little patch of yard, beyond, as though the sunlight in the crown of the one small tree was a cause of wonder. She watched his profile, looking so wonderingly out at the summer foliage, watched the sunlight blurring his thick lashes, with a sense of privilege.

Later he asked her what her plans were, for the day. Since it was Saturday, the day for the weekly shop, he asked, should he come with her?

What a strange time it was.

She almost said not to bother. She felt self-conscious about this offer; but she could see that she ought to accept it. She felt a tenderness in it, though it was so unpromising an outing. And it was unusual. They rarely did anything at all, together, or as a family.

The two of them went out with her shopping trolley, and he walked thoughtfully beside her, not even saying much. He looked around, occasionally, with that same stunned look of wonder, though there was little to wonder at, or be amused by.

For the Saturday shopping, as for most of the shopping,

she always went down to the so-called supermarket in the bleak little shopping centre, down the mildly dilapidated street that crossed the divided highway. The shops in this place were stocked with items of a peculiarly desolate ordinariness and cheap decorum, which she herself found so dispiriting she had no wish to share the sight of them, or of the area.

But that day, wandering among these cramped, untempting shelves, past these slick, tawdry showrooms, they were once again like lovers whose physical attraction is so novel and overwhelming that it casts a glamour over the most unlikely circumstances. Seems, even (however briefly), thrown into relief by such circumstances.

After the shopping, he helped her put the groceries away. They lingered with Ben and Ella over their sandwiches, making idle, companionable talk about books and television programmes. How nice it was, when it was like this. There was a sweetness that showed up in people's faces, when it was like this. There was a particular sweetness in the smiling creases around Ben's eyes, and the shape of his mouth, while Ella's entire face was alight with happiness. They talked about Ben's friend Eddie's new madness for fishing; they talked about whether Peter the guinea pig would enjoy an outing to visit his friend Pokey, across the road, and should he be taken there in a carrier bag; could he be wrapped up in a handkerchief?

After lunch – which, again, he gave her a hand with, and then (just as though it were routine) helped her to tidy up – he didn't immediately turn to his work or pick up the paper, but suggested a walk, just the two of them, since Ben and Ella were already involved with their respective friends.

And still they talked very little, only smiling at each other from time to time. There seemed no need to talk about the quarrel. It would have seemed like a step backwards, a diversion. A waste of time.

They headed off in the opposite direction from the urban nakedness of the shopping precinct, down through the lushness of the old avenues of sycamore and limes that led to the pretty, embowered village by the heath. But Danny didn't stop, as he so often did, to study the windows of the estate agent. Instead, after only the briefest pause, he took her hand, and as they walked on, began to talk about whether they might not, now, actually move house.

43

She'd hardly been able to believe that this long-deferred possibility was actually being discussed as a genuine prospect.

For seven years they'd more or less bivouacked in that dull little house on the estate, never sufficiently committed to quite make a home of it, to explore the neighbourhood and its community or even London, really, yet at the same time, not agreed on a future, either. Perhaps they'd go back to the States, or Canada. Or what about Sweden, possibly, or even Switzerland?

Now it seemed that a new conversation might be possible. They could be talking about how they were living here, and where, and how. They could be talking about now.

Out on their walk that afternoon, Danny had suggested stopping for a drink, and by lucky chance, they found an outside table at a small, decorative pub at the edge of the heath, at just about the spot where they'd usually have turned back home.

It felt like a holiday.

Sitting in the soft, late autumn sunshine while he fetched their drinks, Jessie was buoyed up – despite the effects of sleeplessness, emotional exhaustion, and, probably, a hangover – by an exhilarating breath of holiday. The novelty of the occasion, even of these particular views of heath and village, from an unfamiliar vantage point, was such a treat. Why should there not be more?

'This is so nice,' she said, when he returned. 'Just coming out for a drink like this. It's like the countryside.' And then, as the possibility dawned on her, 'But we could do that, some time, couldn't we? You can get trains to the countryside. Couldn't we do that, some time, with Ben and Ella?'

He hadn't answered, but his look had seemed so loving. 'You're happy,' he said, and she reached to squeeze his hand.

'Oh, yes.'

How easily such expectations and desires could begin to flower.

After a while, as they sat looking out towards the heath, Danny had started to talk about his work, a thing he almost never did, those days. It was as though, having opened up to her so much, he found the temptation irresistible.

It was this piece he'd been so heavily engrossed in, recently; it was something new (he told her). It was meant for an organisation he'd just connected with… It might mean a change of direction.

It had been a long time since he'd even attempted to convey to her what actually mattered to him, what he thought was important or interesting about it, and he didn't do so now. She was aware that he was excited about this topic, but then he evaded her questions, avoided her questioning look. It was… oh, he couldn't say for sure; he really couldn't say, and she saw that mentioning it had brought a cautious elation too near the surface, like releasing the top on some carbonated drink that had got shaken…

But in any case (he went on, as though it was a part of the same conversation), they should think about moving. It was really time they thought about moving.

Wouldn't she like that? There were lots of changes they should make.

Changes. It seemed so good to be looking forward to changes.

When at last they left the pub and wandered off together, he took her hand again and swung it, caught up by another topic – and then another. It was almost as though the pent-up feelings and thoughts of all those months vied for expression: the impressions, fancies, whims…

As they walked back through the village, he stopped her at the windows of a trendy dress shop, a place where Jessie had made some of her few famously successful purchases when they were first in London: Jessie, you really need to buy yourself some clothes. Look – that would suit you; wouldn't you like a trouser suit like that? And look, that hat would be terrific on you…

As they continued, he kept thinking of things to tell her, kept catching her hand and squeezing it again, and then he would be silent a moment, and then begin again.

By supper time, he'd become irrepressibly talkative: perhaps partly the result of his own exhaustion. By the time they were drinking coffee on their own, he'd begun to muse out loud about Karen, about what an odd experience it had been.

'I wonder if you'd have liked her,' he said, once, and she was captured by the peculiar innocence of the remark – as though she, Jessie, were his sister in this respect, for the purpose of entertaining this conjecture: even his twin, or another side of himself, like the persona of a private journal.

They made love hungrily that night, and for a while, there seemed to have been a renewal of that old, magnetic pull that in default of obstacles could always bring them closer, open them up to one another.

It's true that he refused to be drawn, again, about the project he'd seemed so excited by. When she referred to it, once or twice, he brushed it away.

But at the same time, he was longing to talk, longing to share things. He was brimming over with stories about Karen, and her circle, and their views, and how he felt about it all.

For Jessie, listening to the stories was not that easy. Certain anecdotes stung; certain images burned. But while it lasted, she was suffused by the happiness of being together again – being part of his life again – won by his urgency to share it all: his gestures large and vivid, his face bright with communication, and then alight with such pleasure when she got what he wanted to tell her. He loved it when she found a way to tease him. He loved her occasional challenges, loved her drawing him out…

And she found that she, too, had things to share; she even told him about dissecting that white rat. She'd forgotten the look on his face when he'd come home that night –

presumably from his weekend away with Karen. Instead, she got excited all over again, remembering that revelation.

It wasn't something she'd had any interest in, beforehand. The book was already behind schedule (by this time, she was always behind schedule); the truth was, she probably shouldn't have taken on this project with the rat, but the teacher, her consultant, was so young and enthusiastic. She even offered to come round on a Sunday evening, and in the end, Jessie couldn't bring herself to refuse; even (as it turned out) to wield the scalpel.

Then, to her astonishment – to her awe, in fact – the process in which she was instructed turned out to be as precise and beautiful as opening a jewelled watch, unforgettable: the tiny, coloured, marvellous shapes of the creature's organs, when you peeled back the neat, lined velvet of its skin.

Was it the tininess of these interconnected processes? Was it the intimacy of touching things so hidden?

Describing it to Danny, she jumped up and pulled a book from the shelves and stood there leafing through it, trying to find a poem it recalled to her, until she looked down and found him gazing up at her with what seemed almost an equal sense of awe.

'You get so excited!' he said, with a wondering laugh, as though he was seeing something he'd forgotten.

As for her, in the glow of the moment she found so many thoughts arising – things they could share, and do, and talk about – dozens of things. Another rift seemed unimaginable. You wanted only to think of new things to show each other, new things to share and talk about. It seemed as though the days (and nights) to come would not be long enough.

44

They should have had those things, those happy times. Why couldn't they? Why didn't they? Why were the good times always, for ever, deferred? Why, when it could have been so simple?

Instead, before thirteen months had passed, here she was, erasing the last signs of their family's presence in that supposedly permanent, long-awaited home, which they had shared for barely a single winter.

At times, the sheer unfairness of it dried her tears and shrivelled the sense of loss. It was easier to be angry. It gave you energy, didn't it. She needed energy.

But again and again, she would find herself sapped by a stroke of compunction, sorrow, doubt.

… The stupidest things. How proud he had been (for instance) of briefly owning all those glasses of different sizes, bought specially for this new home, and the special cabinet to put them in…

And then, how chagrined he'd been when the solicitor enshrined in legalese the fact that this was all he had asked for from their marriage – just a few modules of the shelving system he had bought so recently, together with a shaving cabinet, a small selection of books and records, and a couple of old cider bottles he was fond of.

It had been a mistake to give that list to the solicitor. She hadn't been thinking; she had just handed it on to him, when she was asked. It was so pathetic. The look on Danny's face, as he held that document, later. She hadn't been thinking.

He frequently accused her of not thinking.

She was so tired of thinking.

45

On the day they'd moved to Albion Grove, she had been happy. It seemed a hopeful thing to be at last in action, working like this, with Danny. He was full of energy and command, pulling them all into a team, chaffing the movers – even laughing at the inevitable obstacles and hold-ups. How she had always loved that particular laugh of his, high-spirited, his head thrown back…

The house that awaited them was impeccably clean; you couldn't have asked for it to have been left in better order. The previous owners had included in the price a number of expensive white goods, nearly new, the kinds of possession Danny particularly liked. There was a big, handsome cooker, an immense fridge-freezer, even a combination washer-dryer with its own room, a utility room. Danny was in his element unpacking, assembling, organising.

Catching sight of him at a distance, carrying a heavy box of books from the car they'd rented for the occasion, it occurred to Jessie that he, too, was an enviable possession. He was one of the beautiful things that seemed, now, to belong to her, and she ought to allow herself to enjoy it, the way she enjoyed those other things. She should think herself lucky.

For oddly, after all the threadbare, shabby years, Danny had done something with their finances and now they could afford new possessions, too.

He had done it all at once.

Having put down the deposit on the house, he chose and bought things for it in just a few brisk lunchtime sessions at a big department store – a whole, complete set of crockery and decent cutlery and different kinds and sizes of glasses and a system of shelves and cabinets to house them all, together with that sleek, expensive dining table with the leaf extensions and the matching chairs, plus a stack of towels, and fresh, new bedding, and feather- and down-filled duvets.

He had insisted that Jessie come with him, but her lunch hour barely gave her time, and she was flurried and distracted. Rushed suddenly into these decisions, after so long and with no time to look and think, and talk it over, she was distressed to find he'd mostly made his mind up, on his own.

Then, there'd been the awkwardness of returning late to work, hauling these great, shiny bags of towels or pillows and facing the expectant gaze of colleagues; and she had to summon a great show of pleasure and excitement to compensate for this repeated lateness, and not appear presumptuous or unsociable.

Yet when the time for the move arrived, she found she was up to it. To be at last in action, enjoying the effectiveness and energy of this big, handsome husband – she was relieved to find in herself a wave of hope As they unpacked and assembled and shelved the new belongings, it occurred to her that at any rate, Danny's choices had been good ones: the new things suited the house, which was also new, although (unlike the last one) so very satisfyingly solid and well built.

She was surprised at how much she was affected by the new surroundings. That felt hopeful, too. The very layout of the house, with its unaccustomed ease of access, lent her a novel sense of self-assurance. How powerful, this experience of ownership. It was as though she herself had become more solid and substantial. As though she could be a different person, now.

Danny's mother came for the holiday, and became their appreciative audience and helper. She cooked for them while they finished the unpacking and shelved the books; she washed and dried the splendid crockery and glasses that Danny had insisted on buying for this house; she admired and praised it all; she played board games with Ella: she played Scrabble with Danny; she gave a hand with all the Christmas preparations.

On Christmas Day, she came down to the main bedroom with a tray of morning tea for Jessie and Danny and exclaimed with pleasure to see them in bed together, sitting up with their backs against the big, new, bouncy pillows, under the white cloud of the new, down-filled duvet. 'Oh, don't you look beautiful!' she cried.

Jessie knew that they looked beautiful like that, together. She was struck by the fact that people are happy to see you looking happy; they like to see you looking rich and lucky and well cared for.

She enjoyed that moment. She basked in the pleasure of it, even though she knew, as Gran did not, that her presence in that bed was just for Christmas, just while they had a visitor.

The big ground-floor bedroom with the adjoining bathroom, and the study across the hall, were to be Danny's, on his own, like a separate flat; Jessie was to have a different room. He didn't want to share a bedroom with her, in this house.

46

There were numbers of new advantages, of course. Their lives were changing. They were going to be people who had things, and showed off those things. They were equipped to entertain, now, and they had neighbours interested in entertaining them, like the couple who asked them round for midday drinks, over the Christmas weekend.

It was another world from their old neighbourhood, where the parents of Ben's and Ella's friends were postmen and dockers, policemen, primary school teachers – people with jobs so regular and steady that Ben and Ella had found it hard to explain the peculiar hours of an academic father. The people at this neighbourhood Christmas party, by contrast, were people who worked in marketing and advertising or had roles in things like record or film production. And it wasn't a family neighbourhood. There were only a few children of Ella's age, or younger; there were no teenagers in the area at all.

During their trips to view the house, after Danny had selected it from his shortlist, Jessie had become increasingly conscious that this was not at all a family project, the way house moving in her childhood had been, when her parents so enjoyed the process – making a story of the impending move, hinting at tantalising new possibilities, creating suspense. Of course, you couldn't expect that kind of thing from Danny; he had his own, very different style, and almost an aversion to thoughts of neighbourhood – perhaps even of family – as though alarmed by the idea of being identified in those terms.

But by the time they made their last trip of inspection, she couldn't resist suggesting to him, 'Shouldn't we ask Ben and Ella to come, this time?'

He shot her a look of sheer rebuke at the idea, and said bitingly, 'I'm not buying this for the children.'

Chilled by his tone, she caught a glimpse of the rift between them, like a chasm that had been obscured by cloud.

He'd got drunker and drunker at that drunken Christmas party. He affected to be much amused by the drunken ravings of their host about the pop singer he was thinking of signing up. Their hostess, a strikingly beautiful French woman, had confided in Jessie, as they stood alone together for a moment at the drinks table, that she and this producer had been separated until very recently; she'd returned for the sake of her own boys' school fees, and was wondering how long she could stick it out.

Jessie, moving away to look out through the windows, was realising only now just how desolate their surroundings were. Aside from the great, walled acres of Crystal Palace (somewhere out of sight), it was a wasteland of urban blight in which they had installed themselves. This cluster of townhouses on the rise near the tiny wood was an anomaly: a small, smug enclave, with park or dereliction stretching away downhill on every side.

The good thing was being able to ask friends round – to finally have enough chairs on which to seat people; and that big, extendable table, not to mention the cabinet full of drink and assorted glassware. During the first weeks, they invited several of their old friends, and even began to make some new connections. These, at any rate, were hopeful, happy times. Marty and Arlis came, to exclaim at their transformed surroundings, and Phil and Lucy, and the Buchardts; they even had Oscar and Britta, once, and one of Jessie's most interesting consultants.

Ben and Ella rose to these occasions with alacrity: greeting the guests; helping to hand things round; adding intelligently, on the least encouragement, to the conversation. It was clear how much they enjoyed the buzz, how much it cheered them to see their family as part of a lively social world. At one point, Jessie noticed Ben in conversation with the consultant, an eccentric historian, who was asking him (with reference to Christmas, presumably) if he had views on the character of the historical Jesus. Ben would be delighted by such a question. He'd always adored such speculative conversations, joining in with her and Danny from the time he was small, when they used to talk like that, with friends like Marty.

·

At first, sometimes, she thought she could deal with the situation, and its demands. She could almost believe that the rewards would provide the energy, especially if there could be more people in their lives. Or maybe after a while it would get easier.

But there was so much to do – the new commute, the different new commutes for each of the children, new arrangements to be made with neighbours on behalf of Ella – new friendships to create and support for Ella, as well as the child-minding –and in addition, new and awkward problems of household supplies, distant as they now were from any shopping district. There was never enough time for all of it.

And on the rare family walks, now, Danny insisted they should all speak French.

He had a number of new ambitions for Jessie herself: her clothes, how she should manage her profession, but above all, she really should learn French; in West Berlin, they'd all had a second language. It was something they could do together, as a family.

Jessie didn't want to do anything more, as a family, that was like work.

After all, there must be moments they could just enjoy, together. Sometimes, there could be normal family pleasures, like feeding the squirrels that came to the porch round the back of the house.

And even now there were nights that she and Danny spent together, in the same bed, like always, making love; and to the last, when they did sleep together, they spent the nights with their arms around each other.

Except that now, it was Danny's bed, his room.

Danny insisted that this arrangement was simply

reasonable. He needed the space, he said. Having his own room, so near the study, meant he could work late and go to sleep when he liked, without disturbing her; or get up in the middle of the night, if an idea struck him. And after all, when they slept together it would be like lovers, by assignation. It would be romantic. Use your imagination.

Jessie's bedroom, for which he'd got a single bed, could easily contain a desk, which meant that effectively, she'd have a study, too. This room was up on the second floor with the children's bedrooms. It was by far the nicest of the three rooms on that floor: a long, light room with a window looking down into the wood. In fact, she could have a draughtsman's table, under that big window – Danny was enchanted with this idea.

A draughtsman's table?

The last thing Jessie wanted was a draughtsman's table. She wasn't a designer, she explained (not for the first time) – she was a writer.

She began to try to explain to him what she did, how she had realised that with these books, the words and images needed to complement each other, and her pencil drawings were just a stage in the process; they were just roughs for a designer to improve on. This was a new way of working; it was actually her own big innovation, one of the things she'd contributed to Otford's; she herself never used a draughtsman's table.

But surely she ought to try it? he insisted – surely she ought to train as a designer? But before she could protest again, he said, oh God, he wasn't interested in the detail; he waved it away, walking away from the discussion, saying only, where was her ambition? She should get herself qualified.

Danny himself was preoccupied with his new project: sometimes mysteriously high-spirited, opaque and teasing; sometimes agitated and important. He was away more and more, or came home late; he refused to explain what it was actually about. Of course, there was some professional connection, but then again, not necessarily.

'That's not how it works,' he told her.

'Not how what works?' she once protested.

But he said, 'Oh, Jessie – you're surely not that obtuse.'

It seemed that as the political climate had begun to change, his intellectual stance was finally, in certain quarters, becoming fashionable – the economics of his Chicago hero, what they were beginning to call 'neo-liberalism', was acquiring supporters, potentially powerful. There was this new woman in politics: 'A grocer's daughter,' he would stress, with a show of irony (as people did); and Jessie gathered that at last he might have a role outside the university.

It would take place, she imagined, in that penumbra of advisory influence of which she understood even less than she understood the convoluted gossip of persons and acronyms that filled the political columns in the newspapers, and which she had long stopped trying to fathom. But she did read the editorials. She glanced through his copy of *The Times* often enough to notice certain names, so she was aware of the relative famousness of a few of the people he occasionally mentioned. He seemed to expect her to recognise several more; sometimes she bluffed.

She wished she knew enough to respond in a spirit of

friendly interest. She wished she could tease him – wished she could nicely puncture the occasional pomposities, and thus perhaps feel less aversion for them.

Once, unexpectedly, he invited her for a drink after work, in town, with some new friends of his.

They were a man and a girl, but they didn't actually seem like a couple – more like colleagues, perhaps. They seemed to have something to do with politics, but it was not clear what, and they engaged in a brittle, bantering verbal shorthand clearly designed to exclude the less knowledgeable. The girl smoked elaborately and tossed her head a lot, showing off by dropping names and references at which the man and Danny laughed or nodded knowingly, the young man glancing at Danny now and then with a faint air of ostentation.

Then she found that Danny was bragging about her. He put his hand on her shoulder, with a public warmth he rarely showed, now, and she realised he was talking about her former academic honours – specifically, the big award with which she'd entered their university.

She could feel his eyes on her, and then the bland smile of the man, the bright, hard, smiling stare of the girl, and she was aghast. What connection did she have with that former self, and its false promises? She said, hoping to forestall their questions, 'And now I work for a mass-market children's publisher.'

'It's a very interesting area,' said Danny, after a moment. Who had found that area so entirely uninteresting. 'Well, it's a marketing innovation,' he explained. 'The publisher's a total newcomer,' he said. 'She'll make his name for him.'

'Ah, no,' protested Jessie, feeling her face grow warm.

'What is the name?' the girl asked.

'You wouldn't know,' said Jessie. Then, aware of Danny's look, 'Not yet.'

'Not a household name, then,' said the man.

'Otford Publishing?'

'No,' he said. 'You're right. I wouldn't know!' He looked round at them all for some sort of come-back. 'Will I?' he asked.

'Oh well,' she said, with an awkward laugh. 'I hope so. Some day.'

But she had no idea what to add. It was one of those times when her own sense of mission about the books seemed almost ludicrous – a fantasy of overweening silliness. It was hard enough to believe in it herself.

There was a short, uncomfortable silence before someone found another topic for conversation, after which, to her relief, they didn't question her any further about the publishing world, or the media world, or any other sphere of that public realm about which she was so entirely uninformed.

She relaxed, after this, and managed to look interested and even almost laugh, once; and so did Danny.

But when the group dispersed, Danny strode away as though he was on his own. He stopped to buy a newspaper, but when she drew up at his side, he walked away without a glance at her. He didn't speak; he didn't look at her again, not all the way home or through the evening.

He ignored her completely, all that evening. He was particularly sociable with Ben and Ella, but he cut off Jessie; cut across any remark she ventured to make, at supper. He could do that, sometimes. It entirely reduced her.

The following night, he finally let go at her.

Why was it, after all, that she was like she was? After all, she did have some few assets – she did have some achievements. Why did she refuse to make any use of them?

No, really, she hid herself – she hid behind her inadequacy; she refused to accept responsibility for her life. She was almost in flight from success; and why was that?

What was it that she wanted?

He hoped she'd work it out, because if not – well, he needed to keep his own momentum somehow; he couldn't allow himself to be weighed down by her anxieties; he couldn't afford to carry her any longer.

If she'd just *think*. What was it, honestly, that she wanted?

He didn't really believe she was just neurotic. He wouldn't have married her if he hadn't believed that deep down, she did have real ambitions – she did have some guts.

Or maybe not.

The problem was, she didn't know how to answer him. What single thing did she want that was, in his sense, real? What simple, accessible objective?

There'd been times she'd thought that this was Danny's secret, this was the attractive power that he had, just that he was prepared to make demands. And he could make them so passionately, so plausibly, with that almost childlike assumption that they would be met: thus providing, to anyone within his orbit, the enlivening excitement of a purpose.

Because this was the secret, wasn't it – this was the great theme that Neitzsche struggled with, the secret of

Dostoevsky's Grand Inquisitor: the source of purpose.

Where else do you get that sense of purpose? Aren't we all trying to explain ourselves in terms of someone else's satisfaction: children, lover, family (what a burden to place upon them!), society at large (with what terrible results!), or (ditto) some fine, great, inevitably deforming cause…

But as for her, she seemed, periodically, to lose connection with her own appetites.

It was her private shame, this thing that sometimes sabotaged her energy – this anhedonia, this incapacity for pleasure. After all, if you couldn't create it for yourself, how could you ever share it with anyone else?

Which would explain why she could never commit herself to real things – those simple, accessible objectives – but only what was immaterial or impossible.

Things like heaven, God, a tribe. A tranquil, unpolluted beach…

47

She began to realise that she was hysterical, as he so often said, now. It scared her, but it made her angry, too, because it was not her fault. Surely she'd tried, she kept on trying, and sometimes it worked, so that she had to keep on trying, but then it didn't.

There would be, sometimes, this hot-house flowering of sex, which might lead to a spell of tenderness, but then again, might not. She tried things and they sometimes worked, sometimes hideously failed.

'God,' said Danny, 'do you need a rule book? Do you need a map? Can't you play it by ear?'

The sex had always been good, between them, but now he said, more than once, that it had been too good; he had to protect himself from her.

She was his weakness, he said. Liking her, even, was his weakness.

At work, one day, after seeing out a difficult designer, she discovered she couldn't get her breath.

She stood on the outside stair, taking deep breaths, again and again, but there never seemed enough oxygen in these breaths, and then the pain began in her chest, and the tingling in her fingers and the dizziness. Luckily, it was the lunch hour. She was succoured by a temp and taken by ambulance to an emergency ward where a contemptuous doctor assured her that her symptoms were meaningless; afterwards, the temp (a kindly girl) said she was sure that Jessie's absence had gone unnoticed.

Her behaviour became increasingly impulsive, wayward, even desperate.

Towards the end of those months, she began to spend the occasional Saturday in the office; this, at least, Danny found acceptable; soon she began to keep a half-bottle of Scotch there. She was relieved at how it restored her energy.

She had spells of curious elation; found herself taking new, peculiar risks.

Stopping at a tobacconist en route to work one day, wearing a dress that Danny had curled his lip at, she encountered a very striking man whom she found at her heels as she ran on up the street. He begged her to meet him later in the foyer of a nearby building; she said she might, and did.

She was relieved and excited by this encounter. This, then, was how people picked each other up; she'd always wondered. It was the sort of knowledge that had seemed exclusive to Danny's world, and to which her inexperience had seemed such a barrier; perhaps it needn't be.

Later that afternoon, she let this stranger kiss her in an archaic passage off the side of the building in which she'd found him; he pressed his card into her hand before she left him.

Her confidence washed back; that evening, she seduced her husband.

Danny was pleased.

Stretched out naked on his naked body, in the lamplight, smiling down into his smiling eyes, she was delighted to have brought about this rapprochement. She was briefly powerful; she was Scheherazade.

She was deluded.

At one point, she persuaded him to take her away for a week in France, before he went off on a trip of his own that he was planning. It was years since they'd been away alone together. She clung to the hope that if only they could be released, for once, into a different atmosphere, away from all the questions and the striving – especially the pointless, endless striving – they'd rediscover each other.

But almost as soon as she'd got him to agree, he began bringing this project into question. He brought up objections and diversions. He dragged his heels.

As she began to see it slipping away, her anxiety itself became an objection to him.

What he wanted, he kept trying to explain, was space. What he wanted her to be was cool. Why couldn't she just allow them to be calm, together?

But what this meant, in fact, was being apart. What this meant was that he didn't want to know. He didn't want to hear about her life – her enthusiasms or frustrations, or her disappointment – he wasn't interested in her interests, he wouldn't follow her. And of course, he wouldn't allow her to follow him.

It was no good confronting him. He was too strong. But still she did, and still her idiocy in doing so enraged him. He believed in people being rational, and why wasn't she?

She offended his essential world view.

She would find herself protesting – stupidly, 'You can't do this to me!'

And he would say (or sometimes even shout, himself), 'Of course I can! I have all the cards! You have no effective sanctions on my behaviour!'

Then, of course, she'd weep, wondering why she was the way she was.

Sometimes, her refusal to see the solid, objective barriers against which she threw herself, drove him to fury. Once, near the end, he simply cried out, 'Let me win!'

If she had even known how she could do that! Well, how to do it through some accommodation she could understand. Or even if she couldn't understand it (Danny, I'd stand on my head three times a day), just work out how she could reliably enact it.

It would sometimes end with a sexual engagement that was intense, but like a blaze that consumed great resources of time and energy, yet had no continuing result: the cold could descend again so quickly – so that she sometimes felt as though these emotional dramas were the only heat-source in their lives, and surely there was something squalid about this, something dissolute, like poor people burning banknotes to get warm, like addicts squandering heirlooms for a fix.

It had started again, those long debates about what a relationship should be about.

He was spending much of his time away now, but when he was home, they didn't talk the way they used to talk. They never talked about books, ideas, experiences, attitudes – at least, not in the old way – but only about how they could manage to live together, about what it was, exactly, that he required, in order to recognise her as an equal.

There were times when he actually tried to explain why he found it so difficult to understand and accordingly respect her. Once or twice, he even tried writing letters to her; then he tried to explain the letters.

They sat in the dining room of the posh new house, with the door closed, and when Ben or Ella called to them, they were told: 'Your mother and I are busy.' 'Your mother and I are talking.'

After all, it was an endlessly seductive puzzle. On the one hand, there was the official version of their problem, which was Jessie: her neuroses, her neediness, her emotional voracity.

On the other hand there was for Jessie even now, at times, the sense of some profound, unacknowledged pull, from Danny. She was haunted by the sense that perhaps he really longed to be controlled, himself – to be rescued from his own bullying energy – like a child tormented by a tantrum.

Hours could go by. Sometimes, most of a weekend was devoured like this, in argument and tears, until at last she would leave the room in which they were closeted, and find a child waiting idly on the stair outside, or near a door…

Ella, sitting outside the closed door of the dining room; just sitting there alone, on that broad, carpeted stair, while inside, her parents plunged again into the all-encompassing conflict that absorbed them.

Ben, disappearing into those dull, thankless streets, that emptied neighbourhood – into the pubs, in fact (as she discovered later) – in a quiet, forlorn search for a little friendly liveliness, for the company of other human creatures.

And it would hit her: this is wrong. It shouldn't be like this.

48

November, 1976

She was alone on her last weekend in Albion Grove: Danny had taken Ben and Ella to his mother's to leave her free to finish packing and clear the house. Six months had passed since she had started the process – a whole season of changing fears and hopes. The summer had arrived and finished. The world outside was growing cool and drab and empty, even as she worked her way through the emptying house, removing the last signs of their passage.

Certain areas were easier than others. The living room had acquired few associations; there were mainly just the books to pack again, Danny having come round one evening to disassemble things like the shelving system and the dining table. The bathrooms were just a cleaning job; ditto the kitchen; it was just work – packing up the food, scrubbing the shelves, defrosting the fridge. Since the day Danny had left for that last trip of his, she'd never used the room that was supposed to be her own room, and the big ground-floor bedroom seemed almost anonymous.

The room that was painful to confront was Ben's.

Ella's room was tiny; it was the room estate agents refer to as the 'box room', which meant (as Jessie understood) the storage room. Danny had charmed Ella with the idea that its very smallness was an asset; it would be her nest; it would be, in fact, a golden nest – one of the first things he did, when they moved in, was paint it a rich shade of yellow-gold, at her behest. Even now, it was almost comforting to fold the new, pretty curtains and the little rug they'd got for it; it was like packing the new good crockery, and glasses, and bedding.

Ben's room was a different story. It had never had that cheering coat of paint, or any other attention. It was a cold, pale, dingy blue, made that much drearier by its outlook on the communal garages. There was nothing in it but his bed and a rather flimsy little desk; there was no lamp – not even a desk lamp. His old curtains, never replaced, failed to meet the battered windowsill.

Looking round it, she was assailed by thoughts of the once-treasured baby, the bright, cherished, lively little boy… How had she let this happen? The room seemed to smell of neglect, like a smell of damp. Why hadn't she at least, right from the start, made sure that he had curtains that actually fit? Why hadn't she noticed that he had no reading light?

She remembered the lamp she'd found for him, when she fixed up the room partitioned off the garage, the room that had served as a makeshift study, to welcome him on his first weekend home from boarding school, three years before. She remembered the zest with which she'd dusted and cleaned and shifted bits of furniture, stuck up posters, found a right-size cardboard box to serve as a bedside table.

The night she and Ella brought him home was one of the high points of that happy, hopeful period.

After three weeks of separation, they'd all been thrilled to see each other. Ben was excited by the adventure of his new regime, chatting happily to her and Ella from the moment they left the College. So many stories of new experiences, friends, discoveries – so many jokes.

She and Ella hadn't arrived at his boarding house till well after 8pm, having had to negotiate two buses after their quick supper; then the three of them immediately had to begin the same long journey back, through the cold October evening; but it was a journey full of news and fun.

All the way home, they told each other jokes. There were elephant jokes, knock-knock jokes, light-bulb jokes – it was a tournament of jokes, ending with an interminable shaggy-dog story about a cornflake, which was only just winding down when they were finally at home, gathered at the kitchen table with cups of cocoa.

Ben had had to forfeit his own bedroom because they'd all had to be shifted round for Jessie's lodger, but when he was taken to this bare little outpost, with no heating and a concrete floor, he gazed round it approvingly. He noticed and praised, with such grace – such endearingly condescending eleven-year-old sweetness – the touches of cosiness she'd given it. In a moment of boyish solicitousness that particularly touched her, he leapt across the room to caution her about a dodgy electrical outlet, exclaiming, 'I don't want to lose you – I've only just got you back!'

Despite the long day, she sat up for hours that night, after the two of them were settled, too happy to sleep. She felt at peace with the world, and full of hope – a hope that seemed to promise boundless energy. She'd finally discovered a way to use her talents; at last, at last she was contributing to the family; and she was managing. If it was an arduous regime, she was proud of that, too; she thought she had enough strength and stamina and initiative. She thought she could save them all.

What a distant time.

It seemed almost as distant as adolescence, which also had been full of purpose and affection. Then, too, she'd had a role; she'd had beliefs and goals and hope. She believed that what she did served the people she loved, and she managed to hope that the goals she aimed for also served them.

Then, too, it had been hard work, but she had thrived on it – the part-time jobs, the cooking and cleaning, looking after the younger ones, being a companion to her father; even, sometimes, finding ingenious ways to coax her mother from the brink of those incapacitating depths that plagued her, to coax her into at least a hug, if not a laugh; though this had its costs. There was a falseness to Jessie's position between her parents, that was the only thing. One of the only things.

But she'd believed she could do justice to it all – to her parents, with all those troubles (the father's illnesses, the mother's depressions, the constant money problems); to the family and friends, the church, the small-town institutions towards which they expected her loyalty, the rebellious brother, the beloved little sisters – not to mention that passionate desire to do her own work, to achieve, accomplish:

that drive to escape to a freer atmosphere, where you were allowed the possibility of distinction.

In pursuit of which, she'd squared the terrible circle of their neediness by promising herself that this would be, somehow, also for them.

Because, in spite of the affection and fun and playfulness, there was that falseness; there were those unignorable currents of anxiety.

It was as though, at some level, they all had to clutch each other, cling together; to never, ever disagree, protest, stand out, make claims, demand – let alone to criticise, to grab attention (as Danny, so refreshingly and beautifully, once) could do…

She was going away (she had told herself) to find something for herself that would be a gift to them.

She managed to persuade herself that she could do this: she would be happy and free for them, too.

She would show them how.

Oh, yeah.

What on earth had she imagined she was doing? She winced, remembering that vague, fatuous dream: that somehow, she'd find something so grand and brave – some liberating idea or ideal – it would make up for all the heartache of her leaving them. She'd meant to prove it was all right to be ambitious!

Later she'd learned that after they'd put her on the train to the university (it was such a long time ago that on that first trip, it was actually a train), her mother cried so unstoppably that Jessie's dad had made her take the wheel on the long drive home, to take her mind off things.

She was right to weep, too. It really was the end – her

daughter never really came home again. There were just those few summers, and then the long years of separation and dispersal.

As for Jessie, what had she done with this wonderful freedom she had got herself? What bright, brave thing had she discovered? What happiness had she found, even for herself – even for her own small family?

And yet, and yet.

Her mind was a relentless instrument of torture. Reflections and recollections of this kind continued to rise up and quarrel with each other as she continued her progress through the increasingly anonymous and denuded house.

She was supported by a sense of urgency. It kept her upright, like a kind of exoskeleton, and propelled her. She even found herself making numbers of minor decisions (where to pack this thing, do we really need to hold onto that one?) with a rapidity and daring rarely available to her.

She was relieved to find she could still summon up the energy, even as the old, pointless, miserable arguments unspooled inside, holding onto the certainty that I have to do this, so I can, I can.

This was true. She did know she had to do it, though she did not know why.

She really did not know why.

Because it seemed to her – it so often seemed to her – that in fact, there was no simple set of wrongs that she held against Danny; it really wasn't anything he'd done.

How easily she'd have forgiven him, if she'd been able to win back their unity, their good humour!

No, it wasn't the things he did; it was the ugly sight of the wounds it left in her. It was her own inadequacy and confusion that she couldn't bear.

He had said to her more than once, at the beginning, people have got to keep each other honest. That had seemed, then, an ideal worth aiming for.

He had said to her, then, 'Don't let me forget I love you.'

He knew about his own weak, trivial side – how much he cared about how he looked, what people thought – and he had asked for help, once; he'd even asked her – almost begged, once, when they were young and ardent – 'Don't let me care about the fucking world!'

As though she could do that.

If only they could have gone away together. If only there'd been a chance to share new things, together.

Oh, Tolstoy was wrong about the monotony of happiness; surely it's misery that's repetitive: the grinding sameness of misery, digging you into the same predictable ruts that never could take you anywhere new or fresh…

Whereas happiness is vivid and particular. Happiness relies on the unexpected, like gleams of sunlight that transform a landscape, little miracles of luck that bring you closer, bring you suddenly into alignment, and then, of course, into each other's arms…

The letter he sent from France dealt the final blow.

It was a cool, cautious letter. After some tentative enquiries about her state of mind, he gave a wryly self-deprecating and amused account of his experiences on the language course he was taking, over the Easter break – the plans for their own joint holiday having been amended and eroded and finally dropped. He ended the letter by saying he'd been asked for an essay about his family; he signed off with a question mark.

His last confidence to Jessie had been about sleeping with a young graduate student at a recent weekend residential graduate seminar – the first he'd ever gone to, the kind he'd once avoided like the plague.

He had slept with her both the nights he was away, he said.

Jessie didn't understand why he was telling her. She hadn't probed; it wasn't anything she'd have expected.

Well, it wasn't anything he had planned, or meant to continue. She didn't mean anything to him, he said. He mimicked the girl; he mimicked her being in awe of him. He rolled his eyes and gasped, then threw his head back to laugh, the way she had once found so engaging.

This was the last thing he confided in her, and then later, almost the last thing he did was hit her across the face.

She'd been disoriented by this communication, and by her own reaction. She didn't know how to respond, couldn't imagine what he had expected – didn't care, really. It was just another diversion, and all she wanted was to shake it off, and tackle the main grievance.

They were supposed to have been going away together. They were supposed to have been about to start being happy.

They had been drinking; she was confused, enraged and incoherent.

She began again her anguished questions of him, wanting to get back to us, the question of us; why can't we ever—

But he jumped up and made a gesture of disgust. 'I've had enough; I'm off to bed,' he said, and left her, heading away downstairs.

She ran off after him. She followed him down the stairs, across the hall, into the bedroom. She actually backed him up against the wall, on fire with rage; she screamed at him, shouting into his face, 'You hurt me!'

And so, of course, he did.

PART TWO

1

In the little house on Greenlea Avenue, with the autumn sun sliding rapidly into the west, she stood irresolute among the upturned furniture.

Somewhere, the phone began to ring.

She remembered noticing where it plugged in, near the bottom of the stair. Moving back in that direction, she found she could see it, high on a stack of boxes in the furthest corner of the hallway, near the door. She worked her way around the packing crates, with their mean, metal corner-guards, and managed to reach it before the ringing stopped.

'Hello?' she said, doubtfully.

'Oh,' said Lucy's voice. 'You're there.'

'Oh, Lucy.'

'I thought it was today. Though God knows how I managed to find your number. Was it all right?'

'Oh,' said Jessie, caught by a deep sigh. 'Oh, it was fine. The movers were fine,' she said. 'It was – you know.'

'And it's all right?'

'Oh, well…'

'Probably not,' said Lucy. 'Never mind,' she said. 'It's always horrible.'

'It is pretty horrible,' said Jessie. She wished she could think of something else to say. She was disoriented. Already, Lucy was someone from a distant past – a time when she herself had been a different person. What would they ever have in common, now?

'Have you got any heat?' Lucy was asking.

Jessie told her yes, she'd heard the boiler start, and the radiators were beginning to warm up – this had actually worked out quite well. Mr Coates had got the boiler going when he came round to patch the ripped-up walls where the new wiring went. Making good, they called it. It looked terrible.

'Well, that's something,' Lucy said, about the boiler.

'Yes,' said Jessie.

'I suppose I'd better let you go,' said Lucy. 'I was just thinking of you. So I thought I'd ring.'

'Thanks for ringing,' Jessie said. 'Thanks very much.'

'Give my love to Ben and Ella.'

At the same moment, almost in Jessie's ear, there was an abrupt loud ringing from the doorbell.

'This must be Ella.'

'So I hear,' said Lucy.

'I'd better go.'

'Take care,' said Lucy.

The children's arrival was an anti-climax. They were not horrified by the chaos. They did not seem anxious.

They didn't seem particularly interested.

Ella was being jostled by the Buchardt boys, with whom, as arranged, she'd been walked home from school. 'Mum!' she cried, as the door was opened to her, 'can I go to Aaron and Joel's to do my homework? Can I? Their mum said.'

And here was Maggie, pushing through the gate, sauntering down the hideous crazy pavement, and Jessie was conscious of a brief surge of hope.

'Everything under control?' asked Maggie, blandly. Without waiting for a reply she added, 'Look, darling, come and join us for a sausage later – and Ben, of course – and tell us all about it, hmm? About six-thirty.'

'Oh,' said Jessie. 'Oh, that would be wonderful. I was just wondering—'

'Yes,' said Maggie, with the smoothest movement of withdrawal. 'But I'd better warn you, I'll have to bid farewell to you within the hour. I need a good half-hour slumped on the sofa before I can face preparation for class tomorrow. But Ben and Ella are welcome to stay while you get on with things.'

'Oh, sure,' said Jessie. 'Thanks.'

She felt her heart knot up, pathetically.

Maggie turned to leave. 'Oh, look,' she said. 'There's the man himself. Must be a free last period today.'

'Ben? Where?'

'That little gang of them. Just up the road.'

And there he was. With – just as Maggie said – a little gang. Ben with a bunch of boys, three or four of them, bumbling companionably down the street. Ben in the centre of a bunch of boys.

Ben got her into action. After taking stock of the situation, when he came to greet her, he went back and made some arrangement with the group of boys waiting on the pavement; then he came in to help her make a start.

He proved astonishingly, disconcertingly good at finding things. First, he found the bag of breakfast supplies, which he stowed in the deep, tiny sink; then he began the hunt for their overnight things. He shifted furniture and delved into crates, undeterred by the dirt beneath and round about, by the disorder of it all – the sheer unlikeliness of so much that met your eyes (bikes and mattresses, old, dusty curtains, the guinea-pig cage, the rusting barbecue, splitting boxes of sea shells and photographs). He clattered up and down the noisy stairs. He poked and peered, heaving aside one obstacle after another to haul out the bags of duvets and pillows, the stash of sheets and towels, the box of cleaning materials, finally the cases packed with their pyjamas and spare shirts and socks, even the little suitcase with Ella's most necessary books and toys, even his beloved tape recorder, which he stowed safely just inside the room that would be his bedroom.

Jessie followed, taking possession and setting herself the slow task of beginning to dispose things in the places most likely to be useful, though probably only temporarily. What could be anything but temporary?

She almost wished he wouldn't make it look so easy.

When he finally left, she carried on, however woodenly and ineptly; she stopped only for the brief meal with the Buchardts, in their bright, spacious, well-appointed kitchen.

It was like the glimpse of a better world from which, almost certainly, she herself was permanently banished, now. How she longed to linger, in that safe place.

'You'll be wanting to get on with things,' said Maggie.

2

In the weeks and months to come, people would say such unerringly wrong-headed things.

'That's something, isn't it,' they'd say, when Ben and Ella went off to Danny on a Saturday, leaving her alone with the terrors of her inadequacy. 'You'll be glad of the chance to get stuck into things.'

They said things like: 'Well anyway, you've got your freedom.'

They said, 'What a good thing you've got your work.'

They even said, 'After all, you've got peace of mind, now.'

Mainly, however, people left her alone.

Arlis came up, once, having offered to help unpack and straighten out, but clearly couldn't imagine how to tackle it – the hall still crammed with packing crates, the kitchen jammed with boxes piled beneath the dirty, dinky shelves of the clumsy dresser. Gazing round, after a brief, unseeing tour, she spied an ungainly ceramic planter left in the cobwebs of a corner cupboard by the former owners, and she pounced on it.

'But this is interesting! This could be valuable! Just needs a scrub – a little elbow grease,' she cried; and entertained herself for the remaining hour of her stay by scavenging for similar inessential and undesirable finds. 'Jessie,' she coaxed, 'You need to investigate. Keep your eyes open!' She never made a similar visit again; after all, it was nearly an hour on the Tube, and then a long walk from the station.

One weekend, Danny came round for an hour or so and put together Jessie's share of the storage system, providing shelving for the books and liberating several square feet of floor space; thus, as day followed day, the great barricade of crates in the hall was gradually diminished.

It had been strange seeing Danny enter this disaster area, and make no comment. He had often and convincingly inveighed against her practical abilities; he had even, in the last, turbulent months of their married life, threatened to make her life so miserable that she would have to go away and leave the children with him, to make sure that they'd be properly looked after.

Of course, that was probably just frustration, a display of power; but all the same. All the same, here it was, the evidence – here were his children in this run-down, chaotic household; didn't he care? Had he so thoroughly disengaged himself from his family?

She and Danny had resumed a certain relationship by this time; yet it was odd to see him like this – see him focus simply on a task (like Ben), business-like and unemotional, blind to the implications, the surrounding problems; then leave her to it. But his focus had changed; his own life had changed and opened up. Things were good for him.

And of course, it had been helpful to have the shelving organised.

As for her work…

Once, after a few weeks, Oscar dropped by her desk, in what she supposed was a kindly attempt to chivvy her.

'So where are the new books, Jess? Where are the new ideas?' He propped himself on her desk for a moment, gazing down at her from above his spectacles. 'You know you're safe, here. You know what we like about you – your joy! Your sense of fun!'

At her stare, he made a restless little movement, pushed the spectacles back on his nose, and looked away. Then he began again.

'Look,' he said, rather more gently, in one of his few, oblique references to her newly vulnerable single state, 'you've got a job. Actually, you've got a good job,' he elaborated, as though he had inspired himself. 'You're not –' he waved his arm, impatiently – 'You're not selling armaments, for God's sake. You're not selling bombs. You're not selling – well, cigarettes' (and now he stubbed out the one he was holding, with an expression of distressed disgust) 'or, you know – pornographic trash! You're not working for some boring, boring civil servant' (he rolled his eyes; after Oxford, he had briefly, horribly been a civil servant) 'or some evil capitalist like Rupert Murdoch! We do good stuff, here. We're making fun for people! So, you know, be happy!

'Or at least…' As he rose from his perch on her desk, his mood seemed suddenly to plummet. He lifted his arms in one last, prayer-like gesture before shoving them in his pockets as he moved away. 'At least, try not to be so miserable,' he finished.

What justified her pay cheque, for the moment, was a six-week series of comic-strips for a Sunday paper – actually just publicity for an Otford series, a sort of make-work. It had been handed over to her when it became clear that she couldn't really be part of what was now considered Marjorie's project.

Across the room, Johnny (whose desk blotter was in itself an almost saleable item, crowded with zooming aircraft and thrillingly foreshortened motorbikes) said, 'Well, that's a nice little project for you! I used to do a strip like that; I loved it. Just a few doodles and you're done with it; piece of pie!'

Every four-panel strip took Jessie at least a week, and sometimes two.

3

Waking up to those November mornings, she could hardly believe this was her life. This was what she'd done, deliberately. This was the life she'd brought her children into.

Ben and Ella didn't seem to care. They didn't seem to notice how bad it was. Perhaps, for them, it was not that bad. How could you tell? In any case, she didn't know what she could do about it.

Ben had a band, now; Ella had a kitten; they walked to school with other kids; they saw their dad quite frequently, at weekends – they probably spent more time with him than before, and he was already planning their Easter holiday, which would be somewhere glamorous and foreign. If they were aware how crowded and shabby their new home was, they ignored it. They were focused on making their lives work, making their way around the neighbourhood, finding friends. If they missed a sense of common background with these friends – well, the truth was, they'd never had that, anyway.

What had she done to them? She could no longer

imagine how to make a life for them. She couldn't see what she'd got for them, out of all the terrible disruption she had put them through. She couldn't imagine how there could ever be anything durable or valuable in their lives again. As she watched them learning to survive in this alien setting, unable to do anything herself but keep the household barely ticking over, she felt functionless. She felt swamped by muddle and drabness and uncertainty.

And her escape from all this was Danny. She'd begun what amounted, more or less, to an affair with Danny.

Getting back with Danny – it was like brandy on an empty stomach.

It had started the evening the decree nisi had arrived – perhaps that had provided the permission.

Ben and Ella were with him, in that flat she'd never seen; they'd been with him on school nights since the start of term, to facilitate the commute to their new schools, while Jessie was still clearing out the house in Albion road. Danny had rung about the papers, which he, too, had got that day; he said the children were already in the spare room, in their sleeping bags, tucked up with their books. They looked very nice, he said.

Then there was a silence.

'It sounds very nice,' she found herself saying.

'You'd like this place,' he said, after a moment. 'You ought to see it.'

She said, perhaps she would. Some time.

'What about now?' he said.

'What – now?'

'Come,' he said. 'Why not.'

'Why not,' she said.

It was like brandy on an empty stomach.

It was a small, old door, next to a shop tucked away on a little side street just round the corner from a Tube stop, in the centre of London. His flat was above the shop. He appeared at the door within moments of her ringing. He was wearing a shirt she'd never seen before, and also a pullover – the flat had no central heating and could be chilly – the light was behind him, coming from an open door some distance above the narrow, crooked stair. In that dim light, she was dazzled by how thin and beautiful he looked, and intensely dear – how familiar and how dear.

For a moment, they just looked at each other, without speaking, taking in each other's presence. Then he put a hand on her shoulder. 'Come,' he said, leading the way upstairs.

And here it was, this new life of his. One large room that served as a living room and study, with windows looking out on the city street, a bedroom with just room for a double bed, a rudimentary galley kitchen, the spare room in which Ben and Ella were now asleep. The two of them looked in on the sleeping children, and they did look nice; they looked beautiful.

The place had all been freshly painted, and the sparse furniture was new – neutral colours, and clean, simple lines; there was a good lamp, a small, bright-coloured rug; there were chrysanthemums on the table, under the lamp.

With much proprietary satisfaction, he showed how

primitive the kitchen was: there was no fridge, and he kept the milk on the windowsill, outside.

Of course he was right about how much she liked it.

'You're right,' she said. 'I do like it.'

He said, 'I thought you would.'

Indeed, it was just the kind of thing she liked, spartan and glamorously minimal.

He poured them each a whisky, in the good glasses in the drinks cabinet that he'd liked so much, one of the few things he'd brought with him, from Albion Grove. It was very good whisky, he said; she should drink it neat.

She held the big glass in both hands, moving round the room, examining the things in it, gazing out of the window at the urban scene, which seemed unreal from here, like a stage set under the streetlights.

At last she finished the whisky and put down the glass. She turned to look up at him and they moved together, wrapping their arms around each other. At first, she just buried her face in his shoulder, inhaling his scent and holding him tight, so tight – then turning up her face to press it close to his face, until his face was turning too, and her mouth met his mouth. Then she was suffused with a sense of gladness and of safety, a wonderful, rare sense of safety, as intense as it was illusory and brief.

To Ben and Ella, Danny passed off her presence in the morning as a kind of joke – 'Why shouldn't your mother come to visit me?' – as though to suggest that after all, life could be full of surreal and marvellous surprises. He almost seemed to imply that perhaps this was just a new way to be a family.

It was very odd to watch him doing this, so buoyant and charming, with that confidence that somehow forestalls any awkward questions; and the two seemed happy enough to accept it from him. Perhaps they hoped, or imagined, it meant something real. Jessie, on the other hand, felt almost drunk with the unreality of what she'd started. Stepping out together like a family into central London – emerging, like a family, from this odd corner to which only one of them belonged – felt almost hallucinatory.

After this, however, they met again, from time to time, and later, when the dust had settled from the move, Jessie frequently met up with Danny after work on Fridays. She'd spend the night in these romantic bachelor rooms; then in the mornings she'd take the Tube back to the ramshackle house up in north London.

They were unaccustomed luxuries, these evenings. Several times, Danny took her to an exceptionally good Indian restaurant just up the street from him, advising her on the nicest things to order. He showed her the landmarks of his new, diverting life: the pub he sometimes went to for a beer, when he'd spent the afternoon and evening at his desk, at home, and the really splendid fish and chips place round the corner, frequented by a bunch of locals he was beginning to recognise and be entertained by.

Further afield, there was an Italian place he'd come to like, and he took her there, too; it was handy for having a pizza after a film, and there was a small, plush cinema not far away, that featured art films. Once he even took her to the theatre, to a witty musical about a one-time star who'd had to re-join the chorus line. They hadn't been to the theatre in years, but he had more money, now.

After these outings, they could just stroll back to that little flat of his on foot, because it was so central. He'd turn on the electric heaters in the big room and the bedroom, offering her a blanket to put round her shoulders while the room warmed up – even tucking it round her shoulders, the first time, so delighted by the joke of his living arrangements – and put some music on his new system, while they had a nightcap. Then, after a bit, the tape would end, they'd put their glasses down, and he'd put out his hand and lead her off to bed.

And of course, it was wonderful to be making love again. Only she wasn't sure you could really call it love. There should be some other term – sex was too cold a word to describe what it was for her, this exchange that gave such comfort to her animal self. Perhaps for him it might be other things.

The first time, there'd been a look on his face that almost seemed like triumph.

Meanwhile, their relationship was calm in a way it hadn't been, before. He gave her treats and she gave him approval for the treats. She smiled and sparkled and dressed up for him. Often she had very little to say, because now she was actually a dead person. Inside, she was dead.

But her skin was still alive. Her skin, her tastebuds, those little secret folds in which her pleasure lay – all this was still alive and could kindle into bursts of pleasure that astonished her. She was surprised at how much feeling there could be, on the periphery of what was actually herself. But she almost never had anything much to say. He didn't seem to mind that she said nothing. Indeed, he didn't seem to notice.

So their relationship had the simplicity of a transaction, just as he'd wanted for a long time, now. She never, now, hinted at how she felt about all this: about the past, or future, about trust or death or even about the children, though sometimes she had some story that would amuse him; after which he would say, with satisfaction, 'Oh, they're all right. They're fine.'

She was learning the discipline. Perhaps she was becoming, at last, a grown-up. She was being rational.

Once he said, 'I'll probably always love you, but I'll never marry you.'

He seemed to have forgotten that technically, they were still married. Even so, what a strange thing to say – as though they were both still young and unencumbered, and he still possessed this lordly power to bestow a promise.

And in any case, what did he mean by love? Did he really think that what he felt for her was love?

Did she love him?

She became conscious of a remarkable quality of coldness in what she felt for him, though it could sometimes melt into affection, or even, occasionally, delight. She could still be delighted by flashes of his old charm.

He said, 'I'll probably still be hooked on you when I'm a very old man.'

She wondered if he had any idea how little she cared. Hooked on her?

Yet she was well aware that she could wish to be married to him, now. The status of being in a marriage, the security, the having a future with someone at her side – more or less;

having an attractive, personable someone at her side, being financially safe and cared for…

How desirable it looked, from here.

She couldn't imagine what to do with the future that now belonged to her. It seemed entirely devoid of promise or of purpose, let alone other adult persons with whom to share it, and she was sometimes fully aware of quite how desperately, how cravenly, she could now wish to once again be married to him.

Standing there in his well-appointed flat, she longed to just hole up in this place for weeks and months, reading the intriguing journals and papers that lay about (and which she could not afford, now), intellectually entertained and stimulated, and with London all excitingly outside your window – just to live there, and never have to return to the frightening muddle of the voracious little house on Greenlea Avenue, with its ineradicable smell of compromise and uncertainty and sheer tackiness, which she was so utterly inadequate to contend with.

Of course, being married to him had not meant living just off Holborn, in central London, with the social amenities of a bachelor academic, but at times like these, she didn't allow such considerations to dilute the pure force of her longing and self-pity.

In any case, whether she wished or not no longer mattered; she had removed herself from a situation in which it could. She had freed herself from the fluctuations of wishes and wanting. She was on her own, now.

She'd done what she needed to do.

And she had no real fear that he'd ever want to marry her again.

4

Quite soon after the move, Ben and Ella's Sundays with Danny became less successful. The lunchtime outings had petered out, the novelty of chess and Scrabble had waned, and for both Ben and Ella, the demands and attractions of the neighbourhood and their own private lives had grown more pressing. Danny suggested he might drop in on them at home, instead, and perhaps go for a walk; Jessie invited him to share Sunday dinner, too.

Perhaps it was easier to fall into such close relationships as these because Danny would be leaving London in the new year. A former colleague, assuming Danny would appreciate a change of scene, had wangled him a high-paid six-month contract. He'd be based again in Berlin, but as a consultant, now, and there would be lots of travel to interesting (and warmer) spots, in the Middle East.

Danny had, in fact, found his metier. Wrestling with ideas for academic papers, attempting to speak out into that vast abstraction, he'd always been haunted by the lack of audience. Who was he talking to, writing for? Who was he thinking for? Now it was clear. Some actual person, or authority, was asking him: he was handed problems to solve. After all, that's what he was: a problem solver He did it well, and got immediate acknowledgement and feedback.

By yet another stroke of fortune, he had landed his first long-term consultancy by August. All those unspecified meetings with odd, new people had borne fruit; one of them knew the head of an important think-tank, and perhaps this person, too, was spurred to action by some brotherly compunction over Danny's newly single state. This appointment (as well as the astonishingly happy solution for him, on the housing front) meant an end to any money problems Danny might have had, and he settled on Jessie, as temporary, added child support, a small proportion of the considerable income from this new role.

In return, it was agreed that he would keep the tax exemption for the children. This was a very sensible exchange; since Jessie's income (and thus her tax rate) was so very much lower, it was unlikely ever to matter to her, anyway.

Jessie was relieved by the new arrangement for the weekend. She'd been shaken by the sense of panic that swept over her when Ben and Ella first went off again to Danny, leaving her alone, trapped in this house of intractable and hateful problems. And often, Danny's arrival was a pleasure.

Coming to see them like this, at his own choice – and, perhaps, knowing how short-term the arrangement was – he arrived like a burst of sunshine, full of goodwill and energy. He was so gorgeous, after all: a tall, strong figure, with that expressive face, the dancing eyes; truly a burst of colour in those drab surroundings. Since he was a guest, he would occasionally bring treats, too, like a bottle of wine, or chocolate, or a cake.

Then they'd have tea, and Ben and Ella would tell him something of their news. For Ben's birthday, Danny had bought him an electric guitar; now he pursued a joke about how Ben would support him as a rock star, in his old age. His other favourite pastime was teasing the kitten, Snowflake, teaching her to bite, and claw, which Ella watched with awe and apprehension. Then he'd say, 'Let me talk to your mother, now,' or he'd read the paper until it was time to go out for a walk.

There were times when Jessie caught Ben watching his father with wistful affection, as Danny read or played with the kitten. It struck her that the look on Ben's face was almost fatherly – as though it was actually Danny who was the child.

To her, Danny seemed a strange, bright, charming object that added novelty and flavour to their lives. Once it occurred to her that she could wish that they might keep him as a pet – a glamorous, even dangerous pet, perhaps: something like a cheetah or a leopard – but there'd be a basis, a protocol. There'd be professional advice on self-protection.

The walk they went on, as a family, was always the same – just as at other times in their lives together – but it was longer, rather more challenging, and to Jessie, at any rate, more rewarding. It was the route Ben took when he began cross-country running. He'd rung from Danny's, at the start of term; he couldn't wait to tell her: 'Mum, it's the country, where we're going to live, now. I've just been there, on my run, and there are fields – real fields, with cows and horses…'

This was true. They now lived within reach of the famous Green Belt that encircled London. If you walked in a certain direction, and up a long, built-up hill against a desolate-looking fence of knitted wire, there was a moment when you rose into a wood, and turned a corner, and suddenly found yourself in a stretch of open country. And it was true that there were horses in the fields, and even cows.

On these outings, they seemed to have little to say to each other, as a family. They no longer tossed a ball around together. There were no playful teases with Ben and Ella; there were no family routines, or jokes; the children hardly entered into the conversation. Danny seemed preoccupied with gossip – gossip of a rather tedious variety: the idiocies of colleagues and remote acquaintances, various stupid people who had let him down.

How small their conversation had become – how tawdry. How she disliked herself for pandering to this tendency, for having nothing of her own to offer. Sometimes, half-guiltily, she just tuned out; it hardly seemed to matter. After all, she said so little, these days.

Once, she even took refuge in a daydream.

It had occurred to her that she might make supper for a neighbour, another newly single person she'd met through Maggie – not someone who particularly attracted her (and in any case, he had a lady somewhere), just a likeable person, with whom there could be, perhaps, some neighbourly sociability. But just the thought of making that supper, of what would be the nicest thing to cook, filled her thoughts so divertingly that as she walked alongside Danny, nodding and smiling at him, she felt both inwardly brightened, and disloyal.

Over this period, Danny was frequently in touch. Sometimes he telephoned, just for a chat. He talked at length about his good fortune, sometimes about women he was seeing – not sleeping with, he rather elaborately qualified, just going out with, for supper or a movie. Jessie responded with the sort of teasing interest that she knew he liked, and made encouraging or curious noises. She also began, occasionally, to make hideous faces at the telephone receiver. Sometimes, she stuck out her tongue at it.

She had long phone calls with Arlis too, from time to time, once Arlis considered that she'd settled in. Arlis took up her old campaign for Jessie's love life and her social life, not realising – how could Jessie have admitted it? – that for the moment, Danny fulfilled this function.

'So what about Martin, what about your neighbour? How's that going?' Arlis would ask, and Jessie would allow some speculation. It hadn't actually been that successful, her dinner with Martin – had in fact been vaguely disappointing – but it was something to say, a way to pretend she had a life, like other people. She couldn't talk about work. She was getting better at what she did, at work, but that was all.

Her life in fact seemed just a succession of more or less unpleasant tasks, to all of which she felt herself unequal. How entirely drab she was, and small. She found herself looking forward to such paltry novelties: the rare invitation to the Buchardts, for example, just for a drink: the brief chance to bathe in the impersonal warmth of that large exuberance that Maggie radiated, the comfort of that solid, stable household. She was aware of how she snatched at such occasions, in which (as with Arlis, now) she lacked the vitality to create any real connection, and from which she went away feeling dissatisfied and ungrateful.

She was immensely, drearily angry.

Legally – financially – Danny had been and was being more than generous. She resented being his beneficiary.

She couldn't hate him. In a sense, she was in mourning for him; how could she hate him? But what could she do with this enormous anger?

It seemed as though God, or the universe, or simply how-things-work went on rewarding Danny, showering him with gifts and luck and chances, while the same agency was bent only on punishing her. And of course, the children, too, through her.

She couldn't understand why it should be this way; how it had all – all – had to go so wrong for her, so right for him.

Of course, she realised she was a fool, as he had always said – she was unrealistic, she was dreamy; she asked too much and saw too little; from time to time she would fully see and appreciate this foolishness and understand what it was that she did wrong; but then it seemed as though the same things had been right, at other times; how did you know? How could you tell? And now, now it was just so unfair.

Danny seemed to have got just the life he wanted, and without losing anything. He would be having adventures and new loves. He would be living in that colourful, inner-city neighbourhood, romantically tucked away but only just a short walk from his work. The post would bring him those inviting journals she could not afford, and there was opening up to him a future mapped out with challenges and travel, old friends and fresh experiences – delights in which he might even include their children; he would have wonderful times with Ben and Ella, too.

And in addition, he was being calm and fair and generous, while she was stuck at the bottom of a sea of broken toys and misplaced paperwork and rotting windowsills, out in a distant suburb, being bitter.

It was one thing to call him a selfish person – though so vivid, so charming and attractive – and she had resented being the boring good guy.

But now, it seemed he was the nice, good person, too, as well as the attractive one, while she wasn't good at all: as well as dull, she was envious, resentful and small-minded.

And Danny's rent cost him only as much, per month, as the monthly ticket for her commute.

She once remarked on this to Maggie, with what she hoped was a touch of sardonic wit, but Maggie saw right through it.

'You're not bitter, are you?' asked Maggie, warningly. 'That won't do, you know. That's not going to help you, in the end.'

Jessie thought it might have helped a little, meanwhile.

5

All the same there began, now and then, to be good moments, though they didn't add up to anything – didn't give you anything that helped make sense of the world or suggested how you could begin to make a future.

One evening, as she walked home from the station toward that house of ineluctable problems, it occurred to her that after supper, she might start to organise the books.

For some reason, this was a cheering thought.

All she'd pictured was just sorting out the fiction, alphabetically; and as it happened, other chores became more pressing. But it pleased her, to have had this plan – to have found herself looking forward to a project.

Then, there were those books of Ella's about the eccentric explorer who went around catching animals and establishing zoos, the bedtime reading of Jessie's own childhood favourites having finally given way to these battered paperbacks, handed on to Ella by Danny's mother.

Gran had an instinct for what was suitable for a precocious reader. The books she gave Ella were not children's books, but books with innocent, childlike themes: that whole series by the adventurous zoologist, first of all, and then a few about a country vet, though Jessie didn't enjoy those books so much.

However, there were lots by the zoologist, and every night, now, for some time – as soon as she'd settled Ella down, and seen to Ben – Jessie escaped to bed with a cup of cocoa and some chocolate biscuits, and lost herself in these descriptions of Greece, North Africa, the gloriously eccentric family of the zoologist, the sunny landscapes and strange, marvellous dwellings – the whole sensual fairy tale of these intimate and charmed encounters with plants and creatures.

All the time, she was aware how private and insular these satisfactions were, as though she no longer really possessed a social being, or even aspired to it, was just being childish, enjoying the warmth of shallow waters.

At Christmas, all four of them went up together to stay for three days with Gran, who greeted them with affection and asked no questions. They did nothing but eat and sit in front of the huge new colour television, and Jessie was surprised to discover, when she got home, that she felt better for it. She hadn't even minded leaving Danny at the station, and going back with Ben and Ella by herself.

Not long afterwards, coming home in the winter dark after work one night, her glance was caught by the light that spilled from the upstairs bedroom. Looking up, she discovered Ben, framed in the window, holding a paint roller, with which he'd already covered half the wall. The ugly, plasticised, patterned beige of the wallpaper had been obliterated; the painted wall was a soft, creamy yellow – it seemed he'd used his Christmas money for supplies.

Jessie knew you weren't supposed to do it this way. Horst had been adamant, and so had Marty. First, there should be all sorts of preparation: stripping the paper, filling the cracks in the plaster, sanding it, washing it, using an undercoat; and really, you should start by doing the window-frames, which were rotting and splintered, and thus presented an impossible obstruction.

She was so glad that Ben had just gone ahead and done it.

And then at work, there began to be some improvement. Gradually, she had got better at that thing she thought of as the charity project. By the time it was finished, her mind had begun to work again, and she'd started to sketch out some possible new ideas. She shared them with Marjorie, to whom she now reported on a more regular basis. Marjorie was surprisingly encouraging. Eventually, Marjorie brought in Oscar for discussion, and he, too, was agreeable.

'Just keep it simple,' Marjorie warned, with a glance at Oscar, and he nodded.

'Marjorie's an old hand; use her. Lean on her!' he exhorted cheerfully.

There passed between him and Marjorie the briefest flicker of mutual congratulation, like parents of a chastened and newly tractable child, and Jessie tried not to resent it. She tried to believe that she really had, now – truly – abandoned her independent and rebellious ways. She thought she could listen to Marjorie. She thought she could do what was required of her.

Of course, she had no idea how wrong she was. She could never have imagined, then, how many times, in the months and even years to come, she would once again be seized by an irresistible idea that would alarm and infuriate those around her.

She didn't realise how long it would be, how much it would take, before she learned how to win them over, to win through – or had the chance to strike out on her own…

Luckily for her.

In the evenings, she began to spend time making lists of what was needed on the house, and what it would cost. She finally bought a small, squared-paper notebook and began toying with plans for making the kitchen workable. There was no way to do this without tearing down the unwieldy built-in cupboards, one of which housed the boiler for the central heating, so it was sometimes hard to continue wrestling with these imponderables. Yet in its way, it was almost grimly satisfying – marking off the obstacles, working out what could be done with what was left.

Horst insisted that the storage tank in the loft should be inspected, too, but Jessie baulked at this, at the very thought of dragging in the old, splintery step ladder from out at the back, hauling it through the house, heaving it somehow or other up the stairs…

Before he left, Danny bought her a week's skiing in the Austrian Alps, just the basic package. Ben and Ella would be joining him a short time later, to spend their Easter holiday abroad with him, and he felt some compunction about their all leaving Jessie, though the two of them talked about meeting for a weekend on the continent, somewhere, during the time he would be away. Long after he'd gone, she clung to this fantasy.

There'd been some tender evenings, though by the end, it seemed to her that he was more remote. She wrote immediately from Austria to his new address, and then again before she left – bright friendly postcards, with certain affectionately erotic references – but the letter that finally came from him, after several weeks, was like a travelogue, except for references to Ben and Ella, and to his suntan.

Of course, as she eventually discovered, he had found someone else almost immediately, though it wasn't serious, and it was a while until this sporadic correspondence with him finally ended. He hadn't wanted to encourage her expectations, he told her later. It would have been unfair.

She had forgotten there was an apple tree in the garden, a big, old tree, and at the front gate there was a stand of lilacs. But it was a late, cold spring, and it seemed a long time before anything came into leaf.

One evening, at a meeting at Ella's school called to introduce a new headmistress, Jessie was accosted by a man she vaguely remembered from years before, as one of Danny's colleagues – a man she would come across at faculty parties, or at the bar, when she was meeting Danny to go out somewhere. He wasn't someone she'd expected to meet again, or wanted to, though he might have hovered in her vicinity, in the old days, when she was new to London, and excited, and had a certain flair. She wondered if she'd even snubbed him, then, trying to copy Danny's confident manner of dismissing people in whom he wasn't interested.

'Well, well, well,' he said, 'what a surprise. I always thought you lived south of the river.'

'Not since the autumn,' she said, meaning to be evasive.

'Not since the split-up with Danny, I suppose,' he said.

She gave an inadvertent sigh, and shrugged.

'You're happy, here?' he asked, but then he added, 'Stupid question, isn't it.'

They'd been given sherry at the door; she offered a small, wry smile and tried to concentrate on this tiny drink, without getting through too much of it, too quickly.

'Danny's looking very good these days,' he said. 'Or was, when I last saw him. He seems to be doing well,' he went on, remorselessly.

His gaze travelled up to her wind-blown, badly cut hair, and down to the old army jacket borrowed from a friend of Ben's when the zip on her own had broken.

He said, 'You're – perhaps not doing quite so well, yourself. Is he looking after you?'

'Oh, yes,' she said.

His gaze was faintly sceptical. He said, 'I never warmed to your ex-husband.'

She made a little movement of her head, not quite a shrug. He was not the ally she'd have wanted. She couldn't remember what his work was, or indeed anything about him, and she felt an aversion to those cynical, heavy-lidded eyes, the thickened alcoholic's nose with its blue veins.

He said, 'One of the most self-absorbed people I've ever met.'

Now she looked up at him. She was ready to spring to Danny's defence; but he continued, meeting her eyes with a bland, blue gaze.

'Well, you both were, I thought. Two of a kind. Very attractive, of course,' he added, raising a hand in mock-defence, and she turned away again, shocked and helpless, because he was right. She could remember how the two of them used to be, together. At least sometimes.

'Never mind,' he said. 'You'll learn.'

Now she recognised what it was about him. There was something in him of the bully – an angry, unapologetic bully. Yet at the same time, there was a note in his voice of almost grudging kindness.

He put his hand on her shoulder, repeating this banal consolation as though she hadn't appreciated its significance. 'You'll learn,' he said again; and then, after catching her glance and holding it for a moment, he finished his drink and turned away, saying, with finality, 'He won't.'

At some point, as the months went by, remembering the exhilaration of her walks that summer week three years before, when the family was in Wales, she started walking Ben's cross-country route again. She would go off on Sundays, on her own, as Ben and Ella were now involved with their own friendships.

There was no such buoyant happiness to look for, now. She was just very tired of her thoughts, tired of her anger, of the endless arguments she found herself rehearsing. She went out hoping for diversion and refreshment, but as she wended the empty, Sunday streets, she was at first so abstracted it almost seemed she couldn't see or hear.

It was when she began the long trudge up that hill that she made a certain valuable discovery.

She found that if she kept her eyes fixed on the pavement,

kept up a good, stiff pace and kept her breathing steady – kept focused on the breathing: in and out, in and out, in and out – by the time she reached the summit, it had happened: somehow, her mind had emptied and was at peace.

The timing of this miracle was perfect, because this was where the country part began. She was present to the trees and fields and distances, and it was all downhill… She walked down past the fields and animals, all at ease. And there might be as much as ten or fifteen minutes of this blessedness before the chatter in her mind began again.

It was just a glimpse, but sometimes you had these glimpses, unexpectedly. You couldn't tell where they might come from. It was a long time before she realised how important it could be to simply keep the faith.

Then there was the memorable moment, when she'd finally decided to get that rickety ladder from behind the house, and drag it upstairs, and climb up and check the storage tank in the loft.

She'd been apprehensive about this project. She assumed it would be quite frightening to go climbing up there, on her own, with no one to hold this dubious-looking ladder; but in fact, it wasn't. The top of the ladder was not that far from the ceiling – it was not that risky, after all. She found she could push aside the trap-door lid with little difficulty, from halfway up the ladder, and then she could hold onto the door frame while she took the next steps, until she'd got up almost into the loft itself. Then she could pull herself up, and sit on the frame, and swing her legs around, and there she was, up there inside the roof space of the house.

She took hold of one of the cross-beams, and stood up. She hadn't expected it would feel like this – seeing the big, arching bones of the house rising up around her, its actual skeleton – almost a sense of awe. She knew you had to walk along the joists, but after all, they were fairly broad, and she liked the smell, too. The place had its own peculiar smell, a not-unpleasant, cool, damp, musty smell.

To be perched there under the roof-tree, high up in this mysterious, shadowy cave, seemed somehow, just in itself, exciting – the new, queer perspectives of the hallway, seen down there through the trap door, beside her feet – the looking down instead of up – the walking gingerly along the joists, part of the bones of the house, exploring it.

She put out her hand and touched the rough, warm surface of a rafter. Mine. She felt the spaces.

Mine.

She became aware of an unfamiliar sense of freedom. It almost seemed as though she was finding some new range of play in the very fingers of her hands, and in her arms, and in her knees and shoulders.

It almost seemed as though a self she had been unaware of had finally emerged, and straightened, and stood upright.

And it seemed to be turning its face in a new direction – turning its face to the breath of possibility.

Judy Hindley is a poet, writer and social justice/environmental activist. She was born and raised in California, and has lived in the UK since the 70s. She is the award-winning author of over 50 books for children, and in 2014 co-founded Citizen's Climate Lobby UK, part of the global citizens' engagement network dedicated to solving the climate crisis through democracy – and relationships. She has two adult children, John and Anna, and is Nanna to Alex.

Printed in Great Britain
by Amazon

39807580R00233